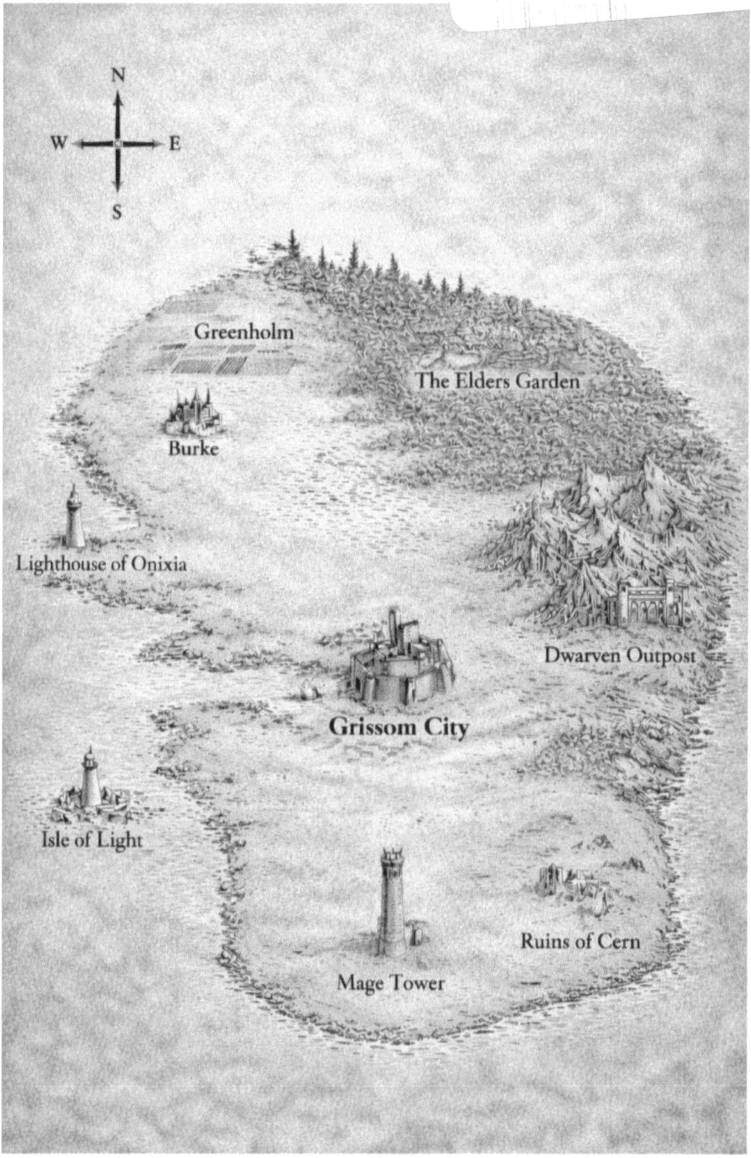
N
W
E
S
Greenholm
The Elders Garden
Burke
Lighthouse of Onixia
Dwarven Outpost
Grissom City
Isle of Light
Ruins of Cern
Mage Tower

THANK YOU

Thank you to everyone who reads this book and to those who encouraged me to write it. Your support made this story possible, and I hope you enjoy the journey.

Special thanks to the brave souls who read early drafts and survived.

Faith, Izzy, Jeremy, Luke, Rachelle

Author
Jordan Thomas

Editor
Daryl Mallet

Copyright © 2026 Jordan Thomas
All rights reserved.
No part of this book may be reproduced or transmitted in any form or by any means, electronic or mechanical, including photocopying and recording, without prior written permission from the author, except for brief quotations used in reviews or scholarly works.

This is a work of fiction. Names, characters, places, and events are either the product of the author's imagination or are used fictitiously. Any resemblance to actual persons, living or dead, or to actual events is purely coincidental.

First Edition
ISBN 979-8-9944141-4-9

Chapter 1 - The Hammer and Anvil

Dwarven ale, a drink that tests even the hardiest of stomachs, especially if you're not a dwarf. At ten in the morning, it feels less like refreshment and more like a dare.

I grin at my mug, swirling the brownish liquid before taking a big gulp, then chasing it down with a bite of dwarvish breakfast paste. It has a proper name, but it's so dreadful-sounding I've long since called it simply "breakfast paste."

The concoction is an odd mix of meat, oats, cream and mountain spices so potent they could knock the wind from your chest. Most gag at first taste, but I've grown to savor it. Growing up among three dwarves has shaped my palate in ways few humans would envy.

I chuckle, remembering my first encounter with it as a wide-eyed eight-year-old. Uncle Grogrick had just returned from the mountains, boasting of spices only true dwarves could craft. I spat the paste onto the ground, declaring it vile. He was furious, had Throm and Gamreal, my other two uncles, not restrained him, I might not have survived his wrath. Judging by their smirks, though, they were more entertained than concerned.

I glanced down at my mug, smiling at the memory. Over time, I came to appreciate Uncle Grog's cooking, and now I count him among the finest chefs in the city. Few would guess it, of course, his gruff demeanor tends to overshadow his talent.

Now I sit in Uncle Grog's inn, a sturdy and welcoming establishment he insists on calling simply "The Inn". The locals, however, know it as "The Hammer and Anvil", after the iron sign out front bearing, what else? a hammer and anvil. To the dwarves, the symbol carries weight, though I've never quite grasped why.

The building itself is stone and timber, with a wide archway leading to wrought-iron doors inlaid with redwood. Inside, the inn feels like a sanctuary, a warm refuge from the harsh world beyond.

Massive beams support the low, vaulted ceiling, some carved with scenes of dwarven legends, battles and symbols of strength. Rough-hewn stone walls are softened by tapestries, shields, and weapons, many said to be trophies from Grogrick's younger days. The golden glow of lanterns and torches lends warmth to the cold stone.

At the rear, behind the bar, a blackened hearth crackles cheerfully, its heat filling the room. Before it stretches a long, polished counter, worn smooth by countless hands and tankards. Shelves behind it display an impressive array of ales, meads, and spirits, many brewed in-house, true to dwarven tradition.

Sturdy tables fill the hall, some etched with carvings and scars left by patrons past. A stairway in the back corner leads to four snug rooms above, each with a stone bed, a thick woolen blanket, a window, and a washbowl.

Though the hour is early and the common room nearly empty, the scents of roasted meats, fresh bread, and simmering stews drift from the kitchen, promising delights to come.

Chapter 1 - The Hammer and Anvil

Dwarves are famed for their hospitality, gruff though it may be, and my uncle embodies it fully. By midday, the hall will ring with laughter, clinking tankards, and the occasional bardic song. For now, the inn is quiet, its warmth a gentle embrace.

A small stage waits in the corner for the next storyteller or musician, though here, conversation often outshines performance.

Everyone is welcome, so long as they respect the house and its patrons.

At that moment, my Uncle Grogrick, Uncle Grog, as I came to call him, stormed in from the kitchen, his scowl sharp enough to curdle milk. His black eyes swept the room with the practiced authority of a man used to commanding any space he entered.

Average height for a dwarf, his bright red hair and beard, set against pale skin, gave him a presence both striking and, in the shadowed doorway, intimidating. To strangers, and even to some who knew him, he could look terrifying. But I knew better. Beneath the iron exterior was a heart softer than he ever admitted. He had a reputation to uphold, and he wore it like armor.

Rumors swirled about his days as a berserker in the border wars, tales of ferocity few dared to question. He never confirmed them, never denied them, only met such talk with silence.

Yet I had glimpsed another side: the day he helped a human child who had scraped her knee. He lifted her gently, pressed a small flower into her hand, and sent her off with a smile, after glancing around to make sure no one had seen. Children sense kindness where adults see only menace.

My thoughts broke at the sound of heavy boots on wood. Suddenly, Uncle Grog stood before me at the bar, arms crossed, gaze sharp as a blade.

"Well, where were you off to in that ridiculous little brain of yours?" he asked gruffly.

I tried to suppress my smile. "Just enjoying the simple pleasures of good ale and a fine meal, Uncle Grog."

He snorted. "At least you've finally learned to appreciate good cooking when you eat it." His tone was rough, but the flicker of satisfaction in his eyes betrayed him. His gaze slid to my empty bowl, and a smirk tugged at his mouth.

"What brings you here so early?"

"I'm meeting Keenan. His ship should arrive this morning."

His brows furrowed. "Still friends with that troublemaker, are you? Has he finished his paladin training?"

I laughed. "Don't worry, Uncle. He's got the title, the oath, and even a proper paladin name to prove it."

Uncle Grog shook his head, snorting again. "I still remember the day he came running to you about those cursed wolves. If Gamreal hadn't overheard your plans, the both of you would've been dead meat."

The memory rose, sharp and vivid. Keenan, eyes alight with excitement, had come to me declaring that wolves were harassing farmers and that he'd tracked them to their den.

"All we have to do is kill them, and we'll save the farmers and be heroes!" he said.

Chapter 1 - The Hammer and Anvil

Who wouldn't want to be a hero? So, I followed my ever-impulsive friend.

We were only ten years old, armed with wooden swords and blind confidence. When we found the den, the wolves were there, just as Keenan had promised. But nothing prepared us for what we saw.

Six dire wolves.

Dire wolves are nothing like their lesser kin. These beasts stood nearly as tall as horses at the shoulder, their coarse gray-and-silver fur bristling, amber eyes gleaming with predatory intelligence. Their teeth were razors; their limbs built for killing.

The Alpha stepped forward, its howl splitting the wilderness, chilling us to the bone. It fixed us with a gaze that weighed our lives.

We froze, wooden swords trembling. Neither of us screamed or ran. Terrified, yes, but we had each other's backs. As the pack circled, we pressed together, back-to-back, waiting for the end.

The Alpha lunged, a blur of muscle and teeth. We raised our toy blades, bracing for death.

Then, light. A sudden flash, and the beast slammed into an invisible barrier.

Out of nowhere, my three uncles appeared, weapons drawn, faces grim with resolve. They fought like seasoned warriors, cutting down the wolves with terrifying precision. We stood frozen, awestruck.

Afterward, Gamreal inspected the den, muttering, "Good, good," though he noted the wolves were unnatural for these parts. Throm and Grogrick marched us home in silence. We both knew how close we had come to death.

As we passed through the city gates and onto the cobblestone streets, I glanced back at the wilderness. I didn't know it then, but that day would shape who I became and the kind of trouble Keenan and I would always find.

When we reached Grissom, Throm gave us his steady gaze. "Keenan, you should head home."

Keenan nodded, but before he left, I blurted, "Thank you for helping us."

Uncle Grog only grunted and went inside. Nudging Keenan, I whispered, "Go on."

Keenan muttered, "Uh, yes...thanks."

Throm smiled, a rare gift, and we parted ways.

I'll never forget that day. It was the day I learned how dangerous the world could be and how much more dangerous my uncles were when protecting those they loved. Keenan and I grew up a great deal that evening.

Snapping out of the memory, I noticed Uncle Grog staring into the distance, his features softer than usual. Was he remembering the same thing I was?

"Hey, Uncle," I called.

He jolted, quickly masking the faraway look with his signature scowl. "What?" he growled.

"What brings you here on a Monday?"

"You haven't heard?" His tone carried a hint of incredulity.

"Heard what?"

"The king's stopping by today," he said, shaking his head.

"King Brom?" I raised an eyebrow.

"Who else would it be?" he huffed, exasperated. "Sometimes you ask the dumbest questions."

Chapter 1 - The Hammer and Anvil

I grinned, knowing my next jab would rile him up. "Why's he coming here instead of staying at that fancy Inn on the Hill?"

That did it. Grog's eyes widened as he sputtered, "The Inn on the Hill? That fancy-pants place with tiny portions, ridiculous cutlery, and food fit for birds? Bah! Of course he's coming here! He wants real food, made for real men, not that nonsense!"

Catching my grin, he growled, "You're just stirring me up, boy. Watch it."

To anyone else, it might have sounded like a threat. To me, it was just Grog being Grog. "I'm sorry, Uncle. Everyone knows your food is the best. I was only teasing."

He snorted, turning toward the kitchen. "Of course it's the best. I'm the one making it."

"Well, maybe I should stick around and meet him. I've never met a king before," I said casually.

He shrugged without looking back. "You need to meet your king."

I frowned. "Except I'm not a dwarf. I'm not allowed in the city under the mountain."

That stopped him in his tracks. He turned slowly, fire flashing in his eyes. "You were raised by dwarves, you passed the trials, you were given a dwarven name. If it were up to me, you'd already be on the registry!" He drew a deep breath, steadying himself, then added, "The three of us will speak for you. It should be a formality."

He muttered under his breath, "Though my word won't mean much, they'll listen to Throm and Gam."

I chuckled, touched by his protectiveness, but Gamreal's words echoed in my mind:

No one who isn't a dwarf has ever been allowed in the city under the mountain, nor are they permitted to know its name. If you pass the trials, we'll take you to the king to see if he'll allow it.

The trials. I shuddered at the memory, especially the final one: seven days alone on the mountain, without supplies.

I remembered overhearing Throm arguing with Gam and Grog when they thought I was out of earshot.

"No one who isn't a dwarf can survive the cold. We can't do this to him," Throm had said.

Gamreal's reply was firm. "If he wants to be one of us, he has to."

Grog had said nothing, only snorted in agreement.

I had stepped into the room then, my voice steady with determination. "Of course I'll do it. I am one of you."

That ended the debate.

The next morning, with quiet wishes of good luck, they watched as I ascended the mountain, their figures shrinking behind me.

The cold struck like daggers against my skin. A blizzard raged for the first three days, and more than once I was certain I would die. Yet somehow, I endured. Perhaps there was something in my blood that gave me an edge. My uncles always seemed to think I was different, though I doubted even they knew why.

I suppose I'll never know for certain.

They had found me as a baby, my dying mother, using the last of her strength to place me in Grog's arms before she passed. Not even Throm's healing could save her. Odd,

Chapter 1 - The Hammer and Anvil

they said, for she was still young. I know little about my family's past, but my uncles are my family now.

On the seventh day, as the sun rose, I had made it. Numb from the cold but exhilarated, I began my descent.

Near the base, I spotted three figures trudging up the mountainside. Their worried faces turned to shock when they saw me.

By then, warmth had begun to return to my limbs, and my sense of humor remained intact. I grinned and called out, "Got anything harder?" Their stunned expressions were priceless. "That was pretty cold," I added with a laugh.

Grog recovered first, muttering, "See? I told you he'd be fine."

Gam smirked. "Is that why you were up before dawn, pacing like a nervous goat?"

"I was making breakfast," Grog grumbled, glaring at him.

"And leading us up the mountain had nothing to do with worrying, I'm sure," Gam teased.

While they bickered, Throm stepped forward, pride shining in his eyes. Resting a hand on my shoulder, he murmured, "You are one of us now, boy."

Warmth flooded through me, chasing away the last of the frostbite, filling me with an overwhelming sense of belonging. As Throm's healing energy washed over me, I thought, *I wish I could learn paladin spells like him.*

They gave me my dwarven name: Halvar.

"He was a great warrior," Throm said. "Carry it with pride."

"I'm honored," I replied, my chest swelling as they beamed at me, though Grog quickly returned to his usual gruffness.

"Enough of this. Let's go home. Supper's waiting," he grunted, stomping off toward the city.

We returned to Grissom, where a feast was prepared in my honor. That night, surrounded by the uncles I had fought so hard to call family, I knew this was where I truly belonged.

I smiled at the memory as my thoughts drifted back to the inn.

Grog laughed as he disappeared into the kitchen. "I still can't believe it, a Noctari paladin!"

I grinned, thinking, Yeah, that is crazy.

Noctari aren't well-liked. Often, they find themselves on the wrong side of the law. They're described as nomadic and hostile, dwelling in the wastelands to the southeast. Humanoid in build, slightly taller and leaner than humans, they carry an athletic, wiry frame. Their origins are shrouded in mystery, though some claim they were born of experiments during the Great War, when humans and demons were forcibly merged.

Their skin ranges from deep reds and maroons to unnatural hues of purple and gray. Their hair is equally striking, black, white, or dark red. Many bear horns like rams or gazelles. But their eyes are most distinctive: solid-colored, faintly glowing, in shades of gold, silver, white, or deep crimson and blue. Some Noctari carry further infernal traits, fangs, clawed nails, marking them as otherworldly.

I'd heard stories of the wastelands they call home, though I'd never traveled that far. No one knows how many

Chapter 1 - The Hammer and Anvil

remain out there. Occasionally, one wanders into town, only to be met with suspicion and scorn, though Keenan, over time, had been accepted.

Even as an orphan, I was grateful he hadn't grown up in that wasteland. Instead, we found each other. We both saw something in the other, something neither of us fully understood, but we believed in it. I was just glad he was coming back. I missed my best friend.

My thoughts drifted to Brom. I'd heard he was kindhearted, but also a fearsome warrior. They said he had a wife and three children, two sons and a daughter. I wondered what they were like.

Just then, the tavern door creaked open. A tall, broad-shouldered Noctari stepped inside, a massive shield slung across his back, a sword at his belt. His deep red skin contrasted with jet-black hair, and his bright blue eyes scanned the dim room.

It took me a moment to recognize him, but when I did, I leapt to my feet. "Keenan!"

His gaze locked on mine, and a slow smile spread across his face. He strode over, leaned his shield against the bar, and extended his hand. I grabbed it, pulling him into a hug.

He sighed, hugging me back begrudgingly. "You know I've never been much of a hugger."

I laughed. "I don't care! I haven't seen my best friend in three years, I'm giving you a hug!"

He shook his head with a small smile. "Well, at least some things never change."

"And some things do," I said, stepping back to size him up. "You've put on, what, thirty pounds of muscle?"

He grinned. "They worked us pretty hard."

We sat at the bar, my curiosity spilling over. "So, how was the training? Was it as tough as they say? And why three years? I thought it was less than two. Did you get a smite? A special weapon? How was the food? The beds? Did anybody die?"

He laughed. "Slow down, one at a time." He took a breath. "Training was good. Yes, it was tough. It shouldn't have taken that long; it's only supposed to be 18 months. But I didn't get the vow and smite I wanted, which is why it took longer." He paused, thinking. "What were the other questions?"

I chuckled. "Weapon, food, bed, and, uh... anyone die?"

He smirked. "No weapon, but I did get a shield. The food could never match Grog's," he said loudly toward the kitchen. "The beds were terrible. And no, I am not dead."

I laughed, but before I could press further, a low grunt came from the doorway. Both of us turned to see Grog standing there, arms crossed, silently listening.

"Of course, the food wasn't as good as mine," he said flatly. "And the reason it took you longer is because you're stubborn." He fixed Keenan with a knowing look. "Throm called it. Said you'd make it, but it would take longer than two years."

Surprised, I looked at Grog. "You never told me that."

He shrugged. "Didn't see why I needed to."

I glanced at Keenan, curious. In the old days, he would've flared up, but now he seemed calmer. If he was upset, he didn't show it.

Chapter 1 - The Hammer and Anvil

Keenan nodded. "Throm has good insight, having gone through the training himself. I'll admit, he was right. And tell him I was only two seconds behind his record on the final challenge."

At that, Grog raised an eyebrow. "Oh, really? Now that's impressive."

He studied Keenan for a moment, then let out a deep laugh. "Well, boy, let's hear it!"

Confused, I asked, "Hear what?"

Still grinning, Grog turned to Keenan. "I want to be the first to hear him officially announce himself as a paladin. Or do you think this establishment isn't worthy of the honor?"

Keenan stood, looking slightly embarrassed. Then, in a voice deeper than I'd ever heard, he declared:

"I am Aegis, Protector of the Innocent, Wielder of the Bulwark of Kings."

Grog's smile faltered at the last words. His expression shifted, and without warning, he vaulted over the bar, rushing to Keenan's shield.

"By my beard, I didn't recognize you at first!" he exclaimed, laughing as he inspected it. "So, you've chosen a new charge, eh? Never thought I'd see the day!"

Keenan and I exchanged bewildered looks as Grog continued. "What's the matter? Cat got your tongue?"

When the shield, predictably, said nothing, Grog muttered, "The silent treatment, huh? I remember your last charge, you rascal. I was there when you..." His voice trailed into a whisper, his expression darkening.

"Let him die, eh?" Grog's voice dropped lower. "Still nothing? Don't worry, he broke his oath. Had it coming, in my opinion, not that anyone cares what I think. And Throm's here too, if you'd like to see him again... if you'll speak to him."

Keenan and I just stared, dumbfounded, as Grog whispered something to the shield. Then, realizing we were still watching, he straightened, scowling.

"All right, Aegis," Grog said sternly, "you'd better take good care of that shield. You hear me?"

Keenan nodded silently.

"Good." Grog grunted and retreated to the kitchen.

I looked at Keenan and chuckled. "Well, that's not something you see every day."

He smirked. "No, I suppose not."

As we sat back down, I leaned toward him. "So... no Oath of Vengeance, then?"

"No," he replied. "Your uncle was right about me. I was stubborn and foolish."

He glanced up with a wry smile. "Well, I still am. But they taught me how to control it."

I smiled back. "At least they managed to do what I never could."

He laughed. "I suppose you're right. There were times when I put you and your uncles through your paces."

"'Times'?" I scoffed. "It was a full-time job. Remember the wolves?"

Keenan chuckled. "Oh, I remember."

I grinned but pressed him. "Don't think you're getting away without answering my question. No Oath of Vengeance, what happened?"

He sighed, his expression darkening. "The first eighteen months of training were perfect. I was developing quickly, almost breaking some of your uncle's records. But then came the Selection…"

His voice trailed off, his gaze distant. I waited, trying to be patient, though curiosity gnawed at me.

Finally, he looked at me. "What do you know about Selection?"

Caught off guard, I frowned. For all I'd heard about Paladins, even with my uncle being one, I realized I knew very little about how their oaths were chosen. "I always thought you could just pick the one you wanted," I admitted.

He shook his head. "So did I. But that's not how it works. Once your instructors approve you, you're brought before... something. A presence. It had no form, only a glowing light. It was... calming. I felt at peace in its presence."

His voice softened. "I've never seen anything like it. Maybe an angel, maybe some celestial. I don't know. But then I heard a voice in my head. It said: 'You, my child, cannot take the Oath of Vengeance, for it will be your undoing. If you are willing to accept another oath, I will bestow it upon you, and you may continue.'"

Keenan's jaw tightened. "I was furious. Why not Vengeance? I trained harder than anyone. I was the best in my classes. Was it because I'm a Noctari?"

He paused, anger rekindling at the memory. "But the voice seemed to know my thoughts. It said: 'This has nothing to do with what you are or where you come from. We see into your soul, and vengeance will destroy you. You have two choices: leave and abandon your path or return to training until your heart and mind are ready to accept the gift we offer.'"

Keenan shook his head, sadness in his voice. "I stormed out. I was furious. Almost two years, I thought it was wasted! And now I'd have to start again. The worst part was, I think my teachers knew. Maybe even the other trainees. But once I calmed down, I realized what I wanted more than anything was to be a paladin. No matter the oath, I'd take it."

He sighed. "So, I went back. Another eighteen months of training. When I was selected again, I didn't argue. This time, I was given the Oath of Protection."

"And?" I asked eagerly. "What about your smite? Does your sword burst into flames? Can you call down lightning?"

Keenan smiled at my enthusiasm. "No smite, no fire, no lightning. Instead, I got Lay on Hands."

I blinked. "What's that? Can you blow someone up by touching them?"

Keenan burst into laughter. "I've missed this," he said, shaking his head. "No, it's a healing ability. I think it can cure diseases, maybe heal wounds. But I'm not sure yet."

I frowned. "How can you not be sure?"

He shrugged. "When we're given an ability, it's one we have to discover and grow into. Lay on Hands was granted to me, but it's a hidden spell I need to unlock for myself. There's no manual."

I patted him on the shoulder. "Well, even if it's not a 'cool' spell, I'm proud of you."

Keenan smiled, but neither of us noticed Grog standing in the kitchen doorway, his expression stunned.

Chapter 1 - The Hammer and Anvil

"Lay on Hands…" he muttered, as though in disbelief. "That hasn't been granted for centuries…"

Then, quietly, he slipped back into the kitchen as I began telling Keenan about what I'd been up to in the years he'd been gone.

After about thirty minutes of catching up, a commotion stirred outside, followed by the sounds of a small party arriving. The tavern door opened, and two halflings slipped inside with the silence of shadows. They moved quickly, scanning booths, peering beneath tables, their green hooded armor blending with the dim light. Each carried a dagger, but it was more than weapons, their movements carried purpose, discipline, and uncanny precision.

As one neared the kitchen, my uncle stepped out, arms folded. "Ah, right on time as always. Go ahead and look, you nosy buggers."

The halflings vanished into the kitchen, reappearing moments later to exchange a nod before slipping back outside.

My uncle turned to us, his tone suddenly sharp. "You two best behave. I don't need any trouble today."

The door opened again, and a giant of a man entered, clad in full plate armor. He removed his helmet, revealing brown eyes beneath a fall of blonde hair that brushed his shoulders. His gaze swept the room with the calm vigilance of a seasoned warrior. He set his massive shield by the door, its polished surface catching the lantern light, and rested a gauntleted hand on the hilt of his sword. On his chest plate gleamed an intricate design: a dove with outstretched wings descending before the roaring head of a lion.

Next came another man, perhaps six feet tall, with wavy blonde hair and bright green eyes. His warm smile softened the edge of the armored presence before him. Behind him trailed a girl of ten or twelve, shy and watchful. She clung to his side, her black eyes darting about the room, her blonde hair tied back in a neat ponytail. She pointed toward a corner table, and the man nodded. She slipped quickly into the seat, the armored giant settling beside her, listening patiently as she whispered to him.

The man in charge wore well-crafted but unremarkable leather armor. His presence was commanding, yet his features radiated kindness. He strode to the bar. "Hey, Grog, what's for lunch today?" he asked with a smile.

Grog clasped his hand firmly. "Fresh bread, stag and boar stew, and I even got some of that nasty mead you like from that island that only trades here once a year."

The man laughed heartily. "See, this is why I come here and not up on the hill." He lowered his voice, glancing around. "Though I should probably be more careful who I say that to."

Turning, he regarded Keenan and me. "So, this must be your nephew you've told me about? And it's not every day you see a Noctari paladin in a bar."

Introductions were made, and Brom shook our hands. What struck me most was his ease with Keenan. For most, a Noctari drew suspicion, if not outright hostility. But Brom's kindness was unshaken, as though Keenan's heritage meant nothing at all. In Grissom, people tolerated him, but elsewhere Noctari were often driven to the docks or the wastelands.

Chapter 1 - The Hammer and Anvil

As Grog prepared their food, Brom lingered, asking about life with my uncle, about Keenan's training. His questions were warm, genuine, and his presence put us at ease. When the food arrived, he excused himself to join his daughter and the armored guardian.

The lunch crowd began to swell, and Grog busied himself behind the bar. At some point, two halflings returned, slipping to separate tables, their eyes scanning the room. I chuckled inwardly. He keeps a low profile, but he's well-guarded. That bodyguard alone would make anyone think twice.

Keenan leaned close, whispering, "I could be wrong, but I think those are two different halflings."

I blinked, studying them. "Hard to tell. Their hoods hide most of their features."

He nodded. "One's taller, the other shorter. The first pair were the same height."

I laughed, smacking his shoulder. "Well, at least they taught you some useful awareness in training." He smiled faintly.

As we rose to leave, raised voices caught our attention. Three men argued at a nearby table, their fear plain.

"I'm telling you, that ship is cursed!" said one, a dockworker with dirty brown hair.

His companion, a traveling merchant, scoffed. "You expect me to believe that nonsense?"

The third man, another dockworker with black hair, leaned in. "No, it's true. There's something about that ship; it strikes fear in your heart. It'll drive you away!"

The first man shuddered. "The crew…dreadful. A stench about them. And their eyes…"

The third man's voice dropped to a whisper. "Yes. Their eyes…they were red."

By now the tavern was loud with laughter and clinking tankards, drowning out the rest. But I noticed Brom and his companions, still, alert, listening intently while the crowd remained oblivious.

I turned to ask Keenan what he thought, but the door creaked open. A wave of unease swept through me, sudden and inexplicable. It was not fear of what I saw, but of what I felt, a terror without shape, like a shadow in the dark you know is there but cannot see.

Two large sailors entered, filling the room with the smell of death and the doorway with their bulk, scowling as they surveyed the room. Their sun-darkened skin, tangled beards, and calloused hands spoke of years at sea. Their patched canvas and leather garments hung loose, worn thin by salt and storm. But it wasn't their size that chilled me, it was their eyes. Red.

A shiver ran through me. One of them growled, "What are you looking at?" His voice was gravel, his stare unblinking. He brushed past me toward the bar, his companion close behind.

I turned to Keenan. He had gone rigid, his hand resting on the hilt of his sword.

"Do you see their eyes?" I whispered. "I've never seen anything like that."

Without looking away, he murmured, "I've heard of it, but never seen it. Demon possession, maybe."

"What? I thought that was a myth!" I hissed.

He shook his head, his expression grim. "Not according to the paladin library."

Chapter 1 - The Hammer and Anvil

The sailors reached the bar. Grog had stopped mid-motion, his gaze narrowing. For a long moment, the three of them stared at one another, the air thick with tension. Then the second sailor pulled something from his pocket and held it out. It looked like a black stone.

"You know where we can find more of these?"

Grog's face shifted, so subtly only I, who had grown up under his watch, would notice. His jaw tightened, his eyes darkened. Anger and concern flickered beneath the mask of his gruff exterior.

"No," he said coldly. "And if you're not going to order anything, I'll have to ask you to leave."

The man snorted. "Come on. Let's try the market. Someone there will know."

They turned and left, their heavy boots echoing against the floorboards. Grog's eyes followed them until the door shut behind them, his stare burning with an intensity that made my stomach twist.

He turned to Keenan. "Keep an eye on them. They're bad news."

Then to me: "If you see your uncles, send them straight here."

I nodded, though confusion gnawed at me. "What's wrong?"

He shook his head, his voice low and final. "Send them straight here."

Without another word, he disappeared into the kitchen.

For a moment, the tavern's warmth returned, the clink of tankards, the hum of conversation, but I couldn't shake the image of those red eyes. They lingered in my mind like embers in the dark, a warning I didn't yet understand.

Chapter 2 - Fight

"Come on!" Keenan urged quietly, already moving for the door.

We burst outside, the sudden sunlight blinding after the dim light of the inn. The cobblestones gleamed white-hot, reflecting the midday glare. For a moment, the world felt too bright, too sharp, as though the city itself was holding its breath.

Turning left, we hurried toward the market, only a few buildings away. Behind us came the sound of armored boots striking stone, Brom, catching up with long, purposeful strides. His expression was grim, his jaw set like iron.

"I'd like to know more," he said, his voice low but steady, nodding toward the market.

Grateful for his presence, we quickened our pace.

The market square was chaos. Milton, the farmer who sold his produce daily, sat slumped on the ground, clutching his shoulder. His wife, Linda, scrambled to gather spilled apples and carrots, her hands shaking as she tried to simultaneously right their overturned cart. The shattered remains of their table lay scattered like bones.

We rushed to help, lifting Milton to his feet. His face was pale, twisted with both pain and fury.

"What happened?" Brom demanded, his tone commanding, already taking charge.

Linda's voice cut in, sharp and trembling. "It was those evil men! They came through demanding information. We

Chapter 2 - Fight

told them we didn't know anything about their cursed stones, and they shoved him down, smashed our table, and walked away like they owned the place!"

Brom's jaw tightened, his eyes narrowing. "Which way did they go?"

Before she could answer, a scream tore through the square. Shouting erupted from the blacksmith's shop, followed by the crash of metal on stone. Then Franklin, the blacksmith himself, staggered into the street, a dagger buried deep in his chest. His eyes found ours, wide with shock, lips parting as if to speak, but only a wet gasp escaped. He collapsed at our feet, lifeless.

The sounds of destruction still echoed inside the shop.

We charged through the open doorway. The air reeked of blood and smoke. Inside, the two sailors from the docks loomed over a town guard struggling to rise. One sailor's shoulder was split open, blood pouring freely, yet he moved as though pain meant nothing. The other turned toward us as he heard us enter the shop, his lips curling into a sneer.

"Well, well," he growled. "If it isn't the little boy who doesn't know it's rude to stare." His laugh was jagged, cruel. "Time to teach you some manners."

His eyes glowed brighter now, a hellish red, and the air itself seemed to thicken with dread. A palpable aura of fear pressed against my chest, making it hard to breathe.

The guard staggered upright, it was Jeffries, one of Keenan's and my childhood friends. His face was bruised, blood trickled from his mouth, but his green eyes burned with defiance.

"You're both under arrest," Jeffries declared, his voice steady despite the tremor in his body.

The wounded sailor barked a laugh. "Come here, runt. I'll break you in half."

Jeffries raised his short sword, but he was hopelessly outmatched. The brute charged, and at the same instant, the other sailor lunged at me. I barely had time to lift my arms when a blur of steel and fury slammed into him, Brom, the king himself, driving his shoulder into the man's chest. The sailor flew backward, crashing into a rack of tools with a howl of pain.

At the same moment, Keenan stepped in front of Jeffries, his voice calm but commanding, ringing with authority.

"I am a Paladin. You have one chance to surrender, or I will stop your unlawful actions by force."

The sailor hesitated, his sneer twisting into something darker. "A Noctari paladin? You should be on our side." With a hiss, he lunged.

Keenan met him head-on. His shield struck like a hammer, slamming the man into the wall with bone-cracking force. Before the sailor could recover, Keenan's blade flashed. One swift, merciless stroke, and the man's head struck the floor with a sickening thud.

The room went still.

Keenan turned, his eyes cold. "You get one chance," he said to the remaining sailor.

The man's grin widened, wicked and unafraid. Slowly, he pulled a small device from his belt. It began to hum, glowing with a sickly red light that pulsed in time with his heartbeat.

"You can't stop us all," he taunted.

Brom's voice thundered. "Everyone out! Now!"

Chapter 2 - Fight

We bolted for the door, dragging Jeffries with us. Behind us, the sailor's laughter rose, high and manic, echoing through the shop.

Then came the blast.

The explosion ripped through the street, a roar of fire and stone that shook the very bones of Grissom. Windows shattered, carts toppled, and the cobblestones themselves cracked beneath the force. Heat seared my back as we dove for cover, the world dissolving into smoke, screams, and the ringing in my ears.

When I lifted my head, the market was unrecognizable choked in dust, littered with debris, and echoing with the cries of the wounded.

As the dust settled, Brom rose and called out, "Is everyone okay?"

Jeffries, Keenan, and I nodded, shaken but still standing. From deeper in the city, the clash of steel and the cries of battle grew louder, echoing like a storm rolling in.

We knelt beside Franklin. It was too late, he was gone.

"I need to get back to my daughter," the king said, his voice taut with urgency.

With no immediate threat pressing in, we followed him, hearts pounding, weapons ready.

As we turned onto the main street, an elf moved swiftly out of the shadows, bow drawn. He glanced at us and gave a curt nod. Reeger was an elf who felt more comfortable in the wild than among people. An adept outdoorsman, he often spent his time with us growing up, keeping us out of trouble. Incredibly stealthy, his green eyes never missed a detail.

"I think some of the guards have turned," he said grimly.

We broke into a run, heading for Grog's inn.

Brom pushed the door open. Torchlight flickered across a wreckage of splintered chairs and overturned tables. Bodies lay scattered, two sailors, three townsfolk.

He scanned the corner where they'd been sitting. "Not here," he muttered. "But they left in a hurry."

The door creaked again. We tensed, until a familiar halfling slipped inside. He walked straight to the king, whispered something urgent, and vanished.

"They're headed to the barracks," Brom said.

I frowned. "Safest place in theory. But if Reeger's right, they're walking into a trap."

Brom gave a dry chuckle. "If Victus is with them, they won't be prepared for what they're about to catch."

I grinned. "Sounds good to me."

Keenan and I exchanged a look, then bolted out the door. "The guards' barracks, which doubled as an armory and prison, stood atop a gentle rise, surrounded by homes and shuttered shops." As we climbed, the sounds of combat grew louder. A deep, guttural voice echoed through the air, speaking in a language none of us recognized.

We rounded the final corner and froze.

In the center of the town square stood two towering demons, each at least ten feet tall. Their red skin shimmered in the firelight, wings twisted and unfurled, claws flexing, hooves grinding into stone. Their black eyes locked onto us with cold malice.

And there, standing alone before them, was Victus, shield raised, sword in hand, laughing as he hurled insults.

Chapter 2 - Fight

Behind him, pressed against a building, huddled a group of children with their schoolteacher. The king's daughter stood among them, a halfling at her side. He trembled but held his ground.

The square was in chaos, wounded guards and townsfolk crying out, steel clashing, blood staining the cobblestones.

To the side, guards fought one another. And atop the steps of the meeting house stood an old, scarred man clutching a glowing orb. He chanted in a tongue none of us understood, and before him, a shimmering portal grew larger by the second.

A wounded guard gasped from the ground, "You must stop the old man! He's opening portals, that's how the big ones got in!"

Jeffries broke into a sprint toward the steps, but snarling imps leapt into his path, claws flashing.

I froze. Too much chaos. Too many cries. I didn't know what to do first.

Then Keenan's voice cut through the noise. "Help Jeffries and stop the old man!"

Snapping into motion, I drew my short sword and axe and sprinted toward Jeffries. As I reached him, I saw Reeger loose an arrow at the old man on the steps, but it struck an invisible barrier and dropped harmlessly to the ground.

Meanwhile, Keenan charged the towering demons, the king close behind him.

Jeffries was being swarmed by imps, small, grotesque creatures with sharp fangs and beady eyes. Their stubby wings barely kept them aloft, but they were relentless, death by a thousand cuts. One lunged for Jeffries' throat, and I caught it midair, slammed it to the ground. It glared up at me, screeching, "You will die, human filth!", just before my axe split it in two.

Another imp darted toward me. I braced for impact, but it dropped lifeless beside me, an arrow lodged in its skull. Reeger appeared at my side, swords flashing as he cleaved another in half, grinning.

"No honor in these little beasts, is there?" he said.

I chuckled, dispatching the last of the imps near us. Together, Jeffries, Reeger, and I charged the meeting house steps, determined to end the old man's dark ritual.

But the barrier held. We couldn't reach him.

Frustrated, I shouted to Keenan, "You know anything about invisible shields?"

"A little busy!" he called back, dodging a massive war maul swung by one of the demons.

"The portal's growing! We need to shut it now!"

Keenan slid aside, dropped his weapon, and clasped his hands together, eyes closed in concentration. The larger demon seized the moment, raising its maul high.

"No!" I shouted as the hammer began to fall.

Victus lunged in, shield raised. The maul crashed down with a bone-shattering impact, driving him to his knees with a grunt of pain.

The demon paused, stunned that Victus still lived. That hesitation was all Brom needed. He leapt onto a half-wall, then sprang onto the demon's back, driving his sword deep into the base of its neck. The creature staggered, blood gurgling from its throat, eyes wide with shock as it collapsed forward, lifeless.

Chapter 2 - Fight

The second demon roared, turning toward Brom, who struggled to free his blade from the fallen beast. Victus tried to rise. The demon raised its weapon, then stopped.

A small projectile had struck the back of its head.

It turned slowly, black eyes landing on the king's daughter, standing defiantly with her hands on her hips.

In a voice both soft and strong, she said, "You leave my daddy alone."

Time froze.

Smoke curled from the demon's nostrils as it locked eyes with the little girl. Ignoring Victus' taunts and Brom's shouts, it gave a cruel, savage smile.

"I will kill you and all your little friends for your insolence."

With terrifying speed, it swung its maul into the building where the children were huddled, collapsing an entire stone wall.

The girl cried out, "No!" and threw herself over the children, shielding them with her small body.

The king, abandoning his sword, launched himself at the demon in a frenzy, punching, stabbing with a dagger, doing anything to bring it down. Victus drove his blade deep into the demon's leg, but the creature, consumed by hatred, didn't flinch. It laughed as it slowly sank to its knees.

Brom stepped in front of it, hand outstretched.

"Victus!" he called.

With a solemn nod, Victus tossed his sword to him.

Tears welled in the king's eyes as he gripped the hilt. His voice trembled with grief and fury.

"For my little girl," he whispered, and drove the blade deep between the demon's eyes.

The creature let out a final, shuddering gasp before collapsing into the dirt.

Keenan sprang to his feet. "Found it!" he shouted, voice ringing across the square.

He began chanting in a foreign tongue, and the shimmering barrier around the old man flickered, then collapsed.

Reeger didn't hesitate. His bowstring snapped, and the arrow flew true, striking the old man squarely between the eyes. The sorcerer dropped without a sound.

The portal behind him convulsed, its edges fraying. With a final, violent swirl, it collapsed inward and vanished.

The battle's fury began to subside. Screams faded into groans. The streets lay broken, littered with the dead and wounded.

Then we saw them, Victus and Brom, clawing through rubble where the king's daughter had last stood.

We ran to help, bracing for the worst. But as we reached the wreckage, someone spotted a faint shimmer beneath the stone, a magical barrier, still intact.

Hope surged.

Together, we cleared the debris, revealing the children huddled safely within a protective dome.

The king dropped to his knees beside it, voice trembling. "Sweetie, can you hear me? If you can, release the barrier."

Chapter 2 - Fight

The shimmer vanished. The little girl collapsed, unconscious. Brom caught her before she hit the ground, cradling her with tears in his eyes.

The other children stirred, dazed but unharmed.

Keenan exhaled, shaking his head. "Well... that was impressive."

As I scanned the wreckage, a cold realization struck, Gamreal was with the council. If the city was under siege, they'd be next.

I turned to Keenan. He was already watching me.

"Gam," I said.

We broke into a sprint, Reeger close behind.

Inside the council chamber, we heard a small voice cry out.

"More are coming!"

I couldn't help but laugh. "No, it's just us, Millhouse."

His head popped up from behind an overturned table, eyes wide with relief.

Millhouse, one of Grissom City's five councilmen, was always nervous, always expecting disaster.

The room was a mess. Several guards lay dead. One wounded man was being tended to by Renard, another councilman. Renard was quiet, his past a mystery, but he'd proven himself steady.

He glanced up as we entered. "Looks like you missed the party," he said, tying off a bandage.

"We had our own," I replied, forcing a smile.

Gamreal stepped forward, his hand wrapped in bloodied cloth. I grabbed it instinctively.

"What happened?"

He shrugged. "Knife wound." Then, lowering his voice, he gestured toward the far corner.

Villaheim sat bound, glaring. Anselot stood over him, sword in hand.

"He was in on it," Gamreal said. "A traitor."

I looked at Keenan, who was checking the fallen guards.

Gamreal continued. "Villaheim came in with two guards, asking about the black stones. When we said we didn't know anything, he called us liars. One of the guards went for Millhouse. I intercepted the blade, hence this." He raised his bandaged hand. "The other two tried to stop me, but Matt", he nodded toward the injured guard..." helped Anselot and me take them down."

Anger surged. I thought of the demons, the children, the destruction. My fists clenched as I stared at Villaheim. I wanted to strike him.

Keenan's gaze was locked on him too. Then he turned to Gamreal. "Want me to interrogate him?"

Though Keenan now wore the mantle of a paladin, he still deferred to those in charge, very different from the defiant youth I'd once known.

I chuckled quietly, remembering. Gamreal caught the look and grinned, reading my thoughts.

"That won't be necessary," Gamreal said, his voice calm but edged. "He started talking the moment he lost. Something's blocking his memories, not magical, at least not that I can tell. We'll either wait for it to wear off or…" He raised his voice slightly. "Just kill him."

Villaheim whimpered. "I told you everything! They came to me asking about the stones, promised me money to

Chapter 2 - Fight

help find them. I didn't know they were going to try to kill you!" His voice cracked, desperate.

I suddenly remembered the inn and told Gamreal about Grog's absence and the wreckage we'd found.

Gamreal gave a knowing smile. "In an emergency, Grog and Throm head home to protect our house."

I frowned. "Why the house?"

Gamreal offered one of his trademark enigmatic smiles, the kind that signaled he wasn't going to answer. "Well, it's our home, isn't it?" he said, with a mischievous glint.

Before I could press further, Brom entered with Jeffries and his entourage. For the first time, I saw all five halflings together. They moved quickly, sweeping the room for threats as Brom approached.

He glanced at me, then at Gamreal. "Well, this sure is a mess."

He reached for Gam's hand, then paused at the sight of the bandages. Chuckling, he said, "Just can't stay out of trouble, can you?"

Gamreal grinned. "Sometimes I get bored with all the meetings and politics."

They shared a laugh, but Brom's expression soon turned serious. "So, you know something."

Gamreal's smile didn't fade. "Maybe. But there's a lot I don't know, and I don't like that."

Brom shook his head. "You not knowing makes me nervous."

"You and me both," Gamreal replied.

Jeffries stepped forward and gave the council a grim update. Half the city guard was either dead or deserted. They were critically understaffed.

He explained that Anthony, the captain of the guard, had refused to cooperate. When the traitors tried to turn him, he spat in their faces. Though outnumbered eight to one, he fought fiercely, killing two before they overwhelmed him.

Gamreal's face darkened. "Well, looks like you've been promoted, Jeffries."

Jeffries blinked. "Uh... I'll do my best, sir."

Gamreal placed a reassuring hand on his shoulder. "I know you will. Start by figuring out who we have left. Organize shifts around the gates and the harbor."

Just then, Keenan stepped over and gently took Gamreal's hand, beginning to heal the wound.

Gamreal smiled. "You're already rather good at that. Didn't burn or anything."

"Burn?" Keenan asked, puzzled.

Gamreal smirked. "Every time Throm healed me, it always burned."

Keenan chuckled. "Yeah... it's not supposed to do that."

Gamreal blinked, then burst into laughter. "Oh, Throm is gonna get it next time I see him." We all laughed with him.

Then, regaining his composure, Gamreal said, "I'll send a runner to the dwarves, see if they'll lend us troops while we regroup."

Chapter 2 - Fight

Jeffries looked surprised. "Do you really think they'll send help?" Like most of us, he was curious about the dwarves beneath the mountain. They rarely ventured out and seeing them in force was almost unheard of.

Gamreal smiled confidently. "Some of them owe me favors. I don't see why not."

As we spoke, several halflings slipped away. I watched them from the corner of my eye as they melted into the shadows. I smiled to myself. I was glad they were on our side.

"Wait," Gamreal said sharply. "What about their ship? The one they came in on?" He turned to Jeffries. "Take a few men and check the vessel in the harbor."

"Yes, sir," Jeffries replied, already moving.

Gamreal raised a hand. "Don't board it. Quarantine and lock it down until we can send a proper team."

Jeffries gave a sharp nod and headed towards the door. Gamreal turned to the council. "We need to search Villaheim's quarters. Anything useful, anything hidden, find it. Then toss him in a cell."

He looked at me. "If you can, head home. Let your uncles know it's over, for now."

I nodded and turned to leave, but Gamreal caught my arm and pulled me aside. His expression was grave as he pressed several black stones into my hand.

"Give these to them," he whispered. "No one else sees them."

I slipped the stones into my pocket, masking my surprise with a nod.

As Brom, Reeger, Keenan, and the council continued their discussion, I slipped out quietly and made my way down Cobblestone Street toward the house.

But as I approached, a strange unease crept over me. My steps slowed. A chill ran down my spine, an inexplicable fear I couldn't shake.

Then a voice rang out: "It's Halvar!"

The fear vanished instantly. Grog stood in the doorway, gripping a massive battle-axe. I'd only seen him wield it once before, during the wolf attack. The sight of the stout dwarf braced with a weapon nearly as large as he was enough to terrify most, but I couldn't help but laugh.

"Did you feel fear, boy?" Throm called, brushing past Grog with a warm grin.

"So that was you?" I asked, smiling.

Throm nodded. "Still working on my aura control."

Grog muttered, "Magic nonsense. Just give me my axe and stay out of the way."

Throm and I chuckled, but as I reached for the stones, Throm's expression shifted.

"Not out here," he said, voice firm. "Inside."

I nodded and followed them in.

Throm was the eldest of the three dwarves. His white hair was pulled into a thick ponytail, his beard neatly kept. His sharp brown eyes missed nothing, always calculating, always alert. Despite his formidable presence, Throm was gentle at heart, protective of all living things. I'd only seen him raise a weapon once, but the memory of the wolf battle made it clear: he and Grog were terrifying when roused.

The house was warm and solid, thick stone walls, redwood beams supporting the angled roof. A large hearth

Chapter 2 - Fight

glowed at the center, casting soft light across the room. A sturdy table sat near the fire, built for four. A small seating area occupied one corner, and four modest bedrooms branched off the main room. It was snug, familiar, and lovingly remodeled when I came to live with them.

Inside, I pulled out the stones. Grog and Throm exchanged a glance, their faces darkening.

"Do you think it's starting?" Grog asked quietly. His subdued tone caught me off guard, I'd never seen him like this.

Throm's reply was grave. "It's getting closer. I never thought I'd see it in my lifetime."

He took the stones and slipped them into his pocket. I couldn't hold back anymore.

"What's going on?" I asked. "What are these stones? Why are people hunting them? Who are the men with red eyes, and why are they attacking?"

The two dwarves exchanged a long look.

"We need to tell him," Grog said.

"I know," Throm agreed. "But Gam should be here. He deserves a say."

Grog grunted. "Then we'd better do it soon. If it's begun, we don't have much time."

I waited, heart pounding, desperate for answers.

Throm gave me a wry smile. "I hate to send you running again, but we need Gamreal here. Tell him to come back soon. We'll speak in private."

Frustrated but knowing they wouldn't say more, I shrugged. "Alright. I'll go get him."

I left the house at a brisk pace, heading back toward the council chamber. The streets had come alive with people sweeping debris, tending to the wounded, and trading stories of what had just unfolded. Every few blocks, a cry of grief pierced the air as someone found a loved one among the fallen.

I felt the weight of their sorrow, but my thoughts were tangled in the cryptic exchange with my uncles. The black stones. The urgency. The secrecy.

I reached the council chambers just as the final threads of discussion were wrapping up. Without pause, I walked straight to Gamreal.

"Grog and Throm want a private meeting," I said.

He nodded, unsurprised. "I figured they would," he replied with a weary sigh. His eyes studied me, calculating how much of that meeting I'd be allowed to hear.

Brom stepped forward. "I'll head home, see what I can dig up. If I can spare any men, I'll send them your way."

Gamreal nodded. "Much appreciated. We'll keep pressing the traitor while you're gone." He cast a cold glance at Villaheim, who whimpered, "It was only business."

Before anyone could respond, one of the halflings burst through the door, breathless. He rushed to Brom and whispered something urgent.

Brom's face drained of color. Without a word, he turned and strode out, his daughter and Victus close behind.

Keenan and I exchanged a glance, then followed.

Outside, the halflings pointed toward the horizon.

There was a column of smoke rising in the direction of Burke. Brom's home.

Chapter 3 - Burke

Brom, visibly shaken, let out a sharp whistle. One by one, the halflings emerged from alleyways and buildings, converging around the king. Victus and Cara joined them, all watching and listening with quiet intensity.

Brom surveyed the group. "We need to get home quickly. Ideas?"

A halfling stepped forward. His voice was small but steady. "The stables were opened during the fighting. The horses scattered. It'll take time to round them up."

Victus frowned. "Walking will take half a day."

Another halfling hesitated. "Could we ask Reggie?"

Keenan and I exchanged confused glances. "Who's Reggie?"

Reeger, who had been standing silently nearby, snickered.

I jumped in surprise, hearing him. "You've got the stealth of a shadow, Reeger. I swear you could vanish in an empty room."

Just then, Cara leaned in and whispered something to her father. Brom turned to her, concern etched across his face.

"Cara, it's too dangerous. You've done enough today."

She planted her hands on her hips, blue eyes blazing. "Dad, people could be dying!"

Brom's expression softened, but he shook his head. "That spell is risky, even when you're rested."

Cara didn't flinch. "Reggie said I'm strong enough now. I can move twenty people if I stay focused. It doesn't drain me like it used to."

Brom looked toward the rising smoke, torn between fear and urgency. Cara gently took his hand. "Please trust me. I can do this."

Victus leaned in. "Sir, this might be one of those moments."

Brom sighed, then gave a faint smile. "You too, Victus? Alright. I trust you both."

Keenan stepped forward. "If you'll allow it, I'd like to join. It's my duty to protect the innocent."

I smiled. Keenan's heart had always been in the right place. If he was going, I couldn't stay behind. The talk with my uncles would have to wait.

Brom nodded. "A paladin's help is always welcome."

"But..." he began, only to be cut off by Cara. "Up to twenty, Dad. They can come."

He laughed. "Who's the king here, you or me?"

Cara flushed. "I didn't mean..."

Brom smiled gently. "It's alright, sweetie. I'm just nervous." He took a breath. "Alright. Into the circle."

We gathered close as Cara closed her eyes. A shimmering field began to expand around us. I inhaled deeply, shut my eyes, unsure of what was going to happen.

A flash of light engulfed us.

When I opened my eyes, we stood in vibrant green countryside. Rolling pastures stretched out beneath a cloudless sky. Wooden fences lined the fields.

Chapter 3 - Burke

To the northwest, a castle and city rose atop a gentle hill. Stone walls and a towering keep dominated the skyline, surrounded by clusters of homes. Bells rang from within as troops poured out of the gates, heading south.

To the west, a watchtower overlooked a small village. Flames licked at rooftops, and the sounds of battle echoed through the valley.

Farther southwest, the great lighthouse of Onixia stood tall, smoke curling from its base.

Victus and Keenan were already sprinting toward the burning village. Brom barked orders to the halflings, who scattered with practiced precision.

The king and I ran toward the smoke, Cara close behind. Reeger had vanished, but I knew he'd return when it mattered. He always did.

As we neared the watchtower, the devastation came into focus. Bodies lay strewn across the ground, villagers, soldiers, and imp-like demons. Burn marks scarred the earth. Homes had been reduced to ash and ruin.

It was worse than Grissom. Far worse.

The sounds of battle faded as we neared the watchtower. Rounding a scorched cottage, we caught sight of Victus driving his blade through the last demon, while Keenan guided a wounded soldier toward a makeshift healer station near the base.

The tower loomed over the landscape, its stone foundation wide and rooted deep. Thirty feet across at the base, it narrowed as it climbed, rising to a height of forty feet. The lower stones were rough and weathered, streaked with moss and lichen, nature's quiet reclamation.

Arrow-slit windows punctuated the walls, narrow and precise, built for vigilance and defense. Higher up, the masonry grew tighter, smoother, evidence of ancient craftsmanship. At the summit, the tower flared outward into a crenellated battlement, where faded flags snapped in the wind.

I followed Brom inside. The air was cool and damp, thick with the scent of old stone. A spiral staircase wound upward, its steps worn smooth by generations of use. At the top, a wooden trapdoor led to the roof.

Inside, soldiers moved with urgency, taking orders from a young man who stood at the center of it all. His presence was commanding, blue eyes sharp, voice steady, movements efficient. He studied a battle map while issuing orders, his shoulder-length blond hair framing a face marked by focus and resolve.

Brom embraced him. "Perseus, what's the situation?"

Perseus's expression darkened. "We were blindsided," he said. "An old man and a boy arrived by boat. The coastal watchers helped them up the cliffs, but once ashore, the old man opened a portal, killed the boy and wounded two guards. A third escaped and warned us. The creatures poured through the portal and surged towards the village."

"Where's Rannoch?" Brom asked.

Perseus gestured toward the lighthouse. "He took his men there. He's trying to close the portal."

"We had to dispel a barrier in Grissom to shut one down," Brom said. "Let's hope they were less careful here. Any word from him?"

Perseus shook his head. "Nothing yet. We've posted guards throughout the city in case the Order of Light makes

Chapter 3 - Burke

a move. The queen is safe, secured in her quarters with protection."

I stiffened at the mention of the Order of Light. I'd heard whispers, fanatics who despised magic, bent on purging it from the world. Paladins were tolerated, sometimes. But even that seemed uncertain. I'd always dismissed it as rumor. Now, I wasn't so sure.

Perseus continued, "With the village secured, we're preparing to retake the lighthouse. We need to shut that portal."

"What about Greenholm?" Brom asked.

"We've sent guards with smoke signals. If they need reinforcements, they'll call. The emissary sent an eagle to warn the elves."

I blinked, trying to absorb it all. Greenholm, that's where the halflings live, isn't it? And who exactly is this emissary?

Reeger appeared beside me, silent as ever. In a low voice, he said, "The emissary is one of my kin. A trusted advisor to Brom. He's working to strengthen ties between our people."

I smiled and mouthed "thank you." Reeger nodded, then added, "I can see the lighthouse. There are wounded, but no more enemies. No portal."

I shook my head, once again amazed by elven sight.

A guard burst in, pale and breathless. "We're bringing back wounded. Rannoch is unconscious, badly hurt."

Brom didn't hesitate. He bolted for the door, Keenan close behind.

Outside, soldiers were already piling imp corpses onto pyres. The flames sputtered, struggling to catch.

Maybe their bodies resist fire, I thought.

A group of armored men approached, carrying a broad-shouldered warrior between them. His armor hung in tatters, revealing deep gashes across his chest and arms. His face was pale, black hair matted with blood, sweat, and dirt. He shivered violently, pain etched into every line of his body.

They laid him down gently. Brom rushed to his side, gripping his hand. "Rannoch!" he called.

Keenan knelt beside him, placing a hand on his forehead and murmuring words I couldn't make out.

One of the healers arrived but froze at the sight of Keenan. "Get him away from the king's son!" he shouted. "He'll kill him!"

Brom silenced him with a glare. The healer backed off, still watching Keenan with suspicion. Soldiers gathered, faces tight with concern. Perseus stood among them, blinking back tears. Time stretched. Keenan remained still, hand pressed to Rannoch's brow, his focus unwavering. Finally, he exhaled, shoulders sagging with exhaustion.

I looked at Rannoch. The sweat had stopped. Color was returning to his cheeks. The wounds remained, but something vital had shifted.

Keenan rose slowly, drained. "He's stable. Fever is gone. But he'll need time to recover."

A ripple of relief passed through the crowd. Healers stepped in.

Brom stood and clasped Keenan's hand. "I've heard stories of paladin healing but never seen it. Thank you. You'll always be welcome in my house." He pulled Keenan into a firm embrace.

Chapter 3 - Burke

Keenan stiffened, unsure how to respond. His awkward half-hug made me smile. He'd spent so long being mistrusted, he didn't know what to do with kindness.

"You're welcome," he muttered as Brom stepped back.

The king turned to his soldiers, exchanging nods before his face hardened. "How many did we lose? And what happened at the lighthouse?"

Cara rushed to Rannoch's side, helping the healers tend his wounds.

A soldier stepped forward, Zander, one of Rannoch's closest friends and a fellow shock trooper.

"We avoided the main fight at the village," he began. "Our goal was to cut off reinforcements. When we reached the lighthouse, the portal had already collapsed. But inside, we found an old man draining the wounded, pulling their life into a sphere. We think it was feeding the portal."

He paused, voice tight. "We attacked and killed him fast. When he died, the orb shattered, knocked us all back. Then the real threat emerged."

Zander's eyes darkened. "A demon. Huge. Nine, maybe ten feet tall. It came out of the lighthouse."

Brom exchanged a grim look with Victus.

Zander continued. "Rannoch and I charged. The rest followed. But then ten, maybe twelve smaller creatures poured out. We were down to five. We tried to hold the line, retreating toward the outer wall. The little ones were relentless. And the big one, it hit like a siege ram."

He swallowed hard. "Fredrick took a direct blow from its club. It sent him flying. Before we could reach him, five imps swarmed him. He was unconscious. Rannoch jumped in, cut down several, but the big one targeted him. Clawed him twice. Then crushed him with its club."

Zander's hands trembled. "Even then, we fought. Killed the imps. Swarmed the demon. It took twenty solid hits, maybe more, to bring it down. And the whole time, it laughed. Said something none of us understood. Ten more shock troopers arrived, cutting down the last of the little ones."

Zander's voice cracked. He lowered his head, struggling to contain the emotion. "Fredrick didn't make it. And we nearly lost Rannoch."

Brom stepped forward, placing a firm hand on Zander's shoulder.

"No," he said, voice steady. "None of that. You should be proud of what you did here. I am proud of you all. This was a surprise attack, and it could have been far worse. You showed courage and resilience. You proved yourselves worthy of this kingdom, and of our family."

He turned to the gathered soldiers, raising his voice. "You are all family. My son and I are honored to fight beside you."

Then he raised his hand high. "For Burke!"

The men erupted in cheers, their spirits lifted. Watching them, I couldn't help but smile. No wonder Brom was so beloved.

I walked over to Keenan, who leaned heavily on his shield, exhaustion etched into his face.

"You alright, brother?" I asked.

He gave a faint smile. "Yeah. Just... haven't done that one in a while. Took a lot out of me."

Chapter 3 - Burke

Reeger appeared beside us, eyes scanning the horizon. "This area's secure," he said quietly, ever watchful.

Brom joined us, his expression was a mix of gratitude and grief. "Thank you again. I won't forget your kindness today." He sighed. "We lost twelve men, sons, fathers. All with families."

His gaze drifted toward Perseus, still directing troops and villagers. "It could've been worse," he murmured. Then he turned back to us with a tired smile. "I'm lucky to have two good sons, and now, three new friends. Thank you for coming with me."

He chuckled softly. "Let's hope there are no more attempts on my family's lives today. I need a break."

I laughed with him, until Cara screamed.

She ran toward her father, her cries slicing through the air. Instinctively, we reached for our weapons, scanning for danger.

"No! No! No! No!" she wailed, panic in her voice.

Brom knelt beside her, alarmed. "What's wrong, sweetheart?"

She didn't answer directly, only sobbed louder. "No! Leave my mom alone!"

The ground trembled beneath us. I looked around, seeing confusion mirrored in every face.

Cara screamed again. "No! Leave her alone!"

A blinding flash engulfed us.

When the light faded, we were no longer in the field.

We stood in a large chamber. A massive bed dominated the center, a warm fire flickering to the right while sunlight streamed through high windows to the left. Stone walls and floors, *castle architecture?* I wondered, confused. Behind us loomed a heavy wooden door.

We stood in silence, adjusting to the sudden shift.

Brom blinked. "My room?"

Cara collapsed, drained.

Reeger drew his bow and whispered, "Company," before melting into the shadows.

Across the room stood a striking woman, dark features, black hair, encased in a glowing magical barrier.

Brom gasped. "Eryn," he whispered, stunned.

Beside the barrier stood a servant girl, clutching a knife. Her face was a storm of sorrow and resolve.

"You shouldn't be here," she said, voice trembling.

Brom stepped forward, cautious. "What's happening?"

She raised the blade toward the queen. Brom froze.

"Stay back!" she warned.

"Annie, why?" Brom pleaded.

Tears welled in her eyes. "You know why," she said bitterly. "You hide her, but she's a danger to us all. She must be stopped."

"Don't do this, Annie. We can help you," Brom said, his voice low but urgent.

She gave a bitter laugh. "Help me? Your arrogance will be your undoing."

Her gaze softened for a moment. "You were always kind to me. And for that... I'm sorry."

Before anyone could move, she turned and drove the knife into the queen's heart.

A twang split the air. Reeger's arrow struck Annie in the shoulder. She cried out, and collapsed, sobbing.

Chapter 3 - Burke

Brom lunged forward, catching Eryn as she fell from the magical barrier. Keenan set his shield down and stood over her, despair in his eyes. He knew the wound was beyond his ability to heal.

Reeger dragged Annie away, his grip firm but not cruel. Brom cradled his wife's limp body, tears breaking through ragged breaths.

"No... please, no," he whispered.

I stood frozen, helpless.

Then I saw Keenan staring at his shield, eyes wide with surprise.

He moved quickly, gently nudging Brom aside. He pulled the dagger free, placed both hands over the wound, and began to speak.

The language was unfamiliar, fluid, melodic, resonant with power.

Energy surged in the room. Light built around Keenan's hands, then burst in a flash.

When it faded, Keenan collapsed.

I rushed to him. "Keenan!"

Before I reached him, Eryn gasped. She coughed, blinking in confusion.

Brom pulled her close, tears streaming. "Shh, it's okay, honey. You're safe," he whispered. "You're safe."

She smiled weakly, resting in his arms.

I turned to Keenan, lifting him gently. "Wake up buddy," I said, shaking him.

His eyes opened slowly, exhaustion etched deep.

"Did it work?" he murmured.

I glanced at the queen, alive and breathing. Relief flooded me.

"Yeah," I said, smiling. "It worked."

Keenan gave a faint nod. "Sleep," he whispered, and passed out.

Guards burst into the room, startled by the crowd. They scanned the windows, Annie, Brom and the queen.

Reeger pointed to Annie. One guard stepped forward and escorted Annie out.

Brom began explaining everything that had happened to Eryn, who listened quietly, her hand in his.

Moments later, Perseus arrived, breathless. He spotted Cara and lifted her gently onto the bed. Then he joined his parents, listening as Brom recounted the events.

Not wanting to interrupt, I touched Perseus's shoulder. "Is there a place Keenan can rest?"

Before he could answer, Brom's voice rang out.

"Absolutely not!"

I turned, startled. Brom stood beside the queen, his usual warmth returning.

"He'll sleep in the family's guest quarters," he declared. Then to the guards: "See that he gets whatever he needs."

I glanced at Perseus, who smiled faintly. He didn't yet grasp what had happened, but he knew it mattered.

With help from the guards, we carried Keenan to the guest room.

It was simple, elegant. Stone walls adorned with woven tapestries softened the chill and celebrated the kingdom's artistry.

Above, a vaulted ceiling revealed carved wooden beams, each one etched with patterns that spoke of legacy and skilled craftsmen.

Chapter 3 - Burke

At the heart of the room stood a grand four-poster bed, its frame carved from dark wood and draped in velvet curtains dyed a deep royal blue. Thick quilts and embroidered pillows layered the bedding, each feather-filled and plush, offering a rare touch of opulence. Overhead, a canopy lined with fine fabric shielded against the draft, completing the sense of quiet luxury.

At the foot of the bed rested a solid oak chest, ready to hold the guest's belongings. Nearby, a polished writing desk stood beside a high-backed chair, its surface artfully arranged with sheets of vellum, a quill, and an inkpot.

Wrought-iron sconces lined the walls, each cradling a beeswax candle whose golden glow danced across the stone. By day, sunlight streamed through a single arched window, casting long, warm shadows. To ward off the evening chill, a small fireplace had been built into one wall, its mantle adorned with delicate carvings. A tidy stack of firewood waited nearby.

In one corner, a washstand held a ceramic basin and pitcher, with fresh linens folded beside them. Above it, a polished metal mirror reflected the flickering candlelight. A woven rug softened the cold stone floor, and two upholstered chairs sat near the hearth, inviting quiet conversation or rest.

The room felt regal, more refined than the king's own chambers, which caught me off guard.

Once I ensured Keenan was settled, the guards led me to an adjoining room. Exhausted from the day's chaos, I lay down and drifted to sleep almost instantly.

Chapter 4 - Questions

I woke up early, the weight of yesterday still lingering in my mind. Crossing the room, I splashed cold water onto my face from the basin, the shock of it clearing the last traces of sleep. I dressed quickly, the castle's quiet pressing around me like fog.

I walked to Keenan's quarters along the eastern wall of the castle, where the windows overlooked the sea. The silence was broken only by the faint rustle of banners stirred by the draft. I passed a pair of guards who nodded respectfully as I made my way to his door.

After a brief knock, I stepped into Keenan's room and found him standing by the window, his silhouette framed by the morning light. He gazed out with a wistful expression, his posture relaxed but distant. Curious, I joined him, my eyes drawn to the breathtaking sunrise spilling over the distant ocean. The horizon blazed with hues of gold and crimson, the sky painted like a living tapestry. For a long moment, we stood in silence, wrapped in the quiet awe of it.

Without turning, Keenan spoke softly. "Do you ever just stop and notice how beautiful this world is?"

I looked at him, surprised by the sudden sentiment. He seemed lost in thought, his voice tinged with something deeper. But then he shook his head, breaking from the reverie. Turning to me with a grin, he said, "Well, I suppose you're here for answers." He chuckled. "Too bad. We're

Chapter 4 - Questions

supposed to head to breakfast, and there will be no answers on an empty stomach."

I laughed. "Alright, you stubborn mule, let's get breakfast."

He grinned, and together we left the room, following a guard through the winding corridors to the great dining hall.

The hall was vast and awe-inspiring, its high vaulted ceiling supported by ancient timber beams, each one intricately carved with swirling patterns and symbols I didn't recognize. Massive stone walls rose around us, adorned with rich tapestries that added warmth and grandeur. A long oak banquet table stretched down the center, polished to a gleam and set with golden goblets, fine pewter plates, and elegant candelabras.

The table was laden with an impressive spread: roasted meats glistening with herbs, freshly baked bread still steaming, platters of ripe fruits, creamy cheeses, and gilded pitchers filled with wine and mead. Above us, iron chandeliers hung from the ceiling, their candles flickering gently. Sunlight poured through tall windows, casting a warm glow that shimmered across the room. The light danced over suits of armor displayed along the walls and the polished metal of ceremonial weapons.

A roaring fireplace, large enough to walk into, dominated one side of the hall. Its flames crackled and filled the space with heat and the faint tang of burning wood. Servants moved swiftly and quietly, attending to every detail with practiced grace. The air was rich with the aroma of spiced meats, fresh herbs, and warm bread.

"Whoa," Keenan murmured, smiling as he took in the scene. "I could get used to this."

I chuckled. "No, you'd get fat."

He shot me a glare, snorting. "And you wouldn't?"

We both laughed as we made our way to the table. At its center, Brom stood waiting, his grin as warm as the fire behind him.

"My friends, come and sit!" the king called out. "We were just wondering if you'd snuck out or decided to sleep the day away."

Keenan and I joined the table, both of us impressed by the feast laid out before us. Keenan, however, looked noticeably uneasy as the servants bustled around him, setting his place, pouring his drink, fussing over every detail. I suppressed a grin, knowing he wasn't used to this kind of attention. Perseus noticed too; he glanced at me, and we both tried not to laugh.

The king waited patiently, his gaze steady as the last goblet was filled and the final plate set. Then, with a subtle nod to a nearby guard, the man moved swiftly to relay the order. One by one, the remaining servants and guards exited the hall. The heavy doors at both ends closed with a deep, resonant thud that echoed through the vaulted chamber.

Brom took his seat at the table. To his right sat Queen Eryndra, regal and composed, with Cara beside her, swinging her legs beneath the chair. On his left was Perseus, upright and attentive, then Keenan, and finally me.

Behind the king stood Victus, silent and vigilant, his sharp eyes sweeping the room. But my attention was drawn to a figure I didn't recognize, a tall, dignified elf standing near one of the arched windows. He seemed lost in thought, his posture serene, his presence quietly commanding.

Noticing my gaze, Brom said, "Ah, I believe you're acquainted with everyone here, except our emissary from the elves, Thalion."

The elf turned slightly and offered a polite nod but said nothing.

Keenan leaned forward. "How is Rannoch?"

Brom's face lit with warmth. "He's resting. The healers say he'll be up and about in a day or two. Whatever you did worked wonders, not just on the wound, but his recovery as well."

Keenan smiled, visibly relieved. "I'm glad he's going to be okay."

"We all are," Brom agreed.

Then, with a playful glint in her eye, Eryndra added, "And I'm doing fine as well, thank you very much."

Keenan's eyes widened in alarm. "I, I'm sorry! I just thought... I mean, you looked fine, and I didn't want to, uh…"

He shot me a helpless look, the classic 'I'm drowning, help me' expression. I couldn't help it, I burst out laughing. Brom and Perseus chuckled too.

Still smiling, Brom placed a hand on his wife's shoulder. "She'll keep you on your toes."

Eryndra's eyes sparkled with amusement, clearly enjoying how flustered she'd made him. Keenan sighed in defeat, and she offered him a gracious smile as Brom chuckled again.

I glanced around. "Where's Reeger?"

Brom answered, "He helped question Annie last night, then left to deliver an update to the elves. Since he's been present in both cities during the attacks, he can give them a more direct report. He said he'll meet you back in Grissom City this evening or tomorrow morning."

I sighed, disappointed. I had questions for Reeger, questions that would have to wait.

Eryndra, Eryn, as Brom often called her, broke the brief silence, turning to Keenan. "In all seriousness, thank you for saving my life," she said, her voice soft but sincere. "I wouldn't be here if it weren't for you."

Keenan flushed a deeper shade of red, clearly unaccustomed to such direct gratitude. "You're welcome," he mumbled, barely audible.

Brom laughed heartily. "Well, why don't you two eat while I explain a few things? But first, you'll need to swear an oath of silence. Nothing said here, especially concerning my wife or daughter, must leave this room."

Keenan and I exchanged a glance, curiosity sharpening. He scanned the faces around the table, his expression cautious, weighing trust. The silence stretched. Then, with a subtle nod to me, he spoke.

"We agree."

Brom's expression grew solemn. "Excellent." He leaned forward slightly, his voice lowering. The air in the room seemed to still.

Out of the corner of my eye, I noticed Thalion watching us intently. His gaze was piercing, calculating, measuring us as surely as we had measured him. I looked away, hiding a knowing smile.

Chapter 4 - Questions

The king stood and began to pace slowly at the end of the table. When he stopped, his eyes softened as they settled on Eryndra.

"I would do anything for her," he said quietly. "A thousand deaths, torture, pain, whatever it takes to keep her safe."

Then Brom turned his gaze back to us, and his expression darkened.

"And yet... she is more powerful than anyone I've ever known," he said quietly. "She could kill all of us with a flick of her wrist. Or a whisper."

Keenan and I exchanged a glance, our faces tightening as we tried to mask our surprise.

Fixing us with a steady stare, the king asked, "Have you ever read about the Great War, the Forming, and the Fracture of the World?"

I shrugged. "Not really."

Though I thought, *most of what I've seen was written by people who weren't even there. How do we know if any of it's true?*

Keenan added, "I know very little, other than what I read during paladin training. Just that some humans rebelled and sided with demons. According to legend, that's how Noctari were created."

Brom nodded. "That much is true. But what isn't widely known is this: the demons created a bloodline among humans. A lineage capable of channeling their dark energy. These individuals became conduits for evil, wielding powers with devastating results."

He paused, his eyes shadowed with sorrow. Eryndra reached out and placed a gentle hand on his arm. Encouraged, he drew a slow breath and continued.

"Most of them burned out quickly. Their life force was consumed by the very power they wielded. The more they tapped into it, the faster it devoured them. Each time they used their abilities, they lost a piece of their humanity, becoming more demonic, more feral, until they were no longer human at all. In the end, they turned into monsters. Their bodies spent. And then... they simply died."

His voice wavered.

"My wife is of this bloodline."

Keenan and I stared at him, stunned. The weight of the revelation settled over us like a storm cloud.

The king's voice softened as he spoke of the past.

"When I found her, she was barely holding on to what remained of herself. She'd nearly burned through everything. My friends and family all told me to stay away. But I couldn't. I fell in love with her."

He smiled faintly, the memory bittersweet.

"It took years, but she recovered enough to live a mostly normal life. Still... if she ever uses her powers again, she might lose herself completely."

Eryndra leaned her head against his shoulder, her presence grounding him.

"We have to keep her safe," he said. "Not just for her sake, but because keeping her safe keeps all of us safe."

Eryndra turned to us, her voice calm and resolute. "I'm not afraid to die. Every day I live here is a gift, one more day I never expected."

Her gaze shifted to her daughter.

Chapter 4 - Questions

"I could destroy this entire castle and city in seconds," she said, her tone flat, matter-of-fact. "It would consume me completely... but I could do it."

I glanced at Keenan. He was clearly shaken, though trying hard not to show it. I felt the same. Two days ago, I would've thought she was mad. Now, after everything I'd seen in the last twenty-four hours, I was ready to believe almost anything.

"If you have the bloodline," I asked slowly, "does that mean your children have it too?"

The king and queen exchanged a glance before Brom answered.

"We weren't sure. Honestly, we thought the bloodline had ended. None of the boys showed any signs. And even when Cara was born, there was nothing unusual. But around her tenth birthday, she started exhibiting abilities we couldn't explain, things no normal human could do. At first, we thought she was cursed. Or under some kind of spell. We'd forgotten about the bloodline. It wasn't until we consulted Reggie, after several sessions, that he confirmed what we feared."

"We are that bloodline," Eryndra said quietly. "And it's passed to Cara."

"Wait," Keenan cut in. "Reggie?"

Brom smiled. "Yes. The mage who lives in the mage tower on the southern end of the island."

I blinked. "The southern end? You're kidding, right?"

He chuckled. "Well... the southwestern end. The southeast is too dangerous, if you believe the stories."

I thought of the rumors, Noctari and wild creatures said to roam the southeastern wilds, making the region supposedly impassable.

"So, you're saying some old man lives out there?" I asked, incredulously.

The king laughed. "Not just an old man. An ancient tower full of mages."

Keenan and I exchanged stunned looks.

"How is that possible?" Keenan asked.

"Yeah," I added. "I thought no one could survive out there."

"They've cloaked themselves with powerful magic," Brom said, grinning. "I don't know how it works, but Cara's been training with them for the past three years."

I shook my head, trying to process it all. *How many more surprises am I in for?*

"What's Reggie like?" Keenan asked.

Brom paused, then chuckled. "That's something you'll have to find out for yourselves. It's not my story to tell." His smile lingered, touched by something fond, or perhaps funny.

"Wait," I said, the realization hitting me. "Cara is part of that bloodline, and she's been using her powers, a lot, over the past few days. How is she not being... ruined by it?"

The king's expression darkened. "We don't know. Reggie thinks she's some kind of anomaly. Something special. A lot of the history he's uncovered is incomplete, burned, lost, or deliberately erased. But so far, Cara hasn't shown any of the usual side effects. None that we've seen, at least."

Chapter 4 - Questions

"Dad," Cara cut in, shaking her head with the exasperation only a child can summon when they think their parent should know better. "You're forgetting the most important part."

Brom looked at her, puzzled.

"Good magic," she said simply.

Brom and Eryndra exchanged knowing smiles as Cara continued. "I can use good magic, healing, teleportation, protection, even some illusion spells."

Brom gave her a sideways glance. "Although I hear you're not taking your illusion training very seriously, young lady," he added, feigning sternness.

Cara rolled her eyes. "Reggie talks too much," she muttered, which sent Keenan and me into a fit of poorly stifled laughter.

"So, Eryndra," I asked, curious, "you can't use those kinds of magic?"

She shook her head, her expression tinged with sadness. "No, I can't. That's one of the things that makes Cara different. We don't know why, but she's able to use both light and dark magic. It shouldn't be possible... but somehow, she can."

Keenan turned to Brom. "Is that why this so-called 'Order of Light' is targeting your wife?"

"Yes," Brom said, his voice heavy. "We hoped to keep Eryndra's identity, and Cara's abilities, a secret. But somehow, they found out about Eryn. The Order's goal is to eradicate magic entirely. They've been hunting Reggie for years, but he's always five or six steps ahead. They believe all magic, light or dark, will one day destroy the world, just as it nearly did during the Fracturing."

"But your wife agreed not to use her powers," Keenan pointed out. "Why should they be worried?"

"Ha! That's exactly what I said," Brom growled, thumping his fist on the table in frustration.

Perseus, who had been silent until now, finally spoke. "I've been working to quietly root them out," he said. "But their network is vast, spread across the entire island and beyond. It wouldn't surprise me if they've gained allies among the elves and dwarves, though likely not many. Those with longer lifespans tend to be more even-tempered."

Thalion spoke for the first time, his voice calm but firm. "Be vigilant of everyone," he said. "Even me. Trust your friends but never give them a reason to doubt you. Be cautious and always make sure your actions can be verified."

Perseus nodded, and Brom chuckled. "You should write that down."

Thalion gave a faint smile. "I'm over a thousand years old. Who says I haven't?"

The king laughed, and even Victus allowed himself a rare smile.

But then the king's expression darkened as he turned to his wife.

"Annie was rescued from slavers ten years ago," he said quietly. "She's been a loyal member of our household ever since. The fact that they got to her…" He trailed off, shaking his head. "It's unsettling."

"How is she?" I asked softly.

Eryndra answered, her voice gentle. "I spent the night with her and Reeger. She's... broken. She believes she did

Chapter 4 - Questions

the right thing but never intended to hurt us. It's tearing her apart."

Her gaze drifted, distant and sorrowful. "I told her I forgave her, and she just collapsed, sobbing, saying she'd failed in every way. I reminded her that things happen as they must. But now, she'll have to reconcile what they taught her with what her heart and mind know to be true."

Keenan nodded slowly. "It's strange. We were warned about them during paladin training. They're trying to recruit paladins to help eliminate magic, claiming paladin magic is somehow 'acceptable.' Our leader believes they'd just use us to do their dirty work, then discard us when we're no longer useful. Maybe even enslave us. No one really knows."

Perseus nodded. "Yes, that lines up with what I've heard. They're desperate to bring a paladin or two into their ranks, it would give them a veneer of legitimacy."

By now, we'd finished eating and were preparing to leave when Brom leaned forward, his gaze settling on Keenan.

"If you don't mind," he said, his tone serious, "I have one last question. Something Eryn and I have been wondering."

Keenan nodded, cautious. "What would you like to know?"

The king's expression softened, though his eyes remained intent. "How does a Noctari become a paladin... and learn to bring the dead back to life?"

Keenan offered a faint smile. "Necromancy is strictly forbidden," he began. "And even if it weren't, it can't reattach a soul once it's gone. At best, you'd end up with a walking corpse."

The king nodded. "All right, then. What about someone who's nearly dead? She was dying, she had seconds left."

Keenan smiled. "Well... that's a bit of a story."

Brom glanced at Eryndra, who gave a small nod. He turned back to Keenan with a warm smile. "We've got time, if you don't mind."

Keenan leaned back slightly, gathering his thoughts. Then he began.

He spoke of being rescued by strangers as a child and left at an orphanage in Grissom City. He admitted he'd always been a troublemaker, which earned a few chuckles from the royal family, especially when I jumped in to share some of the chaos he'd dragged me into over the years.

"But I always wanted to be a hero," Keenan said quietly. "To help people. To protect others. To stand against those who hurt people like me. That's why I wanted to become a paladin."

He paused, then added, "To join, you need a paladin to vouch for you. Throm is the only one I know, so it must've been him, though he never actually told me."

He hesitated, then added, "Although it didn't go quite how I imagined."

His voice softened. "I wasn't given power to destroy my enemies. Instead, I was given the power to heal."

The room grew still, the weight of his words settling over us.

Chapter 4 - Questions

"The spell I used... it's incredibly rare. Only granted to a select few. As far as I know, it hasn't been bestowed in over two hundred years."

"What was the name of the spell?" Brom asked.

"Oh," Keenan said, almost absentmindedly. "Lay on Hands. Funny thing is, I didn't even know what it did until I used it." His tone shifted slightly, and I caught it, there was something he wasn't saying. I knew better than to ask about it now, but I made a mental note to bring it up later.

The king leaned back and laughed, gesturing toward his wife. "See, Eryn? Even the universe wants to keep you alive."

"At least someone outside our family does," she replied with a soft smile.

Keenan's expression turned serious. "I'd appreciate it if you didn't spread this around. If the wrong people find out... I could become a target."

Brom grinned and clapped him on the shoulder. "Of course. And after what you've done, you're part of this family now."

Just then, a knock came at the door. A guard stepped inside, and Brom turned to Keenan with a smile.

"I have a surprise waiting in your room," he said.

Curiosity sparked between us, and we quickly stood to follow him. After brief farewells to his family and Thalion, the king, Victus, Keenan, and I made our way down the corridor.

When we entered Keenan's room, we were greeted by several attendants standing on either side of a magnificent suit of armor.

The king chuckled, eyes twinkling. "This was mine when I was your age," he said. "Now it's yours."

The armor was breathtaking. Its polished surface gleamed with a silvery sheen, crafted from an alloy of mithril and silver. Engraved across the chest and pauldrons was an image of a dove with outstretched wings descending before a roaring lion. Delicate etchings traced every edge, glowing faintly with an azure shimmer.

Keenan stood frozen. "It's beautiful," he murmured, eyes wide.

"The smiths worked through the night to adjust the feet," Brom said, laughing. "Since you are... unique."

Victus leaned in and whispered something to him, and the king nodded. "I've enjoyed our time together, but there's still much for me to do," he said, turning to us. "Know this, you're always welcome here. I've instructed the staff to prepare provisions for your journey back to Grissom."

We exchanged farewells, and Keenan thanked him sincerely for the armor.

Once the king had gone, I turned to Keenan with a look. "All right, talk."

"About what?" he asked, trying to sound innocent.

"The spell," I pressed. "How did you know to use it? I saw you look at the shield first, what was that about?"

Keenan glanced over at the shield resting on the stand. His expression tightened. He muttered something under his breath, then sighed.

"Fine."

"What?" I asked, confused.

Chapter 4 - Questions

He studied the shield for a long moment, then nodded to himself and said quietly, "The shield told me to use the spell."

I stared at him, waiting for the punchline. Then I laughed. "Okay, that's funny. But seriously, how did you know?"

He didn't smile. "The shield told me," he repeated, dead serious.

The laughter caught in my throat. "You're not joking."

He shook his head. "No."

"The shield told you," I echoed, still trying to process.

I squinted at him. "You're serious?"

He nodded once more.

"How can a shield talk?" I asked, incredulous.

"I don't know," Keenan admitted. "But I have a hunch. I read once about a group of paladins, centuries ago, who imbued their spirits into weapons to protect the world. The weapons were said to have special powers, and the ability to communicate with their wielders. Maybe even others, though I'm not totally sure."

He stared at the shield, a mix of awe and disbelief on his face.

Thinking back, I said, "Wait, that would explain…"

"Yes," Keenan cut in, "your uncle's reaction when he saw the shield."

"This is insane," I muttered, shaking my head.

"You're telling me," Keenan chuckled. "I didn't believe it either. At first, I thought I was losing my mind. But in that moment, it was the shield, colorfully and rudely, I might add, telling me to use Lay on Hands."

I laughed. "Well, at least it would get along with Grog."

Keenan sat down heavily on the edge of the bed, running a hand through his hair. "Why me, though?" he muttered. "There's nothing special about me. Why did I get the shield? Why Lay on Hands? I just... don't get it."

I walked over and sat beside him. "Man," I said quietly, "I don't know why all this is happening. But I'd rather it be you than anyone else in the world."

He glanced at me, eyes glistening. "Come on, man..."

"I'm serious," I said with a smile. "You saved those people. You saved the queen. That's proof enough for me."

At that moment, a voice echoed through the room.

"Oh, for crying in public, is this how you two are gonna be all the time?"

Startled, we both looked around. The room was empty.

And then it hit me.

It was the shield.

"Ugh, you two are duller than a butter knife," the voice continued. "Yes, it's me. For the love of all the celestials in the heavens, I chose this one, and all I get is waterworks! Next time you want to have a sweet, heartwarming moment, leave me in the hallway."

I stared, then burst out laughing. "Wait, so you can't hear us if you're in another room?"

"Eh," the shield replied. "I can always hear K. We're telepathically linked now. Which sucks for me, by the way, but I guess I'll manage."

Keenan scowled. "I liked you better when you were quiet."

Chapter 4 - Questions

The shield laughed. "Now you're getting it. But first, I'm done with being called 'the shield.' Ugh. 'The shield this, the shield that', no respect. My name is Merek Ironguard, third paladin of the First Order."

A pause followed.

Keenan and I exchanged puzzled looks.

Merek let out a dramatic sigh. "You should both be impressed, but whatever. I guess we'll just have to make the most of this situation. Oh, and if you see Grog, kick him for me. Better yet, push him down a flight of stairs. Outing me in public like that... he's lucky I'm stuck in this shield, or I'd thrash him in the pits."

"Wait, what?" I asked, startled.

"Eh, I'm done talking," Merek said. "Wake me up if there's a fight."

No amount of prodding got him to speak again.

Keenan and I sat there in stunned silence before finally bursting into laughter. Either we were both losing our minds... or Keenan really did have one of the sacred weapons. With our spirits lifted, we packed our belongings and joined a caravan heading back to Grissom City.

Chapter 5 - The Ship

We didn't talk much as we traveled, mostly listening to gossip and chatter of others in the caravan. Occasionally, someone would throw an odd glance our way or ask if Keenan was really a paladin. We tried to discuss the halflings, their role for the king, how that arrangement worked, but interruptions kept breaking our focus.

As the city drew near, the weight of the previous day settled over us again: Franklin dying outside his shop, the fight in front of the council hall, Cara saving those children, and the sheer size of the demons we'd faced. We glanced at each other, both thinking the same thing, wondering if things would ever return to normal.

At the western gate, a child darted out of the shadows and approached us. He was maybe ten or eleven, thin-faced and smudged with dirt. His blue eyes scanned the street with sharp, restless energy. His hair was a tousled mess, uneven, like it had been cut with a dull blade. It might once have been light brown or blonde. His clothes were patched and mismatched, the fabric worn thin and riddled with stains. Yet despite the rough exterior, he carried himself with defiant confidence. Beneath it flickered a spark of curiosity, a yearning for adventure or something exciting.

I smiled. "Hello, Philip."

Philip was the leader of Grissom's orphaned and street children. I'd befriended him a few years ago, right after Keenan had left. With Gamreal's help, we'd built a network

Chapter 5 - The Ship

to give those kids a sense of family, something to anchor them and keep them out of trouble. Though I suspected my uncle also used them to keep tabs on the city's undercurrents.

Philip stood there trying to look cool, glancing around like he had something important to share. I chuckled to myself. This kid cracked me up, but I was glad he was staying out of trouble.

Once he was sure no one was listening, he leaned in and asked, "Is he safe?" nodding toward Keenan.

Keenan suppressed a smile while I leaned in, answering seriously, "Yeah. He's okay."

Philip studied him for a moment, then nodded. "Well, if you say he's alright, then he's alright with me."

Trying not to laugh, I replied, "Don't worry, if he goes sideways, I'll let you know."

Satisfied, Philip continued, "It's been crazy here since some of the guards switched sides and those red-eyed men attacked the other day."

I nodded. "Are all you guys okay?"

"Yeah," he said. "I made sure we got to our safe houses. We even found this new place in the sewers, but we can talk about that later."

Philip paused, glancing around nonchalantly before adding, "Your uncle wants to talk to you. That ship they came in on, it's messing with people. Some say they're hearing voices. Most can't even get close without freaking out and running off."

I glanced at Keenan, who was listening closely. "Alright. Thanks for the heads-up, Philip. Do you know where my uncle is now?"

"He was headed home, but he might stop by the blacksmith's shop," Philip replied.

"Why would he stop there?" I asked.

"Oh, you didn't hear?" Philip's expression turned somber. "Franklin was killed by those red-eyed devils. Throm's filling in until they find a replacement."

Keenan and I exchanged a look, the reality of Franklin's death returning. He'd been a quiet but steady presence in the community. Not one for many words, but his absence would be deeply felt.

As was our custom, I pulled a couple of coins from my pouch and discreetly handed them to Philip. He slipped them into his bag without missing a beat.

"If you need anything, I'll be around," he said, then he headed back into the city, vanishing into the crowd.

That kid's something else, but he's a good one." Keenan smiled. "He remind you of anyone?"

I laughed. "Yeah, too much. Hopefully, we help this one turn out better than you did."

Keenan smirked. "One can only hope."

We stopped by the blacksmiths, where Throm was finishing up some work on the guards' armor. He told us Gam had headed home, so we made our way there.

When we arrived, Gam greeted us at the door.

"Oh, good, good, you're here. I was just about to head down to the ship to check it out. We'll grab Throm on the way."

"What about Grog?" I asked.

Gam shook his head. "He wouldn't be much help, unless we need someone to chop the boat into kindling.

Chapter 5 - The Ship

Which... might come later. For now, I want more information."

He grabbed a few items from a chest, and we headed back toward the blacksmiths. After picking up Throm, we made our way to the dockyard.

The dockyard sprawled along the edge of a wide, murky harbor, where the salty tang of seawater mingled with the earthy scent of wet wood and fish. Weathered piers jutted into the water, their beams slick and darkened with brine and algae. Ropes and rigging hung in tangled webs along the posts, some frayed from years of use. Masts rose like skeletal fingers from the moored ships, and the rhythmic creak of timber mixed with sailors' shouts and the distant squawk of gulls flying overhead.

Lining the shore, warehouses and workshops stood in uneven rows, their stone foundations and timber frames worn by years of salt-laden wind. Open doors revealed busy workers stacking crates or mending nets. Dockhands hauled heavy sacks of grain and rolled barrels up gangplanks, while merchants haggled and scribes scratched notes into ledgers. Fishermen unloaded their catches, calling out to passersby with the day's offerings.

We made our way toward the largest pier, where a ship with two masts and black sails loomed into view. It sat alone at the end of the dock, an eerie, unnatural presence. Nothing, no gulls, no dockhands, not even rats, ventured near it.

At the edge where the dock met the road, two town guards stood uneasily as we approached.

Gam greeted them. "Has anyone tried to board the ship?"

"No, sir," one guard answered. "Not that anyone would want to. Just getting close makes you feel like you need to run. There's something... wrong with it."

As they spoke, I studied the ship. The wood itself seemed to seep a dark, oily blackness that defied logic. It radiated danger and decay. Even from this distance, the smell of rot was sharp and oppressive. And yet, despite the revulsion curling in my gut, I felt myself drawn to it, an invisible pull, as though something deep inside wanted me closer. My instincts screamed at me to run.

I shook myself out of it and glanced at Keenan. He was staring too, unmoving. We both blinked, snapping out of the trance at the same time, only then realizing how quiet it had become.

Gam, Throm, and the guards were watching us.

"Well?" Gam asked.

"Yes?" I said, confused.

"You've been staring at the ship for five minutes. You didn't hear a word I said," Gam replied, concern etched across his face.

Keenan and I exchanged uneasy glances, unsettled by what had just happened. Gam's expression turned grim.

"I need you two to deliver a message, to someone who might be able to help us."

Keenan frowned. "Shouldn't we at least try to board it first?"

In response, Gam picked up a rock and hurled it toward the ship. It struck something midair, an invisible barrier, and dropped into the water with a soft splash.

"Oh," Keenan muttered, clearly feeling a bit foolish.

Chapter 5 - The Ship

Throm chuckled. Gam shrugged. "Don't worry. If this contact of mine can't help, then we'll revisit the 'chop-it-into-pieces' plan."

He turned back to the guards. "Keep rotating shifts. No more than two hours per group per day."

"No argument from us," one of them replied quickly, nodding in agreement.

As we walked away from the docks, Throm explained that the magic surrounding the ship was beyond his ability to handle, even as a paladin. But hopefully Gam's contact would be able to help.

"Although," Gam muttered under his breath, "I just hope the little bugger will cooperate."

We arrived at the stables, and I raised an eyebrow. "He's not in town?"

Gam smiled. "Nope. And this could be dangerous, but I need you to reach him as soon as possible."

"Well, who is it?" Keenan asked, curiosity peaked.

Gam let out a sigh. "His name is Reggie."

Keenan and I exchanged stunned glances. "You mean the one at the mage tower?" I blurted.

Throm and Gam shared surprised looks. "How do you know about him?" Gam asked.

We quickly shared the little we knew, carefully side-stepping anything that tied back to the king's family from earlier that morning. Gam narrowed his eyes, clearly sensing there was more to the story, but he let it slide, for now. Instead, he handed me a sealed letter.

"Follow the road, when you get there, just call out his name and, for your own sake, try not to be out after dark. That doesn't always end well."

With that, two horses were led out of the stables. They were northern mustangs from the rolling hills. Keenan's mount, Ember, was a red roan, rusty red with a dusting of white spots across her coat. Mine was Storm, a striking dapple gray with a white blaze down his nose.

"How will we know when we're there?" I asked, glancing south toward the unfamiliar road ahead.

Gam chuckled. "Oh, you'll know."

Before we could ask anything else, he and Throm turned and walked off, leaving us standing there, exchanging uncertain looks.

Keenan shook his head. "If I didn't know better, I'd think he was trying to get us killed in the Badlands."

I laughed. "Yeah, same. Either way, we'd better get moving if we want to get there before dark."

We set off at a steady pace, the wasteland stretching endlessly before us. It was a desolate expanse, devoid of life. The ground was a patchwork of cracked earth and ashen dust, broken only by jagged rocks and the occasional tuft of withered grass. Scattered across the barren landscape were remnants of old stone and wooden structures, once sturdy, now crumbling into decay. Blackened stone walls leaned precariously, riddled with cracks and choked by dying vegetation. Splintered beams jutted at odd angles, their surfaces bleached by years of exposure.

The air was dry and heavy, carrying the faint scent of rot. A persistent, eerie silence hung over the land, broken only by the groan of a collapsing beam or the soft whisper of wind stirring the dust. This was a place where decay marched steadily forward, swallowing the last traces of a once-thriving world.

Chapter 5 - The Ship

We rode quietly, eyes scanning the horizon, hoping we wouldn't run into anything. I glanced at Keenan. He was watching a half-collapsed structure near the road, its roof long since caved in.

"Great place for an ambush," I said, nodding toward it.

Keenan kept his eyes on the ruins. "If this road saw more traffic, I'd probably be more nervous. Still, even with paladin training... numbers and surprise can kill you."

"Thanks, Captain Sunshine," I said with a chuckle. "With that kind of optimism, how could we possibly lose?"

Keenan smiled. "I'd love to take a contingent of paladins out here like in the old days and just clear it all out. There can't be much left out here that could stand against a unit of trained paladins."

"Maybe," I said, shaking my head. "But I remember my uncles talking about how they used to send raids into the wastes. Then one day they just... stopped. Never said why. I don't think they were afraid exactly, but they were concerned."

"Hmmm," Keenan said thoughtfully. "Interesting."

We rode on, the strain of constant alertness making the hours stretch longer than they were. The landscape remained bleak, and the silence pressed in like a weight. Eventually, we reached the end of the road, only to find... nothing.

We stopped and dismounted. Our horses shifted uneasily, ears pricked, eyes scanning the horizon with nervous energy. Dust swirled around their hooves as we exchanged puzzled looks.

"Is this it?" I asked, scanning the empty surroundings.

Keenan looked just as confused. "Your uncle said to call out, so... I guess, hello?"

Nothing.

The silence deepened.

"Wait," I said. "Try his name."

"Oh, right." Keenan cleared his throat, then called out, "Reggie!"

A sudden thunderclap echoed across the wasteland, and before us appeared a towering figure, a massive man, easily ten feet tall. He stood like a living monolith of muscle and menace. His shoulders stretched impossibly wide, his chest rising and falling with the slow, deliberate rhythm of a predator watching prey. Every inch of him was corded with sinewy strength, his thick arms like tree trunks carved from stone.

His face was a chiseled mask of intimidation, deep-set eyes burning with cold, calculating intensity. His battered dark armor bore the scars of countless battles, and at his side hung a colossal weapon, its dulled blade no less threatening in his grip. An aura of menace clung to him, thick and suffocating, enough to make even the bravest hesitate.

When he spoke, his voice was a low rumble that seemed to vibrate through the very air.

"Why are you here?"

For a moment, we were too stunned to respond. Then I remembered the letter. I held it up.

"I have a message for Reggie, from Gamreal, in Grissom City."

The giant said nothing, staring at us like he could see straight into our souls.

Chapter 5 - The Ship

I glanced at Keenan and shrugged. "Can you take us to him? This is urgent. People are dying."

Still, no response.

Frustration welled up in me, but before I could press further, Keenan stepped forward.

"I am Aegis, Protector of the Innocent, Wielder of the Bulwark of Kings," he declared, sweeping off his travel cloak to reveal the king's armor beneath. "We are friends of King Brom. He gave me this armor as a brother, and as a friend."

The man's voice grew lower, rougher, cracking like dry stone. "Did you kill him to get it, Noctari? Your kind are always scheming. But it won't work on me."

The sting of those words hit Keenan hard. I saw it in his eyes. But he held firm, steady.

The two locked eyes for what felt like minutes.

Then, unexpectedly, the giant laughed, a deep unsettling sound that rolled through the dust like thunder. "Well, I'll be. The king says you're alright."

"Wait, how did he..." I started, but before I could finish, a flash of light engulfed the massive figure.

And just like that, he vanished.

Before we could react, a blur of movement erupted beside us, a small, hyperactive gnome bursting onto the scene like a wind-up toy with no off switch.

He stood just under three feet tall, his wiry frame barely containing his boundless energy. Wide, luminescent green eyes darted in every direction with manic curiosity. Unkempt green hair spiked wildly from his head, and even his skin seemed to carry a faint green tinge. His patchwork clothes looked like they'd been sewn together from every fabric known to man. His vest was a chaotic masterpiece of tiny pockets, each one stuffed with trinkets, vials, tools, and shiny odds and ends.

He started speaking so fast it was hard to keep up.

"So! You helped the king, huh? Good, great…" He grinned like he hadn't slept in days and didn't need to. "How's his daughter doing? I'm sure she's great! Yep! Gotta be great, I trained her! But don't tell anyone. Since you've got the armor and he said you're alright, you probably already know, don't you? Yep, she's something special. Different."

He glanced up at us and sighed. "Too fast, huh? Okay, slowing down. I always forget how fast us gnomes talk when we're excited." He paused, then nodded to himself, realizing he'd started speeding up again.

Keenan and I exchanged lost looks as the gnome made a visible effort to slow his speech.

"She's gotta be great," he said, more deliberately. "Knew she could do it. Portaled you from Grissom to Burke, huh? Hot coals, that's impressive! Told her it was easy, just needed the right push."

He paused just long enough to take a breath before barreling ahead again.

"Sooo... what's going on in Grissom? I sensed some nasty portals over there. Bad news, yep. You're not hiding a mage, are you? Hmmm?"

He squinted at us, his piercing gaze darting back and forth like a lie detector on overdrive. Before we could answer, he waved a hand dismissively.

"No, no, I'd have known! Figured it out already. No mage. But bad? Or not good? Definitely!"

Chapter 5 - The Ship

I opened my mouth to respond, but he cut me off with a raised finger.

"Yes, yes, the letter! But first, how about we get indoors, hmm? Not safe out here at night. Come on, you two!"

He turned and gave Keenan a long, amused look, tilting his head. "A Noctari paladin, huh? Who'd have thought? Hah!"

Without another word, he spun around and strode off with purpose. Keenan and I exchanged bewildered glances before shrugging and following him, our horses close behind.

The wasteland fell away the moment we crossed an unseen threshold.

Before us unfolded an oasis, hidden deep within the desert's heart, veiled by illusion. Lush and almost otherworldly, it stood in stark contrast to the desolation we'd left behind.

At its center shimmered a crystal-clear pool, its surface rippling gently as a breeze carried the scent of fresh greenery. Reeds and cattails lined the water's edge, swaying in quiet harmony with the wind. Clusters of date palms and acacias circled the pool, their leafy canopies casting cool shade across the vibrant ground. Bright wildflowers speckled the earth, their vivid colors a bold contrast to the muted hues of the desert beyond.

Rising above it all stood a sturdy stone tower, its weathered facade scarred by countless sandstorms. Ivy crept up its base, a sign of nature reclaiming its place. Narrow windows caught the sunlight, glinting faintly, as if watched by unseen eyes. From its height, the entire oasis could be surveyed: serene waters, winding paths, and dense foliage forming a haven where peace and vigilance coexisted, sanctuary and sentry in equal measure.

Reggie smiled. "You can release the horses; they'll be safe here."

He turned to us, still grinning. "Well? What do you think? I come out here sometimes to garden. Some of the others do too. Not bad, huh?"

We let the horses go, watching them trot toward the shade, clearly at ease.

Keenan nodded, smiling. "This place is incredible. You've done an excellent job hiding it."

The little gnome beamed with pride, then turned and made his way toward the tower.

We followed as Reggie rambled on, pointing out various plants and explaining their uses. Most of it went over our heads, his words tumbling out in a rapid, scattered stream. Eventually, we reached a large door at the tower's base. He opened it and we stepped inside.

The entryway was narrow, with a stone staircase spiraling upward along the outer wall. At the far end stood a slender door set flush into the stone, barely noticeable at first glance. Reggie walked straight to it, paused, and muttered something under his breath. The door shimmered, its surface shifting from a dull red to a luminous blue.

Keenan and I exchanged startled glances. Reggie just grinned.

"Lots of doors to lots of places," he said, patting the frame. "Short legs hate long walks. So, no hallways. We use a door storage device! I call it the walk-not, but the other mages call it the arcane archway."

Chapter 5 - The Ship

He paused, then added, "Still waiting for a better name. If you think of one, let me know."

With that, he opened the door and stepped through, into a space far larger than the tower should have allowed.

It was a massive study.

The hearth, built from dark stone etched with faintly glowing runes, radiated a warm, steady heat. Above it, a mantle held many curious artifacts: a crystalline orb, small jars of shimmering powder, and trinkets whose purpose we could only guess at.

Towering bookshelves lined the walls, crammed with ancient tomes and brittle scrolls. Some were bound in cracked leather with strange lettering, others wrapped in threadbare cloth. Between them nestled gleaming vials, oddly shaped stones, and jars of black ink cradling feathered quills.

A large oak desk dominated the center of the room, its surface scattered with parchment, open books, and half-melted candles. An ornate inkpot and a raven-feather quill suggested recent use, while a stack of neatly written notes hinted at the gnome's latest project.

The air was thick with the scent of aged paper, burning wood, and something stranger, an almost metallic tang that hinted at recent magical experiments. Shadows danced across the ceiling as the fire flickered, casting the whole room in a warm, golden glow.

It was cozy, chaotic, and full of boundless discovery.

"Well?" the gnome asked, looking at us expectantly.

"What?" I replied, confused.

Keenan shook his head and silently mouthed, *the letter*.

"Oh, right!" I fumbled to pull it from my pack and handed it over as Reggie tapped his foot with theatrical impatience.

Keenan chuckled as I passed it along. While Reggie read, his eyes darting across the page, Keenan's attention drifted to a small, curious-looking bag on the desk. He stepped closer, intrigued, but stopped himself from touching it. Probably wise, not everything in a wizard's study was meant to be handled.

Reggie finished reading and grinned. "Interesting... Haven't had a mystery like this in years. Could be fun. Or..." His eyes flicked to Keenan. "Could be an old mage's practical joke."

"What?" Keenan asked, puzzled.

Reggie pointed to the bag. "That. Draws you in, makes you want to open it." He picked it up, turning it over in his hand. "Pops out random potions. Might turn you into a frog. Might make you fall in love with a dwarf. Who knows?" He casually tossed it back onto the desk.

"But this..." he continued, tapping the letter. "This ship, possessed crew, possessed hull? No, no. Can't be. Maybe a spell... but something more. Could it be one of the Three? Bound to it, maybe? No, no... too old. Too evil. Unless..."

He drifted into silence, muttering to himself, eyes unfocused.

Keenan and I exchanged glances, waiting. After a long pause, Reggie suddenly looked up and blinked, as if seeing us for the first time.

Chapter 5 - The Ship

"Oh, you're still here? You should go home. I'll help with the ship in the morning. Need to study first, figure out what we're dealing with. Takes time."

He paused, then added, "Oh, pocket dimension. Forgot to mention. That's why the room's so big."

I glanced around, finally realizing just how impossibly vast the study was. "Uh... thanks."

Reggie waved a hand dismissively. "Well, you asked, so I'm answering. Now off you go. I've got research to do. You two are too noisy. Although..." He squinted at us, head tilted. "There's something about you. Something old..."

He sniffed his own armpit. "Or maybe I haven't bathed this year."

He wandered off mid-thought, mumbling to himself. I looked at Keenan, shrugged, and mouthed, *Okay*. We turned toward the door.

Just as I reached for the handle, Reggie called out, "Wait, what are you doing?"

We froze.

"You're crazy! You could die out there at night! Wild animals, rampaging Noctari, and worse..." he squinted, ", other, smaller animals. Not safe! Hang on."

He grinned and snapped his fingers.

I blinked, and suddenly, I was standing outside Grog's Inn. The night was quiet, the streets mostly empty. I glanced around, disoriented... and realized Keenan was nowhere in sight.

A commotion echoed down the street. Hand instinctively on my weapon, I jogged toward the noise. It led me to the bathhouses, where I arrived just in time to see Keenan being shoved out of the women's bathhouse by a furious housekeeper. His face was even redder than usual as he apologized repeatedly, dodging swats from her broom.

I couldn't help but laugh as he finally escaped and walked over to me, flustered.

"Wait till I see Reggie again," he muttered.

I shook my head, still grinning. "Oh, Keenan. Only you."

"At least it was empty," he said with a sigh. "That could've been really bad."

We both laughed as we headed home, still trying to make sense of the day, and what was easily one of the strangest encounters of our lives.

Chapter 6 - Boarding

We were up early, eating a quick breakfast with Throm. He told us Gam and Grog were already at the docks, getting things ready. Once we finished, the three of us made our way down to the waterfront, where a somber silence lingered in the air.

Usually alive with noise and motion, the docks were strangely subdued. Word had spread, most of the townsfolk already knew what was coming. They stood at a distance, watching, waiting.

The council members were present, all except Villaheim, who remained in a cell awaiting judgment. Reeger had returned late last night and now sat in a chair, petting his all-black cat, Ralphie, his constant companion on hunting trips.

Not far off, Grog leaned against a stack of crates, his axe resting within arm's reach. He puffed on his pipe, looking smug as we approached the edge where the pier met the cobblestone road.

"Well, about time you showed up. We've been waiting all morning," he said gruffly.

I glanced at Throm, who shook his head and replied, "No, we're still waiting on Reggie."

Keenan chuckled, looking at Grog. "You haven't changed a bit."

Grog's lips curled slightly in response.

Gamreal stepped forward. "Once Reggie gets here, we'll finalize everything. None of the guards are willing to board the ship, and I don't blame them, so they'll hold the line back here with Grog and Throm. If you're up for it, you boys can come aboard with me and Reeger. Reeger's agreed to scout ahead. We're the quietest and most familiar with traps, in case there are any... or worse."

I looked at Keenan. He gave a nod.

Smiling, I said, "Yeah, we'll help."

Gam nodded. "Good, good." He placed a hand on my shoulder. "No taking chances."

I grinned. "When have I ever done that?"

He snorted. "If I made you a tabard, it'd have wolves on it."

I winced but smiled at the jab. "Fair enough," I chuckled.

After saying good morning to Reeger, Reggie suddenly appeared beside Gam.

"Well, are we ready?" he asked, his words tumbling out in a blur. "I stayed up all night preparing. We've got what we need, plus a few contingencies, but this won't be easy. The ship is full of energy... and one type I still can't identify."

Gam waited patiently as Reggie rambled, knowing he'd have to breathe eventually.

"My energy reserves are full," Reggie continued, barely pausing. "And I've been charging my emergency reserve container too." He pulled out a small crystalline orb, glowing bright with stored power, and set it on a nearby crate. "Yes, yes, yes, should be able to drop the force field. Give you ten, maybe fifteen minutes, depending on what's

Chapter 6 - Boarding

powering it. I can probably clear the fear effect too. But there's something else... I don't know what it is. Smells bad. No, good? No... I can't tell. But it's new. Definitely new."

Gam jumped in, outlining the boarding plan with crisp efficiency. Reggie nodded along, then added, "Look, no guarantees I can hold it. I have no idea how fast the energy will burn. This is all uncharted territory. I've only read about demons, never tested any of this. If the field regenerates, you may have to disable it from the inside. Worst case, it could take me hours to recharge and try again."

Leaning toward Keenan, I whispered, "Energy reserves? What's he talking about?"

Keenan whispered back, "Everyone has some base level of magical energy. It's like a muscle, you can train it, but your ceiling depends on your natural strength. Some people have bigger reserves. You can supplement with artifacts or stored energy, but that can be risky."

"Ah," I nodded. "Got it. Thanks."

As I mulled over his explanation, my thoughts drifted to the Queen and the Princess. Their power had to come from somewhere. How deep did their reserves run? And how far were they from reaching their full potential?

Suddenly, Reggie muttered a few words and cast a spell, then looked up. "Ready?"

"Wait, what did you just do?" I asked.

"Oh, I put a shield around the shield," he said casually.

I frowned. "Why? I thought we were taking the shield down."

Reggie shrugged. "In case disabling it triggers an explosion. No reason to blow up the entire town," he added, nonchalantly.

"Great," Keenan muttered. "That makes me feel so much better."

"Wait, explode?" I asked, alarmed.

Reggie shrugged again. "Doubt it. But let's go."

With that, he turned his attention to the glowing orb and began focusing on whatever spell he had in mind.

My fear eased slightly as I stood waiting, watching for any sign of movement. I glanced at Gam, about to speak, but he cut me off with a quick, "No... don't do that."

He picked up a rock, gave me a sly smile, and tossed it. The rock struck the side of the ship with a dull thud before plopping into the water.

"The shield's down now," Gam said, still grinning.

I shook my head, smiling despite myself.

Reeger darted silently up the gangplank and vanished onto the ship, with Gam close behind. I took a deep breath and followed, Keenan right behind me.

The ship felt grimy, slick with a kind of oily residue. I hesitated to touch anything. We moved forward, checking the bow for anything unusual before heading toward the stern. But aside from the ship's all-black hull and the filth coating its wood and ropes, nothing stood out. Reeger and Gam were already below deck by the time we reached the ladder.

Just as we were about to follow, Gam reappeared and signaled for silence, gesturing for us to come down.

We crept after him and found ourselves in a room filled with bunks.

Chapter 6 - Boarding

Each bunk held what looked like skeletons, peaceful at first glance, but their jaws were twisted at unnatural angles, and skeletal fingers clutched rusted weapons. A chill crept down my spine.

Keenan focused on one of the skeletons, eyes closed, sensing for something unseen. Reeger silently motioned to Gam that he was heading further below. Gam nodded and gestured for me to follow him toward the aft section.

Sword in hand, I moved beside him to a closed door. He drew his daggers and mouthed, "One... two... three..." before slowly easing it open.

Dim light filtered through nearly blacked-out glass panes. The flicker of an oil lamp revealed a cluttered desk piled with papers and charts. A disheveled bed sat in the back, surrounded by several locked chests. In the darkest corner of the room stood a large birdcage, and inside, a crumpled, motionless figure.

Gam began rifling through the papers as I approached the cage.

As I drew closer, the figure stirred. Her head snapped up.

A young woman, mid-twenties, malnourished, filthy. Wild red hair framed a face streaked with grime, and her fierce green eyes burned with fire. She spat at me and spoke in a harsh, rapid language I didn't recognize.

Startled, I looked at Gam, who had paused mid-search, staring at the cage.

"That sounds like a Northern tongue," he said. "From the cold lands up north."

I shrugged, unfamiliar.

Then the woman switched to flawless Common, her accent heavy but clear. "Why are you here?"

Gam stepped forward cautiously. "The people on this ship attacked us. We want to know why."

Her expression darkened. "Did you kill them all?"

"As far as we know," Gam replied.

She exhaled slowly, her posture softening just a little. "Good," she muttered. "They killed my family."

I watched her, heart tightening. "What's your name?"

She struggled to speak, her voice dry and cracked, but managed, "Valkara."

I turned to Gam. "I'm letting her out," I said, voice low and resolute.

Gam didn't take his eyes off her but gave a small nod.

Valkara lifted a trembling hand and gestured toward the desk. "The key's in there."

I retrieved it, unlocked the cage, and helped her step out. She could barely stand, though it was clear she had once been strong, athletic, even.

"How long were you in there?" I asked.

She sighed, staring into the distance. "I don't know... but it felt like weeks."

Gam quietly moved to her side and eased her into a chair beside the cage.

"What happened?" he asked gently.

Her voice was distant, hollow. "They opened portals to my island and started attacking. The men were away, fighting off another island that had raided our fisheries. All we had left were women and children... but we fought. Fought until only five of us remained."

Chapter 6 - Boarding

Her jaw tightened. "They found where we'd hidden the children and promised to spare them if we surrendered. So, we did."

Her voice faltered, but she pressed on. "Once we laid down our arms, they killed everyone. Including the children. Everyone but me. They discovered I was the chief's daughter and kept me as a bargaining chip."

She paused, swallowing hard. "Two days later, our men returned. The invaders demanded they surrender. My father looked at me... and I smiled. Told him with my eyes: *Don't surrender. They'll kill you anyway.*"

Tears welled, but she didn't let them fall. "They fought. Valiantly. But they all fell. I watched my people be annihilated." Her voice dropped to a whisper. "The leader spared me. I never found out why."

She spat on the ground at the mention of him.

I looked at Gam and shook my head. His expression was tight, processing, calculating. Like he was piecing together a puzzle too awful to finish.

Just then, Keenan stepped into the room, drawn by the sound of our voices.

The moment Valkara saw him, her eyes went wide with fury. Her hand shot out, grabbing two small axes from the wall. She turned on Keenan, rage twisting her face, but her body gave out. She collapsed to her knees, the axes hitting the floor with a dull thud.

"You'll pay for what your people did!" she rasped, trembling, trying to lift the weapons again but too weak.

Keenan stood frozen, watching her struggle. She tried once more, then finally slumped, spent.

"I'm sorry, Father," she gasped. "I've failed you."

Keenan moved. Slowly, silently, he knelt before her. He lifted her chin with gentle hands, his voice low and full of sorrow. "I'm not your enemy."

She stared at him, confused, pain clouding her eyes. Then her eyelids fluttered, and she collapsed, unconscious.

Keenan gently lifted her into his arms. Grief spread across his face as he looked at us, trying to speak, but no words came. He lowered his head and turned, carrying her out of the room.

Gam exhaled and shook his head. "So much senseless violence... and for what?"

Shaken by what we'd just heard, but mindful of the ticking clock, we resumed our search of the cabin. Several chests were filled with weapons, likely trophies taken from victims the crew had slaughtered. I moved to the desk while Gam rifled through one of the larger trunks.

As I searched the drawers, my fingers brushed against an odd seam in the wood. I pulled gently, revealing a false bottom. Inside lay a cluster of smooth, dark stones, twenty or so in total, each one unnaturally cold to the touch.

"Gam," I called quietly.

He stepped over, and his expression darkened the moment he saw them.

"How?" he whispered, shaking his head. "This... this can't be good."

He swiftly gathered the stones into a small cloth bag. "Tell no one," he added grimly.

I nodded, saying nothing.

Reeger appeared in the doorway, face unreadable. "I need you downstairs," he said flatly. "I... I don't know." He

Chapter 6 - Boarding

paused, searching for words, then just shook his head and turned away.

We followed Reeger immediately, but as we passed through the bunkroom, something caught my eye. Between two warped planks in the wall, I noticed a subtle gap. Avoiding the skeletons, I knelt and pried it open, revealing a small compartment. Inside sat a wooden box with a folded parchment resting on top.

I unfolded it carefully. The parchment was covered in entries, dates, locations, names, cargo notes. The top corners were smudged with saltwater, erasing the writer's name, but the content remained legible.

One section described the crew's unease when men with red eyes began joining their ranks. Some sailors left. Others grew quiet, strange... and then they too began to change. The writer's fear bled through the page. He stayed only for the money, one final run to rescue his family from the slums.

The last entry was scrawled in frantic, shaky handwriting. It spoke of a burning sensation inside, growing worse by the day. *"I fear I don't have much time,"* it read. The writing ended abruptly.

I stared at the page, fists clenched. Another innocent life twisted and destroyed by whatever darkness was behind all this. Three days ago, we didn't even know these demons existed. Now we were just trying to understand how and why.

I sighed and slipped the parchment into my pocket before heading below deck.

The hold reeked of heat and decay. At its center pulsed a strange, glowing orb, organic and unnatural. Tubes ran from it into nearby burners, each filled with a goopy, grayish paste I didn't want to examine too closely. The sight alone made my stomach turn.

Gam and Reeger were already there, discussing the orb in hushed tones. They guessed it might be a power source, but neither could figure out how to disable it safely.

Then I heard something.

A voice. Whispering. Calling.

I spun around. No one was there.

Again, the voice, faint but clear. It was coming from the orb.

Before I realized what I was doing, my hand had started to rise.

Gam and Reeger shouted, but I couldn't stop.

The instant my fingers touched the surface, a blinding flash erupted.

I found myself standing in a stark white void. No walls. No floor. Yet the space felt impossibly vast, and claustrophobically small. In front of me, a wisp-like figure floated in the air, pulsing faintly.

"Hello," she said softly.

Startled, I replied, "Hello. Where am I?"

"You are not like the others," the voice answered.

"No," I said cautiously. "They're a dwarf and an elf."

The wisp paused, then spoke again. "No... Why are you here?"

"We're trying to stop evil men from hurting people," I said.

A strange calm washed over me, soothing but also draining. My limbs felt heavy. My eyelids drooped.

Chapter 6 - Boarding

"You do not have much time," the voice said gently. "Please... help me."

I sank to my knees, breath shallow. "What do you need me to do?"

"You must freely allow me to bind my spirit to you," she urged. "So I can use you as a bridge to escape. So I can attach and be carried away."

"I don't understand," I whispered. "Will you hurt anyone if I do?"

"Please help me! Time is gone!"

Before I could fully grasp her meaning, the white space vanished and I collapsed onto the floor of the ship, gasping.

Gam and Reeger knelt beside me, faces lined with concern.

"Your mind was... somewhere else," Reeger said quietly.

Before I could respond, shouts rang out above deck.

"Time's up!" Gam snapped. "We need to move!"

They helped me to my feet, but something inside me stirred, an instinct I couldn't explain. I could still hear her voice, soft and pleading.

Please.

And with that, I reached toward the orb again, shouting in my mind: *I want to help!*

The orb flared with a surge of violent energy, shaking the ship as Gam and Reeger dragged me up the stairs. The pulse intensified. Waves of force tore through the vessel, the deck shuddering beneath our feet.

Chaos had erupted above. Throm and Grog shouted for everyone to take cover on the dock, while Reggie stood at the edge of the gangplank, struggling to contain the magical surge. His face was pale, drenched in sweat. Keenan pushed against the roaring energy, trying to reach us, barely able to stay upright.

The ship groaned, wood creaking, cracking. A deafening screech split the air, and we all cried out in pain.

Then, with a final explosive pulse, the world went white.

When I opened my eyes, I froze.

The ship... was pristine.

Gleaming wood. Bright white sails. Everything clean, renewed as if untouched by corruption.

Gam and Reeger helped me to my feet, but before we could move, a voice rang out, firm, commanding.

"I would not do that, if I were you."

We turned. A glowing wisp floated before us, hovering just off the deck.

"If you intend to harm him," she warned, "you will die."

"No!" I said quickly. "They were helping me."

The wisp drifted through me, her presence brushing against my thoughts.

I sense no fault in you or your companions, she said silently. *I accept your word.*

The light shifted, reshaping into the form of a woman, featureless, yet graceful, cloaked in flowing white.

"I am a life form without physical shape," she said. "I was taken from my world by the evil ones. My energy was drained to power their devices. I am sorry for any harm that was caused."

Chapter 6 - Boarding

She turned to me. "When you freed me, we became linked. I can now communicate with you telepathically."

I nodded, still stunned.

"You are different," she continued. "That is why I could speak to you and why you were able to break me free... Thank you. I have created a field around this ship using the small one's knowledge. It allows me to remain here. I do not yet know how to return to my world, but until then, I will help you."

She paused, her glowing form flickering softly.

"Halvar," she said, facing me.

"Hello," I said, finding my voice again. "These are my friends." I introduced the others, who still stood in stunned silence.

"I must rest," she said, already fading back into her wisp form. "I find your method of communication... taxing."

Her voice echoed in my mind one last time:

Thank you, my champion.

And then, she was gone.

We stood in silence, looking at each other, unsure what to say.

Suddenly, Reggie popped up on deck, his face alight with excitement.

"Well, that was amazing! I never thought I'd see or experience anything so incredible! Did you see the wisp lady and the magic, hah!" he exclaimed, words tumbling out so fast they blurred together. His eyes sparkled, his energy contagious.

Keenan leaned toward me and whispered, "He lost me at 'never.'"

I laughed as Reggie continued his animated rambling. Around us, the dock began returning to normal, the air buzzing with chatter about the ship's transformation and everything that had just happened.

Grog grumbled about the lack of a fight, grabbed his axe and headed back to the inn. Throm mentioned he had orders to fill for the armory and made his way to the blacksmith shop. Gam said he needed to speak with the council, about holding a vote to replace Villaheim, and to decide his fate.

Reggie was still going, his words now approaching another language in speed, when, just before Gam could leave, he darted over, said something completely unintelligible, and vanished in a flash of light.

Keenan chuckled. "He's like a kid on those sugar sticks we had growing up."

"Man, those things were crazy," I said, smiling at the memory.

Around us, the dockworkers, now more at ease, whistled and sang as they worked. Some offered handshakes and smiles as we passed, the tension of the morning finally lifting.

Reeger approached, his expression unreadable. "Can you join me at the inn? There's something we need to discuss."

We nodded. With nothing left to do and everyone else already gone, we followed him out of the dockyard district, through the market, and into the inn. It was bustling with the lunch rush, filled with noise, laughter, and the clatter of mugs and plates. Proof that, for now, the ship was no longer a concern.

Chapter 6 - Boarding

We found an open table in the corner and ordered drinks. Reeger, the quiet, skilled elf who had mentored us in hunting and tracking as teenagers, leaned in once the drinks arrived.

"The elders think this could be the start of the Second War," he said gravely.

I raised an eyebrow. "Way to ease us in with some light conversation."

Keenan sighed. "Yeah, nothing like a world-ending event to brighten your day."

Reeger continued, "This has all the signs of the First War, the one that scattered the people and tore the land into islands. The elders believe someone is searching for the dwarves' homeland. They think an ancient weapon, or power, is hidden there."

I frowned. "The dwarves are secretive, sure, but an ancient weapon? That sounds far-fetched." Still, after everything we'd seen lately, even the unbelievable felt possible.

"There's more," Reeger added. "Demon possessions are increasing. Portals are opening again. My father believes they're coming back, to finish what they started centuries ago."

"Why now?" Keenan asked.

Reeger lowered his voice. "Because the magic of this world is fading. Some of the oldest elves say an ancient power once protected us. But it's weakening."

"That's a good question for Reggie," I muttered, glancing around the room.

At the bar, Grog was watching us. When our eyes met, he shook his head and turned back to his work.

Keenan chuckled. "Us talking probably reminds him of our childhood schemes."

Reeger smiled. "You two were a handful back then. Glad to see you've matured, mostly."

We laughed, then I asked, "So, what can we do?"

"Gather information," Reeger said. "Knowledge is power. But we're short on numbers to fend off any large-scale invasion. Scouts have already been sent to other islands for intel."

A thought struck me. "What about Villaheim's house? Maybe there's something there."

Reeger and Keenan exchanged glances.

"The guards already questioned him and searched his home," Keenan said.

"Yes, but they might've missed something," I replied.

Keenan nodded. "As a paladin, I'd have the authority to search it." He paused, then smiled. "Just like old times. Let's go."

We exchanged quick smiles, downed our drinks, left a few coins on the table, and filed out, none of us noticing Grog watching us closely as we left.

When we arrived at Villaheim's house, a note pinned to the door read:

Under investigation for the coup on Grissom City. Subject is under arrest.

"Must be the right place," I said with a grin.

We opened the door and stepped inside.

The house was a modest one-room structure of timber and stone, topped with a thatched roof. It felt lived-in, functional... and cold. A tall, slightly tarnished mirror leaned

Chapter 6 - Boarding

against one wall, reflecting light from a single window. The hearth was dead and dark, adding to the chill.

In one corner, a simple wooden bed with a neatly folded woolen blanket sat beside a pile of scattered books and clothing. Across from it stood a sturdy desk, cluttered with parchments, ink bottles, and half-written business notes. Nearby, a small table with two mismatched chairs rested near the hearth, bearing the remnants of a meal: a half-loaf of bread and a half-empty tankard.

The space was organized but neglected, like someone who valued function over comfort.

Reeger frowned, scanning the room. "This doesn't feel like the home of a councilman."

"Yeah," I agreed. "He was a last-minute addition in the most recent vote. He came from another island, supposedly. No one I know ever figured out which one. Just seemed odd how quickly he won everyone over."

Keenan shook his head. "I don't miss politics at all." He knelt beside the bed, beginning to search for anything hidden. Reeger moved to examine the desk, while I turned my attention to a chest near the mirror on the far side of the room.

I knelt beside the chest, careful not to disturb the scattered books and folded clothes nearby. The lid creaked as I opened it, revealing a jumble of blankets, old boots, and a few sealed jars. Nothing suspicious, at least not yet.

We were so focused on our searches that none of us heard the footsteps approaching.

The door burst open with a loud thud.

Startled, I turned too fast, tripped, and bumped into the mirror. I caught it just before it fell, steadying it with both hands. Then I looked up.

Grog stood in the doorway, arms crossed, scowling. "Don'tcha know it's illegal to break into someone else's house?" he grunted.

I chuckled, setting the mirror upright. "You scared me half to death."

Keenan stepped forward calmly. "I've taken it upon myself to help investigate the murders," he said. "One of the suspects lived here. We're searching for anything that might lead to more evidence, and more answers."

Grog scratched his head. "By the mountain, they really did a number on your noggin. You sound like some kind of lawyer." He shook his head, then laughed. "I know what you're doing. Just came to see if I could help."

I grinned. "Though you did nearly curse us all by breaking that mirror."

Grog's smirk faded. "Bah, superstitious nonsense." He grabbed a nearby mug and hurled it at the mirror.

"No!" I shouted, reaching out instinctively.

But instead of shattering, the mug vanished, straight through the glass.

We all froze, staring in stunned silence.

The mirror shimmered faintly, its surface rippling like water. The room fell quiet. Even Grog stopped moving, his hand still raised from the throw.

Keenan stepped closer, eyes narrowed. "Did that just…?"

"Yeah," I said, voice low. "It went through."

Chapter 6 - Boarding

Reeger moved beside me, studying the mirror with intense focus. "It's not glass. Not anymore."

Grog grunted. "Well, that's new."

Keenan reached out, hesitated, then touched the surface. His fingers passed through like mist. He pulled back quickly, eyes wide.

"It's a portal," Reeger said. "But to where?"

I glanced at the others. "Only one way to find out."

Grog snorted. "You're not seriously thinking of stepping through that thing."

Keenan looked at me. "We've seen worse."

"True," I said. "But let's make a plan first."

Grog broke the silence, his voice low and wary. "Please don't do anything stupid."

Keenan smiled and without hesitation, stepped through the portal.

Grog shook his head. "like that."

Reeger nodded to Grog. "If we don't come back in an hour, send word to Gam."

Grog let out a heavy sigh as Reeger followed him.

I lingered, watching the mirror ripple faintly. Grog shook his head.

"Well," I said with a grin, "I guess you know what's about to happen."

"And they say dwarves are stupid and stubborn," Grog muttered, a wry smile tugging at his lips. He stepped closer, placing a hand on my shoulder. "Please be careful."

I didn't notice at the time, but he slipped a small stone into my pocket as he turned and walked away.

I chuckled quietly. "Old softy,"

Grog muttered something under his breath, then grunted. "But if you end up in a demon's pantry, don't come crying to me."

I took a breath, stepped forward, and reached into the mirror. It felt cold, like plunging my hand into a mountain stream. Then I stepped through. The sensation was strange, like falling sideways through cold mist. Then I landed, boots crunching softly on damp rock.

Chapter 7 - Portal

I emerged into a dark cave.

It took a moment for my eyes to adjust. Jagged walls surrounded me, and the ceiling, about eight feet high, looked roughly carved from the rock. The air was cool and damp, carrying the faint scent of wet earth. Shadows flickered along the uneven walls, cast by torches in iron brackets. Their warm, amber glow barely pierced the heavy darkness.

The floor was slick and uneven, littered with pebbles and patches of moss. Somewhere in the distance, water dripped in a steady rhythm, echoing through the cavern like a heartbeat.

Ahead, Keenan stood silently, holding up a finger to signal for quiet. I crept up beside him, careful not to slip. He gestured toward a bend in the tunnel. I glanced behind us, just a dead end.

Reeger appeared around the corner, mouthing the word *big*, and motioned for us to follow.

We moved cautiously. When we turned the corner, we froze.

A massive troll sat on a boulder at a junction where three tunnels converged. He was enormous, his bulk nearly filling the entire space, with a club resting beside him that looked capable of crushing a man in a single blow. His skin was mottled gray, thick and leathery, and his eyes glowed faintly in the torchlight.

I heard Merek's voice echo in our minds: *Keenan, if you let him hit me, I will be very upset.*

Keenan stifled a laugh, despite the towering figure in front of us. *You're a shield! It is your job to get hit and protect me!*

We both sobered quickly, exchanging uneasy glances. A fight with a troll in these cramped quarters would be brutal.

But before we could decide what to do, the troll began to speak.

"Frank hate lonely. Frank promised friends, Frank must guard tunnel. Captain says tunnel important, Frank must impress Captain. Then Captain be Frank's friend. We do friend stuff. That be fun. Frank always wanted friend…"

His voice trailed off, and we stared at each other in disbelief.

Merek chuckled in our heads: *Oh, this is so much better. You both finally have someone who can match your intellect. If you fight him now, I'll be mad at you for other reasons. Now I'm off to sleep. Enjoy your new friend.*

Keenan closed his eyes briefly. Reeger leaned in and whispered, "I don't know if I want to kill him unless we have to."

I nodded. The troll seemed more like a child than a monster. An extremely dangerous child, judging by that massive club, but still, a child.

Keenan opened his eyes, sadness etched into his expression. "I detect no evil in him," he said softly. "And I'm with Merek. He's probably being manipulated by whoever's behind all this."

"Wait," said Reeger, puzzled. "Who's Merek?"

Chapter 7 - Portal

Keenan whispered, "Tell you later," then took a deep breath and smiled at us. "Time to turn on the charm."

I gave him a reassuring nod. "We've got your back, brother."

He nodded confidently, then stepped forward into the troll's view.

"Hi, Frank," Keenan said nonchalantly.

Frank startled, jumping up and smacking his massive head on the ceiling. Small rocks tumbled down as he rubbed the spot, wincing. "Ow," he muttered, his bulky form nearly filling the tunnel. Seeing the Noctari, he relaxed slightly. "Uhhh... hi," he replied uncertainly.

Keenan smiled and walked right up to him. "Hey, we need to talk to the captain. Is he here?"

Frank gripped his club tightly, eyeing Keenan with suspicion. "Well... maybe yes. Maybe not. You gotta give the password." He stopped rubbing his head and glanced up, eyes squinting as if trying to remember. After a moment, he seemed to recall it, then folded his arms and smirked, clearly trying to look important.

"Good job, Frank!" Keenan said warmly. "The captain will be proud you're checking everyone. You can't be too careful."

Frank beamed, his large face breaking into a grin. Then, putting on his most serious expression, he nodded. "That's right! Gotta be careful. Captain says bad people who hurt others are everywhere. But I help."

Reeger and I exchanged glances, shaking our heads slightly as this surreal scene played out in front of us.

"You don't know how true that is," Keenan said sincerely. Thinking quickly, he leaned in and lowered his voice. "So, Frank... which password is it again? I always get them mixed up. Is it the ship one, the island one, or..."

He paused, stroking his chin like he was deep in thought.

Frank's face lit up. "The backdoor one for the cave!"

"Right!" Keenan snapped his fingers. "The backdoor one. So... what's the password again?"

Frank puffed out his chest proudly. "It's backdoor!"

"Of course! The password is backdoor. Excellent job, Frank. Now you don't have to smash me."

Frank laughed, visibly relieved. "Yeah! No smashing. That's good."

"Maybe we can even be friends," Keenan added with a grin.

Frank's eyes widened. "Really? That would be great! We could do friend stuff, like smashing and helping and... fun!" He clapped his massive hands together, the sound echoing through the cave like distant thunder.

"Exactly," Keenan said. "That sounds amazing. And hey, there's a good chance we'll be working together in the future. I think we can get you lots of friends with how good of a guard you are."

Frank snorted happily and stood up straighter. "Yep! I am good guard. Don't worry."

"I'm sure you are, friend," Keenan said smiling. "Now, I've got to go relieve the captain. He's got other stuff to do. But I brought two trainees," he added, motioning toward Reeger and me. "They're not ready for the password yet, though, so don't tell them, okay? It's hush-hush."

Frank nodded eagerly. "Okay! I won't say nothing."

Chapter 7 - Portal

Keenan turned to us and waved us over. As we approached, Frank loomed above us with a broad smile on his face.

"You trainees do good, maybe one day you guard hallway with me. But be good to... uh..." He looked at Keenan uncertainly.

Keenan smiled. "My name's Keenan."

Frank nodded, as if he'd known it all along. "Yeah! You better follow Chief Keenan. If not, and he asks me to bonk you, I gotta do it. Might save people, you know."

Reeger smiled. "Don't worry. We'll be good, no bonking necessary."

"Good," Frank said, nodding in approval. "Now I gotta guard. You guys go."

We started forward, but Frank wasn't quite done.

He leaned down slightly, lowering his voice. "If you see Captain, tell him Frank still guarding. Still waiting. Still good."

Keenan placed a hand over his heart. "We will. Promise."

Frank grinned, then resumed his post, standing tall and proud.

As we walked past him, we heard Frank mumble to himself, "I made new friend today. Hah, that makes Frank happy." Then, louder, he called after us, "Oh, remember friends stay out of water!"

We turned back and thanked him, then continued down the tunnel, exchanging amused glances. The echo of Frank's happiness bouncing off the walls.

The tunnel eventually opened into a natural cavern.

A narrow bridge spanned a stream flowing from a crack in the stone wall, feeding into a dark, still pool to one side. The water shimmered strangely, almost as if it were calling to us, inviting, clear, and beautiful.

Without realizing it, I took a step toward it.

Reeger placed a hand on my shoulder. "Careful."

Keenan closed his eyes, focusing intently.

Reeger added, "The water's moving against the current in some spots. There's definitely something in there."

Keenan opened his eyes and nodded. "There's magic in it, but not like anything I've seen before. Let's stay on the bridge and keep moving."

Shaking my head as if snapping out of a dream, I muttered, "Yeah... that was wild."

We crossed the bridge without incident and followed the tunnel for several hundred yards. Eventually, the rough stone gave way to shaped masonry, a stone-lined hallway that looked like it belonged in a castle. The transition was so sudden it felt almost surreal.

The floor beneath our boots was smooth and level. The arched ceiling rose ten, maybe twelve feet high, and the corridor stretched about twenty feet across. Ahead, it branched off to the right, while a pair of massive double doors stood to the left, reaching all the way to the ceiling. Torches lined the walls, casting a steady, warm glow.

We approached the intersection cautiously. As we reached it, we glanced right and saw another hallway with five doors, two on each side and one at the far end.

We decided to investigate, starting with the first door on the right.

Chapter 7 - Portal

Inside was what looked like a combination of a mess hall and kitchen. Large wooden tables were scattered throughout the room, and at one end stood a hearth and a prep area. The air smelled faintly of old smoke and dried herbs. Finding nothing of interest, we moved on.

The second room on the right was a barracks and armory. Most of the weapons were gone, but sharpening stones and bunks, stacked four high, lined the walls. A few dented helmets and cracked shields lay forgotten in the corners. We searched the space, turning up a few stray coins but no useful information.

Finally, we reached the door at the end of the hall.

What waited inside was beyond anything we were prepared for.

The room resembled a laboratory. Along one wall stood several hospital beds, their sheets stained and rumpled. The opposite wall was lined with shelves filled with vials, strange chemicals, and glass tubes bubbling with unknown contents. The air was thick with the scent of metal and rot.

Standing on one of the beds was a gnome with white hair and yellow eyes, muttering curses under his breath as he flipped through a book, switching languages mid-sentence. His robes were stained with ink and something darker.

Above him, stuck to the ceiling, writhed a grotesque mass of flesh. It vaguely resembled a humanoid form but moved with jerky, unnatural spasms. Its limbs stretched and contracted like wet ropes, and its head, or what passed for one, twitched erratically. The gnome hadn't noticed us yet, but the creature had. It let out unsettling, wet noises as its limbs reached in our direction.

"I think it might be a flesh golem," Reeger whispered, drawing his bow and melting into the shadows.

Keenan gave me a look, shrugged slightly, and said under his breath, "Might as well play the part again."

He stepped forward and barked, "Report!"

The gnome spun around, eyes narrowing with suspicion before launching into a furious tirade.

"Report this, report that! That's all you demons ever want, reports! Well, here's your blasted report: I used the townspeople you gave me to make this, gesturing towards the creature. Everything was going fine until I tried to make it immune to magical damage. Somehow, that spell levitated it to the ceiling, and now I can't undo it. So here I am, stuck and frustrated, and you waltz in demanding updates!"

Keenan clenched his jaw, forcing a calm smile. "So... you used townspeople for this?"

"Yes, yes!" the gnome snapped. "And they were alive, just like you asked when I started! You lot love causing pain, don't you?"

Keenan's smile tightened, his rage barely contained. "So, you were forced to do this? Against your will?"

The gnome let out a bitter laugh. "Forced? Of course not! Why would I be? I enjoy this kind of work."

At that, he suddenly stopped. His eyes narrowed, and his tone turned sharp.

"Wait... who are you? And why are you here?"

Keenan drew his sword with calm authority. "I am Aegis, Protector of the Innocent, Wielder of the Bulwark of

Chapter 7 - Portal

Kings. For the murder of these townspeople, you are sentenced to death."

As he stepped forward, the gnome shrieked, "You'll never take me alive!" He hurled a vial to the ground. "Smoke bomb!" he cried triumphantly, vanishing into a cloud of thick smoke.

Almost immediately, his laughter turned into hacking coughs. "Tear gas!" he wheezed, crawling out of the cloud with red eyes and streaming tears.

Keenan stood, dumbfounded, as the gnome scrambled onto a nearby table. Clutching another vial, the gnome pointed it shakily at him. "Not another step, or I'll hit you with this!"

Keenan paused, raising an eyebrow. "What is it?"

The gnome opened his mouth, glanced at the vial, and hesitated. "Honestly? I have no idea." Still, he held it up like it was a weapon.

Straightening with a shred of regained bravado, he sneered, "Besides, you can't harm me while my creature lives! I bound its life force to mine as insurance!"

From the shadows, a quiet twang echoed, followed by a heavy thud as Reeger's arrow struck the flesh golem. It let out a grotesque cry but stayed alive, stuck to the ceiling.

The gnome waved the vial even more frantically. "Pssh! It can't be killed that easily. Stay back, or I'll drink this!"

Keenan tilted his head. "Why would I care if you drink it?" he asked incredulously.

"Because!" the gnome snapped. "I'll turn into a bear and tear you to pieces!"

Keenan glanced at me and shrugged. Then, dryly replied, "Or you'll turn into a mouse, and I'll step on you."

The gnome froze, eyes darting. "That's... a valid point," he admitted. Then his face lit up. "How about you drink the vial, and we go from there?"

Before anyone could respond, another twang sounded. Reeger's arrow struck the gnome square between the eyes. He dropped instantly. Above us, the flesh golem let out a final, shuddering moan before collapsing, still stuck to the ceiling, now lifeless.

Keenan sighed, shaking his head. "I think he reversed the spell. If he dies, the golem dies too."

I stepped forward and crouched beside the gnome's body, eyeing the vial still clutched in his hand. "I kind of wanted to know what this does."

"Same," Keenan said with a chuckle.

Reeger emerged from the shadows, slinging his bow over his shoulder. "He was... something else," he said, shaking his head.

"That was anticlimactic," I said, smiling.

"At some point, we should come back through here and figure out everything going on in this place," I added, glancing around the cluttered lab. "But knowing the guy who was working on it... who knows how much of this actually works or even does what it says."

"Agreed," Keenan said with a nod. "Let's keep moving."

We left the lab and headed for the second door on the left. Inside, several cages lined the walls, each one containing a lifeless body. In the center of the room stood a table with a softly glowing orb resting on it.

Chapter 7 - Portal

Reeger sighed heavily. "I was afraid of this."

"What is it?" I asked, uneasy as I stared at the orb.

He glanced from the corpses to the glowing sphere. "I think these are soul orbs. They drain the life energy from people and store it. That's how they power their magic, by consuming lives."

Keenan shook his head in disgust. "That's horrifying."

"Not the way I'd want to go," I muttered, staring at the eerie glow. I couldn't help but wonder how many souls were trapped inside.

Keenan, seeing my look, placed a reassuring hand on my shoulder. "Best not to dwell on it. Let's just make sure they don't make any more of these."

"Agreed," Reeger said, stepping back into the hallway.

Keenan lingered for a moment, then raised his sword and brought it down on the orb. It shattered with a flash of light and a faint, sorrowful cry.

We stood in silence.

Then Keenan turned and walked out, his voice low. "Let's finish this."

We approached the final door but froze as a sound escaped from the other side, movement. Instantly, we were on alert, weapons ready. Reeger signaled a silent countdown, then threw the door open.

Keenan led the way in, followed by me and Reeger. The room was large and dimly lit. A bed stood to the left; a massive desk dominated the center. Behind the desk stood a hulking man at least seven feet tall with jet-black hair and black eyes that locked onto us the moment we entered. To the right, a large mat occupied most of the floor, and on it sat a massive wolf, its head level with mine even while seated. It watched us without blinking, poised and waiting for a command.

For a moment, the air was thick with tension. No one moved.

Keenan finally broke the silence. "I am Aegis, Protector..."

"Yes, yes," the man interrupted with a deep, dismissive voice. "I know who you are. The question is: why are you here? How did you get past the troll... and where is Remy?" He gestured vaguely toward the hallway. "That fool gnome promised me his golem was unbeatable."

We tried not to smile at the captain's irritation, but he noticed. His expression darkened as he stood, grabbing a massive great sword from behind the desk.

"You may be amused now," he said with a cruel grin, cracking his neck, "but you won't be in a moment. So, which one of you wants to die first?"

"Before you kill us," Keenan said calmly, "just one question."

The man chuckled darkly. "No promises but go ahead."

"Are you the captain?" Keenan asked.

The man's grin widened. "Guilty as charged."

At that, Keenan pulled something from his pocket and shouted, "Smoke bomb!" He threw it at the captain, striking him square in the chest. The vial shattered, releasing a thick cloud of white smoke.

The captain laughed. "You think..." but immediately broke into violent coughing as the gas surrounded him.

I grinned. Keenan must have swiped one of the gnome's tear gas vials from the lab.

Chapter 7 - Portal

Through his coughing fit, the captain managed to shout a command to the wolf.

The beast lunged at Reeger, who dodged just in time. It barreled into me instead, slamming me to the ground. I jammed my weapon between its jaws as it bit down, shattering my blade.

This is it, I thought.

Just as the wolf opened its mouth for another strike, I heard the twang of a bowstring. An arrow pierced its skull, and at the same instant, Keenan's sword plunged into its heart. The wolf gave a final gasp before collapsing on top of me with a heavy thud.

The captain burst out of the smoke, his bloodshot eyes blazing with fury. He charged at Keenan, swinging his sword. Keenan raised his shield just in time, and a burst of energy erupted on impact, knocking the captain back several feet and stunning him briefly.

I struggled to slide out from under the wolf's weight as another arrow struck the captain's shoulder. He roared in pain, turned toward Reeger with murderous intent, and kept advancing, even after a second arrow hit his other shoulder.

Reeger tried to retreat, but the captain caught him by the arm and raised his sword to strike.

Before the blow could fall, Keenan's blade burst through the captain's chest from behind.

The captain froze, eyes wide, and then crumpled to the floor, lifeless.

We stood there in silence, catching our breath.

Reeger looked up at Keenan and gave a weak smile. "It's good to have friends."

"Yeah," Keenan said, grinning. "Just ask Frank."

I finally managed to push the wolf's body off me and sat up, wincing. "That was... intense."

Keenan offered a hand and pulled me to my feet. "You held your ground."

Reeger nodded. "And you didn't scream. That's progress."

I laughed softly. "I was too busy thinking about how much I liked my old sword."

Keenan glanced at the captain's fallen weapon. "We'll find you a better one."

I stood and brushed myself off. "And once again, I'm almost useless in a fight," I said dryly.

They both laughed.

"At least we're okay," Reeger said with a tired smile. "That's what really matters."

The adrenaline was wearing off, and the weight of what we'd just been through started to settle in. We were lucky to have made it out without serious injuries. Keenan exhaled slowly, hoping our luck would hold out just a little longer.

We scanned the room, finding letters and correspondence that linked several of the town's traitors to the captain's plans. Some notes referred to distant islands, but the most disturbing discovery was a detailed plan outlining how they were using the townspeople to feed the soul orbs. They would then power weapons and portals meant to bring even more demons into our world.

Nothing new, I thought grimly. Then Keenan opened a drawer in the desk and pulled out several black stones. The moment I saw them, I froze.

Both of them turned to look at me.

Chapter 7 - Portal

I let out a slow breath. "I don't know what they are, but these... these had my uncles rattled."

Keenan and Reeger exchanged a glance. Reeger was the first to speak. "If something shakes your uncles, I don't feel good about it."

"Me neither," Keenan agreed. "We'd better bring them back. Maybe your uncles can tell us what we're dealing with."

I nodded, my curiosity rising. What were these stones, and why did they matter so much?

"Well," Keenan said, slipping them into his bag, "I guess that just leaves the last room."

"Please let it be something helpful," I muttered as we stepped back into the hallway.

We walked in silence, the echo of our footsteps bouncing off the stone walls. As we reached the final set of doors, we all paused, each of us feeling the same creeping unease. It was like the air itself was holding its breath.

"Maybe it's like Reggie," I said, trying to lighten the mood. "Whatever's inside might not be as bad as the outside makes it seem."

Keenan chuckled. "One can hope."

Together, we pushed the massive doors. With a creak and a groan, the doors began to open, revealing a vast chamber beyond.

It looked like a throne room. At its center sat a massive chair, ornate and ominous. On the left side of the room stood a towering statue of a demon, easily fifteen feet tall. The room itself was shaped like a sphere, with a domed ceiling stretching at least twenty feet above us. The walls were etched with runes that pulsed faintly, as if reacting to our presence.

But what truly made our blood run cold was what lay to the right.

Three portals.

Identical to the ones we'd seen yesterday, and all active.

One reached nearly to the ceiling, while the other two stood about seven or eight feet tall. All three pulsed with sickly energy, drawing power from several glowing soul orbs arranged on a table nearby. The air around them shimmered with heat and menace.

I exchanged a glance with Keenan and without a word, we sprinted forward, grabbing the nearest soul orbs and smashing them on the ground. The moment their connection broke, the portals began to flicker and fade. But just as we turned to deal with the last, largest orb, a massive foot and leg stepped through, slamming into the ground and knocking us backward.

We scrambled to our feet just in time to see the largest creature I had ever laid eyes on emerge from the portal.

He was massive, towering at least fifteen or sixteen feet tall, with a muscular, red-skinned body that radiated raw power and menace. Leathery, bat-like wings unfurled behind him, casting monstrous shadows across the room. Glowing yellow eyes locked onto us. Two jagged horns curled back from his forehead like a crown of bone and fire.

In each hand, he wielded a weapon: a massive, curved sword in one, and a heavy hammer in the other, both humming with terrible, magical energy. A long, barbed tail

Chapter 7 - Portal

swayed behind him like a serpent, and his hooves ground into the stone as if claiming the ground itself.

Smoke curled from his nostrils as he exhaled brimstone and flame, his gaze filled with hatred and hunger.

And then he smiled.

"So... these are the little creatures giving my pawns so much trouble?" His voice was deep and thunderous, rumbling up from the bowels of the earth. He sniffed the air, lip curling in disdain. "Pathetic. You are nothing. How have you made it this far?"

I turned toward the doors, but they had closed, sealed shut behind us. Panic surged in my chest. I looked at Keenan, who met my gaze with the same grim determination I'd seen in his eyes when we'd faced the dire wolves as kids. No escape. No running.

I grabbed my axe and a dull sword we'd found in the captain's room, my own sword still shattered, and Keenan turned to Reeger. The two exchanged a silent look. One of understanding. Of acceptance.

It was fun while it lasted.

The creature pointed a clawed finger at Keenan. "You," he sneered. "A paladin. A betrayer. My generals will roast you on a spit for what you've done."

Keenan stepped forward, calm and resolute. "I am Aegis, Protector of the Innocent. Wielder of the Bulwark of Kings. And for your crimes against this world, you will be judged."

The demon paused, surprised by Keenan's unwavering resolve. Then he laughed, a booming, guttural sound that shook the very walls.

"If my men had half your courage," he said, "I would have already conquered this world. That's too bad, betrayer. You could have gone far."

Keenan raised his weapon. The demon did the same, letting out a roar that shook dust from the ceiling.

"Know that you die by the hand of Nerathor, World Destroyer!"

He slammed his hammer into the ground.

The shockwave hit like a tidal wave of stone and fire. We were hurled across the room, limbs flailing, weapons torn from our grasp. I slammed into the wall, the impact driving the breath from my lungs. My vision blurred. Keenan and Reeger crumpled to the floor, unmoving.

Laughter echoed through the throne room, deep, cruel, victorious.

I tried to rise, but my body refused. Pain shot through my ribs. Blood filled my mouth. I coughed, the sound wet and ragged, and the world tilted sideways.

Nerathor loomed in the center of the room, his wings unfurled, his hammer resting on the cracked stone. He surveyed the wreckage with satisfaction, eyes glowing like coals in a furnace.

"You were warned," he said, voice low and venomous. "This world belongs to me. Your defiance is a whisper against the storm."

I reached for the weapon beside me, fingers trembling. Too far. Too heavy. My arm collapsed beneath me.

Reeger groaned, barely conscious. Keenan didn't move.

Chapter 7 - Portal

Nerathor turned toward Keenan's body, raising his hammer once more. "The Bulwark dies with its bearer," he said. "And the light fades forever."

I wanted to scream. To fight. To do something. But the darkness was closing in, thick and final.

My thoughts scattered. Memories flickered, Reeger's laughter, Keenan's stubborn grin, the quiet resolve that had carried us this far. Was this how it ended? Not with triumph, but with silence?

The throne room spun. The demon's laughter grew distant. My heartbeat slowed, each thud a fading drumbeat.

I coughed again, weaker now. The blood tasted like iron and ash.

Nerathor's shadow fell over me. I felt the heat of his presence, the weight of his gaze.

"You should have stayed in the shadows," he said. "You were never meant to stand in the light."

And then, nothing.

Darkness enveloped me.

Chapter 8 - How

Pain. That was all I could feel as my senses slowly returned. My ears rang. Everything was dark. I tried to open my eyes, but the effort sent a wave of agony through me. I coughed, a wet and rattling sound, feeling blood rise in my throat. A hand pressed firmly against my chest.

The pain gradually gave way to a strange tingling in my lungs, like frost melting from within, slow, aching, alive. Breath returned in shallow gasps, each one sharper than the last.

When my eyes finally fluttered open, I saw Keenan kneeling over me, his hand glowing faintly as he slowly healed my wounds.

"Take it easy," he said, helping me into a sitting position.

Reeger sat nearby, his face streaked with dirt, cuts, and bruises. We all looked awful, battered, bloodied, and coated in debris. I glanced down to see bruises spreading across my chest and legs through the tears in my clothes.

"What happened?" I asked weakly, trying to stand.

Keenan and Reeger exchanged glances before helping me to my feet. As they stepped aside, the room came into focus, and the sight before me stole the breath from my lungs.

Nerathor was frozen solid.

His face was locked in an expression of pure terror, arms raised as if trying to shield himself. His eyes, wide,

Chapter 8 - How

glassy, were fixed on a point fifteen feet above the floor, near the door. The space before him was coated in thick ice, jagged icicles erupting from his back as if he'd been struck by an impossibly powerful freezing force.

The temperature had dropped sharply. I shivered as I looked around, breath misting in the air.

Behind us, the doors remained shut. We had collapsed directly in front of them, whoever opened them would've had to push us aside. The third portal was sealed, its orb knocked from the pedestal and lying dark on the floor like a dead star.

"How?" I whispered. "Who could have done this?"

I looked at Keenan. He shook his head, his expression grim.

"It wasn't me. Even if I had the power... something like this would require an unimaginable amount of energy."

I turned to Reeger.

He met my gaze with something I'd never seen in him before: fear. Real fear. And uncertainty.

Quietly, he said, "The elves... we can't do this."

I stretched, wincing as pain flared through me. Keenan had healed the worst of it, but I still felt like I'd been tossed around like a rag doll.

"We should be dead," Keenan murmured, staring at the massive, frozen demon.

I followed his gaze. I remembered Nerathor's hatred, how he looked at us like we were insects beneath his heel. Now his eyes were locked in a mask of fear, the worst I'd ever seen. It wasn't just death that had claimed him. It was something older. Something powerful.

"Did you see anything?" I asked.

Reeger shook his head. "No. I hit the wall and blacked out. When I came to, you and Keenan were still out cold. I crawled to him, woke him up, and he healed both of us. Then we got to you."

I scanned the room, confused. "Is there any other way in or out?"

"I don't think so," Reeger said, coughing, a trace of blood on his lips.

"Then someone must have portaled in," I said. "We need to tell my uncles. Immediately. This is serious."

I shook my head, mumbling, "We should be dead…"

"Agreed," Keenan said, slowly shaking his head in disbelief.

The three of us pulled open the large doors and stepped into the hallway, every movement slow and cautious as we tried to process what had just happened.

As we walked, the soreness in our bodies gradually faded, letting us pick up the pace. We still didn't know how to leave the area, or even what time it was. The silence of the corridor pressed in around us, heavy and strange.

Retracing our steps, we finally came across Frank. We gave him a vague explanation, telling him that some "bad guys" had attacked and killed everyone, but we'd managed to stop them.

He shook his head solemnly, then broke into a wide grin.

"Well, my new friends are safe and strong and beat bad guys," he said cheerfully.

Keenan smiled back. "Frank, we want you to have the captain's room. You're in charge here until we return."

Chapter 8 - How

Frank's face lit up with pride. "Frank will take care of the mess and make sure place is safe!" With that, he turned and excitedly walked off.

Keenan called after him, "Only let us or our friends through, okay?"

"Okay!" Frank shouted, disappearing around a corner.

"We should've asked where that other tunnel leads," I muttered, wincing as I stretched, trying to loosen up my stiff muscles.

"They had to get out somehow," Keenan said. "Hopefully it leads somewhere near Grissom."

We turned and started down the tunnel.

As we pressed forward, the faint sound of waves crashing against rocks reached our ears, distant, rhythmic, like a heartbeat calling us home. We exchanged hopeful glances and quickened our pace. Soon, we emerged into a hidden cove where the ocean lapped against dark stones, the air thick with the salty tang of sea spray.

Above us, the sky was painted in soft oranges and golds, the sun hovering near the horizon like a watchful eye.

"Wait," I said, stopping. "Is the sun going down... or coming up?"

We stepped further out, and to our surprise, spotted Grissom Harbor in the distance to the north.

"That means," I said, turning to Keenan, "we were in there for nearly a full day."

"Or a full day and night," Keenan added wryly.

"I hate caves," Reeger muttered.

Keenan and I couldn't help but laugh, though the motion sent sharp jabs of pain through our sides, quickly silencing us. Still grinning, we began the long walk toward town.

By the time we reached Grissom Harbor, the sun was fully risen, and its warmth felt glorious on our cold, aching bodies. The town looked unchanged, quiet, familiar, almost surreal after what we'd endured. We headed straight for the inn, where Grog met us at the door.

He took one look at us, battered, bruised, exhausted, and without a word, turned and disappeared into the kitchen.

We collapsed into chairs at a table, completely drained. Moments later, Grog returned with mugs of mead, three steaming bowls of hog soup, and fresh bread. He sat across from us, silently watching as we devoured every bite.

Five minutes later, Throm and Gam entered the inn, having heard we were back, and joined us at the table. They waited patiently while we ate. Each of us had multiple servings. It was, without question, the best soup I'd ever tasted. When we finally leaned back, full and content, we exchanged a look that said everything without a word.

The dwarves seemed to understand. Grog stood, locked the inn's front door, and flipped the sign to Closed. Returning to the table, he sat down and said, "Now, from the start. You walked through the mirror. What happened next?"

We glanced at one another, then began to recount the entire ordeal, taking turns filling in the details. My uncles listened carefully, asking the occasional question for clarity.

Chapter 8 - How

When we got to the part about the bumbling gnome, Gam chuckled, and even Grog cracked a rare smile. But Throm frowned, his expression shadowed with concern.

"You three are the luckiest group I've ever seen," he said, shaking his head. "But luck like that doesn't last forever."

We shifted uneasily, knowing full well the story was only going to get harder to believe.

When we described the moment the massive demon stepped through the portal, silence fell over the room. You could've heard a leaf hit the floor.

Then Keenan repeated what he'd told the demon.

Grog jumped to his feet. "By my beard! You told him that, you bugger?" he roared with laughter. "This one's got some brass on him! I would've paid good coin to see his face when you said it." Still chuckling, he sat back down.

Throm and Gam allowed faint smiles, but their focus remained sharp as we continued.

When we described being thrown against the wall, Grog glanced at the shield resting beside Keenan and barked, "Hey, you silent cretin! Why didn't you help them out?"

At that moment, Keenan and I both remembered Merek.

To everyone's shock, the sentient shield spoke aloud.

"The moment you stepped into that room, a suppression field activated," Merek said, his voice low and edged with regret.

We listened in stunned silence as he continued.

"No magic could function in there. None, except perhaps the most basic healing touch. I couldn't speak, couldn't draw on my energy, couldn't even see. I was completely cut off. I've never experienced anything like it."

He sighed, the sound heavy with sorrow.

"I'm only just now regaining my voice. It's been returning slowly since we left the cave."

"Well, that's odd," Throm said, stroking his beard. "I don't think I've ever encountered a suppression field that strong before."

"Okay, so how did you beat him, then?" Gam asked, leaning forward with interest. "After he knocked you into the wall?"

We exchanged uneasy glances, fidgeting in our seats. Finally, I sighed and admitted, "We didn't."

"What do you mean you didn't?" Grog asked, confused.

Throm's expression turned grim. "They didn't beat him. They lost."

Our heads dropped under the weight of his words.

"But how?" Grog pressed. "How are they here, then, eh?"

"We don't know," Reeger said quietly.

"He spared you?" Gam asked, incredulously.

"No," Keenan said firmly.

"Well then how…" Grog began, but I cut him off.

"When we woke up, he was frozen solid," I said. "We don't know what happened."

The dwarves paled, glancing at one another with a strange mix of dread and awe. Even Throm leaned forward in his chair, his normally stoic expression cracking with curiosity.

"What do you mean 'frozen solid'?" he asked.

Chapter 8 - How

"I mean exactly that," I replied. "Frozen. Completely. And he had a look of pure terror on his face."

Suddenly, the three dwarves jumped up and cheered, startling us so badly that Reeger nearly spilled his drink. We exchanged wary glances, unsure if they'd lost their minds or if we'd missed something crucial.

But after a moment of raucous celebration, fists pounding the table, mugs sloshing, and Grog letting out a war cry that rattled the rafters, they settled down again, breathless and grinning.

"Can you take us there?" Gam asked, eyes gleaming like a child who'd just been promised a new toy.

"Right now?" I asked, stunned.

"Yes!" he said, barely containing his excitement.

Throm stepped in, eyeing our battered and exhausted forms. "Gam, maybe let them rest first?"

"I could go scout it out myself," Grog offered, already half-standing.

"No!" we all said in unison.

"You'll hurt Frank," I added quickly.

"The troll?" Grog asked, frowning.

"Yes," Keenan said. "He's, our friend."

Gam raised an eyebrow. "A troll? A friend? Trolls aren't exactly known for companionship. We should probably kill him, for safety."

Our reactions were so serious and immediate, Reeger's hand tightening on his belt knife, Keenan's jaw clenching, my glare sharp enough to cut, that the dwarves hesitated. After a tense pause, they backed off, and Grog reluctantly agreed to wait until we had rested.

"Oh," Keenan said suddenly, reaching into his pouch. "I almost forgot." He pulled out several small black stones we'd found and placed them on the table.

Gam snatched them up quickly, slipping them into his pocket without a word.

To our surprise, he didn't explain a thing.

"Uncle," I said, eyeing him. "This is important. We need to know what those stones are."

Gam exchanged a look with the others, then nodded. "But not here," he said quietly. "Somewhere safer."

The three of us exchanged curious looks but were too tired to argue. Our bodies ached, our minds buzzed with unanswered questions, and the weight of the day pressed down like a mountain.

We agreed to rest only until after lunch, then make plans to return to the cave.

Dragging ourselves to bed, I lay down, but the image of Nerathor's frozen face stayed with me, locked in terror, eyes wide, mouth twisted in a silent scream. And the way the dwarves had reacted to hearing he was frozen? It was almost more thrilling to them than the fact that we'd survived.

I let out a soft chuckle as I fell asleep.

A knock at the door dragged me from a deep sleep. Moments later, Grog burst in, grinning like a boy on a festival morning.

"Come on, boy! Daylight's burning!"

"You're killing me," I groaned, sitting up slowly. I stretched and winced, Keenan's healing had done wonders, but I was still sore in places I didn't know I had.

Chapter 8 - How

"Yeah, yeah," Grog said. "We're all ready to go. You're the last one, as usual."

Shaking my head and smiling, I got dressed in the fresh clothes they'd brought from home and headed downstairs. The three dwarves were already geared up, packs on their backs and weapons in hand, grinning like kids before an adventure. Our gear was laid out and ready. I chuckled, grabbing the new sword Throm had brought for me. Keenan and Reeger smiled as we stepped out together and made our way to Villaheim's house.

When we arrived, Gam headed straight for the mirror.

"We need to move this somewhere safer," he said thoughtfully.

"Agreed," Throm added.

Keenan gave him a crooked grin. "Paladins lead the way," he said, stepping through the mirror.

Throm chuckled and followed. One by one, we all passed through, emerging in the same section of the cave as before. The air was cool and damp, the stone walls glistening with moisture. The memory of our last passage through here clung to us like mist.

We warned the dwarves about the water, but we made it through to the hallways without incident. As we walked, Throm slowed, running his fingers along the smooth stone walls, a thoughtful look on his face.

"I wonder..." he murmured.

"Wonder what?" I asked.

He smiled faintly. "There was a city once, partially built underground, south of Grissom. This stonework looks like it might've been part of it. But" he added, "that's a story for another day."

Before we could ask more, we heard the thudding of heavy footsteps echoing through the hall.

We exchanged amused glances and warned the dwarves to stand back as they instinctively reached for their weapons.

Frank came stomping around the corner, his face twisted into a scowl. But when he saw us, his expression immediately brightened.

"Friends! Hah! You back soon!" he bellowed happily. "Don't worry, Frank cleaned up! No more stinky dead guys!"

Then his eyes landed on the dwarves. His smile vanished. He pulled out his club and raised it high.

"Look out, friends!" he shouted. "Those enemy, evil dwarves! They kill children and eat them!"

Keenan quickly stepped between Frank and the dwarves.

"Wait!" he yelled.

Frank froze mid-swing, blinking in surprise.

Keenan approached slowly and whispered, "I've been turning the dwarves to our side, to fight the bad guys."

Frank squinted at the dwarves. "Really?"

"Yes, really," Keenan said with a nod. "These three? One hundred percent good now."

Frank stared at them blankly for a long moment. "So... they friends too?"

Keenan considered, then nodded. "Yeah, they are."

Frank thought it over. Then, at last, he nodded. "Hmm... okay. More new friends. But don't hurt old friends, or I will have to bonk you."

Grog chuckled. "By the mountain..."

Chapter 8 - How

Gam smirked. "Well, now I've seen everything."

Throm, shaking his head, mouthed "eat children" before leaning toward them, lowering his voice. "There's no evil in him. I've never seen that before."

We introduced the dwarves to Frank properly, letting him shake their hands and hearing him explain his new cleaning system, which mostly involved throwing bones into a pit and stomping on them until they were "not gross anymore."

Then we continued to the large chamber. Together, we opened the door.

There, still frozen solid in the center of the room, stood the massive demon.

Frank looked in and gasped, his face contorting in horror.

"No!" he cried out. "He hurts me!"

He turned and ran.

Startled, we looked at one another.

Keenan sighed. "I'll go talk to him," he said, and left the room.

The rest of us stepped inside, staring in disbelief.

Throm immediately approached the demon, inspecting its icy form with a craftsman's eye. He circled slowly, fingers brushing the frost, studying the frozen expression locked in terror. The silence in the chamber was thick, reverent.

"You're the only one who would know," Gam said, watching him closely.

Grog and Gam exchanged glances, silently waiting for Throm's verdict. After a long pause, he smiled.

"Yes," he said simply.

Grog and Gam clasped hands, grinning like boys who'd just uncovered a long-lost treasure.

"Haha! This is great news!" Grog exclaimed.

Gam rubbed his hands together with a grin and gave his signature, "Good, good."

"How do we find him?" Grog asked, eyes still fixed on the frozen form.

"He'll reveal himself when he's ready," Gam replied. "I'm just glad he's here somewhere, especially if they're coming back." He nodded toward the demon, his tone darkening.

Gam turned to Throm. "Should we crack him?"

"Wait, crack him?" I finally spoke, having remained silent until now.

Gam began, excitedly, "There's a spot that…"

He trailed off, glancing at the others. His tone turned deadly serious.

"We can't say more without permission," he said firmly.

"He's a dwarf in my book," Grog grumbled.

"Yes, but you're not the king," Throm replied.

Gam sighed, then looked at Throm. "But you could…" He hesitated, then said, "Short answer, shatter him. But we can't explain further."

Throm crouched, examining the base of the frozen demon. After a moment, he smiled.

"Found it," he said.

Just then, Keenan returned with Frank. The troll looked frightened but determined, tears streaking his

Chapter 8 - How

cheeks as he tried to appear brave. His massive hands trembled slightly, and his eyes darted around the chamber like a cornered animal.

I watched him, thinking he must still be a child, or at least stuck in a child's mind.

As if reading my thoughts, Reeger muttered, "I'd put him in what you humans would call his teens."

I smiled. "Thanks, you old mind reader."

Reeger chuckled. "Learn to stop announcing your thoughts with your face."

"Okay, Mr. Insightful," I replied with mock indignation.

Keenan spoke in a low voice. "He was tortured by demons when he was young. They killed his family. The captain probably kept him around because he thought Frank was entertaining."

At that, my blood boiled. The image of all the kind creatures the demons had hurt, or killed, flooded my mind. The weight of it pressed against my chest like a stone.

Keenan looked back at Frank and said gently, "See, Frank? We stopped him. He can't hurt you anymore."

Frank took a hesitant step toward the room, his movements uncertain, swaying as if dodging blows only he could see. He was clearly reliving something awful, his breath shallow, his eyes wide.

Then, in a rare show of emotion, Throm stepped forward. He cast a spell, soft and golden, and stood beside Frank, whispering something in his ear. None of us could hear what was said, but Frank's eyes widened.

"Really?" he asked softly.

Throm smiled warmly. "Really."

Frank straightened up, wiped a tear from his eye, and tightened his grip on his massive club. Brimming with new courage, he said, "I member you, what you did to my family..."

He paused, glancing at Throm, who gave him an encouraging nod. Frank turned back toward the demon and said with conviction,

"Frank gonna bonk you now."

We couldn't help but smile.

Frank walked to the spot Throm had pointed out earlier, set the end of his club down briefly, then turned to beam at us with childlike excitement.

"You are best friends," he said.

Then with a mighty swing, he brought the club down hard. The impact cracked through the chamber like thunder. The demon shattered into a thousand icy shards, each one catching the torchlight like a falling star.

Frank jumped up, triumphant.

"You see? You help Frank be strong!"

We all laughed, the tension breaking at last. The sound echoed through the chamber.

After a few moments of celebration, we gave my uncles a quick tour of the remaining area. The halls felt less haunted now, the shadows less sharp. Before we left, Throm collected the last two orbs still humming with energy then smashed them on the ground releasing the souls trapped inside.

Frank agreed to stay behind and protect the cave. He was so happy to have defeated his enemy, and we could see the pride in his eyes as he stood tall, guarding the place like a knight before a sacred tomb.

Chapter 8 - How

We left the tunnels behind, and the walk back was silent. Each of us was lost in thought, replaying everything we'd witnessed. The wind whispered through the trees, and the crunch of our boots on the ground was the only sound.

When we arrived at the city, Throm and Gam looked at us, saying they had an idea for the underground chamber and needed to discuss it.

"We'll meet you at the inn shortly," Throm promised.

Keenan excused himself too, saying he had something to check on. He left with a brief, reassuring smile.

Reeger and I headed to the inn, where we were greeted by Rosalind. She often helped my uncle run the place. A sweet, freckled girl with light blonde hair, inquisitive brown eyes, and a soft smile, she was our age and had grown up watching us get into trouble. She used to joke we'd either become great men or die before we had the chance.

Rosalind loved to read. In the evenings, she'd sometimes read aloud to the patrons, her gentle voice lulling them to sleep. Grog always complained it cost him profits, but we knew he secretly loved it.

Reeger and I took our usual corner seats with drinks in hand, letting the warmth of the inn and the comfort of routine settle around us. The fire crackled. The scent of bread and roasted meat drifted from the kitchen. For a moment, it felt like the world had righted itself.

After a while, Keenan returned. When we asked if everything was okay, he just smiled and nodded. I was about to press him further when my three uncles entered the inn.

Their faces were serious.

Throm stepped forward.

"This is very important," he said gravely. "But it's not a decision you can take lightly. If you agree, there's no turning back. What we're about to ask of you... may cost you your life."

We exchanged stunned, uncertain glances.

Throm continued, his voice heavy.

"We'd like to take you to the King Under the Mountain."

Chapter 9 - The Mountain

We all looked at each other in surprise.

I had always expected to meet the king eventually, after passing my trial to officially become a citizen, but for an elf, and especially a Noctari, to visit the dwarves was practically unheard of. Their kind was intensely secretive, their culture wrapped in layers of tradition and silence. They kept a small trading post outside the mountain, a modest outpost where goods were exchanged with the surface world, but no one truly knew the size of their city beneath it, or how many dwarves lived there. It was said to be vast, ancient, and fiercely protected.

Rumors hinted that gnomes also dwelled underground, hidden even from the dwarves themselves, their presence more whispered legend than fact. Some claimed they were master inventors, others that they were cursed beings who had fled the surface long ago. People often gossiped about what might be found beneath the mountain, vaults of gold, ancient machines, forgotten gods, but aside from my uncles, no one we knew had ever been there. Even then, they refused to talk about it. I always suspected they enjoyed letting the more outlandish rumors run wild, feeding the mystery like stoking a fire.

I glanced at Reeger. He wore a faint smile, clearly intrigued. Keenan, on the other hand, frowned, his brow furrowed with concern.

He turned to Throm. "If I go in there and they decide against me... what happens?"

Throm sighed. "You can't leave."

Keenan nodded solemnly. "I see."

Gam, always the diplomat, offered some reassurance. "I don't think they'd do anything drastic, considering the news you bring, your role as a powerful ally in Burke, and your standing with us as a paladin. But..." He paused, choosing his words carefully. "There's always a chance, however small, that the king could oppose you."

The weight of that possibility settled over us like a heavy fog. The silence that followed was thick with unspoken fears, intrigue and calculations.

Finally, I leaned toward Keenan. "Whatever you decide, man, I'm with you."

He looked at me, surprised. "But this is your chance to finally become a citizen."

I placed a hand on his shoulder and smiled. "Our friendship is more important."

Reeger nodded in agreement, his quiet solidarity speaking volumes.

Grog snorted. "You three are something else."

Gam chuckled. "Almost reminds me of another stubborn party of three, doesn't it?"

Throm smiled, but Grog cut in before he could speak.

"That's what I mean." He turned and started walking away. "Too much like us. And look where that got us."

I glanced at Gam and Throm, both of whom sighed and looked down. I couldn't help but wonder what Grog meant by that, what scars they carried, what choices they regretted.

Chapter 9 - The Mountain

At last, Keenan exhaled and said, "Well, I don't know about you guys, but I'm curious. Sounds like the only way I'm getting answers is from the dwarves. So... let's do it." He smiled.

The two dwarves smiled back, and the three of us launched an excited conversation about what we might discover, momentarily forgetting the danger. For a brief moment, the weight lifted, replaced by the thrill of the unknown.

From the kitchen, Grog watched us with a small, almost hidden smile.

"That's my boy," he muttered, before disappearing into the back.

After a bit more discussion, we agreed: we'd leave first thing in the morning.

After a restless night, we were up early and ready to go. The sky was still dark when we gathered our things, the air crisp with the promise of change. It was about a half-day's walk to the small dwarven town or outpost of Dwoldrem, and though it was a long shot, we hoped to get an audience with the king by day's end.

We set off on a well-traveled road, used heavily for trade between the three cities of Grissom, Dwoldrem, and Burke. The path wound through low hills and dense thickets, the trees whispering secrets in the morning breeze. While few dared venture into the northern woods, elves would occasionally come down to trade in all three cities, whether to gather information or simply check on the state of the world, no one could say for sure.

As we walked, we chatted about dwarven customs, determined not to embarrass ourselves by accidentally offending anyone. From what we'd gathered, the key was simple: honor their traditions and never mock their beliefs. Respect was paramount and we intended no offence.

After a quiet stretch of walking, I turned to Gam and asked, "The halflings?"

He looked at me, surprised. "What about them?"

"Why does the king have an entourage of halflings sneaking about?"

Throm laughed, and Grog snorted. Gam just smiled. "Have you ever been to Greenholm?"

Keenan and I shook our heads, but Reeger nodded. Gam continued. "It's a beautiful little place between Burke and the Old Woods. The story goes that centuries ago, the halflings were nearly wiped out. They had nowhere safe to go until the King of Burke took them in. In return, they now supply most of the kingdom's crops. And while they're not known for fighting, they're incredibly quiet and nimble. Every three years, five halflings volunteer and are vetted to join the king's guard."

"Ah," I said, nodding. "That makes sense."

Gam added, "Normally, no one hears all this. But considering this one", pointing at Keenan..."is walking around in the king's armor, I think it's safe to say you're cleared for a bit of privileged knowledge."

Keenan blushed slightly and grinned. I chuckled. "Yeah, Keenan, stop saving people's lives. Give Reeger and me a chance at some glory."

Reeger laughed. "I'm perfectly fine hiding in the back."

Chapter 9 - The Mountain

Keenan shrugged, still smiling. "Alright then, next time you need magic to save someone, it's on you."

I shook my head. "Not fair. I can't do that. You'll have to save them, and I'll just take credit."

Everyone burst into laughter, even Throm and Grog smiling.

As we drew closer to the mountains, they rose like sleeping giants on the horizon, their jagged peaks slicing into the sky. Dark, shadowy rock jutted from the earth in uneven spires, sharp and foreboding. Snow clung to the upper ridges, a stark contrast against the charcoal-gray stone. The mountains radiated mystery, as though they guarded ancient secrets buried deep within their craggy heart, secrets older than any kingdom, older than memory itself.

We arrived just after lunch. What we found looked less like a town and more like a fortress. A fifteen-foot-high stone wall enclosed the perimeter, inside were ten to fifteen stone buildings arranged in a neat grid along two main streets. At the far end stood a larger structure, clearly the central hub of the settlement, its architecture more refined, its stonework etched with runes that shimmered faintly in the afternoon light.

Dwarven soldiers patrolled everywhere, along the walls, through the streets, and at each gate. Their armor was heavy, their movements precise, their eyes sharp.

Keenan leaned in and whispered, "I count at least fifty."

I nodded. "Same here."

As we passed through the gates, the soldiers took immediate notice of Keenan. It wasn't just that he was a Noctari, rare enough on its own, but the plate armor of Burke he wore made him stand out even more. Their whispers and furtive glances betrayed a mix of curiosity and unease. Some stared openly, others looked away quickly, as if unsure whether to salute or draw their weapons.

Throm led us toward the large building at the back of the compound, guiding us past various shops and facilities: a blacksmith hammering out a blade that sparked with enchantment, an armory displaying weapons and armor of dwarven make, stores selling food and potions, and several supply warehouses stacked with crates marked in runic script. The air smelled of iron, stone, and fire, a place built for survival and simplicity, not comfort.

As we approached the main building, four guards stepped forward to block our path. Gam greeted them, and they responded with slight bows to him and Throm, an unusual gesture that caught my attention. Dwarves rarely bowed to anyone. The gesture spoke of respect, or perhaps old debts. Without a word, they stepped aside and allowed them through.

Grog remained with us, his mere presence drawing reactions from the people around us, fear, reverence, or perhaps disgust. I found their response intriguing. He was clearly known here, though not necessarily welcomed. But before I could ask him about it, Throm returned. Two of the guards saluted and departed, and with a motion from Throm, we were signaled to enter.

"I'll be at the armorer's," Grog grunted, turning to leave.

"No!" Throm said, his voice sharp and commanding.

Chapter 9 - The Mountain

Grog froze mid-step and turned, clearly surprised. Throm's tone carried such weight that even Grog, unshaken by most, seemed momentarily stunned.

"You too," Throm added, leaving no room for argument.

Grog paused, muttered an apology, lowered his head, and followed us inside. His unexpected compliance left us all quietly stunned.

The building's interior was sparse but imposing. At its center stood a large wooden table scattered with parchments, inkpots, and quills. Banners and tapestries adorned the walls, likely representing various military factions, though I couldn't be sure. Each bore symbols I didn't recognize, axes crossed over mountains, hammers beneath stars, shields etched with ancient runes.

In the far corner, a dwarven scribe sat reading, his presence so still he nearly faded into the background. His robes were simple, but his eyes flicked up as we entered, sharp and calculating.

We gathered around the table, uncertain of what awaited us. The only sound was the soft rustle of the scribe turning pages. I opened my mouth to ask Gam what the plan was, but before I could speak, a door at the back of the room creaked open.

Ten guards marched in, their heavy armor clanking in perfect unison. They swept the room with practiced eyes, then positioned themselves behind us, weapons in hand. For the first time in my life, I felt truly nervous, not just afraid, but deeply unsettled, as though the ground itself had shifted beneath me.

I glanced at Keenan. Though sweat beaded on his brow and his eyes darted about, he remained outwardly composed. Reeger, on the other hand, stood stiffly, looking down and fidgeting, as if wishing he could disappear from the center of attention.

The room fell silent again, heavy with tension. Then, a dwarf walked in.

He had a commanding presence, piercing black eyes, jet-black hair cascading to his shoulders, and a beard just as dark, intricately braided and adorned with beads and trinkets, each likely holding some personal or cultural meaning. His gaze was cold and sharp as mountain air, cutting into each of us as he studied us one by one.

When his eyes met mine, I felt as though he could see straight through me. I could do nothing but meet his gaze, though it was uncomfortable, like your soul being laid bare.

Finally, his attention turned to Gam. He held up a parchment and spoke with a voice devoid of emotion, yet brimming with authority.

"I'm assuming your information on this is accurate?"

"Yes," Gam replied with a slight nod. I found myself wondering, was this the king? Or perhaps a high-ranking official? His bearing suggested royalty, but his manner was more soldier than sovereign.

The dwarf turned to the guards. "You may leave."

We exchanged surprised glances. The guards hesitated for a moment, as if wanting to speak, but said nothing. One by one, they filed out. In the corner, the scribe looked up from his book with a smirk.

The dwarf began walking slowly around us, eventually stopping beside Throm. He paused.

Chapter 9 - The Mountain

"Throm."

Throm stood at attention. "Yes, my king."

Suddenly, the king broke into laughter. "You old badger, give us a hug!" he boomed.

Throm smiled as the king embraced him tightly.

"Twenty years, brother, and you didn't return even once!"

I froze. Keenan leaned in and whispered, "Did he say brother?"

Throm nodded. "You know I couldn't," he said softly.

"Yes, yes," the king said, waving a hand before glancing at Grog. "The trouble with the mission."

He squinted at Grog, who lowered his head. The king watched him for a moment, then smiled.

"Well, I think twenty years is enough penance, don't you?" he asked, glancing at Throm.

At that, Grog's head snapped up, eyes flickering with hope, though he quickly masked it with his usual gruff demeanor. "Eh," he grunted, as if debating whether to speak and deciding against it.

The king turned to Gam with a grin. "Still the loyal friend to this lump of granite, eh?" he said, extending his hand.

Gam smiled and shook it. "Someone has to keep him out of trouble."

"Truly," said the king. "I'm glad to see you all again." He chuckled, turning to Grog. "Even you, you old codger, still as friendly as ever, I see."

"Always the softy," Throm added with a grin.

Grog grunted and muttered under his breath.

I was stunned. Throm, the king's brother? I'd always assumed Gam was their leader. He carried himself with quiet authority, always the one to speak first, to calm tensions. But Throm, stoic, grounded, and now revealed as royalty, stood with a presence that made the room feel smaller. And what had Grog done to have them exiled for twenty years? Questions swirled in my mind as I watched Throm, who stood completely at ease, as if he belonged here more than anywhere else.

He approached me and placed his hands firmly on my shoulders, pride in his eyes.

"This is Halvar," he said. "The boy we raised to be a dwarf. He has completed the trials and is one of us. I ask a favor, my king, make him a citizen of the mountain and a son of the Celestial Mother, here and now."

The king smiled. "You know the rules, Throm. You may speak for him, but where are the other witnesses?"

"Gam and Grog were there," said Throm.

The king turned to them, eyeing them thoughtfully.

"Well, Gam will have to do, since Grog is still listed as a traitor in the records."

At that, Grog winced. The pain in his eyes was unmistakable. It wasn't just shame, it was the ache of being remembered only for your worst moment.

Throm stepped forward. "Brother, I object to such language! You and I both..."

The king raised a hand, silencing him. "You and I both know he isn't, but not everyone agrees, and I can't afford divisions right now. We have bigger problems."

Chapter 9 - The Mountain

He sighed, then turned back to me with a gentler expression. "But this one... this one will be easy," he said with a smile.

He stepped closer. "Kneel, Halvar."

I knelt before him, heart pounding. The stone floor was cold beneath me, but I barely felt it. My breath caught as the moment stretched, sacred and surreal.

"Halvar is a strong dwarven name," the king said. "Wear it proudly. I, Tormund, King of the Mountain, hereby declare you a citizen, with Throm standing for you and Gamreal serving as your witness. Rise and let me be the first to welcome you home."

He extended his hand, and I took it, overwhelmed by the moment I had waited for my entire life. The grip was firm, warm, and final, like a door closing behind my old life.

As I stood, I glanced around. My three uncles beamed with pride, while Keenan and Reeger grinned warmly at me. Their smiles carried no envy, only joy.

"Now," Tormund said, turning to Reeger and Keenan, "the harder cases."

He studied them in silence, deep in thought. His gaze was not unkind, but it was calculating.

Gam spoke up. "I assume we still have good relations with the elves?"

"As always," the king replied with a shrug. "But we still have strict rules about non-citizens."

The room fell quiet again until the scribe cleared his throat. "Sire, if I may?" he said.

Tormund nodded.

"According to the law, you have two options that won't stir up further division," the scribe continued. "You could convene a war council and appoint them as representatives of their people, that would grant them entry. Or…" He hesitated. "You could name them prisoners."

At that, Keenan and Reeger leaned forward, exchanging uneasy glances.

The king didn't even look up. "No. We're not making them prisoners, and we're not at war with anyone officially."

We all exhaled, tension easing slightly as the dwarves returned to their discussion.

"Reeger will be easy," Throm said. "He can come in as counsel for his father."

Tormund nodded. "That'll work. Some won't like it, but it's defensible."

"Keenan will be much harder," Gam added. "What about his status with Burke?"

Tormund shook his head. "He's not officially part of the family. I'm sure they'd vouch for him based on that armor, but it doesn't change his status."

As the debate continued, I noticed Grog sitting quietly off to the side. His usual bluster had faded into something more introspective. I walked over and took a seat next to him.

He glanced at me and grunted.

"How are you doing?" I asked.

"Hmph. I'm fine," he muttered. "I just hate all these rules and arguments. Just point me at the enemy and let me go, then you'll see something worth watching."

Chapter 9 - The Mountain

Reeger and Keenan came over. "What about the paladin angle?" Reeger asked. "There's got to be something there."

We exchanged glances.

"That's an idea," I said. "Now we just have to get their attention."

Grog chuckled, then suddenly bellowed across the room, "Hey!"

The room fell silent as everyone turned toward Grog, who pointed directly at Keenan.

"He's a paladin!" he declared.

Tormund raised an eyebrow. "Wait, really?" He let out a hearty laugh and slapped Keenan on the back. "A Noctari paladin! Now I've seen everything!"

But then his expression shifted.

"Wait," he said more seriously, grabbing Keenan by the shoulder and turning him around. Keenan stood frozen as the king stared intently at his shield.

"Where did you get that shield?" Tormund demanded.

Caught off guard, Keenan stammered, "Uh... from paladin training?"

"No, no," Tormund cut in. "How did you get it? Did you select it yourself?"

Keenan hesitated. "Well... no. I didn't choose it. They told me it was mine. Assigned it, I guess." He let out a nervous chuckle. "I wanted a sword or a mace..."

The king slowly sank into his chair, eyes still fixed on the shield. His face had gone pale, his breath shallow. Grog, watching him carefully, spoke in a quiet voice.

"Yes. It's him."

The king's voice dropped to a reverent whisper. "Merek, you old billy goat... if you can hear me and wish to speak for this one, I'll accept it."

A hush fell over the room.

Even the scribe stopped writing.

Then, to my utter astonishment, a voice rang out, deep, powerful, and resonant, as if echoing from the stone itself.

"I, Merek Ironguard, third paladin of the First Order, hereby speak for this Noctari named Keenan. I vouch for his character and vote yay on allowing him entry."

The words hung in the air like a sacred bell toll, reverberating through the chamber. The torches flickered. The stone beneath our feet seemed to hum. For several seconds, no one moved. No one breathed.

Stunned silence followed.

"Did... everyone hear that?" I asked, my voice barely above a whisper, breaking the stillness.

They all nodded, even Grog, who sat unusually quiet, his usual scowl softened into something unreadable. The scribe's quill hovered mid-air, ink dripping onto the parchment unnoticed.

Throm stepped forward, his voice clear and strong, as if summoned by ancient rite. "I, Throm Gravelbringer, wielder of the Hammer of Arzouth, vote yay."

I was overwhelmed, unsure of what any of it meant. Keenan looked equally stunned, his gaze lowered humbly to the floor, as if afraid to meet anyone's eyes. His hands trembled slightly, resting on the hilt of his sword.

The king rose to his feet. He looked slowly around the room, meeting each gaze in turn.

Chapter 9 - The Mountain

"I, Tormund Ironshield, wielder of the Spear of Justice, vote yay."

The words rang with finality, like a seal pressed into wax.

The scribe, who had been furiously scribbling notes, stood with a rare smile on his face. His eyes shimmered with something close to reverence.

"Never thought I'd see this in my lifetime," he said, shaking his head in disbelief. "A quorum of paladins..."

Chapter 10 - Entrance

"A couple of things we need to go over," said the king, his voice firm but not unkind. "Anything we discuss while in the mountain, anything you see there, stays there. Break this rule, and the punishment is death."

The room fell silent.

He pointed at Reeger and Keenan. "Just because we had a quorum doesn't mean you're free. You must be accompanied at all times. If you lose contact with your escort for even a moment, you'll be considered enemies and killed. If your escort gives you an order, you are to follow it immediately or be killed. Is that understood?"

Reeger and Keenan nodded soberly, the weight of the warning settling over them.

"Great," said the king. "Excellent." He glanced at me. "You, of course, are free to do as you please, though it might be wise to listen to your..." He paused, glancing at the three dwarves.

They smiled, and Gam added, "Uncles."

"Right," said the king. "Listen to your uncles." He chuckled briefly, then straightened. "Anyway, I must get back to being serious. This has been a pleasant diversion, and I thank you all for it. Once we're underground, where it's safer, we'll go over everything you've seen. But first, Baldrek will give you a brief tour and some backstory. I have a few matters to attend to, and I'll meet you afterward."

Chapter 10 - Entrance

He paused, then smiled again, a flicker of nostalgia in his eyes. "No... I think I'll at least walk with you through the front gate. I haven't done that since I was a boy."

Turning, he called out, "Guards!"

They entered immediately, armor clanking in rhythm, and the king gave instructions regarding the guests and Halvar, the new "dwarf." Two guards broke off to escort Reeger, and another two for Keenan.

Keenan leaned toward me and whispered, "Nothing like the threat of death and a babysitter to make you feel like a real man."

I leaned back and replied, "Well, if I see any real men, I'll let you know. Although, for the record, one of us doesn't need a babysitter."

He chuckled and said, "just like old times," as we headed out the door. The king, surrounded by four guards, led the way. Then came me and my uncles, walking in pairs. Keenan and his escorts came behind us, with Reeger and his guards bringing up the rear with Baldrek, the scribe, at the very end of the procession, his robes fluttering slightly with each step.

The back of the outpost was built into the foot of the mountain, which rose sharply on both sides, with a pathway winding into the valley between the ridges. Guard stations perched above us, each one detached from the next to prevent a breach from spreading. The road twisted and turned, forming a formidable kill zone. Narrow choke points, angled walls, and hidden alcoves made it clear, this place was designed to repel invaders with brutal efficiency.

I wouldn't want to be the one attacking this place, I thought. Keenan glanced at me, and we exchanged a smile, both knowing we were thinking the same thing.

Ahead, I heard running water. As we rounded a sharp corner, the path opened into a larger clearing. Crescent-shaped walls framed either side, leading to a massive drawbridge spanning a deep chasm. To the far right, a high waterfall thundered into the depths below, its mist rising like breath from the mountain.

Flanking the drawbridge stood two massive stone dragon statues.

The dragon on the right was enormous, its tail coiled around a rock spire, mouth open, claws bared, its massive body poised as if ready to leap. The sheer scale was staggering. Its wings were folded, but even so, they stretched nearly the height of the wall behind it.

To the left, a slightly smaller dragon statue crouched as if about to breathe fire. Though not as large, it radiated a sense of agility and deadly purpose. Its eyes, carved from deep amber stone, seemed to glow faintly in the sunlight.

As we marveled at the sight, the scribe stepped forward with a dramatic flourish of his arm. "Gentlemen," he said, pausing for effect, "The Hammer and the Anvil welcome you."

I quickly looked at Grog and whispered, "The inn?"

He smiled knowingly. "Never forget your roots," he replied.

As we passed through the archway and crossed the bridge, it felt like the dragons' gazes were following us. I chuckled to myself. That's unsettling, I thought.

Chapter 10 - Entrance

The king smiled at the dragons and said, turning to us, "Until the meeting hall," and strode away, followed closely by his guards.

The scribe took the lead, barely able to contain his excitement. It was clear he cared deeply about the history and architecture of this place, and either rarely got to share it or never grew tired of doing so. His voice carried a reverent tone, like a priest guiding pilgrims through a sacred temple.

I noticed my uncles taking in the surroundings with quiet pride. Leaning toward Throm, I asked, "Happy to be back?"

He smiled warmly. "Yes," he said. "This is truly home."

We crossed the drawbridge and passed through a massive gate, moving past several guard posts and defensive structures before entering a grand hall, its sheer scale humbling. The ceiling arched high above us, supported by massive stone columns carved with scenes of dwarven history, battles, coronations, and moments of triumph etched into the very bones of the mountain.

The scribe stopped abruptly before an immense mural and, with a dramatic gesture, declared, "Now, this... this is our masterpiece."

The mural stretched nearly thirty feet high and spanned at least a hundred feet along the wall. It was a breathtaking testament to dwarven craftsmanship, carved directly into the mountain's rock face. Every figure and detail were rendered with stunning precision, each feature brought to life by the hands of countless artisans.

At the center stood a mighty dwarven king, his massive war hammer raised high. Glowing runes were etched into the weapon's surface, and his flowing beard seemed almost alive, like a river of stone. His eyes burned with fierce determination. Around him, dwarven warriors formed an unbreakable phalanx, their intricately detailed armor gleaming, shields locked together as they held the line against an onslaught of demons.

To the left, elven archers drew their bows, their arrows frozen in mid-flight. Their forms were graceful, their robes flowing like water, a sharp contrast to the rugged dwarves. Their faces bore resolute expressions, unshaken amidst the chaos.

The humans were divided. Some fought alongside the dwarves, charging on powerful steeds, their lances glinting in the light. Others stood with the demonic horde, their forms twisted and corrupted by darkness. Each horse was so masterfully carved that they seemed ready to leap from the stone.

Above it all, two massive dragons dominated the sky. The smaller spewed flames, while the larger unleashed an icy torrent. Their scales shimmered as though alive, and their sheer size and power left us awestruck.

In the foreground, dwarven ballista fired massive bolts, their crews working in unison. Strange, ancient weapons we couldn't identify stood alongside them, their craftsmanship equally impressive and mysterious.

The edges of the mural were framed with intricate knotwork, interwoven with runes that told the story of the great battle in the ancient dwarven tongue. At the bottom of the mural, a single line was inscribed in glowing gold lettering:

Through Ice and Fire, We Endure.

Chapter 10 - Entrance

The mural was illuminated by gems strategically embedded in the stone. These gems caught and reflected the torchlight, creating the illusion of movement. As we stood before it, the flickering light made the entire scene seem alive, a vivid, living history carved in stone, a testament to the courage and unity that defined the dwarves and their allies.

I exchanged a glance with my companions, and we all shared the same expression: awe.

Looking at Keenan and Reeger, I nodded toward the dragon spewing ice. "You see that?" I whispered.

They both nodded silently.

"I think I'm team Ice," I said with a grin.

Keenan immediately shook his head. "No, I'm fire all the way."

Reeger smiled and added, "As long as they're on our side, I like them both."

We all chuckled quietly, the sound small beneath the weight of the mural's grandeur.

The scribe began his history lesson, his voice filled with reverence. It was difficult to focus, torn between listening to his words and trying to take in the intricate details of the mural. Every time I looked, I noticed something new, a hidden rune, a subtle expression, a forgotten name etched in the border.

"Thousands of years ago," Baldrek began, "three celestial beings came to this world, a mother and her two sons. The mother shaped the dwarves, the mountains, and the forests. The eldest son created elves and the oceans. The youngest son crafted humans, the plains, and horses."

Hammer and Anvil

I leaned toward Keenan and whispered, "No love for the gnomes, huh?"

He shushed me, curiosity lighting his eyes, and I smiled before turning my attention back to Baldrek.

The scribe continued, his voice rich with the weight of history. "At first, there was peace. But over time, the youngest son grew consumed by his desire for control, a flaw reflected in humanity. He forged a pact with demons, seeking to dominate and destroy all who opposed him. In his arrogance, he believed his brother and mother would not intervene.

"But his mother rallied the dwarves and elves, while the eldest son channeled his creativity and power into crafting two mighty guardian dragons. The war that followed was long and brutal, with neither side gaining the upper hand."

Baldrek's voice softened, heavy with sorrow. "In the end, the mother and eldest son, determined to save their creations, sacrificed themselves. The eldest son closed the demonic portals and slew the demons' general, but he was mortally wounded by his younger brother, who by then had lost himself entirely to rage and hatred.

"The dragons tried to save him. The smaller fell in the effort, mortally wounded. The larger dragon disappeared, its fate unknown to this day."

He gestured toward the mural, his eyes shining. "The celestial mother, in her final act, poured her life force into the planet itself, stabilizing it. The demonic magic had fractured the continents and islands, scattering them like pebbles across a pond. Her sacrifice saved the world, but at a terrible cost."

Chapter 10 - Entrance

Turning to Keenan, Baldrek nodded at his shield. "Of the original twelve paladins who fought in that war, only five survived. They poured their essence into powerful weapons to protect future generations.

"Four of those weapons have since fallen silent, their voices long gone. The weapons remain potent, but when the final wielder passes, their power will fade entirely."

Baldrek smiled warmly at Merek and bowed slightly. "It is an honor to hear the youngest of them speak."

He sighed, his voice growing grave once more.

"Before the portals were sealed, the youngest brother, seething with hatred and rage, vowed to return and destroy all who opposed him. In the aftermath, the dwarves and elves, with the help of some humans, purged the world of demonic influence. Noctari, born of humans and demons, were left behind as children and were spared. Since then, the dwarves have been preparing, ever watchful for the demons' return."

His words lingered in the air, heavy with the weight of the past and the uncertainty of the future. The flickering torchlight danced across the mural, making the dragons seem to shift, the warriors to breathe, the battle to rage anew.

I thought to myself, no wonder dwarves are so serious if this is what they believe is going to happen.

Turning to the scribe, I asked, "If the brother closed the portals, how are they being opened again?"

The scribe looked at me, his expression unreadable.

"I cannot answer that. You'll have to ask the king."

With that, he motioned for us to follow. He led us into a large circular meeting room, its centerpiece a massive map of the island carved directly into the rock. Surrounding the map were arrows pointing outward toward the ocean, each labeled with names I didn't recognize, ancient cities, lost ports, perhaps even forgotten battlefields.

The scribe bowed to Throm. "Glad to have you back," he said warmly.

Throm nodded in acknowledgment as the scribe departed, his footsteps echoing down the stone corridor.

I turned to my uncles. "Let me guess, you all believe everything he said back there?"

They all nodded solemnly, no hesitation.

I glanced at Keenan. "Thoughts?"

He shrugged.

"I've never heard such an in-depth historical account of the world. This is all new to me."

He paused, his eyes distant.

"It does make some things make sense, though. It definitely gives me a lot to think about... even about my own people's past. Although," he added, his gaze lingering on his shield, "some answers might be closer than others."

I looked at Reeger, who sat in quiet contemplation. "Same question," I prompted.

He looked up thoughtfully. "Our origin story is very similar, though we have no mention of dragons or celestial beings. Either my people have become too pragmatic and lost parts of our history, or..." he hesitated, choosing his words carefully, "some things may be... different than they should."

Grog snorted. "You've got guts saying that here. But we don't expect everyone to believe. We won't kill you for having an opinion, just don't slight what we believe."

Chapter 10 - Entrance

Reeger nodded. "That's fair."

The door opened, and the king entered the room, his presence commanding immediate attention. The air shifted with him, as if the stone itself acknowledged his authority.

"So," he said, glancing at us with a smile, "how was the mural?"

We all agreed it was the most magnificent carving we had ever seen.

Tormund smiled, his pride evident. "I agree," he said, "but I'm glad you do too. Now we don't have to kill you."

We looked at each other nervously as Throm shook his head and Tormund laughed.

"Sorry, bad joke," he said, chuckling. "Dwarven humor doesn't always translate."

"But that's not why we're here, is it?" the king continued, his tone shifting.

"No, it is not," Throm replied.

"So," said the king, leaning forward, trying to hold back his excitement, "you have news of the Anvil?"

Throm nodded. "We found a frozen demon... and the ice had all the markings of being him."

"It's true," I added. "But how did he get into the room? Can he portal? Because there was no other way in."

"Agreed," said Reeger. "The doors were sealed, and there was an anti-magic field. Even Merek was blinded by it."

Keenan nodded. "That's right."

The king frowned in thought. "How big was the room?" he asked, looking at Throm.

"He would have barely fit," Throm replied. "But I'm telling you, the ice matches."

I looked at Throm, curiosity sparking. "How do you know all this, Uncle?"

Throm glanced at me, then at his brother, clearly hesitant. Tormund leaned back in his chair, gazing up at the ceiling with a heavy sigh. Turning to another dwarf who appeared to be an advisor, he said, "We have to confirm it."

The advisor hesitated. "But, sire, do they all have to go? They may have all seen it, and you know... five in agreement would make it fact. We don't need all six."

"Yes," the king replied, "but who would you leave out, then?"

The advisor's eyes shifted to Grog. "I know who I would leave out," he said bluntly.

My blood boiled. I stood up, glaring at the advisor. "How dare you!"

Fire flashed in my eyes, but I felt a hand on my arm, calming me. Quickly, I sat down and muttered my apologies, glancing at Keenan, who was trying hard to hold back a smile.

The moment the words had left my mouth, I regretted them. I'd acted without thinking. The advisor, clearly shocked, turned to the king for support.

The king raised his hand, a smile playing at his lips. "Please, let's keep everything civil. I have no desire for unneeded infighting or unnecessary disagreements."

I felt Grog's hand rest heavily on my other arm. Leaning closer, I whispered, "I'm sorry, Uncle... but he shouldn't speak like that about you."

Grog forced a smile, his words catching me off guard. "I deserve it," he said softly.

Chapter 10 - Entrance

I stayed silent, unsettled by his response. There was no bitterness in his voice, only weariness.

The king, seemingly amused by the exchange and in good spirits at the possibility of one of their dragons being alive and nearby, jumped to his feet.

"Well, I don't know what it is about you all, but I like to think I can trust you."

He stared at each of us for a moment before smiling and declaring,

"We will bring them into the inner sanctum for the sole purpose of confirmation."

The advisor reluctantly nodded. "As you wish, sire."

Tormund grinned, turning to the advisor. "If they get out of hand, I'll let you decide the punishment."

The advisor seemed satisfied with that arrangement.

Turning back to us, the king said, "Now, it's time for a walk. And need I remind you, what you're about to see..." He paused, giving us a pointed look.

Keenan chuckled. "Yep. Death. Got it."

"That's my boy!" the king exclaimed with a laugh, motioning for us to follow as he walked out.

As we filed out, Keenan leaned toward me and whispered, "Do I look like a boy to you?"

I smirked. "You do have a certain boyish charm."

Keenan grinned and whispered back, "Watch it," as I tried to suppress a laugh.

"Hey," I said, nudging him, "did you really cast Calm on me back there?"

Keenan smiled. "Maybe," he said, and I shook my head.

"Man, how the tables have turned," I muttered.

Keenan chuckled. "I like being on this end for a change."

Following Tormund and his guards, we approached an area sealed off by a massive, shiny black obsidian door, flanked by guards clad in the same material.

Then it occurred to me, this stone looked exactly like the small ones the demons had been asking about.

I froze in shock as Keenan and Reeger exchanged the same realization.

The king turned to us, his expression suddenly serious. "This is why we were so concerned about the demons asking about those stones. They are found and mined exclusively here and are used to protect the inner sanctum due to their unique properties and how they are created."

He sighed heavily. "How they acquired so many of these is beyond me. They were created by..." He paused, catching himself. "Well, we'll discuss that soon enough."

He signaled for the guards in obsidian armor to open the door.

As we passed through, the other guards accompanying us stopped. Keenan and Reeger hesitated, glancing back at them.

"Umm...?" Reeger said. "We can't be away from our guards, can we?"

The king turned back, his tone casual but firm.

"Only certain dwarves are allowed here, our best and most powerful. Except maybe Throm, although," he added playfully, grinning at his brother, "I think I can still take him."

Throm smiled back. "Sure you can."

The king laughed and waved us forward.

Chapter 10 - Entrance

"There are more than enough guards here. You won't need your escorts."

We stepped into a long hallway.

The walls were lined with the same polished obsidian, towering at least twenty feet high and twenty feet wide. Torches flickered along the corridor, their light reflecting off the glossy black stone and casting eerie, dancing patterns. Guards clad in gleaming obsidian armor stood stationed every ten feet, motionless but watchful.

The air was cooler here, and the silence deeper. Even our footsteps seemed hushed.

As we neared another door, the king paused, taking a deep breath.

"Here we go," he said, signaling to the guards to open it.

The heavy doors creaked open, revealing a vast chamber beyond.

We filed in one by one.

I heard Grog and Keenan gasp audibly.

As the last to enter, I stepped across the threshold, and my breath caught in my throat.

There, lying in the center of the room, frozen solid, was a dragon.

Chapter 11 - The Choice

I couldn't believe it. Right there in front of me was a massive dragon, its body filling the entire chamber like a cathedral of scale and sinew. Its wings were folded tight against its sides, yet even in stillness, it radiated power.

I stared in shock as thoughts raced through my mind: *Wait, which dragon is this? It couldn't have frozen itself... That meant this was the fire dragon.*

This is the smaller one!?

Keenan, seemingly arriving at the same conclusion, stepped forward slowly and asked aloud, "So, this is the mortally wounded one?"

The king nodded solemnly. "Yes. She was frozen by her brother to keep her safe. We're not sure of her current condition, but when she was frozen, she was dying."

"Can she be unfrozen?" Reeger asked, placing a hand gently on the ice.

The guards immediately stepped forward, weapons half-drawn, but the king raised a hand, halting them. Reeger withdrew quickly, apologizing, his eyes darting around the room as if he'd heard something, searching for a source, visibly unsettled.

The king continued, "Yes, she can, but only by her brother, as far as we know. After the war, he disappeared about a hundred years later. Some say he was searching for a cure; others believe he's waiting for the demons to return. It's probably a mix of both.

Chapter 11 - The Choice

But since he hasn't checked in and no one has seen him, we assumed he was lost... or dead. However, if you've seen a demon frozen like that, then he must still be alive. At least, that's my hope."

He turned to us, his voice full of restrained urgency. "If the six of you would be so kind, inspect the ice and confirm if it matches the ice the demon was frozen in."

He stepped back, anxiously waiting for our report.

Keenan moved closer to me and whispered, "I think most ice looks the same, but there are two things I notice immediately: it's not that cold in here, and it's not melting. This has to be magically bound somehow."

I nodded, and without thinking, reached out and touched the ice.

A faint voice echoed in my mind: *Brother? Is that you?*

Shocked, I recoiled, heart pounding. I glanced around. Reeger was staring at me, his eyes focused, and in that instant, I realized he must have heard it too when he touched the ice. "You?" I asked. He just nodded, his expression unreadable.

I turned back to the ice, inspecting it more carefully now. The surface was smooth, almost glassy, but beneath it, the frozen dragon's body shimmered faintly with internal light, like embers trapped in crystal. I looked at Keenan. "Man, I don't know... I think it's the same, but it's not like I'm an ice expert."

Keenan smiled faintly. "Yeah, but it does have similarities, like the way the ice froze horizontally. That means it had to freeze fast, not just settle from gravity."

"That's fair," I said with a sigh.

"I think it's the same ice," I said aloud.

"So do I," said Keenan and Reeger, almost at the same time.

Throm stepped forward. "I agree."

Grog and Gam both nodded silently.

The king clapped his hands, his face lighting up. "Excellent!" he exclaimed, rubbing his palms together. "Then he's alive! And hopefully, the girl is still alive too."

"She is alive," I said quietly, almost without realizing it.

The room fell into a heavy silence.

Tormund turned to me, frowning. "How can you be sure?"

I hesitated, then said, "When Reeger and I touched the ice, we both heard a voice... asking if we were her brother."

"What do you mean she asked you?" the king said, his hands trembling slightly.

"Uh... when we touched the ice, she spoke into my mind," I explained, glancing at Reeger, who nodded in agreement.

"What exactly did she say?" the king pressed, stepping closer, his face tight with anxious hope.

"She just said, '*Brother? Is that you?*'"

The king's hands shook as he turned to Throm. "She's alive," he murmured.

Throm nodded, a slow smile spreading across his face. "This is very good news."

The king could barely contain himself. "The sister lives! This is wonderful!" He turned back to us, his voice rising with excitement. "We need to find and get her brother here, maybe he can help her. Throm, with your paladin healing... is there anything you can do?"

Chapter 11 - The Choice

Throm shook his head, regret heavy in his voice. "I can't heal mortal wounds, especially if she was already dying when she was frozen."

Keenan sighed quietly from the corner. "But I can," he said. "Though judging by her size..." He glanced at the massive dragon encased in ice. "It might kill me."

The king, who had looked hopeful, quickly tempered his expression. "Well... we should at least think about it. There's no need to do anything rash. From what I've read, she would hate to see someone sacrifice themselves for her."

The room quickly devolved into excited discussions, everyone brainstorming ways to find the brother, save the sister, and melt the ice.

Ideas flew around: building a massive bonfire, using fireball spells from dwarven mages, even invoking ancient rites of thawing. But while I listened, my attention was drawn to Keenan, standing quietly at the back of the room, his head bowed.

He looked up at me and said, "What's the point of being able to bring someone back from the brink if you don't use it?"

"Hold on," I replied quickly. "We might find another way. We must think this through."

I smiled, trying to reassure him.

He met my gaze steadily. "Look at the dragon."

Instinctively, I turned. She was magnificent, elegant, beautiful, and dangerous, even frozen. Her wings were curled like sleeping serpents, her horns arched like obsidian crowns. Even in stasis, she looked ready to rise.

"Who would be better at fighting the demons?" Keenan asked softly. "Me... or her?"

I tore my eyes away from the dragon. "Yes, but let's find a way to keep you both alive, huh?" I said, clapping a hand on his shoulder.

He smiled back. "Yeah... I guess you're right."

Meanwhile, the king had summoned a scribe to bring more information about the dragons, scrolls, maps, anything that might help. The room buzzed with motion and purpose.

I was watching and listening to my uncles, distracted. Keenan was no longer beside me.

He had drifted closer to the dragon, his glove off, one hand pressed gently against the ice.

"You truly are the most beautiful creature I've ever seen," he murmured.

He thought back to when the Light had gifted him the power to heal.

This is what you had in mind all along, isn't it? he wondered. *I was made for this moment, to give hope to many.*

Keenan turned briefly, casting one last look at me and my uncles. "Goodbye, my friends," he whispered.

Then, he took a deep breath and began to channel his energy.

One of the guards noticed first and shouted a warning.

We all spun around to see Keenan, radiant energy pouring from him into the ice, his face etched with determination, his body trembling under the strain. Light surged from his hands in golden waves, wrapping the frozen dragon in a shimmering cocoon.

Chapter 11 - The Choice

"No!" I yelled, heart pounding.

I tried to rush toward him, but the wave of magic held me back like an invisible wall. The air crackled with power, and the floor beneath me vibrated with the force of the spell.

Helpless, I watched as Keenan grew visibly weaker. His shoulders sagged, his eyes drooped shut, and his breath came in shallow bursts. Then, finally, the energy faded, and he collapsed.

I scrambled to his side, cradling him carefully. My fingers frantically checked his neck, his chest, searching for any sign of life.

"He's still breathing," I said, relief crashing through me like a tidal wave.

Keenan coughed and sat up, groaning. "Ahh... my head hurts."

Everyone crowded around him, staring in stunned silence. I yelled, "What are you doing, you idiot? Can you stop being impulsive for ten seconds and help us figure out a plan?"

He shrugged, wincing. "I thought it would work."

"Wait," Throm said, kneeling beside him. "It didn't work?"

Keenan shook his head. "No, it didn't. She's not mortally wounded anymore, at least, I don't think so. I channeled the spell, poured all my energy into it, and was about to use my life force when I heard a voice say, 'No, my child. Not now. Not like this.' Then she said, 'Sleep,' and I passed out. Other than the headache, I feel fine. My energy's back, too."

"Wait," I said, stunned. "The dragon's voice said that?"

"I don't know," Keenan admitted.

"Did it sound like a very young woman?" Reeger asked.

"No," Keenan said. "Much older. Like... like a mother talking to a child."

The room went dead silent. The guards. The king. Everyone just stared at him, frozen in place.

Reeger and I exchanged a glance, then looked around. The dwarves were staring at Keenan as though they'd just seen a ghost. Clearly uncomfortable, Keenan muttered, "Could you stop staring? You're creeping me out."

That snapped them out of it. The king stepped forward, slowly and reverent. "What was it like?" he asked, voice low.

Keenan hesitated. "Well, I don't know... the energy was..."

The king cut him off. "No. Her voice. What was it like?"

"Oh," Keenan said, thinking. "It was... sweet. Kind, I guess."

"And?" the king pressed.

I glanced around and noticed even my uncles were hanging on every word.

Confused, I leaned toward Reeger and whispered, "What's the big deal?"

Reeger leaned back and whispered, "Assuming what Keenan experienced was real... I think he just spoke to their god."

"Ah," I said softly, finally understanding.

The dwarves crowded closer, even the guards edging in. Keenan, still looking uncomfortable, kept answering

Chapter 11 - The Choice

questions about the voice, how it sounded, exactly what she said, whether it felt like warmth or light or something else entirely.

Just then, the scribe burst into the room, arms full of books. "Sire, I've brought all the texts on..."

The king cut him off, practically shouting with excitement. "She spoke to him, Baldrek! You old fossil!"

The scribe's eyes went wide. "She hasn't spoken since your great-great-grandfather's time," he said, his voice full of awe.

"Yes, yes," the king said, waving him forward. "While it's fresh, get the exact quote from him!"

The scribe rushed over to Keenan, much to Reeger's and my amusement, and began carefully writing down every word he said, quill scratching furiously across parchment.

Watching the scene unfold, I thought to myself, *If I'd believed in something my whole life and suddenly got even the smallest confirmation... yeah, I'd be this excited too.*

Soon, the scribe pulled the king aside, pointing excitedly at some papers he carried. They spoke in hushed tones, the king nodding seriously as Baldrek gestured animatedly, flipping through ancient texts with trembling hands.

Keenan, finally free from questioning, walked over to Reeger and me. "What do you think they're talking about now?" he asked.

Reeger grinned. "Whether or not to make you a citizen."

"What?!" Keenan and I said in unison, whipping our heads toward him.

I laughed. "You old, pointy-eared eavesdropper! You've been listening to them this whole time, haven't you?"

Reeger put on a face of mock offense. "I don't know what you're insinuating, but my ears are no pointier than any other elf's. And eavesdropping is a dishonorable act meant only for gossips and spies, of which I am neither. So, if you're attempting to insult me, you're well on your way."

We all burst out laughing at his long and drawn-out way of responding.

But the laughter quickly faded as the king approached, his expression grave.

"We cannot take one person's word as fact," he said solemnly. "We'll record it, but there is something we must show you. Hopefully, it will confirm everything... though it's a long shot."

I quickly asked, "What about melting the ice?"

Tormund shook his head sadly. "We'll have to wait for her brother. We won't risk cracking it. Every dwarf in this mountain would rather die than let harm come to her."

Without another word, he turned and gestured for us to follow.

We trailed behind the king and his guards, moving down a long, winding hall carved deep into the mountain's heart. The air grew cooler, heavier, as if the stone itself held its breath. The flickering torchlight cast dancing shadows across the walls.

As we progressed, the number of guards stationed along the corridor steadily increased. Their armor gleamed, their expressions solemn. Each one nodded respectfully as we passed, but their eyes never left us.

Chapter 11 - The Choice

Finally, we reached the end, a massive doorway guarded by at least a dozen dwarves, each one standing like a statue, unmoving and alert.

The door itself was breathtaking, a masterpiece of dwarven craftsmanship.

It was richly carved with intricate patterns, interlocking runes, flowing lines, and symbols older than the kingdom itself. The frame was a massive stone archway adorned with twisting vines, glimmering gemstones, and ancient dwarven sigils. The soft lighting above it highlighted incredible depth and detail, giving the carvings an almost lifelike, moving quality, as though the stone remembered what it had once seen.

Reeger smiled, admiring it. "Such beautiful craftsmanship," he said quietly.

Tormund nodded with pride. "Indeed," he replied.

A spell sealed the door, and it took nearly five minutes for the mages to remove it. Their hands moved in practiced gestures, murmuring incantations as the runes slowly dimmed and faded. When the final glyph vanished, a series of precise knocks signaled those inside that we were friendly.

Keenan leaned over to me and whispered, "What could they possibly have in there that needs this much security?"

"I have no idea," I muttered back.

One of the dwarven guards overheard us and promptly shushed us. We immediately fell silent.

When the door finally opened, we were ushered inside.

The chamber was dome-shaped, vast and echoing, its walls gleaming with a polished, almost metallic finish that shimmered like starlight. The air was cool and still, charged with a quiet energy that made the hairs on my arms rise.

Four mages stood equidistant from one another, forming a perfect square around the room's center. Each was flanked by two heavily armored guards, their armor etched with runes that pulsed faintly in the dim light. Four additional guards remained stationed by the door, their expressions unreadable, their posture rigid with reverence.

In the center of the room, atop a bed of black obsidian, lay a large, oval-shaped object, much like a heart.

Its surface was smooth and slightly translucent, like frosted crystal. Beneath the pale exterior, faint pulsing veins glowed with a soft, rhythmic light. Long, sinewy vines extended from its base, burrowing deep into the stone floor and ceiling, anchoring it as if it were the root of the mountain itself. The tendrils shimmered with ethereal energy, their glow shifting gently between hues of silver, violet, and gold.

The heart itself seemed alive, rising and falling in a slow, steady rhythm, as if breathing. A dim, calming light radiated from within, casting subtle shadows across the chamber and bathing everything in a serene, otherworldly glow. The silence was not empty, it was sacred.

The sight was both tranquil and awe-inspiring.

"Are you seeing this?" Keenan whispered, his voice barely audible.

He stared at the heart, an unusual expression of peace softening his features. "For the first time in my life, I feel truly at peace," he murmured.

"Aye," said the king, his voice reverent. "This is our most sacred place. Only the strongest and most disciplined

Chapter 11 - The Choice

are permitted to guard this chamber. These dwarves," he gestured to the guards and mages, "are the best we have to offer."

Turning to us, the king's expression softened, his eyes shining with pride and something deeper, devotion, perhaps. "Gentlemen," he said, "I would like to introduce you to the Celestial Mother."

"The one from the mural?" Reeger asked quietly.

Before anyone could reply, a soothing voice filled the chamber.

"My ever-faithful dwarves, you have served me well, but I must speak with the travelers alone."

The voice was not heard so much as felt, like a vibration in the bones, a warmth in the chest. It was neither loud nor soft, but it carried with it the weight of ages.

I quickly glanced around. "Everyone heard that, right?"

Reeger and Keenan nodded, as did my uncles. Even the guards looked shaken.

Tormund, though visibly shocked, immediately gave the order. The guards began filing out, their movements slow and reverent. Even the king and my uncles, though stunned, turned to leave.

But then the voice returned, calm and resonant.

"My beloved Tormund, you have earned the right to stay, as have Throm, Grogrick, and Gamreal. However, I must ask for your silence as we discuss our future."

The four dwarves, still dazed, nodded their agreement. Once the door closed behind the last of the guards, the voice spoke again.

Its tone was so gentle and calming, it felt like being wrapped in a warm, protective blanket, in the embrace of a mother. In that room, I felt an overwhelming sense of safety, as though nothing in the world could harm us. The air itself seemed to hum with comfort and sorrow.

The voice continued, "The decisions for the world's future must now be made by you. I have watched over this world for millennia and have grown weary. You will be this world's last hope."

Then her tone shifted, the warmth fading away. "I am dying."

We froze, exchanging uneasy glances. The words struck like a blow, echoing in the silence that followed.

"I have been the heart of this world for far too long. In less than one week, there will be no chance for my survival, and within half to a full season, my life force will be spent. I have healed the world, stabilized it, and kept it from breaking apart. However, I no longer have the strength to hold back the demons' portals."

There was a long, heavy pause. My mind reeled. *So that's why the demons were appearing now.*

The voice resumed, steady but tinged with sorrow. "This world must make a choice. My loyal dwarves are incapable of being objective in this matter; therefore, they cannot decide alone."

The four dwarves shifted uncomfortably; their faces etched with worry and grief.

The voice softened. "You are incapable in the best possible way."

She paused, as though gathering her thoughts, then continued, "We have at least four races represented here:

Chapter 11 - The Choice

Dwarf, Elf, Noctari, and Human. That is enough to make the decision. Although I already know how the dwarves will vote."

The dwarves exchanged uneasy glances, clearly unsettled. Their loyalty was absolute, but the weight of what was being asked pressed visibly on their shoulders.

For a moment, the chamber fell into a tense silence before the voice spoke again.

"Your world has two choices regarding me," the voice said.

"The first: I will continue to protect this world, holding my shield as long as I can to give you time to prepare for what is coming. In this choice, I will perish, but it may give you a better chance at long-term victory, while saving more lives in the short term."

The dwarves began murmuring among themselves, shaking their heads in disagreement.

"The second choice," the voice continued, "is for me to hold the portals for a few more days, then detach and rest, preparing myself for the final battle. I would survive, though I would not be at full strength when the time came. This path carries a faint possibility of summoning my mate, who still wanders the heavens, though the chance of his return in time is very slim.

"Those, my children, are your choices. Please, take a moment to discuss them among yourselves."

Keenan frowned. "Why us? Why not the other leaders?"

The voice answered gently, "Because you are here. Everything happens for a reason, even if we cannot always see those reasons. Even I must move forward.

"Make no mistake, people will die, but those deaths will not be on your hands. They will be on those who cause them. We all need direction, and sometimes, decisions fall to the unworthy or the unprepared, but we must do the best we can in the moment, learning and growing stronger with each step."

Reeger turned to me and Keenan. "What do you think?"

Keenan sighed. "If I understand her right, we either sacrifice her to buy time, or let her live and face the attacks earlier and less prepared."

"Well, not immediately," I said. "We'd have a couple of days to warn people. Maybe we could even get Reggie to help seal some of the portals?"

Reeger shook his head. "I'm sure Reggie could handle small-scale portals, but on a global level? No. There's no way he could protect every island. Only ours might be ready."

Keenan groaned. "Ugh. I hate this."

"Yeah," I said with a faint smile. "But I guess this is what being a paladin is all about."

Keenan glanced at me. "Hard decisions," he muttered.

I nodded. "The kind that leave scars."

Several minutes passed in tense silence. The air felt heavier with each breath, as if the world itself were waiting for our answer.

Finally, I spoke. "Well, we have to decide. And hey, no pressure, just the fate of the world and every living being on it."

Chapter 11 - The Choice

Reeger let out a long, heavy sigh. "I can see the wisdom in both paths," he said, discouraged. "But either way, someone pays."

Keenan shook his head. "I think we should save her. The right decision isn't always the easy one."

They both turned to me.

"What do you think?" Reeger asked.

I thought about my friends. About the people I'd met along this journey, through all its twists and turns. I reflected on her words: *We are not responsible for others' deaths. Only for the choices in front of us.*

After a moment, I sighed.

"I can't vote to kill someone just to make my life easier," I said. "Especially not someone who's done so much for us, without us even knowing."

"So... we're in agreement, then?" Keenan asked.

Reeger and I both nodded.

I stepped forward, heart pounding. "Okay. We've made our decision."

Chapter 12 - Moving Forward

I took a deep breath, meeting the anxious gazes of my uncles and the king. "You will stop blocking the portals. We won't sacrifice you for helping us. It's our turn to help you now."

The dwarves smiled and sighed in relief.

The voice responded, calm and resolute, "Very well. I will hold on for as long as I can, without passing the point of no return."

And then, I heard her voice directly in my mind.

Thank you, my child. There is more to you than you realize. When you are ready, I know I can count on you.

And just like that, she was gone.

I looked around. The others wore the same dazed, reverent expressions. She had spoken to them too.

Keenan approached, his expression unusually sober. "Did she speak to you too?" he asked quietly.

I nodded.

He sighed, a tear welling in his eye. "She knew exactly what I needed to hear."

"What did she say?" I asked.

He hesitated, then shook his head. "I think I'll keep that to myself."

I placed a hand on his shoulder. "I understand."

He added, voice softer now, "She did thank me, for trying to save the dragon. But she's been healing her while she was frozen."

Chapter 12 - Moving Forward

I smiled. "So that's why it didn't work."

The dwarves were ecstatic, their joy unmistakable. Even Grog, usually gruff and stoic, was smiling, a rare sight I'd hardly seen before.

Tormund beamed and turned to Keenan. "There is much to prepare," he said, "but she wanted me to give you a gift."

He gestured to the shield. "I'll need Merek for a bit, though."

Keenan looked to Merek, who agreed and allowed himself to be handed over.

As we stepped out of the chamber, the soldiers stationed outside bombarded us with questions. The king raised a hand and gave a brief explanation of what had transpired. The scribe scribbled furiously, then suggested an announcement at an assembly. The king agreed.

Finally, Tormund said, "We have much to do, but we all need rest. It's late, and Merek won't be ready until tomorrow."

The dwarves escorted us to a series of small, cozy rooms carved into the stone. Heavy blankets and plush furniture softened the rock. Exhausted from the day's events, we each fell asleep almost instantly, our minds swirling with everything that had just unfolded.

We woke up early and were immediately summoned to the king. The throne room was alive with motion, dwarves running in every direction, maps spread across tables, voices raised in planning and purpose.

Tormund motioned us over and smiled. "Not sure how you slept, but I haven't felt this energized since I was a small boy."

We all smiled. His excitement was contagious. Even knowing what was coming, morale was high.

At his signal, someone brought Merek forward.

He had been transformed, his frame now covered in a sleek layer of black obsidian that gleamed with a brilliant, glossy finish.

Merek chuckled aloud. "They really did a number on me. I can channel energy much easier now, and they even infused some small energy storage orbs into my framework."

He laughed mischievously, "I haven't felt this good in several hundred years. If we get into a good fight, I might even surprise you with something new."

The king smiled warmly. "Good to hear your voice, Merek. I'm glad you approve. Our blacksmiths and mages worked through the night to upgrade you."

He handed the shield to Keenan. "The Celestial Mother named you as one of her champions. You'll need something that lets the world know. And they will know now," he said, pride in his voice as he glanced at the shield.

"But there is much to do. I recommend you travel to Burke and Grissom to inform them of what's coming. They have much to prepare. In the meantime, our mages are working on something critical. We'll have more information in a few days. We may need your help again soon."

Keenan thanked the king. After exchanging farewells, we gathered our gear and left the mountain, beginning our journey back to Grissom City.

Grog had mostly returned to his usual grumpy self, though his mood had noticeably improved after visiting home. Whatever he had heard seemed to have helped.

Chapter 12 - Moving Forward

Throm was whistling cheerfully, and Gam kept marveling at the beauty of the dwarven city beneath the mountain.

"Even after all these years, the splendor of the mountain remains," Gam said, smiling. "Good, good," he added, rubbing his hands together.

We set a brisk pace and arrived in Grissom City just before lunch. Gam immediately headed to the council to discuss preparations for the impending attacks. Throm announced he'd return to the blacksmith to reinforce the city gates and repair or forge as many weapons and pieces of armor as possible. Grog, ever practical, said he'd begin stockpiling food reserves in case of shortages.

Snorting, he added, "I've got some dwarven spices that preserve food, and will knock your boots off."

I shook my head. "Well, if it's dwarven, it probably makes it taste terrible. And now it's also going to take my boots?"

Grog grinned. "You never complained about my cooking before. And your smart comments won't get to me today."

"Too bad," I said, smirking. "Always fun seeing you get riled up."

Grog shook his head and headed toward the inn.

Reeger spoke up next. "Since I'm closest to Jeffries, I'll speak with him about what's coming, see how we can help."

As the group dispersed, Keenan and I stood watching children dart through the streets, their mothers laughing as they called after them to slow down.

Keenan sighed. "The hidden casualties of war... children."

"Yeah," I agreed. "Too bad we can't make them safe."

An idea sparked between us. Our eyes widened as we turned to each other.

"What if..." Keenan began.

"...we hide them in the tunnels," I finished.

"Yes!" Keenan exclaimed. "Philip could oversee it, he'd be perfect. He can help stock everything while we're away."

He chuckled. "He does love feeling important. And this would be pretty important."

It didn't take long to track Philip down. We found him in the harbor district, haggling over some old fish.

"Philip," I called casually, trying to sound nonchalant.

He paid for the fish, shook his head in irritation at the price, and walked over. With an exaggerated air of importance, he hopped onto a barrel and asked, "What's up?"

Keenan and I struggled to keep straight faces.

"Hey," I said, "we've got a special, top-secret mission for you."

Philip's eyes lit up, though he tried to play it cool. "Yeah, I figured you'd need my help eventually," he said, glancing around like he was already plotting his strategy.

We smiled. "We need you to take charge of an underground fortress and prepare it to house refugees. Stock it with as much food, water, and clothing as you can."

Philip's eyes nearly popped out of his head. "Are you serious?" he asked, suspicious. "What's the catch?"

"No catch," we assured him. "You'd even have a friend reporting to you. You'd be in charge."

Philip frowned, still skeptical. "Sounds too good to be true."

Chapter 12 - Moving Forward

"Tell you what," I said. "Why don't you come with us to check it out? You can decide for yourself."

He shrugged. "I guess that can't hurt."

We took Philip to the house with the mirror and stepped inside. To our shock, the mirror was gone. Keenan and I immediately panicked.

"Where is it?" I shouted, running around the room.

"This is not good," Keenan muttered, face pale.

Philip stood there, confused. "What's wrong?"

"There was a mirror here, a very important mirror, and now it's gone!" I sputtered, still searching frantically.

Philip tilted his head. "Oh, Gam had me move it."

We both froze.

"He what?" Keenan demanded.

"Yeah," Philip said, surprised at our reactions. "He said it was valuable or something and had me put it in his small warehouse for safekeeping. A couple of my boys keep watch over the place for him. He pays them a bit of coin and they tell him what goes on."

I groaned. "Wish he'd told us that!"

"Right?" Keenan said, shaking his head with a smile.

Without wasting another second, we followed Philip to the warehouse. When we arrived, he spoke briefly with a young boy watching the entrance, then led us inside. In the far corner, covered by a sheet, stood the mirror.

"There it is," Philip said, pointing.

Relieved, I smiled and pulled the sheet off. Turning to Keenan with a grin, I gestured toward it.

"After you."

Keenan smiled back and stepped through the mirror.

Philip's eyes went wide. "Hey, what's going on here?" He ran behind the mirror and back around to the front, looking utterly baffled. "Okay," he said, grinning. "How did you do that?"

I chuckled. "Why don't you walk through and find out?"

He hesitated, then curiosity got the better of him. "Ah, what the heck," he said with a smile and stepped through the mirror.

I let the sheet fall back over it and followed.

On the other side, we made our way through the tunnel. As we walked, the sound of heavy footsteps echoed toward us.

I turned to Philip. "Okay, don't freak out."

"Why?" he asked nervously.

Just then, Frank rounded the corner, his large frame nearly filling the tunnel. Philip stumbled back, nearly losing his balance as he tried to hide behind us.

"Look out...a troll!" he yelled.

Frank spun around, his booming voice shaking the walls. "WHERE?"

Keenan started coughing, trying to stifle his laughter, while I couldn't help but chuckle.

"Sorry, Frank," I said, still smiling. "We brought another friend to help out down here."

Frank turned back, looking around. "So... no troll?" he asked, confused.

"No," I said, motioning to Philip, who was peeking out from behind me.

Philip whispered, "You're friends with this guy?"

"Yep," I replied. "Frank, I'd like you to meet Philip."

Chapter 12 - Moving Forward

Philip hesitated, then stepped out, trying to act calm, though his hands were visibly shaking.

Time for a confidence boost, I thought.

I turned to Frank, who was eyeing Philip curiously. "Frank, this guy here is basically the king of the underworld in Grissom."

Frank's eyes went wide. "He a king?"

"Well, what I mean..." I began, but Philip cut me off, puffing out his chest.

"Yeah, that's right. So, you must listen to me!"

Frank's face lit up. "Wow! Friends with a king!"

Philip grinned. "Yep. Now listen up, we need to get this place ready to save people. We'll need beds, food, and supplies."

Frank nodded eagerly. "If bad guys come, I can bonk them with my club!"

"Perfect," Philip said, crossing his arms. "But you have to check with me first. We can't go around bonking the wrong people."

Keenan and I exchanged amused glances.

"Well," Keenan said, chuckling, "this is going well."

"Yeah," I agreed. "Two peas in a pod."

I turned back to Philip. "Okay, we need to show you how to get back and where this place is located. After that, you can start coming here and getting everything ready. Frank can show you around."

Philip nodded. "Don't worry, I got this."

As we walked away, Frank called out, "Bye, King Friend Philip!"

Philip turned and waved. "See you later, Frank! And hey... just call me Philip. Not everyone can know I'm a king, it's hush-hush."

Frank nodded seriously. "I can keep secret! Don't worry, just ask the boss about the password."

Keenan shook his head, chuckling as we disappeared around the corner.

As we walked back, Philip grinned and mumbled to himself, "This is gonna be awesome."

We made it back to the city, and after saying goodbye to Philip, who hurried off to start getting things ready, we grabbed a quick dinner from Grog at the inn. We asked if there was any news, but he simply shook his head, too busy preparing for the evening rush and everything else that was coming.

After a quick meal, we headed to the barracks to look for Reeger.

When we arrived, we found him being bandaged by Jeffries, who was talking excitedly. As Jeffries finished wrapping Reeger's shoulder, I blurted out, "What happened?"

Keenan stepped forward, placing a hand on Reeger's shoulder and closing his eyes.

Reeger sighed. "Apparently, some priest from another island was poking around in the sewers. Claimed he accidentally summoned a sea hag or something ridiculous. Turns out it was a trap, he summoned the thing on purpose to steal our gear and who knows what else."

"So what happened to your shoulder?" I asked, frustrated we hadn't been there to help.

Chapter 12 - Moving Forward

Jeffries chuckled. "Well, the priest tried casting spells, but he kept botching them as we chased him through the sewer. When I finally got close enough to arrest him, he pulled a knife on me. But the floor was slick, he slipped and dropped it into a huge pile of..." Jeffries trailed off, glancing at Reeger.

Reeger grinned. "Poop. It was everywhere."

"Yeah, that," Jeffries said, trying not to gag. "He started digging through it, looking for the knife. The smell was so bad I had to back off. He couldn't find it, so he panicked and... threw poop at me."

"Wait," I said, shaking my head, trying not to laugh. "He lost his knife in poop and decided the next best thing was to throw poop at you?"

Jeffries shrugged. "I guess? If he'd hit me, it might've helped him. But as he went to throw it, he slipped and fell right into the sewer water."

"He drowned before I could pull him out," he added, voice grim. "Too slippery."

Keenan shook his head, finishing up with Reeger's shoulder. "That's disgusting... what a way to go."

I shook my head, trying not to imagine it. "What about the sea hag?"

Jeffries continued, "We weren't even sure at that point if the sea hag was real, thought maybe he made her up to lure us down there. But no, she was real. Came out of nowhere and blasted Reeger in the shoulder with a fireball. Then she and Reeger just vanished."

I chuckled. "Yeah, he does that."

Jeffries paused, shaking his head. "So there I was, standing alone, surrounded by filth, listening to her sing about how she was going to eat us. The sound was bouncing all over the place, it was hard to tell where it was coming from."

Keenan and I exchanged a glance, both imagining how eerie and disgusting that must've been.

Jeffries went on, "I kept turning, trying to find her. Suddenly, I heard a twang, an arrow flew out of the shadows, missed my head by inches, and hit something behind me. Turns out, Reeger got her. Nailed her right as she reappeared next to me and saved my life."

He shook his head again. "Those sewers need to be cleaned out and investigated, but man, I don't want to go back down there. It was everything I could do not to throw up."

"Maybe we can help check it out," Keenan said with a smile. "After all the demon stuff is taken care of."

Jeffries sighed. "I'd appreciate that. Besides," he added with a grin, "you guys are making a habit of saving my life. I think I owe you now, not the other way around."

"Don't worry," Reeger said with a smile. "Just glad you're still here."

"Me too, brother. Me too," Jeffries replied warmly.

I laughed while Keenan smiled and looked to Reeger. "You'll be good by tomorrow," he said reassuringly.

Reeger nodded. "Thanks."

I turned to Keenan, curious. "Hey, how does that healing thing you do actually work?"

Keenan chuckled. "I'm not entirely sure, to be honest. But basically, it stitches blood vessels back together to stop the bleeding, then supercharges your body's natural repair cells."

Chapter 12 - Moving Forward

"Huh. Interesting," I said.

Reeger spoke up. "By the way, while you two were off smelling the flowers, the council declared an official emergency. They're hiring as many guards as they can and encouraging folks to arm themselves and fortify their homes and the outer walls."

"That's all well and good," Keenan said, "but it won't matter if we can't stop the portaling. They can just pop right into the city."

I nodded, thinking for a moment. "Hey! What about Reggie? Couldn't he help?"

At that moment, a faint *pop* sounded, and a small portal appeared at head height. Reggie's face suddenly emerged, looking at me expectantly.

We all froze.

"You called?" he asked.

"I... uh..." I stammered, startled by his sudden appearance.

"You said my name, didn't you?" Reggie prompted.

Reeger chuckled. "He wants to ask you about blocking portals. The magic holding them back is weakening, more are coming."

"Hmm," Reggie mused. "Good thing I attuned to you telepathically."

"You did *what*?" I asked, alarmed.

Reggie ignored me and turned to Reeger. "I've been working on the portal issue since they started showing up. I'll focus on it fully now."

"Thanks," Reeger said with a smile.

Reggie's face disappeared into the portal, but popped back out a moment later.

"Just say my name, and if I'm not too busy, I'll stop by." He vanished again, only for the portal to reopen.

"Actually," he said, poking his head out, "try to only call me if it's important."

He disappeared once more. I shrugged, about to say something when, *pop*, the portal reopened again.

"Actually," Reggie said with a smirk, "you better be *dying* if you call me." Then he vanished for the final time, and the portal snapped shut.

We all stared at the now-empty space, then burst into laughter.

We left Jeffries and agreed to meet early the next day to head to Burke and warn them of what was coming.

After a restless night filled with worry, we woke up early, gathered at the inn for a quick breakfast, and set off. By early afternoon, we reached the city and were quickly allowed through the gates.

As we made our way through the bustling streets, Keenan muttered, "We really need to ask the gnome about portaling. It'd save us all this time walking."

Reeger and I chuckled at the thought.

Soon, we arrived at the palace and were ushered before the king.

He listened closely as we explained the situation, the weakening magic, the looming threat.

"We need to prepare," I concluded.

Brom sighed heavily and turned to his two sons, who stood beside him. "If what you say is true, and I've no reason to doubt it, we're in serious trouble. We have too much land to protect and far too few troops."

Chapter 12 - Moving Forward

His eldest son nodded grimly. "Even if we set up killing fields or defensive lanes, it'll be tough. We just don't have the numbers. We'll need to pull all the halflings into the city and let their homes and farms burn."

Brom shook his head. "We can defend the city, but we don't have the strength to meet them outside the walls."

"How much food do you have stored?" I asked.

Brom offered a faint smile. "Enough to keep us alive for a while. But tell me, can these creatures, these demons, portal anywhere?"

We exchanged uneasy glances.

"We hope Reggie can find a way to block that soon," Reeger said.

Brom nodded grimly. "If they can portal inside our walls at will, we won't stand a chance. And that's not our only problem. The Order of Light has been launching probing attacks. If we commit to this defense, we won't be able to fight on two fronts, especially not inside the city."

"Maybe we can talk to them," Keenan suggested.

Brom scoffed. "Good luck. They're a bunch of thick-headed zealots who don't listen to reason."

Perseus added, "We've already tried. Every time it's either been a trap, a no-show, or a flat refusal to talk."

Keenan spoke up. "What if *we* try?"

Brom raised an eyebrow. "A Noctari in their midst? They'd hate the sight of you. But... you *are* a paladin, and they've been looking for one to join them for a while. That might be enough to get them to listen."

"If you have someone we can talk to, we're willing to try," I said.

"It'll be dangerous," Rannoch warned. "They're not exactly known for conversation."

Perseus smirked. "I'm surprised you don't get along better with them, little brother."

"Watch it, big brother," Rannoch growled, making Perseus laugh.

Brom cut in. "Keeping the maid alive gave us a contact name and a meeting location. We were planning a raid there tonight, but if you'd rather try reasoning with them, I'm all for it. That would let us focus on more pressing matters."

I glanced at Reeger and Keenan. Both nodded.

"Let's do it," I said with a smile.

"Excellent," Brom said. "We'll give you the contact info and the meeting spot."

They briefed us on the details, and the emergency signal that would summon troops if things went sideways.

Once ready, we headed for the meeting place: a small grove of trees near the city's outer wall.

As dusk settled, we exchanged determined glances.

"Let's do this," I said, and we stepped from the trees into the grove.

Chapter 13 - Order of Light

We approached the campfire slowly, eyes scanning the small gathering. A traveling bard strummed a lively tune, drawing laughter from a merchant, his wife and a couple of guards. Off to one side, an elf scribbled notes on parchment, his gaze flicking between the performers and the shadows.

Toward the back, a lone figure sat apart, pipe glowing faintly in the dark. His features were obscured, but his eyes tracked us as we took our seats.

We began talking, weaving the phrase we'd been given into our conversation, loud enough for anyone listening to catch it. Once. Twice. A third time. Still, no reaction.

One by one, the audience drifted away. The bard packed up. The guards stretched and wandered off. The merchant couple disappeared down the path into the trees. The grove emptied.

We exchanged uncertain glances. Maybe he wasn't here after all. With a shrug, we turned and started back toward the city. But just before the gates, the lone man from the grove stepped out of the shadows.

"So," he said, voice low and even, "you seek to know more about the Order."

I stepped forward. "Yes. We do."

He nodded once. "Then come."

We hesitated. Keenan raised an eyebrow. Reeger's hand hovered near his weapon. But we followed.

The man led us into the hills, saying nothing. The moon rose higher as we walked, the city lights fading behind us. After nearly an hour, my patience frayed.

"Where exactly are you taking us?" I asked.

"If you want answers, follow. If not, turn back," he said, never breaking stride.

I glanced at Keenan, who smirked. "I'm supposed to be the impatient one, remember?"

I exhaled and kept walking.

Eventually, the path narrowed between two hills. The man stopped beside a grassy slope.

"Are you sure this is what you want?" he asked, a smirk tugging at his lips.

I kept my hand away from my weapon, but my voice was firm. "Yes."

Keenan nodded. Reeger scanned the hills, then gave a small nod of agreement.

The man knelt, brushed aside a patch of grass, and revealed a hidden handle. With ease, he pulled open a concealed door, perfectly blended into the hillside.

"Nice," I muttered, impressed.

We stepped inside. The door closed behind us with a dull *thud*, sealing us in a small, hollowed-out chamber. A single torch flickered on the wall, casting long shadows across a plain wooden table and bench. A second door faced us.

"Now what?" Keenan asked.

Before anyone could answer, a narrow slit in the door slid open. A pair of sharp eyes and a crooked nose peered through.

"Weapons and armor. On the table," the man barked.

Chapter 13 - Order of Light

"Not happening," Reeger said flatly.

The man snorted. "Then no admittance." The slot slammed shut.

Keenan crossed his arms. "Yeah, not going in unarmed."

"Same," I said.

As we debated, the door creaked open. A tall man stepped through, broad-shouldered and blond, with piercing blue eyes and a presence that filled the room. He had to stoop slightly beneath the low ceiling.

His gaze swept over us, then locked onto Keenan.

"You're a paladin, yes?"

Keenan blinked. "Yes."

"Then your word is your bond?"

"It is," Keenan said, voice steady.

"If I have your word that you and your companions won't fight, and will leave peacefully if asked, you'll honor that?"

Keenan exhaled slowly. "Yes. Unless we're attacked."

The man nodded. "Good. My name is Oryn. We know who you are and why you're here."

We stood in stunned silence.

Oryn chuckled. "Come now. How stupid do you think we are?" He pushed the door open wider and gestured. "This way."

We followed him down a tunnel carved deep into the hillside, where compacted earth formed narrow walls and a low ceiling that forced us to hunch as we moved forward. The air was cool and stale, heavy with the scent of damp soil. As we passed through, a gnome glared at us, muttering something under his breath.

The corridor twisted and turned, lined with doors marked by strange symbols. I frowned, trying to decipher them, but none made sense.

The path was deliberately confusing, no straight lines, no clear exits. As if reading my thoughts, Oryn spoke without turning.

"This place would be difficult to assault... or to flee."

He stopped before a heavy wooden door, then opened it and stepped inside.

The room beyond was circular, lit by lanterns set into the stone walls. A large round table dominated the center, surrounded by mismatched chairs. A side table held bread, cheese, and a pitcher of water.

At the main table, a human man scribbled notes with quick, precise strokes. Across from him sat a cloaked figure, utterly still, their face hidden in shadow.

Oryn gestured for us to enter. "Welcome," he said. "Please, take a seat. Hopefully we can come to an understanding." He sat at the circular table and waited for us to join him. We did so cautiously, our eyes darting around the room looking for dangers. His presence was commanding, not cruel like the pirate captain, but heavy with the kind of gravity that warned: cross me, and you'll regret it.

His gaze settled on Keenan. "What do you know of the Order of Light?"

Keenan chose his words carefully. "From what I understand, you aim to eradicate all magic from the world."

The man scribbling notes scoffed. Oryn shook his head. "A common misunderstanding," he said. "The Order believes magic should be reserved for the righteous, paladins, clerics, and those who undergo strict, disciplined

Chapter 13 - Order of Light

training. In the hands of anyone else, it's volatile. Dangerous. It must be controlled, for the safety of the world."

He locked eyes with Keenan. "Someone like you is permitted to wield it because you're bound by a code. Justice. Protection. Your intentions serve the greater good. But even then, its use should be limited and overseen by a council of elders."

I thought grimly, *and who decides who gets to be on that council?*

Keenan shared my skepticism, asking. "Who decides who sits on the council?"

"The council would be elected by city leaders from across the world," Oryn replied without hesitation.

"Then why operate in the shadows?" Keenan pressed.

"Because most people don't see the danger magic poses," Oryn said. "They mock us. Call us zealots. Force us underground. But we're working toward a safer world."

Keenan's voice sharpened. "Why assassinate the queen?"

Oryn's expression darkened. "A regrettable but necessary action. She harbors a power capable of ending the world. With demon attacks escalating, we no longer have the luxury of time."

"So, you still intend to kill her, and her entire family?" Keenan demanded.

"The males are merely carriers," Oryn explained. "They possess no abilities and pose no threat. Her daughter hasn't shown signs of power, though we've heard troubling rumors. Nothing confirmed."

We exchanged glances, caught off guard. Keenan recovered first.

"So, their children are safe?"

"For now," Oryn said. "We have no desire to harm anyone who doesn't pose a threat. But the situation is dire. If the demons gain control of the queen, she could bring ruin to us all. The only way to prevent that..." He paused, reluctant. Then, with a heavy sigh: "...is to remove her."

Keenan leaned forward, his voice steady. "The king and his family are prepared to die to protect her, all of whom are innocent. Which means you would have to kill them all." Oryn nodded grimly. "Perhaps. But what's coming will overwhelm them. If one of them is captured, she'll do anything to protect her family. That won't end well."

"The king will never give her up," Keenan said. "I understand your fears. But unless we find a solution together, turning on each other is a waste of time, and lives, we can't afford to make."

Oryn gave a slow nod. "Which is why we're asking you to convince her to sacrifice herself. For the greater good."

The boldness of the request struck me like a hammer. Asking someone to willingly give up their life felt unthinkable, especially when they had done nothing wrong. Beside me, Reeger shifted, visibly uncomfortable. But Keenan remained composed. "As a paladin, I'm sworn to protect life. She's done nothing wrong. I won't condemn her to death without just cause."

The man taking notes finally spoke, voice sharp with bitterness. "She murdered several people in her youth. Including my brother."

We stiffened. Keenan turned to him, tone even. "If that's true, and she admits it, then justice must be served."

Chapter 13 - Order of Light

I couldn't stay quiet. "You can't be serious," I said, incredulous.

"Not now," Keenan hissed under his breath, before turning back to Oryn. "If there's truth to his claim, we'll handle it. But not here. Not like this."

Oryn's eyes narrowed. "We want what's best for this world. A paladin among our ranks would bring stability. Make everyone safer."

I clenched my fists. The entire conversation felt twisted. Disloyal. Underhanded. How could we even entertain betraying Brom's family?

But Keenan didn't flinch. "I'll consider your offer. But tell me, is there any solution besides death?"

For the first time, Oryn glanced at the hooded figure seated silently beside the note-taker. After a pause, the robed figure passed him a slip of parchment.

Oryn read it. His jaw tightened. Something in his expression faltered.

Without a word, the hooded figure rose and left the room.

"There is... another way," Oryn said at last, his voice taut. "We could place her in stasis. If the king agrees to surrender her, we avoid bloodshed and focus on fortifying the city against what's coming."

Reeger stood abruptly. I followed the motion instinctively. Oryn stared down at the table, visibly working to regain control. The note-taker leaned in, hissed something sharp, then stormed out.

Oryn straightened, eyes locking onto Keenan.

"Please. Consider joining us. You could become a leader in the Order. We have powerful connections. With your help, we can make the world safer. More stable."

His final words hung heavy in the air, less command, more plea.

He rose to his full height, radiating calm authority. "Speak to the king about what we discussed. I ask for your word that you won't lead his men here for the next seventy-two hours under the Paladin negotiating terms."

Surprised, Keenan hesitated only briefly. "You have my word."

Oryn extended his hand. Keenan grasped it, firm and solemn. Without another word, Oryn led us back through the winding tunnels until we emerged once more onto the path in the hills.

"I look forward to your response," he said, then turned and vanished back into the concealed door.

As we walked back toward Burke, frustration boiled in my chest. "I can't believe they expect us to deliver that kind of message," I muttered, fists clenched.

Keenan glanced over, sensing my anger. "As a paladin, I'm bound to act as a neutral mediator during negotiations. That doesn't mean I agree with them. When the time comes, I'll fight for the side I believe in. But some people are clever enough to exploit that neutrality, and they did." He shook his head. "They're smarter than I thought."

His words eased the edge of my fury, though the sting of Oryn's request still burned.

Reeger, quiet until now, finally spoke. "I don't think Oryn is evil," he said thoughtfully. "I think he's just... misguided."

Chapter 13 - Order of Light

I shot him a skeptical look, not convinced. But when Keenan nodded, I forced myself to consider it. Maybe I was missing something.

Reeger continued, "It's the robed figure that bothers me. Why hide your identity? Either we'd recognize who he is, or what he is."

Keenan's expression darkened. "The secrecy around their leadership makes things harder. I tried to detect evil on him, but it was... blocked. Or maybe there was nothing there at all. It felt like trying to sense a void."

Merek's voice cut in from behind us, sharp and certain. "That's because he was using a magical field that blocks detection. I haven't seen one like that in a long time. Few possess that level of skill."

Keenan nodded. "That makes sense. It felt like... like trying to peer into empty space."

"Exactly," Merek said. "And that kind of power is only used for one thing... deception. If you're hiding that much, it's because you don't want to be known. And Halvar," he added, voice rising, "you bumbling idiot, it's hard enough negotiating as a paladin with people we don't agree with. It's even harder when our friends start turning on us in the middle of the meeting."

His words hit hard. Guilt flushed through me. I sighed, anger giving way to regret.

"Hey, Keenan... I'm sorry. I wasn't mad at you. I just..." I shook my head. "I just can't believe they'd ask someone to die because of what they believe. And our friend, no less."

Keenan gave a quiet nod, his voice soft. "I understand."

We continued walking in silence, each of us lost in uneasy thoughts.

We arrived in Burke late, but Brom was still awake, waiting. He summoned us to a meeting room, where we took our seats. After offering food and water, which we accepted gratefully, he asked, "How did it go? What happened?"

Keenan was just about to begin when the Queen and her two sons entered and sat down. The Queen smiled warmly. "I hope you don't mind us joining you."

"Of course not," Brom replied with a smile.

Once everyone was seated and the guards, except for Victus, had left, Keenan began recounting the events of our meeting.

When he explained the enemy's demand that the Queen sacrifice herself for peace, the royal family sat in stunned silence.

"They just want my mother to offer her life for peace?" Perseus asked, incredulous.

"Over my dead body," Rannoch muttered.

"Agreed," Brom said, jaw tight. "I'll die before that happens."

Keenan continued, explaining their second proposal: to place the Queen in stasis and hide her away.

"Well, that's not suspicious at all," Perseus scoffed. "How do we know they won't try to use her?"

Keenan and I exchanged surprised glances. That possibility hadn't even occurred to us, but it added a troubling new dimension.

The family launched into a heated debate. Perseus argued for keeping the Queen safely in the palace. Rannoch

Chapter 13 - Order of Light

pushed for a direct assault to eliminate their enemies entirely. His frustration boiled over, and he began questioning Keenan's loyalty for not revealing their location, until Brom stepped in, voice calm but firm, and defused the tension.

Finally, Eryndra, who had remained silent through it all, spoke softly, her voice trembling. "Maybe, for the sake of the many…"

Brom gently cut her off. "It's important to all of us that you never finish that sentence or think it again." He offered her a warm, reassuring smile. "That will never happen. Please don't consider it."

She smiled and nodded.

At that moment, there was a sudden *poof*, and Cara appeared beside the Queen, sleepily wrapping her in a hug.

"Mother, why are you sad?" she asked.

Eryndra sighed and smiled faintly, returning the embrace. "It's okay, honey. Just tired of people dying, that's all." She looked around the room. "Very well. No more talk of that option. I just don't want anyone else to die on my account."

The king chuckled gently, looking at his daughter. "Cara, we talked about this. You can't keep flashing your ability like that."

She yawned. "It's okay, Daddy. There's no one else in the room."

Brom raised an eyebrow. "How can you be sure?"

Struggling to keep her eyes open, Cara mumbled, "Because I can see around you… wherever you are… if I try hard enough."

We exchanged astonished glances, suddenly aware of how powerful her abilities might be. She curled into her mother's lap and drifted off almost instantly.

Eryndra smiled, brushing a strand of hair from her daughter's face. "The hard life of a young lady," she whispered, gently caressing her forehead.

Keenan's gaze lingered on Cara, his expression darkening. "They don't seem to have her on their radar... but if they ever find out..." He shook his head grimly.

Brom followed his gaze, then looked at the rest of us. "What do you three think?"

We exchanged glances. Keenan spoke first.

"We should try to negotiate directly with their actual leader, not a proxy. Something feels off. They've sent their most honorable face, but even he doesn't seem fully aligned. If we can drive a wedge between them, create a fracture, they might turn on each other. Then we'd only have half of them to deal with."

I leaned in and whispered, "You're getting good at this."

Keenan smiled.

Reeger nodded. "At the very least, we need more information."

It was agreed: we'd return in the morning to attempt further negotiations and try to arrange a direct meeting with the Order's true leader. We were shown back to our rooms and slept uneasily, hoping for better news with the dawn.

At sunrise, we grabbed breakfast and received a final wish of luck from the king before setting out. As we walked away, Rannoch turned to his father.

"You want me to track them?" he asked.

Chapter 13 - Order of Light

The king kept his eyes forward, watching us disappear over the horizon. "Do I want to? Yes. But you're not going to." He paused. "There's something about those three I can't explain. But after saving your mother once, I have a feeling they'll do it again."

"I hope you're right," Perseus said, staring into the distance.

"Me too, son," Brom replied. "Me too."

Rannoch grunted. "If not, they won't get near her again."

The king surprised them both by laughing. "You know I love you boys, right?" he said, grabbing them both and pulling them into a hug.

Perseus smiled. Rannoch muttered, "Men, Dad. We're men."

"Of course. Men. Got it." Brom chuckled, and they headed back inside.

We returned to the rolling hills, as close as we could figure to where the hidden door had been. We scanned the area in silence until I finally broke it.

"So... what now?"

Keenan shrugged, just as Reeger said, "Quiet..."

We listened. A trapdoor creaked open, and the same man who'd guided us before popped up and waved us over.

We chuckled and followed him to yet another concealed entrance. As we descended into the twisting tunnels, I leaned toward Keenan and whispered, "Remember when we camped out here in the hills? We always thought people were watching us."

Keenan whispered back, "Yeah. Don't remind me." He shook his head.

Hammer and Anvil

Our guide led us into a massive underground chamber. The space stretched at least a hundred feet wide and two hundred feet long, with a twenty-five-foot ceiling supported by reinforced stone pillars. Torch sconces lined the walls, their flickering light casting long shadows across the smooth dirt floor.

At the center stood a raised speaking platform of dark stone, flanked by wide staircases. Rows of sturdy wooden chairs filled the space. Long tables lined the perimeter, each meticulously organized: weapons, swords, bows, spears, reinforced shields, light armor, coils of rope, lanterns, maps, parchment, quills. Provisions were laid out: fresh bread, cured meats, fruits, barrels of clean water.

Despite its utilitarian purpose, the chamber was immaculate. The floor, worn by countless boots, was polished and debris-free. The acoustics were exceptional, voices carried clearly without echo, perfect for strategy and command. Heavy wooden doors reinforced with iron bands marked the main entrances, while smaller, concealed doors hinted at escape routes and hidden passages.

Oryn stood waiting, flanked by seven or eight bodyguards in unusually tight formation. We exchanged puzzled glances as Keenan stepped forward and shook his hand.

"I know you have no reason to trust me," Oryn said quickly, "but I have a bad feeling about what's happening. I think it's coming to a head right now. Please, hang back and observe. I know I have no right to ask this, but if things go sideways, we'd appreciate any help you can offer."

Keenan nodded. Bewildered, we stepped back and did as he asked, watching the event unfold.

Chapter 13 - Order of Light

Over the next thirty minutes, people began pouring in, many cloaked, their features deliberately concealed. Reeger elbowed us and whispered, "Notice how Oryn's positioning specific people near the doors on both sides?"

"That's odd," Keenan agreed.

"I don't like it," I said, uneasy. "Something doesn't feel right."

"Agreed," Reeger nodded.

"I don't think he's trying to deceive us," Keenan added.

Reeger nodded again. "But something is definitely off."

I said nothing more. Just kept watching the room, unease growing with every passing minute.

The chamber was packed, with at least 150, maybe 200 people. The air buzzed with tension.

Oryn returned to us, his voice low and urgent. "If things go really bad," he said, pointing to a narrow door behind us, "and it looks like we have no chance, take that exit. It leads into the hills."

Before we could respond, he turned and walked away.

We were on edge. Nerves fraying. The hair on the back of my neck stood up. Something felt profoundly wrong.

Then, at the back of the stage, an old man rose and began to speak. His voice was slow, droning, a sermon on the Order's sacred mission and their pivotal role in the coming battle.

Keenan's eyes narrowed. "Wait... I think it's an illusion."

"A what?" I leaned closer.

"I've seen it stutter twice. Very subtle. That's not an old man. It's something else."

"Can you dispel it?"

"I don't know," Keenan said. "It'll be tricky."

A scowling voice cut in from below. "I can help."

We looked down. The gnome from the night before stood at the edge of the platform, glaring up at the stage.

"I've known that man for years," he growled. "That's not him."

Keenan nodded. "All right. Here we go."

He closed his eyes, focusing. The gnome began chanting in a low, deliberate rhythm, his voice like gravel grinding over stone.

Ten seconds passed. The illusion began to ripple, like heat rising from a fire. Then, with a sharp *pop*, the image shattered.

In the old man's place stood a towering demon, ten to twelve feet tall, its skin the color of scorched iron, its eyes burning coals. It froze, exposed, scanning the crowd with cold, predatory calculation.

Oryn stepped forward, undaunted.

"I knew you weren't him," he said, drawing his sword. "We will fight for this world. And we will stop you."

His bodyguards closed in beside him. He raised his voice.

"Men, join me! For our world, and our children's future! Now is the time for the Order to show these demons we will not be an easy fight!"

The men in the room rose from their seats.

The demon laughed.

Chapter 13 - Order of Light

It was a horrible sound, deep, guttural, soaked in malice. As it echoed through the chamber, dozens of cloaked figures dropped their disguises. At least a hundred, maybe more, stood revealed. Eyes glowing red. Already turned.

"Good speech," Keenan muttered, unsheathing his sword. "But they don't stand a chance if that many have turned."

Reeger had already vanished into the shadows.

Keenan turned to me, his voice low and solemn. "Warn the king," he said, nodding toward the hidden door. "Bring reinforcements. I'll try to slow them down."

My heart dropped. I froze, torn between duty and loyalty, between the big picture and my friend. I couldn't bring myself to abandon him.

Keenan continued toward the stage just as the demon's laughter subsided.

"You pathetic creatures will do anything for power or money," it sneered, its gaze settling on Oryn. "Look around, demon slayer." He said sarcastically.

Oryn stood surrounded. Of the two hundred in the room, more than half had turned. Only a handful of his men still stood with him. Even with all of them, bringing down that demon would be a monumental task. And Keenan, powerful as he was, couldn't turn the tide alone.

I clenched my fists.

I could freeze him again.

The thought came out of nowhere. But doubt followed fast.

No... how? That wasn't us who did it before...

My thoughts spiraled. Heart pounding. Breath shallow.

What do I do?

Desperation surged through me. But I forced myself to breathe. To be steady.

"I can help," I whispered, drawing my weapon.

The demon raised its clawed hand. The possessed surged forward, closing in on Oryn and his defenders.

Keenan reached the base of the stage.

"I am Aegis, protector..."

The demon cut him off with a roar of laughter.

"The traitor will be the first to die!" it bellowed, raising its weapon toward him.

I shut my eyes and shouted, "No!"

And then,

A voice.

Deep. Ancient. Thunderous.

It didn't just echo through the chamber, it *shook* it. The very stone trembled. The sound surged through my chest like a tidal wave. I had heard it before. In a dream? A vision? I couldn't say. But its call stirred something buried deep within me.

My fear vanished. My breath steadied. My resolve returned.

I opened my eyes.

Power flooded through my limbs, hot, like molten steel, alive. The demon and its minions turned toward me, but they no longer seemed so large. Or terrifying.

I stepped forward.

And felt the ground shudder.

I looked down.

A dragon's leg.

Not armor. Not illusion.

Mine.

Chapter 13 - Order of Light

I stared ahead, heart thundering. Realization struck like lightning. Memories surged, flashes of fire, Ice, flight, ancient words spoken in a forgotten tongue.

I am Anvil! I am the other Dragon!

Chapter 14 - Good News

My voice thundered through the chamber, shaking the stone and commanding every soul to stillness. "Demons," I bellowed, "you will surrender and drop your weapons!"

The words echoed like a war drum, crashing off the walls. The vast chamber suddenly felt small, as if the very air recoiled from the force of my voice.

For a heartbeat, silence reigned.

Then the demons laughed.

The lead demon sneered from the stage. "Kill as many as you can!"

At his command, the possessed surged forward, swarming the defenders around Keenan and Oryn.

I roared in anger as I moved forward.

My tail swept through the crowd like a battering ram, smashing fifty of them against the wall. Most died instantly. The enemies were too intermingled with our allies to risk freezing them all. I had to pick my way through the fight one by one, careful to avoid any collateral damage.

So, I turned and grabbed them with my claws.

I tore through the possessed, hurling them into stone, ripping them apart. I fought with fury and precision, carving a path toward the stage.

I saw the demon knock Keenan to the ground, hammering his shield again and again. Nearby, Oryn was being driven into a corner, fending off six attackers. His loyal men were scattered, bloodied, but still fighting.

Chapter 14 - Good News

I reached the demon.

With a roar, I seized him in both claws and tore him in two. His body went limp, lifeless. I flung the remains aside and kept moving, clearing the room with brutal efficiency.

When the last possessed fell, silence returned.

The chamber was in ruins. Bodies lay in heaps, blood pooling across the stone. Only twenty, perhaps twenty-five, of Oryn's men still stood, most wounded or worse.

Exhaustion hit me like a wave. Holding my dragon form had drained more than I expected. I hadn't fully recovered from my near death all those years ago. But my time healing beneath the mountain, thanks to Mother, had done more than I realized.

Keenan approached, wiping blood from his hands. His face was pale, but his eyes were steady.

"Thank you," he said. "You saved all our lives. That's twice now you've saved mine. I owe you a great debt."

He glanced around the wreckage, managing a faint smile. "I only wish my friend Halvar were here to meet you. He would've loved this."

I chuckled, the sound rumbling through the floor. "Oh, I think you'll be the one who loves this," I said, a knowing grin spreading across my face.

Keenan blinked, confused.

I chuckled again and shifted.

The transformation rippled through me. Bones shifting, wings vanishing, scales retreating. In moments, I stood before him in human form once more.

Keenan stared, eyes wide. "No," he breathed. "You're messing with me. This is projection. Illusion. Something."

"No tricks," I said gently. "It's really me."

Reeger stepped into the light, grinning. "Did you just remember?"

I nodded. "It came back to me when I was about to leave... but I couldn't go."

Keenan's brow furrowed. He reached out with his senses, trying to detect magic. His expression stayed tense, uncertain.

Reeger spoke again. "The ship said you were different. This must've been what she meant."

I nodded slowly. "That's right. I'd forgotten."

Reeger continued, "The other dragon asked me where her brother was. But she called you 'brother.'"

I blinked. "Wait... I thought you said she asked you the same thing?"

Reeger gave a sly smile. "Nope. I just nodded when you said that. You assumed."

Keenan's expression shifted, part disbelief, part frustration. "All this time, you could've turned into a dragon? And you didn't? What about when we were kids? Was that all fake?"

I shook my head. "No. None of that was fake. Back then, I was vulnerable. I'd been poisoned. I needed time to heal. Children grow, and that growth is full of healing energy. I needed that time."

I hesitated, then added, "Some of my memories have come back, but some are still sealed. I couldn't tell you... because I didn't know."

I met his gaze, voice soft. "I'm sorry. If I'd known, I would've told you."

He stared at me in silence. My heart sank. Fear crept in, fear that I'd just lost my best friend.

Chapter 14 - Good News

"Please, Keenan," I said, voice trembling. "Don't be mad at me."

He studied me, unreadable.

Then he burst out laughing.

"Mad at you?" he said. "Are you kidding me? My best friend is a dragon. *The* dragon. Do you have any idea how much more trouble I would've dragged us into as kids if I'd known that?"

I laughed, relieved. "It's probably for the best that you didn't."

He laughed again, shaking his head. "Oh, this is fantastic." His smile faded into curiosity. "Does it hurt when you change?"

I shook my head. "Not really. Feels more like a good stretch after a nap."

"Huh." He nodded thoughtfully. "Well, I've got a ton of questions, but…" He gestured to the wreckage. "We should probably deal with all this first. Then I can start planning how to use you to conquer every island and then the rest of the world."

He grinned mischievously.

We turned to Oryn, who had been quietly watching. For a moment, all of us simply stood there, breathing in the aftermath.

Then Oryn sighed.

"Well," he said, "I suppose Brom has succeeded in his mission, stopping the Order of Light."

He glanced at the twenty-five bloodied survivors. "Looks like our leaders failed us."

Keenan stepped forward and placed a hand on his shoulder. "Or maybe," he said, "it just made us stronger for the fight ahead."

Oryn gave a dry smile, then looked at me. "Is he always this optimistic?"

I smiled. "Yeah. And sometimes it's nauseating."

Keenan glared at me. Reeger and I just laughed.

Oryn straightened, his tone turning serious. "I'd rather not fight a dragon or see more of my men die needlessly. I'll surrender myself. But only if you promise to spare my men. Let them go free."

At that, the man who'd sat at the table the night before stepped forward. "I go where he goes. If that means the dungeon or the gallows, so be it."

Oryn groaned. "Ever the drama queen, eh, Alric?"

Alric shrugged, smirking.

One by one, the other men stepped forward, each pledging to surrender alongside Oryn.

He shook his head, clearly frustrated. "The whole point of me surrendering was to get you all out of trouble."

One of them stepped closer. "You are our leader. We are family. The Order stands together, even at the end."

I glanced at Keenan, who gave me a knowing smile and whispered, "Told you. I knew I sensed good in him."

Then, louder, he addressed the group. "Very well. We'll take you all to the king."

We burned the bodies, then began the journey back to Burke. The remnants of the Order walked with quiet pride, heads held high despite the weight of defeat. The mood was somber. None of us spoke much, each lost in thought.

Chapter 14 - Good News

We liked Oryn. But we all knew his role in the plot to kill the queen would not end well. So did he.

When we reached the castle, the guards were stunned to see us leading prisoners. More arrived quickly, flanking them with weapons drawn. The prisoners stood tall, but despair clung to them. They knew what awaited.

We arrived at the castle and were ushered into the throne room, guards flanking the prisoners at least two to one. Brom entered, flanked by his sons, and surveyed the scene. A flicker of a smile crossed his face.

"So, you defeated them all? Excellent. Perhaps now the queen can live in peace, and we can turn our attention to more pressing matters."

Keenan stepped forward, gesturing to Oryn. "This is Oryn, the last ranking lieutenant of the Order. The rest of the leadership…" He paused, glanced at Oryn, then lowered his gaze. "…perished in combat with demons."

Brom's brows lifted. "Demons?"

Keenan nodded. "Yes. Most of the Order was overrun. We fought alongside the survivors to defeat them."

Brom's expression grew thoughtful. "Interesting."

Oryn stepped forward. "King Brom, I surrender myself to your judgment. I only ask that you spare my men. They were following my orders."

Rannoch scoffed. "You're in no position to make requests, not after nearly killing the queen."

Perseus leaned toward him, muttering, "Not now."

Brom shot a glance at his son, then approached Oryn, locking eyes. "And why should I do that? You and your men are sworn to kill my wife and purge magic from the realm. Except, perhaps, a few paladins."

Oryn nodded solemnly. "Would you not do what you believed was right to protect your people, if our roles were reversed?"

A faint smile tugged at Brom's lips. He let out a short laugh. "So you ask for mercy, though you've given none and don't deserve it?"

"I don't ask for myself," Oryn said. "I ask for my men. They are my family. Please…" He paused. "Would you not do the same for yours?"

Rannoch muttered, "A family who murders women."

The king didn't respond immediately. He studied Oryn in silence, then spoke.

"So tell me... what would you have me do? Release twenty-five men who would kill my wife the moment they had the chance?"

Oryn struggled to respond, clearly at a loss, searching for some way to save his men.

Then the queen entered.

Quietly.

The room fell still.

Soldiers tensed, hands tightening on hilts. The men of the Order stiffened at the sight of her, their sworn target, now standing before them, unarmed. The air thickened.

Brom stepped toward her and murmured, "Honey, I think it's best if you leave."

She shook her head, bare feet gliding across the stone floor, her white dress flowing to her ankles. Black hair framed a calm, resolute face.

"I would see my killers," she said softly.

Silence followed as she approached Oryn, who stood frozen, uncertain.

Chapter 14 - Good News

She looked him in the eye. Her voice was gentle, but clear. "Do you want to kill me?"

Oryn hesitated. Confusion crossed his face. Finally, he said, "I don't want to kill anyone. I just want my world to be safe."

"Is that so?" she asked, never breaking eye contact.

Without warning, she reached into her dress and drew a dagger, holding it out to him.

Brom's sons and the soldiers surged forward, but she raised her hand. They stopped.

"Take the knife," she said.

Oryn stared at her in shock, then glanced at Brom. The weight of the moment took all the air out of the room.

"Take it," she repeated, more firmly.

He exhaled, shoulders sagging. "I... can't." His head dropped. "I can't," he said quietly.

"Why not?" she pressed. "Isn't this what you want? Isn't this what you stand for?"

Still staring at the floor, he muttered, "I can face men in battle... but I can't kill an unarmed woman."

She leaned in slightly, voice barely above a whisper. "Why not?"

He shook his head faintly, at a loss. "I don't know."

"I think I know," the queen said, still watching him.

Alric stepped forward, voice sharp with anger. "I'll do it."

The queen turned to him, calm. "You look familiar. What's your name?"

Alric's eyes blazed. "Alric Graves. You murdered my brother twenty-two years ago. In an alley. Burned them all to a crisp." He spat at her feet.

She studied him for a long moment. Finally, she said, "I remember."

Alric turned to Keenan, fury boiling over. "See? She admits it! And you do nothing?"

Keenan, caught off guard, turned to the queen, waiting.

"I didn't admit to murder," she said evenly. "I said I remember."

Alric laughed bitterly. "Remember what? That you torched my brother and three innocent men on their way home from the inn? They were eighteen. Nineteen. And you murdered them. For what?"

Her voice softened, though her composure held. "Your brother... he had blonde hair, didn't he?"

Alric blinked. "What?"

"Blonde hair," she repeated gently.

He nodded stiffly, uncertain.

"Yes," she said quietly. "He was burned. But he was already dead when I set the fire." Her voice carried a shadow of grief. "He died in my arms."

Alric was taken aback, shaken. "What? You expect me to believe that?" He stammered, struggling to form the thoughts swirling in his mind.

The queen's gaze didn't falter. "I was sleeping in that alley. Alone. Dealing with my own failures. A group of young men found me. They mocked me. Threatened me."

Alric stood frozen, his fury wavering beneath growing confusion.

"As I tried to defend myself," the queen said softly, "your brother intervened. He told them to stop. Told them to walk away. But they were drunk, laughing, egging each

Chapter 14 - Good News

other on. One of them shoved him... and he fell. On a knife."

"I don't know whose," she added. "I tried to help him, but there was nothing I could do."

Alric's lips parted, but no words came. Tears filled his eyes.

"He died in my arms," she said. "He was the first person who ever tried to help me. Who showed me kindness." Her voice wavered. "When he was gone... I lost control. In my rage, I burned the entire street. I didn't think. I just reacted in sorrow."

Alric dropped to his knees, tears streaming silently down his face.

The queen knelt beside him, placing a gentle hand on his shoulder.

"I am sorry," she whispered. "But your brother was a hero to me."

The room fell so silent that even the torches seemed to hold their breath.

The queen rose, stepped back, and turned to the king. "I see no threat here."

Without another word, she turned and left the chamber.

We stood in uneasy silence, unsure what to do next. Brom remained where he was, studying the men before him, his expression heavy with thought. After a long pause, he gestured for his sons to approach. They gathered around him, speaking in hushed tones. The conversation stretched on until it felt like time itself had paused.

At last, Brom stepped forward, stopping in front of Oryn with a sigh.

"What are we going to do with you?"

Oryn opened his mouth, but the king cut him off.

"Yes, yes... 'spare your men.' I know." He looked up, exhaling sharply. "You swore to kill the queen. And yet, when she stood before you, unarmed, not one of you made a move."

He began to pace slowly, shaking his head.

"Normally, I'd send you all to the quarries or the labor fields for a few years. That would be lenient. But surviving demons? That counts for something."

He paused, locking eyes with Oryn, who straightened, the faintest glimmer of hope on his face.

"Some would counsel me to hang every one of you, and they'd be justified. Even the paladins wouldn't protest, I imagine." He glanced at Keenan, who met his gaze with a look of sadness and gave a slow, solemn nod.

"But there's a war coming," the king continued. "And we're not ready. Losing twenty-five trained fighters would be... unwise."

He stood straighter now, his tone shifting. "Do any of you have skills worth keeping?"

Eager to spare his men, Oryn stepped forward, outlining the Order's internal structure, their scouts, their spies, the unique skills of each soldier.

Brom raised a hand, halting him. "Wait. Are you saying you have spies in every major city? Including among the elves and dwarves?"

Keenan and I exchanged tense glances.

"Well... not the dwarves," Oryn admitted. "But yes. The elves. Even one of the Noctari clans."

Brom looked intrigued.

Chapter 14 - Good News

Perseus stepped forward. "What if we used them for intelligence work? Couriers. Scouts. Informants. They could monitor demonic activity across the island, give us the chance to act before it spreads."

Oryn nodded quickly. "We could do that."

Brom considered the suggestion, then said, "Alright. But Perseus will oversee the network." He turned to Oryn, gaze sharp. "You, however, won't be leaving here."

Oryn's shoulders sagged. He nodded. "Understood."

Then, to everyone's surprise, Brom burst out laughing. He strode up to Oryn and clapped a firm hand on his shoulder.

"See that big guy over there?" he said, gesturing to Victus, who stepped forward, towering and stone-faced. "While we were talking, I learned something interesting. Turns out, you two are practically brothers."

Oryn blinked. "But... I don't have a brother."

Brom smirked. "You do now. You look enough alike, and that's the story we'll go with. If you're willing to train under him, you and Victus will serve as my personal bodyguards."

Victus stepped closer, his presence looming. Oryn looked at him, then back at the king, unsure if this was a reward or a sentence.

I couldn't help but chuckle. "Just when I thought one giant was enough... now there are two."

Brom laughed. "Before all this, before you came back, before my wife entered, I spoke with Keenan. He's a fine judge of character. And both of you now assure me there's no evil in Oryn. So here's your chance: serve the realm, stay out of prison, and help us stop the demons."

Oryn nodded eagerly. "Yes. Thank you."

Brom winked at Rannoch. "Keep your friends close and your enemies closer, eh, son?"

Rannoch sighed. "I suppose that's one way to do it," he muttered.

Perseus and Rannoch escorted the remaining prisoners out with the guards, while Victus led Oryn away. The king came over to us, smiling warmly, shaking our hands one by one.

"I'm truly glad we met," he said. "But I've got preparations to oversee. And as much as I'd love to stay and chat, duty calls."

We nodded, letting him know we had to be on our way as well. There were updates to deliver to my uncles and the dwarves.

As we made our way out and headed back toward Grissom City, Keenan laughed. "I can't wait to see you explain to your uncles that you're basically one of their gods now."

I shook my head with a chuckle. "Even after all I've seen, I'm not ready for that conversation."

Reeger grinned. "This is going to be very entertaining."

We all laughed, and with lighter hearts, continued our journey toward Grissom. We arrived late and went straight to sleep.

Chapter 15 - The Woods

The next morning, we were up early and grabbed breakfast at the inn. The place was alive with clinking dishes, murmured conversations, and the scent of fresh bread and roasted meat.

Keenan leaned in with a smile. "So, when are you going to tell them?"

I glanced over at Grog, who was grumbling about something. I couldn't make out his words over the morning rush.

"I don't know," I said quietly. "But I'd like them to be my uncles for just a little bit longer."

I turned back to Keenan and smiled sadly.

"I miss the days when we didn't have a care in the world. Back when life was simple. When I was just a human kid with a troublemaking best friend, and an elf who knew better than to hang out with us, but did anyway, because we were entertaining. And he saw something in us that no one else did."

Reeger grinned. "Let's just stick with entertaining," he said.

Keenan and I burst into laughter.

I sighed, looking around the inn. "I'm going to miss this."

Keenan rolled his eyes. "Good grief. It's like you think you're dying tomorrow. Nothing's changed, you're just not worthless in a fight anymore," he said, laughing.

"Oh, thanks a lot," I replied, laughing too. But the feeling lingered, that quiet sense that things might never be the same. Still, in that moment, I made a silent vow: I would protect my friends, no matter what happened.

Reeger stood up. "Well, I'm off to warn my father and give an update."

"And I really should wake up Lily," I said with a smirk. "Though I'm not sure my sanity will survive it."

"Wait," Keenan said. "Who the heck is Lily?"

"Oh, sorry," I replied. "Lily is my sister."

"You have a sister?" Keenan asked, eyes gleaming with mischief.

I groaned. "No, Keenan. No."

"What?" he said innocently. "I haven't even said anything yet."

"You're going to ask if she's single, and the answer is no."

"Wait," he said slyly, "no to me asking, or no to her being single?"

I just glared at him while Reeger chuckled. "See? This is why I stick around," he said, grinning.

We all laughed, and I added, "In all seriousness, we should stick together while we travel. With everything going on, it's safer. We can swing by the woods first, then go wake up my sister."

"Wait," Keenan added, frowning. "Who's, ?"

"The other dragon, you dolt," I interrupted.

Reeger laughed. "Sometimes, Keenan, you miss the mark so badly, I'm not even sure you knew where the board was."

"Oh...yeah...Sorry," he said sheepishly.

Chapter 15 - The Woods

We laughed again, then agreed: after visiting the forest and the elves, we'd head to the mountain.

And with that, we set off.

We headed toward the mountains, then turned north toward the forest. Reeger's excitement was contagious as he described the elven cities, majestic, ancient, alive with magic and memory.

He spoke of "the Big Tree," a giant oak cultivated for over a thousand years. Of the maple shop nestled high in its canopy. Of troop slides, ingenious structures designed for rapid movement or ambushing trespassers.

His storytelling painted the forest in vivid color.

"It sounds amazing," Keenan said, eyes wide with wonder.

"It is," Reeger replied with a smile. "It'll be good to be home. I haven't been to the cities in almost fifteen years."

"Hah!" Keenan exclaimed. "What's that, like one year for us?" Then, glancing at me, he furrowed his brow. "Wait... how old are you, anyway?"

I laughed. "I don't know. A couple thousand years, I guess?"

His eyes widened. "A couple thousand years?" he muttered, turning to Reeger for confirmation.

Reeger chuckled. "Don't look at me. I'm only ninety-three."

"Good grief!" Keenan said, smiling. "I'm the child here!"

We all laughed.

"Finally, something we can agree on," I said with a smile.

We reached the woods shortly after lunch. Reeger approached a narrow road that disappeared into the trees and let out a shrill whistle that echoed over the hills and through the forest.

Moments later, two elves emerged from the trees about ten yards away. They greeted Reeger and began speaking in low, hushed tones.

After a while, Reeger's gestures grew more animated. Finally, he returned to us, shaking his head.

"They've closed the woods," he said grimly.

"What does that mean... 'closed the woods'?" Keenan asked.

"It means we can't go in," Reeger replied, frustration clear.

We were both disappointed, but Keenan recovered quickly. "Well, that's okay. Just go in, tell them what you need to, and we'll wait here."

Reeger sighed. "They've closed it to me too."

"What?" we both exclaimed. "What do you mean, 'closed it to you too'? You're one of their people! I thought your dad was one of their leaders!"

"Yes, well, he is," Reeger said. "But with the demon possession, they're taking no chances. To enter, you must be screened, and that takes time we don't have. It seems my father will be coming here instead."

Trying to lighten the mood, Keenan said, "Well, we can always admire the trees from out here. Besides, if we went in there and someone startled this one", he nodded toward me..." he might knock over a few trees. And we can't have that, can we?"

I shook my head while Reeger stared at him.

Chapter 15 - The Woods

Finally, he said, "Once again, Keenan, your logic and wisdom astound even me."

"I am pretty impressive with my logics and wisdoms," Keenan said, making a ridiculous face.

We both burst out laughing.

"Ladies and gentlemen, the mighty paladin!" I said. "Talk to him at your own risk, for all the wisdoms and logics you can handle."

Keenan grinned. "Don't be jealous."

"Jealous?" Reeger snorted. "He's a dragon!"

"Okay, okay," Keenan laughed. "Just go straight for the ace and play it right away."

I looked at my two friends, warmth swelling in my chest. These moments, this laughter, this loyalty, were the ones that made life worth living. I couldn't help but smile.

We waited fifteen, maybe twenty minutes before four elves emerged from the forest and approached. They stopped a few feet away, and one stepped forward.

"You'll need to set your weapons down here," he said firmly.

Reeger's expression shifted to disbelief. "Are you serious, Saevel?"

Saevel turned to him and replied evenly, "You too, Reeger."

Reeger stared, stunned. "You must be kidding me. This is ridiculous."

I smiled faintly, thinking to myself, *I don't need my weapon anyway.*

Keenan, ever the diplomat, offered a reassuring smile. "It's okay, Reeger. We'll set them down."

Before Reeger could argue, a voice piped up out of nowhere.

"Well, I'm not a weapon, so don't put me down. And if these pointy-eared fellows irritate me, I might just burn their luscious locks off."

The three of us froze.

Keenan closed his eyes and muttered, "Merek…"

"Ah, don't worry," the voice continued. "They can't hear me. I'm just feeling a little spicy today, especially since I got my old buddy back yesterday."

I couldn't help but smile, replying silently, *We did have some good fights.*

Merek chuckled. *Yeah, but keep in mind they can't hear me, so stop standing around like scarecrows and act natural.*

Noticing the elves' puzzled expressions, we quickly smiled and began setting our weapons on the ground. Saevel gave a subtle nod and motioned for us to follow, leaving the others to guard the weapons.

We made our way to the forest's edge, where another group of elves waited. One stepped forward, flanked by twelve archers with bows out and eyes scanning the surroundings.

The lead elf looked like an older version of Reeger.

As he approached, his age became more apparent. Silver streaks threaded through his long, chestnut hair, tied back neatly. Fine lines etched the corners of his eyes and mouth, signs of centuries lived with both hardship and humor. His sharp, almond-shaped eyes were a deep forest green, intense and thoughtful. Though his posture held a

Chapter 15 - The Woods

hint of stiffness, it radiated strength, precision, and authority.

His hands were slender but calloused, marked by years of crafting, writing, or wielding a bow. He wore a cloak of earthy browns and greens, blending seamlessly with the woods around him. His movements were deliberate, fluid, and calm.

He stopped before us, his gaze settling on Reeger, who still looked visibly irritated.

"Father," Reeger said with a curt nod.

His father returned the nod, his expression unreadable, before shifting his steady gaze to the rest of us.

"This is Keenan and Halvar, my friends," Reeger said, gesturing to us. "And this is my father, Thaylan, one of the three elders of my people."

Thaylan studied us with a sharp, assessing gaze. "I see your companions are still beneath your station," he said coolly.

Reeger muttered, "Here we go," then added, "Father, one of these companions you consider 'beneath my station' is a paladin from the Isle of Light."

Thaylan's gaze shifted to me. "You are a paladin?" he asked, tone dripping with skepticism.

"Well, that was rude," Keenan muttered under his breath.

A faint smile tugged at Thaylan's lips. "Of course. My mistake," he said smoothly, before turning his piercing eyes on Keenan.

"So," he said, voice sharp and cold, "we're to place all our trust, and hope of survival, in a Noctari?" His gaze bore into Keenan, unrelenting.

Despite his training, Keenan visibly struggled to maintain his composure.

"Father," Reeger interjected, "I think it would be unwise to provoke a paladin needlessly."

Thaylan turned to him, unimpressed. "Oh, if only you'd taken up music instead of ranger work. How much prouder we would have been."

Reeger's jaw tightened. "And if only you'd had a daughter…"

"Yes," Thaylan interrupted smoothly. "If only."

He stared at Reeger for a long moment, then turned back to me.

"And what about you?" he asked, eyes narrowing. There was no fear in me, but something in his stare was deeply unsettling. After a pause, he added, "You stink of dwarves."

The insult was deliberate, aimed not just at me, but at my people and my friends, who would gladly die for me as I would for them. I stepped forward, ready to respond, but Merek's voice rang out loud and clear.

"Well, Thaylan, you worthless piece of dead undergrowth, your hospitality has always been questionable, but it seems to have nosedived into the sewers. What happened in the last century to make you such a bugger?"

The shock was immediate. Everyone froze, eyes darting around the group.

Thaylan broke the silence. "So," he said quietly.

"Yes," I replied cautiously.

"I heard him," Thaylan said, narrowing his eyes at Keenan. "So, he chose you, did he?"

Chapter 15 - The Woods

A faint smile appeared on his face, and his demeanor softened.

"I would like to apologize for my behavior," he said, almost sincerely.

Turning to Reeger, he added with a sly smile, "I would have hated a daughter."

Reeger's expression eased a little as Thaylan continued. "The possessed lose their cool when taunted. They can't control their rage."

"Wait," Keenan said, frowning. "That was a test?"

"Yes," Thaylan replied, the corner of his mouth curling slightly. "Of course, it won't work on you again now that you know. But I still can't let you into the forest. A portal opened near our coast. We've lost three to demon possessions in the last week. We've had to become... cautious."

"Well, we have news," Reeger said, launching into a summary of everything that had happened over the past several days.

Keenan and I exchanged a glance when Reeger carefully omitted the fact that I was the dragon, and that the Order of Light had infiltrated the elves.

When he finished, Thaylan scoffed. "The dwarves. Always making decisions without consulting us."

"Father," Reeger said evenly, "I was there as a representative."

Thaylan laughed. "You're too young to offer wisdom on matters of that scale. They should have come to me, or one of the other elders."

Reeger clenched his jaw but remained silent.

Thaylan gave a small, approving nod. "At least you know when to hold your tongue."

Then, to all of us: "Now, tell me about this egg, or heart, under the mountain."

We exchanged uncertain glances. Keenan was the one to answer.

"We only saw it once. She spoke to us, said she wouldn't be able to hold the portals back much longer."

Thaylan waved a hand dismissively. "Too bad. Would've been helpful if she could hold them off longer. Buy us more time to prepare."

I clenched my fists, fighting to keep my anger in check. I was glad Reeger was the one representing the elves instead of his father. Keenan, equally irritated, tried to steer the conversation elsewhere.

"Have you learned anything?" he asked.

Thaylan looked at him coolly. "Nothing you don't already know."

Then he turned back to Reeger. "Any sign of dragons?"

Reeger flinched. He'd left both dragons out of the story on purpose.

"Why do you ask?" he said carefully.

Thaylan's voice turned speculative. "If such a power exists, whoever controls it could turn the tide when the need is great. Many things could be... solved... with a weapon of that magnitude."

Reeger hesitated, then glanced at us before answering. "It's in the lore. But as for evidence? I think we'd all know if there were dragons."

Thaylan studied him in silence for what felt like an eternity. Finally, he said, "Well. Hopefully this exchange will help us all prepare for what's coming."

Chapter 15 - The Woods

Reeger nodded. "We need to return and report to the dwarves. Get everyone on the same page."

Thaylan nodded. "It was wise to come to us first. But yes, informing the dwarves is the right next step. Tell them we must convene soon, so we can plan how best to defend our world together."

Reeger nodded again. With that, Thaylan turned and disappeared into the forest with his guards. As he passed, Saevel gave us a polite nod.

We made our way back to retrieve our weapons in silence.

"Well," Keenan said, pausing as he thought aloud, "I'm not sure if he was about to invite me for dinner or mount my head on a pike."

I chuckled, and Reeger added with a faint smile, "My father has a good heart, but he comes across as a pompous, arrogant old fool."

"Ah," Keenan said, nodding thoughtfully. "So, he just acts that way, but isn't actually those things?"

Reeger smirked. "No, no, he is absolutely all those things. But he does have a good heart."

We laughed, the tension finally breaking as we prepared to move on.

We headed south toward the mountain, leaving the forest behind. As we walked, Reeger said, "When all this is over and they allow us back in, I promise to show you everything."

"Well, if that's not reason enough to stay alive, I don't know what is," Keenan quipped with a grin.

We arrived at the dwarven outpost by nightfall and were escorted to the king's meeting chamber. While we waited, I began telling them about Lily, a mix of excitement and nervous anticipation in my voice.

"I should probably warn you," I said with a laugh, "she's a bit much sometimes."

Keenan frowned. "What does that mean?"

I grinned. "Oh, just wait. You'll see soon enough."

At that moment, the king entered, his voice booming with excitement.

"Boys! We've had a breakthrough, finally, some good news!"

He was grinning from ear to ear.

We exchanged curious glances.

"Good news would be great," I said.

He laughed. "My mages have been working for centuries on a way to take the fight to the demons' home world. We were finally introduced to someone named Reggie, and he had the missing piece we needed."

"Wait, really?" Reeger asked, surprised.

"Yes," the king confirmed. "He reached out to us, claiming he had critical information. Turns out Gamreal had been working with him, and we had no idea how big it was."

"So, what's the news?" Keenan asked, leaning forward.

The king picked up a black stone from the table. "These stones carry residue from the demon's world. With that, we've managed to open a small portal to their world... and back again."

We stared at him, stunned.

"You're serious?" Keenan asked.

"Yes," the king said, still smiling. "And it gets better. These stones also resonate at a frequency that blocks portal-ling, when properly attuned."

"What?" we all exclaimed in unison.

The king grinned. "Yes! We've already given several stones to Reggie. He and some of our mages are enchanting them to protect the mountain and other cities from unauthorized portals."

"That's incredible," I said, smiling, already imagining how proud Mother and the Eldest would be of the dwarves.

"Well," Keenan said, "our news is good, but not quite that good." He then brought the king up to speed on Burke, the Order of Light, and their dealings with Thaylan.

The king spat on the ground. "The elves' pride will be their undoing." He glanced at Reeger. "No offense. You seem better than most."

Reeger smiled. "I'd have to agree with you on all counts. But they're still my people. My family. And part of this world."

The king nodded. "Don't worry. We'll be giving them stones as well."

"Thank you," Reeger said sincerely.

"And thank you," the king added, "for not mentioning the dragons."

By now, a crowd of forty or fifty dwarves had gathered, drawn by the rising energy in the chamber. Their eyes flicked between us and the king, eager, uncertain, hungry for hope.

Keenan glanced at me, a sly smile playing on his lips.

"We have news," he said to the king, voice steady, "that may make you happier than anything else in your life."

The king laughed, booming and bright. "I'm in a good enough mood to let that slide, Paladin, but it'll be hard to top what we've discovered today."

Keenan leaned in, lowering his voice just enough to pull the room tighter.

"We've found a way to unfreeze your dragon."

The room fell silent.

The king's smile vanished. His eyes locked onto Keenan's with sudden intensity, the warmth gone in an instant.

"We do not joke about that," he said, voice low and sharp. "If this is some kind of trick, I suggest you choose your next words carefully."

Still smiling, Keenan pointed at me. "He'll show you how."

I shook my head at him, exhaling slowly. Around me, the dwarves had drawn closer, their faces lit with disbelief, hope, and curiosity. They had waited so long for this moment. For a sign. For a miracle. For anything.

I felt the weight of their longing settle on my shoulders.

I smiled to myself.

Here goes.

Chapter 16 - Awake

I transformed into my dragon form, towering nearly fifteen feet tall. My scales shimmered like frosted silver, crystalline under the light, reflecting a cold, pale blue hue. Piercing, glowing eyes radiated icy brilliance. Jagged, icicle-like horns crowned my head, and frozen spines lined my back. My translucent wings, edged with frost, resembled razor-sharp sheets of shimmering ice. A long, powerful tail trailed behind me, ending in a frozen spiked club.

I gazed down at the dwarves, who stood frozen in shock. The king recovered first. Placing his right fist over his heart, he dropped to one knee and shouted, "Kisago!"

His men quickly followed suit, chanting the name in unison.

In that moment, I felt the pride of a mother whose loyal children had served faithfully for centuries, unwavering amid the chaos of the world.

Then I spoke, my voice booming and echoing through the underground fortress:

"My dear dwarves, I am proud of all you have done in my absence. Now, with your help, and the help of others, we shall drive those foul demons back into the abyss and save our world once and for all!"

The dwarves erupted into cheers, their voices reverberating through the caverns. The noise drew more and more of them, excitement spreading like wildfire.

Keenan leaned toward Reeger and whispered, "Why have I been the one giving speeches? He should be doing them!"

Reeger chuckled. "Well, he does have two thousand more years of experience."

Keenan laughed. "Fair point."

I looked down at the king, who beamed with pride, staring up at me in awe.

Smiling, I said, "Now, my dear Tormund, if you would permit me to awaken my sister, I would be grateful."

Snapping out of his reverie, the king nodded. "Of course, Kisago," he said, turning to lead the way toward the hidden chambers deep within the mine.

I returned to my human form, which I had grown quite fond of, and followed him. Keenan walked beside me, grinning.

"You do the speeches now."

I laughed. "No, I prefer yours."

We both chuckled. Then Reeger interjected, "Kisago?"

I smiled. "That is a name I have not heard in a long time. Mother gave it to me."

"Ah," Reeger said. "Well, now I feel left out. You both have multiple names, and here I am with just one."

Keenan smirked. "Oh, I can think of a few for you."

Reeger laughed. "No thanks. I'm good without any of your suggestions."

We arrived at the chamber and stepped into the room where my sister lay frozen. I approached, gazing at her locked in ice.

"Ah, sister," I said with a chuckle. "I may regret this, but I suppose I should let you out."

Chapter 16 - Awake

Turning to the others, I instructed, "Everyone, stand back."

I shifted into my dragon form again, it was becoming easier now, though still draining. Facing my sister, I exhaled a deep breath, releasing a powerful blast to reverse the deep freeze she had been in.

There we go, I thought.

The ice melted quickly, revealing a dragon about half my size. Her scales ranged from deep crimson to molten red, as though forged in fire. They shimmered like embers, glowing faintly in the dim chamber. Her fiery orange eyes burned with intensity, radiating a piercing light. Curved, obsidian-like horns swept back from her head, and a jagged ridge of flaming spines ran down her neck and back.

Her wings were large and bat-like, their leathery membranes threaded with flickering veins of flame. When they were fully spread, they resembled a raging inferno. Her thick tail ended in a spiked club that looked capable of igniting on impact.

I smiled to myself. *I'm glad you didn't die.*

Her eyes fluttered open. She looked around, then locked onto me.

"Regret letting me out? Are you crazy?" she snapped, her voice sharp. "I've been stuck in there since your so-called saving me." She groaned and stretched, glaring. "Next time *you* get mortally wounded and frozen."

I shook my head. "Yep. You haven't changed a bit."

Shifting back to my human form, I watched her raise an eyebrow.

"Oh, okay. We're humans now?" she said, then transformed into a young woman.

Her human form had jet-black hair with a bright red streak, pale freckled skin, and faintly pulsing red veins that shimmered like molten lines beneath the surface. Her burning red eyes lit up when she got excited, glowing like hot embers. She crossed her arms and smirked.

"Well," she said, "are you going to introduce me, or should I just keep talking until I find someone willing to help me cause the most trouble?"

I sighed. "Everyone, meet my sister, Lily."

She gave a mischievous smile and a small wave. "Hello."

Keenan shook his head. "You both look so harmless right now."

Lily snorted. "Harmless?" Her grin widened. "I'll show you harmless."

She inhaled deeply, and I quickly stepped in. "Lily! Not here."

She paused, then smiled impishly. "You're always spoiling the fun." She punched me playfully in the shoulder. "You're worse than Mother."

I glanced at Keenan. "Now you understand how I managed to survive you growing up."

Keenan laughed. "I guess so."

Before he could say more, Lily zipped over and grabbed Keenan's arm, her eyes narrowing with curiosity.

"He always tells me who the troublemakers are without realizing it," she said, squinting at him. "So, you've switched sides? Team dwarf instead of demon?"

Keenan gave me a helpless look.

I grinned. "You know what, Keenan? She's your problem now."

Chapter 16 - Awake

"Hey, wait!" he called after me. "That's not funny!"

As I walked off, Reeger quickly walked past Keenan to catch up. "Hey, wait for me."

The king followed behind, shaking his head. "She is... not what I expected."

I laughed. "It's okay. You'll either grow to love her or want to kill her."

The king stiffened. "Kisago, I would never try to kill her!"

I smiled. "Oh yes, of course. My apologies."

He bowed solemnly, as if to reassure me of his sincerity. It made me smile.

Meanwhile, behind us, Keenan struggled to keep up as Lily bombarded him with questions, still latched onto his arm while he tried to drag her along.

"Hey! Wait for me!" he shouted, his voice echoing down the hall.

"So, what is he like when I'm not around?" Lily asked, eyes gleaming with curiosity.

Keenan glanced at me, mouthing silently, *Why me?*

Reeger and I laughed as we made our way back toward the king's chambers, Lily's endless stream of questions trailing behind us like smoke after fire.

When we arrived, the king was smiling and said. "The Hammer and Anvil back together at last!." Though clearly thrilled to have both of us back, his expression quickly turned grave.

"We're stretched thin," he began, "and now even more so. But I must ask for your help with two pressing matters, if I may."

I nodded for him to continue.

"We sent a patrol toward the northern peak of the mountain," he said, "but they haven't returned. Worse, the scouts we dispatched to investigate also vanished. We're certain something has gone wrong, but we can't afford to lose more men. Still, we can't allow the enemy to establish a foothold, if that's what this is."

He paused, then added, "I have no right to ask this of you. You should be commanding me, not the other way around. But would you consider investigating?"

I offered a reassuring smile. "Of course. We'll help."

Relief softened his features. I turned to Reeger and Keenan. "You two in?"

"Of course," they said in unison.

I glanced around, suddenly realizing Lily was no longer with us. A flicker of concern crossed my mind as I scanned the room.

"Lily?" I called out. The others joined me in the search.

A guard approached and bowed. "She's at the mural."

We quickly followed him. There, we found Lily in her dragon form. Her enormous paw rested gently on the image of our creator. She didn't turn as we approached.

"You know," she said quietly, "he died saving me."

Even whispered, her words carried a crushing weight. We stood in respectful silence.

"That's why…" she faltered, voice trembling, "…that's why I got reckless." She collapsed onto the stone floor. "It hurt so much to lose him."

She shifted back into her human form and walked slowly over to me. I wrapped an arm around her as she whispered, "I'm sorry, brother."

Chapter 16 - Awake

I smiled softly. "It's okay. I miss him too."

"No," she said, shaking her head. "I'm sorry for being reckless. You had to risk everything to save me... and you almost lost me anyway."

Tears streamed down her cheeks.

I gently lifted her chin. "Hey. That's what family is for."

She gave a faint smile. Then, realizing we were all watching, she quickly wiped her tears away and smirked.

"Just so we're clear, this time, we're going to kill them all."

We all smiled, nodding in agreement.

Lily took a deep breath and turned to me. "So, where to first, brother? I need to stretch my wings... and torch some demons." She glanced at Keenan and added with a wink, "But we'll keep this one around."

Keenan raised his eyebrows and looked at me. "Does she know I'm only half demon and also a paladin?"

I sighed, shaking my head. "Wouldn't matter if she did."

We laughed, the weight of the moment lifting just enough.

Then, together, we set out for the northern peak, unsure of what awaited us.

We carefully climbed the path the guard had shown us, following it as it wound around the mountain. Snow whipped through the air, driven by howling winds that slashed visibility down to fifteen, maybe twenty feet. We had to shout over the storm just to hear each other. As we navigated the craggy peaks and jagged rock formations, we moved cautiously, always aware of the sheer cliff face on our left.

The dwarf guide led the way, with Lily and me close behind. Keenan and Reeger brought up the rear.

As we rounded a sharp bend, the guide suddenly dropped to one knee and raised a hand for us to stop.

I looked over his shoulder and saw two dead dwarves lying in the middle of the path. Their bodies were battered, heads and shoulders crushed.

I shouted back to Keenan, "Be ready!"

Turning to the guide, I asked, "Could it have been a rockslide?"

He shook his head and yelled over the wind, "There'd be more signs, sir!"

"What's your name?" I asked, catching him off guard.

He hesitated. "Thuldur, sir."

"You seen combat before, Thuldur?"

"No, sir."

I gave him a reassuring smile. "If things go sideways, get behind me. Got it?"

He nodded firmly, and we pressed on.

As we passed the bodies, now partially buried under fresh snow, we spotted a flickering light ahead, coming from a cave cut into the hillside.

I pulled Thuldur close. "Go report to the king. We'll take it from here."

He nodded and hurried back down the path.

We moved toward the cave slowly, weapons drawn. At the entrance, we heard raised voices, deep, guttural, and sharp, speaking in a language none of us recognized.

Chapter 16 - Awake

Reeger gestured that he'd go in first to scout. Without a word, he slipped inside, leaving the rest of us waiting outside, tense and ready.

Ten long minutes passed before he returned.

"Well," he said, shaking his head, "you're not going to believe this, but I'm pretty sure it's frost giants."

"What?!" Keenan exclaimed. "I thought those were just myths."

Reeger shrugged. "So did I. But I've seen the drawings in the library. These match the descriptions perfectly."

Lily furrowed her brow. "How did they end up here? I don't remember Mother or either of the brothers creating them."

I shrugged. "Maybe the demons opened portals to other worlds and brought them in."

"But why?" Reeger asked.

"Good question," I said. "Maybe we should go ask them."

Lily cracked her knuckles with a grin. "Oh, good. Time to kick some frost giant butt."

"Slow down, Lil," I said. "Let's try to get information first."

Reeger leaned in. "I heard at least one dwarf deeper in the cave, but one of the giants was blocking the way. I couldn't get to them."

"Noted," I said. "Alright. Let's see if we can communicate first."

We stepped inside, out of the biting wind that whistled through the cave entrance and cautiously approached the flickering light ahead. Rounding a slight bend, the passage opened into a massive cavern.

Near its center, two towering frost giants sat around a fire, while a third, smaller, but still enormous, stood guard in front of a tunnel behind them.

The seated giants were easily ten to twelve feet tall; the smaller one stood around eight or ten. Their hulking frames were wrapped in heavy furs and pelts. Their pale blue, frostbitten skin looked cracked and weathered like ancient stone, and their eyes glowed faintly in the dim light. Each one gripped a massive iron hammer, brutal weapons that could easily have crushed the dwarves we found on the trail.

Keenan shook his head and muttered, "Well, what could go wrong?"

"Right," I replied dryly, stepping forward. "Hello!"

At the sound of my voice, both seated giants leapt to their feet, grabbing their hammers and scanning the cavern, searching for the source.

I raised my hands in a peaceful gesture. "We mean you no harm."

They glared suspiciously, shouting in that same harsh, guttural language, louder now, and anything but friendly.

"I don't understand you," I said, shaking my head. "Can you speak Common? Or Dwarven?"

The giants exchanged uncertain glances, but before they could answer, a voice called out from behind the smaller one.

"We've tried. No luck."

Reeger emerged from the shadows and attempted a few words in Elvish and another language I didn't recognize. The giants just looked more confused, and more agitated.

Chapter 16 - Awake

As the rest of us entered the cavern, their tension spiked. They raised their weapons again, shouting louder.

The smaller giant, a female, judging by her voice and build, yelled at the other two in their language, clearly arguing.

"Hey, Keenan," I asked, "did they teach you any languages at paladin camp?"

"It's not a camp," he muttered, rolling his eyes. "And yeah, I know some Infernal."

As Keenan stepped forward to speak, the giants reacted violently. They slammed their clubs on the ground and roared in rage. Even the female giant fell silent, her expression turning fearful.

Keenan barely got a word out before the two males charged.

I moved to shove him aside, but before they could reach us, both giants were suddenly flung backward like rag dolls.

Lily stood in her dragon form, smoke curling from her nostrils. She snorted a jet of fire at the ground in front of them. The giants scrambled back, pressing themselves against the cavern wall in terror. It was clear they had never seen a dragon before.

Letting out a thunderous roar, Lily froze them in place. They slumped to the ground, cowed and silent.

I sighed. "Thanks, Lil."

She shifted back to human form and smirked. "You're welcome. The shouting was getting annoying anyway."

I chuckled. "You violent little psycho."

She laughed and turned toward the tunnel. "Come on out, whoever's back there!"

Hammer and Anvil

Three dwarves cautiously emerged from the shadows, their expressions a mix of awe and confusion. The leader stepped forward, eyes wide.

"What... what roared like that?"

I smiled. "We'll explain later. The king sent us to find out what happened here."

The dwarf gave a nod. "I'm Tholdrun, lead scout and siege engineer."

I introduced our party, and Tholdrun squinted at me. "Ah, yes. I remember you arriving a few days ago, though I was out at the time."

He continued, "We were patrolling the ridge, doing a routine sweep to make sure nothing dangerous had moved in, predators, scouts, anything. That's when a portal opened behind us, and those giants came charging out, swinging their weapons. We lost three instantly and had to retreat into the caves."

"We only found two bodies," Keenan noted.

Tholdrun's expression darkened. "Yes. Sadly, the third was thrown off the cliff."

He went on, "We tried to communicate, but they just shouted back. Eventually, the female stepped in and stopped the other two from finishing us off. She seems to have some authority over them, but we didn't know how long that would last. We've been holed up in here since last night."

"Have you seen the other scouting party?" I asked.

Tholdrun shook his head. "No. Not a sign of them."

"Great," Keenan muttered. "Another missing patrol."

I sighed. "Wonderful. So, what now?"

Chapter 16 - Awake

Tholdrun shrugged. "Unless you know someone who speaks their language, talking's a dead end."

Reeger glanced at Keenan and me with a mischievous grin. "We could call you-know-who."

I laughed. "Yeah, but you remember what he said last time about summoning him unnecessarily?"

"Wait... who?" Lily asked.

"A gnome named Reggie," Keenan answered before we could stop him.

Reeger and I groaned.

Too late.

A portal shimmered open behind us, and a short, irritated figure stepped through, wild hair, scowl, arms crossed.

"You better be dying," the gnome snapped, glaring.

Keenan mouthed *sorry* in my direction.

"Hey, Reggie," I greeted sheepishly.

He squinted at me. "You don't look like you're dying. In fact, you look annoyingly alive."

Reggie scanned the cavern, unimpressed, until he turned around.

His eyes widened. "Frost giants?!" he shouted. "How in the blazes did you capture frost giants?!"

Chapter 17 - Misfits

"Reggie," I called, but he was lost in his own world.

"Would you look at that," he murmured, almost to himself. "I've always heard they were myths, but here they are. But how? We don't..."

"Reggie!" I said louder, but he kept rambling. "Perhaps if they..."

Before I could finish, Lily strode over, picked him up like a child, and gave him a good shake. That snapped him out of it.

"My brother is trying to talk to you," she said sharply setting him down.

Looking thoroughly disgruntled, Reggie turned to me. "That was rude," he muttered.

I chuckled. "We need to communicate with them. Can you help?"

"Yes, yes, let me try," he grumbled, throwing a glare at Lily before stepping forward.

He began speaking in a strange language. No response. He tried two more. Still nothing, just blank stares and a couple of shrugs.

Finally, Reggie threw up his hands. "Well, they don't know many languages. Wait!" He held up a finger, then vanished in a blink.

"Wait... where did he go?" Lily asked, walking to the spot he'd just been.

Keenan shrugged. "Yeah, he does that sometimes."

Chapter 17 - Misfits

"Is he coming back?"

"I hope so. But with him? Who knows."

I was about to suggest a backup plan when Reggie popped back into existence, holding up a strange stone tablet.

"Sorry, took me a while to find it," he said.

"You were only gone for..." I started.

"Yes, yes," he cut me off, glaring again at Lily. He stepped over to the giants, scribbled something on the tablet, and handed it to them. The two males passed it to the female, who studied it, then scribbled something in return.

Reggie read it, nodded, then handed the tablet to us. "Some old mage made this translator pad. Always thought it was junk."

"Well, it's useful now," I said.

Reggie scoffed. "No, it's still mostly useless. But I want it back when you're done." With another glare at Lily, he vanished again.

Keenan took the tablet from me and grinned. "How hard can it be?" He walked toward the giants.

Thirty minutes later, the only thing we'd learned was that they were a family.

Reeger, laughing, took the tablet from a very frustrated Keenan and started writing himself.

Keenan returned and muttered, "They don't teach this in diplomacy."

I laughed. "Oh, you mean first contact with creatures from another world?"

He grinned. "When you put it that way, I feel a little better."

Ten minutes later, Reeger returned with more progress.

"They say they were pulled from their world and forced to fight in some realm of rock and fire. Eventually, they escaped, or were sent, here. They warn us to be cautious of the red one." He pointed at Keenan. "Apparently, he resembles their captors. That's why they attacked."

He continued, "It's a father, his son, and the son's mate or wife, translation isn't exact. She's the only one who can read or write. The father says he'll fight for the 'big one.'" He nodded toward Lily. "They seem to value strength above all else. They hate the demons, so they could help us. But for now, they're content to stay here and fight for her."

I glanced at Keenan. "I don't think the dwarves will tolerate them on the mountain. Not after they killed three of their men."

"That's right we won't," Tholdrun growled from behind us.

"So, what do we do with them?" Lily asked. "I wouldn't mind them as bodyguards."

I rolled my eyes. "Lily, that's a terrible idea."

She just smiled. "Okay, bro. Whatever you say."

Reeger looked thoughtful. "What if we put them in the cave with the troll?"

"You mean Frank?" Keenan asked.

"Yeah. They mentioned losing their tribe. Maybe they could start a new one, with Frank."

Keenan laughed. "Quite the group of outcasts we're assembling."

I nodded. "It could work. It's either a great idea or a terrible one... and I don't have a better idea."

"Then it's settled for now," Reeger said. "Assuming they don't kill each other."

Chapter 17 - Misfits

We decided to take the old path down the mountain to avoid leading the giants through the dwarven city. The other dwarves had already departed to report to the king, and with the storm finally easing enough to see clearly, we began our descent.

By the time we reached the river that led to Grissom, Keenan turned to me.

"Why haven't we learned how to teleport from Reg... I mean, the gnome."

I laughed. "Great question. You can ask him next time."

"Ugh," Keenan groaned. "All this walking is killing me."

Reeger smirked. "Gotta keep our paladin in shape."

Keenan shook his head. "We really need to get those horses back."

"Wait," Lily said suddenly. "You guys have horses? I used to love horses! They go great with bread, butter, and cheese."

Reeger and Keenan froze, staring at her in horror, until she burst out laughing.

"Oh, the looks on your faces!" she said, doubled over.

I chuckled as they glanced at me for reassurance. "Don't worry. She doesn't eat horses."

Lily leaned in close to them, her voice low and playful. "But in dragon form, I do sometimes eat humans."

"Lil, leave them alone!" I called out as she skipped over to me, still snickering.

"Sup, bro?" she said with a grin.

"You're hilarious, you little turd," I muttered, shaking my head.

She laughed, and we continued walking. Behind us, Keenan and Reeger exchanged uneasy glances.

It was well after dark by the time we arrived at the cave. We guided the frost giants through the entrance, making our way toward Frank's area.

"Wait," Keenan said, stopping suddenly. "We never got their names."

"Whose names?" Lily asked.

"The giants'," he replied.

"Oh, right," Reeger said. "Their names are Thraegar, Kaelrik, and Sylvara."

Each time he said a name, the corresponding giant perked up and glanced our way. They grumbled to each other in their own language, crouching to navigate the narrower tunnel sections.

Eventually, we reached the fork in the tunnel, where Frank stood up.

"Friends!" he called, his crooked-toothed grin lighting up his face. "I miss you! Philip tells me what you did and how strong you are."

The frost giants began speaking rapidly and pointing at Frank.

Frank frowned nervously. "These new friends? They... big." He eyed them cautiously. "They'd be hard to bonk," he muttered, gripping his club a little tighter.

"We hope they're friends," Keenan said. "But keep an eye on them, Frank."

"Well... okay," Frank said slowly. "But they think I stronger than you guys, and I don't think that's true."

"Wait, what?" Keenan blinked.

Frank shrugged. "They speak Giant."

Chapter 17 - Misfits

"You understand them?" I asked, surprised.

"Yes!" Frank puffed out his chest. "I grew up with giants in the bad place."

"These giants?" I asked.

"No. Stone giants."

Reeger sighed. "I can't tell if we're the luckiest or unluckiest group in the world."

"Duh," Lily said, grinning. "Obviously the luckiest. I'm here."

We just shook our heads as Frank eagerly introduced himself to the frost giants. They seemed thrilled to finally communicate with someone directly.

We continued into the living quarters, where Philip was organizing supplies while a handful of kids ran about. He looked up and started to say, "Don't worry, boss, I've..."

Then the frost giants entered.

Philip's eyes went wide, and his jaw dropped. "How...?" he managed, staring in disbelief. The kids froze mid-step, eyes locked on the towering newcomers.

Frank beamed. "Philip! They brought us more friends! He the best!" He slapped Keenan on the shoulder, nearly knocking him over.

Keenan grumbled, "You get to be a dragon, and I get a troll."

I chuckled.

Lily smirked. "I got frost giants."

"Not helping," I said, shaking my head.

"They are my bodyguards," she added, still smirking.

Reeger grinned. "I'm fine with nothing, thanks."

We all laughed, despite ourselves, as the frost giants settled in and Philip slowly returned to his work, still shaking his head in disbelief.

We left and headed back into town, agreeing to tell my uncles the truth first thing in the morning.

After a night's rest, we woke up early and gathered at the inn. Grog grumbled about needing to be in the kitchen, but eventually, we got everyone seated around a table. Reeger and Keenan were grinning like idiots, while I was a bundle of nerves.

My uncles looked curious, their expressions expectant as they waited for the "important news."

I took a deep breath and began. "You know you'll always be my uncles, no matter what happens, right?"

Grog squinted at me. "Have you been drinking, boy?" he asked gruffly.

Surprisingly, that made me laugh. "No, Uncle."

He muttered something about "too much emotion," but I pressed on. "I don't want our relationship to change based on what I'm about to tell you."

Grog narrowed his eyes. "What is this? Are you turning into an elf or something?"

Reeger shot him a look, and Grog mumbled an apology. Reeger chuckled, but Throm smacked Grog on the back of the head.

"Shut up and let the boy finish," Throm said.

Grog rubbed his head but stayed quiet.

I took another breath, but for the first time I could remember, I had no idea what to say. I just stared at them, frozen.

Chapter 17 - Misfits

Grog muttered, "Ah, great. His brain's stopped working. He'll start drooling now."

Throm smacked him again.

I glanced at Keenan, silently begging for help.

He smiled and said, "As much as I'm enjoying this, it's time to rip the bandage off." He turned to the three dwarves and added simply, "Halvar is the Anvil."

The dwarves blinked, confused.

Gam asked, "He has an anvil?"

Grog laughed. "Is that all? Throm's got one too!"

Reeger, still chuckling, clarified, "No, Halvar is the dragon. You know, the one on the mural."

The room fell silent. The dwarves' expressions shifted from amusement to something much more serious.

"If that's a joke," Throm said slowly, "or an attempt at being funny... we don't think it is."

I finally found my voice. "It's true."

Grog squinted at me. "Have you been into the southern spices? Or that western tobacco? That stuff will take you on a trip."

"No," I said firmly. "I am Kisago."

Their eyes widened. Gam was the first to speak.

"How do you know that name?"

"Because it's mine," I replied.

"But it can't be," Throm muttered.

At that moment, Lily walked in. "So, did you tell them? How'd it go?"

The dwarves spun to face her, then back to me, completely bewildered.

I gave a faint smile. "This is Lily. I unfroze her yesterday."

Throm stood and began pacing. He stopped and stared hard at me. "We raised you from a child. Kisago is over 2,000 years old."

"Ahhh," Lily said, plopping into a chair. "We're in the denial phase," she added with a smile.

"Lily, knock it off," I said.

"Well," she grinned, "I told you, just go outside and change. Then we can get through all the phases quickly." She glanced at the dwarves. "Although, I can see why you're enjoying this."

"I'm not enjoying this," I said, shaking my head. "I just didn't want to shock them too much."

She picked up one of our drinks and swirled it in the glass. "Oh yeah, this is going so much better," she said sarcastically, then laughed and took a sip. Her eyes lit up.

"Hey, this is actually pretty good." After finishing the glass, she sighed contentedly. "Ahhh. I haven't had dwarven mead this good in at least 2,000 years."

She glanced at the dwarves, clearly enjoying their stunned silence.

"They've all cracked," Grog muttered. He grabbed his empty tankard and stared into it. "What did I put in here?"

Keenan smiled. "This is going well, don't you think?"

I shot him a glare, but he just laughed.

"Alright, everyone," he said. "Outside. Time for a show."

We stepped outside and glanced around. It was still early, and the streets were quiet, with only a few townsfolk milling about.

Taking a deep breath, I said, "Alright, here we go," and transformed into my dragon form.

Chapter 17 - Misfits

Gam and Throm immediately dropped to one knee, heads bowed in reverence. Grog, still clutching his tankard, let it fall to the ground with a dull thud. He shook his head in disbelief and muttered, "But we raised you from a child..."

I was about to respond when a scream pierced the air. A woman stood frozen, pointing at me in horror before bolting down the street, shrieking.

I quickly shifted back to my human form.

Keenan burst out laughing. "I can't believe you just did that, right here!"

Reeger shook his head, clearly exasperated. "Yeah, I would've at least gone to a warehouse or something."

Moments later, several guards came rushing over, weapons drawn. Jefferies was with them, his expression stern.

"Where is the creature?" he demanded, scanning the area.

Gam stepped forward, raising a calming hand. "Sorry, lad. We're testing an illusion spell for the upcoming conflict. Didn't mean to alarm anyone."

Jefferies looked skeptical, eyes narrowing, then he relaxed and chuckled. "Alright, Gam. But you really scared Betty. She ran off screaming. You might want to apologize to her."

"Of course, of course," Gam replied with a quick nod. "I'll take care of it."

As Jefferies and the guards moved off, the dwarves crowded around me, peppering me with questions.

Lily sauntered over with a smirk. "You know I'm just as cool as he is, right? Probably even cooler, and better looking, in my dragon and human form."

"Lil, not here," I said firmly.

Too late. With a mischievous grin, she transformed into her dragon form and let out a deafening roar.

The town exploded into chaos. Shouts and scrambling footsteps echoed through the streets.

Lily shifted back, laughing. "See?" she said, smiling.

"Lil, sometimes I wonder what the Eldest was thinking when he created you," I muttered, shaking my head.

She grinned. "You'd be lost and bored without me." Then she strolled back into the inn, leaving us behind to hear Jefferies down the next street, desperately trying to calm the townsfolk.

"It was an illusion!" he called out, clearly struggling to convince the panicked crowd.

We all shook our heads, grinning at the poor guard's plight, and headed back inside.

Back at the table, the dwarves, now buzzing with excitement, immediately resumed their questioning.

"So, it was you that froze the big one?" Throm asked eagerly.

I smiled. "Yes, although I don't really remember doing it. Must've been some kind of defense mechanism."

Throm nodded thoughtfully. "Then the king must know by now, especially with your sister awake."

I nodded. "He knows."

"Excellent!" Throm beamed. "This is great news."

Gam leaned in, curious. "So... when did you find out?"

Chapter 17 - Misfits

We recounted the events of the last couple of days, explaining everything that had happened. My uncles listened intently, hanging on every word.

When I finally finished, Throm stood and bowed low.

"It was an honor to have you in our care," he said solemnly. "To keep you safe during your recovery. I hope we've honored you with our actions. If you ever need anything, just ask."

I sighed, rubbing the back of my neck. "See, this is exactly what I was worried about. I want our relationship to stay the same."

Gam interjected gently. "But Kis... Halvar... you must understand, for us, this changes everything. As much as we might wish it didn't, we've waited for this moment our entire lives."

Keenan chuckled. "You've got an entire race of loyal dwarves at your beck and call." He smirked. "And I've got Frank."

Reeger laughed, while Grog grumbled, "Well, I don't care who you are. You'll always be a little pot-licker to me. This changes nothing... except maybe you'll give me more of a fight when we train."

That made me laugh, easing the tension in the room.

Throm leaned forward with a smile. "We'll try to keep things the same as much as we can. But in front of other dwarves, we'll have to act a little differently."

I nodded, smiling warmly. "That's all I ask. You're my family. I wouldn't change that for anything."

Throm and Gam beamed with pride. Grog, true to form, just huffed and muttered under his breath, but I could tell he was proud too.

We all shared a laugh, each of us grateful in our own way. Lily rolled her eyes and shook her head, clearly amused but pretending not to care.

Suddenly, the door to the inn burst open with a loud bang.

A strong, young woman with bright red hair strode in, dressed in worn leather armor with two battle axes hanging at her sides. Her piercing gaze swept across the room, fury burning in her eyes.

"Alright," she growled, her voice echoing through the inn, "where is the Noctari?"

Chapter 18 - The Sea

Her gaze fell on Keenan, and she stormed over, eyes locked on him.

"Well?" she demanded, fire burning in her stare.

I chuckled, leaning back, curious to see how this would play out. Lily leaned in and whispered, "I don't know what he did, but I like her."

I smiled at Lily as the woman's glare flicked briefly to us before snapping back to Keenan.

Keenan, clearly confused, hesitated. "What do you mean?"

"Oh, you know exactly what I mean," she shot back, slamming her fist on the table. Her stare looked hot enough to set him ablaze.

Keenan turned to me with a helpless shrug. "I really don't."

Then it hit me. "Wait," I said aloud. "You were the girl on the boat!"

Her eyes flashed as she turned her glare on me. "Do I look like a girl to you?"

"Woman! Sorry," I corrected quickly.

She snorted and turned back to Keenan.

Keenan spoke carefully. "Well, we saved your life."

She nodded. "And?"

"And we brought you to the healers," he added.

"And?" she pressed, arms crossed, voice sharp.

Keenan threw up his hands, glancing at me in bewilderment.

"You paid for my healing," she continued, "and told them you'd cover any future costs."

Keenan shrugged. "I was just trying to help."

"Oh really?" she scoffed. "Well, where I come from, there are only three reasons someone would pay for everything: they're family, they're claiming an indentured servant, or…" She paused, fixing him with a sharp look. "They're declaring an intention to marry."

I turned to Keenan, who looked like he was about to combust from sheer embarrassment.

"That's not what I… I mean, I was just…" He stammered, flustered. "I don't want… I mean, you seem nice, but…"

I glanced at Lily, who was struggling to keep a straight face. I couldn't hold it in anymore and burst out laughing. She quickly joined me. Even my uncles started to smile.

When the laughter finally died down, the woman had relaxed a little, a small smile cracking through her irritation.

"So, you're not trying to marry me, then?" she asked, raising an eyebrow. "Or make me your servant?"

"No!" Keenan said quickly. "I'm sorry, I didn't realize that's how things worked in your culture. I was only trying to help."

She huffed. "Well, good. Because I plan to return to my island and see if anyone survived. I can't be indebted to a stranger."

Keenan offered a reassuring smile. "It was a gift. As a Paladin, it's my duty to help those in need."

Chapter 18 - The Sea

She crossed her arms. "Hmph. Well, I'll find a way to pay you back."

I leaned toward Keenan and whispered, "If she finds survivors, or anyone who can help, she could bring them here. Help defend the town."

He nodded and turned back to her. "Once you know what's left of your people, you're welcome to return, if you're willing to fight alongside us."

She laughed. "That's the first thing you've said that makes sense. But first, my people."

I glanced at Lily, who was grinning. She caught my eye and said, "Yep. I like her."

I just shook my head.

She sighed. "Well, now that that's taken care of... which way is the dock?" she asked with a smile. "I need to find a ship to take me north."

I smiled back. "We were just finishing up. We can take you there."

With that, we all stood and made our way outside, heading down to the docks.

When we arrived, Gam spoke up. "We don't have many ships running north, especially with winter setting in soon."

"Yes, I was hoping you might know someone who could take me," she replied.

As we discussed it, our eyes fell on the gleaming white sails of the ship we had saved and cleansed. A thought struck me.

"Wait, could she take you?" I asked, pointing toward the ship.

Throm shrugged. "It's possible. But we'd have to ask her."

We approached, and a man standing on the deck leaned over the railing with a smile.

"Ahoy! How can *The Lady in White* help you?"

Keenan frowned. "*The Lady in White?*"

The man nodded. "That's what she has decided to call herself, or rather, what the ship will be named."

Gam, curious, asked, "And who are you?"

The man hesitated, glancing down thoughtfully before responding, "I am what remains, but I am new. I help make the ship appear more..." He paused, then continued, "human."

At that moment, the glowing female spirit of the ship appeared beside him.

"They are an extension of me," she explained. "They create the illusion that this is, in fact, a real ship, and not just a possessed vessel with no crew."

Throm chuckled. "That's clever."

Grog huffed. "Why am I even here?" he muttered, turning and heading back toward the inn.

I chuckled, then turned back to the spirit. "We have a favor to ask."

She nodded, listening quietly.

"Can you take this woman back to her island, to see if there are any survivors?"

The spirit's expression softened. "Of course. You saved me, and I want to help this world in any way I can, so that what happened to mine won't happen here."

I nodded. "Thank you."

Chapter 18 - The Sea

She smiled at me. "I see you've begun to understand why you are different. That is good. Evil will be drawn to your energy and knowing who you truly are will help you."

Then she turned to the red-haired woman. "What is your name?"

The woman straightened slightly. "My name is Yrsa." She gave a small bow of her head, and I suddenly realized none of us had asked her name before. I shook my head over the oversight.

The Lady in White nodded. "Please, come aboard. We are ready to depart whenever you are."

Yrsa turned back to us, a determined glint in her eyes. "I will return, if it is meant to be, and help you drive those wretched creatures off this world and back to whatever disgusting cave they crawled out of."

She reached out, shaking our hands one by one, then boarded the ship.

With almost effortless grace, the vessel slipped from the harbor. Yrsa waved goodbye, and we waved back, turning toward the city as the white sails vanished beyond the breakwater.

Just as we were about to leave the docks, Throm stopped and looked at Keenan. We all paused, waiting.

"Have you heard from the school?" he asked.

Keenan smacked his forehead. "No," he groaned. "I hadn't even thought about it."

"We need to warn them," Throm said, his voice low and urgent.

"Okay," Keenan replied. "I guess we should talk to the fisherman."

"Agreed," Throm nodded.

We made our way to the far end of the docks, where the fishermen moored their boats. A small building stood nearby, cluttered with nets, hooks, and the briny scent of seawater. Inside, an old man sat behind a desk, absently threading a lure with a hook that looked older than the desk itself.

"Good morning, Mackey," Throm greeted.

Without looking up, the old man replied, "Throm. Good to see you. What brings you to our side of the tide?"

"We need to charter passage," Throm said.

Mackey finally looked up, eyes sharp despite his age. "Why us? There are other boats," he said, glancing at Keenan, who nodded politely.

"You know where we need to go," Throm said. "And only a few can get us there."

A slow smile crept across Mackey's weathered face. "Tomorrow at sunrise. Be here, and we'll take you." Then he returned to his lure, saying no more.

Outside, Lily turned to Throm. "What was all that about?"

He smiled. "Not everyone can just go to the Isle of Light."

She rolled her eyes. "I was never good at cloak-and-dagger stuff," she muttered. "I'd rather just punch them in the face." She threw a mock jab at the air.

I laughed. "Careful, Lil. You might hurt yourself."

She shot me a glare. "See if I help you next time you're in trouble."

We all laughed.

After a few more words, we split up. Keenan went with Throm to settle things with the healers and check his

Chapter 18 - The Sea

weapons. Gam had a council meeting. Reeger headed to the cave to check on Frank and the frost giants. Lily promised not to start trouble and vanished into the crowd, already exploring.

I returned to my uncles' house, wrote letters to each of them, sealed them, and placed them on their pillows. Then I sat in silence, reflecting on everything, Keenan's return, the king and his family, the ship and Yrsa, the Order of Light, the demons. I had regained most of my memories. And once again, I was helping the dwarves prepare for war.

I fell asleep quickly and woke early. Throm and Grog were already up; Gam had left before dawn. We gathered our gear in silence.

"Where's Lil?" I asked.

Throm smiled. "Already down at the dock. She's been pacing since sunrise."

I shook my head, laughing. "She can't sit still."

We made our way down to the harbor, meeting Reeger and Keenan along the way. The horizon glowed with the first light of day, soft gold spilling over the edge of the sea. The sky was a breathtaking blend of orange, rose, and lavender. Wisps of cloud drifted overhead, tinged with fire.

The stillness of dawn was broken only by the creak of wood, the rustle of gear, and the distant calls of waking birds. The shimmering reflection of sunrise danced across the water, rippling gently in the breeze.

I paused, letting the moment settle. The salty tang of the sea filled the air, mingling with the scent of fish, damp rope, and sun-warmed wood. A briny trace of drying seaweed clung to the breeze, carrying the essence of the harbor.

Around me, the docks stirred. Seagulls cried overhead. Fishermen mended nets. Metal clanked against wood. Ropes groaned as boats swayed with the tide. Footsteps echoed across the planks. The murmur of waves provided a constant, soothing rhythm.

Then, *smack*, a sharp thud to the back of my head.

"No time for daydreaming, doofus. We gotta go save the world... again," Lily's voice teased.

I opened my eyes to see her standing with her hands on her hips, giving me that look, the one that always made me smile.

"Alright, you little brat," I said, grinning. "Let's go."

Together, we walked over to where the rest of our party was speaking with a middle-aged fisherman.

Throm gestured to the man. "This is Ramus."

Ramus stood with the quiet confidence of a man who'd weathered a lifetime at sea. His posture was relaxed yet grounded, like someone who'd grown roots in the deck of a ship. His sun-worn skin was tanned and rough, his face etched with deep lines carved by wind and salt. A neatly trimmed salt-and-pepper beard framed his weathered features, though his hair was wild and windblown. His hands, thick-fingered and calloused, bore the unmistakable marks of decades spent hauling nets and steering vessels through unpredictable waters.

He wore faded brown pants crusted with salt and flecked with fish scales, a thick wool sweater, and boots caked with sand and sea spray. His sharp brown eyes scanned the harbor constantly, reading the mood of the sea like a book. When he spoke, his gravelly voice carried quiet authority.

Chapter 18 - The Sea

He looked us over as we approached. "So, five of you then?"

"Yes," Throm said. "And we're ready to leave immediately."

Ramus gave a curt nod, then gestured subtly toward a larger ship farther out in the harbor. "Keep an eye on that one," he said lowly. "They've been known to run with pirates."

Without another word, he led us down the pier to a modest fishing vessel, where a dozen crew members moved in efficient coordination. Final preparations were underway as we stepped aboard, entering the ordered chaos of sailors shouting commands, tightening ropes, and loading gear.

Thick mooring lines groaned as they were loosened from the posts. The furled sails rustled as the wind tugged at them impatiently. The deck creaked under steady footsteps, while from below came the rhythmic thump of barrels and crates being secured in the hold.

As the tide nudged us free, a final order rang out and the sails were loosed. They snapped open, catching the breeze and propelling us forward. The dock receded behind us, shrinking with every passing second as we glided into open waters. The prow of the vessel sliced cleanly through the waves, sending up white spray on either side.

I smiled and glanced at Keenan. "I've always loved how a crew moves as one, how they all work with the wind together."

Keenan groaned softly, eyes fixed on the horizon. "I prefer solid ground," he muttered. "Last time I was on a boat... I got seasick."

We kept an eye on the ship Ramus had pointed out, noting how they watched our departure but made no move to follow. Satisfied, we turned our attention back to the journey ahead.

For a couple of hours, the voyage was calm. The ship creaked and swayed as we moved about the deck, asking the sailors questions and watching them work.

Eventually, the captain summoned us aft. He wore a faint smile as he gestured us closer.

"Who here has been to the Isle of Light before, besides the two paladins?"

Reeger, Lily, and I shook our heads. The captain's grin widened.

"Then you're in for a treat."

He opened a small wooden box beside the ship's wheel and held up a glowing orange device. It pulsed softly in his hand.

Lily leaned in toward me. "Hey... can I have one of those?"

I shushed her, too intrigued to answer. The device began emitting a series of energy pulses. Suddenly, glowing bubbles formed around the ship, drifting upward like paper lanterns in the wind. As we continued forward, the ship abruptly shuddered, like it had struck something solid, though it never slowed.

A deep vibration rippled through the hull as we pushed through an invisible barrier. Then, just as suddenly, we burst through. The sensation was like breaking the surface of water into open air.

The captain tucked the device back into its box and gave us a knowing smile.

Chapter 18 - The Sea

"Welcome to the Isle of Light."

We all looked up, gasping in awe.

Before us stood a castle perched atop a rugged island, rising like a monument to what we could accomplish when we all worked together instead of fighting. It loomed with commanding presence, its walls crafted from pristine white stone that shimmered in the sunlight. The structure rose majestically, its soaring towers piercing the sky like blades of light. The stone glowed faintly, as though infused with energy drawn from the island itself, alive, vibrant, and ancient.

At the heart of the castle, a beacon of radiant light surged into the heavens, an ethereal column cutting through the clouds and stretching endlessly skyward. The light pulsed with quiet power, a rhythm like a heartbeat, visible for miles, if not for the protective barrier that cloaked this place.

To the side, a small, weathered pier jutted from the rocky shoreline, its wooden planks worn smooth by time and the sea. The distant roar of waves crashing against the cliffs echoed through the air.

"Well, that's a pretty sight," Reeger said, a smile tugging at his lips.

"Agreed," I replied, unable to take my eyes off the castle.

Lily gave a short snort. "You know this place has to have secret passages," she said, eyes narrowing with excitement. "And I'm going to find them."

Throm only shook his head, getting used to her by now, while Keenan grinned. "Lily, I'm glad I didn't meet you until after my paladin training. You'd have gotten me in so much trouble."

Lily smiled mischievously.

I laughed, already picturing the chaos they would've caused together.

Ramus steered the ship gently up to the dock, then turned to Throm. "Should we return tonight or in the morning?"

Throm considered it. "Better tonight. Too many eyes watching around the harbor, we don't want to draw attention."

Ramus nodded. "We'll fish offshore for a while, then tie up and wait. Try to be back a few hours before dusk if you can."

With that, we disembarked as the crew moved out a little way and cast their nets into the water.

We turned to face the winding path that led from the pier up to the towering castle. My heart stirred as I took it all in. I had always dreamed of seeing the Isle of Light, and now I stood on the island, looking up at its gates.

Throm took the lead, followed by Keenan and Lily, with Reeger and me trailing behind. The climb was long, the stone steps carved into the island's slope winding higher and higher until we reached the massive castle doors.

Throm stepped forward and called out, his voice firm. "Gatekeeper! I am Throm, here with Keenan and companions. We bring news for the Master and the teachers, news that cannot wait."

A moment passed.

Chapter 18 - The Sea

Then, with a deep, echoing groan, the massive doors began to creak open.

Chapter 19 - Bad News

We waited as the massive gate creaked open, inch by inch, before grinding to a halt. From behind it, an old man emerged, silent as stone, and waved us in.

Surprised, I glanced at Keenan. He looked just as stunned. Throm muttered something under his breath, but we couldn't make it out as we stepped into the wide courtyard.

Training equipment lay scattered across the space, abandoned mid-use. A long table stood off to one side. Several doors led to other wings of the castle, but the eerie silence wrapped around us like a shroud as we crossed the open ground.

"Excuse me... where is everyone?" Keenan asked hesitantly.

The old man turned to look at him. A single tear welled in his eye and slid down his cheek. Without a word, he turned and continued toward a door on the far side of the courtyard, leaving it open behind him.

Throm had already drawn his weapon. "We're heading toward the barracks and then the keep," he murmured. "Something's not right."

Apart from the faint whistle of wind and the fluttering of torn banners, the castle was deathly quiet.

The old man led us through a doorway into a dimly lit hallway. Bedrooms lined both sides, but the sight that met us made our stomachs turn.

Chapter 19 - Bad News

Broken doors hung from their hinges. Shattered furniture lay strewn across the stone floor. Tattered remnants of once-elegant tapestries clung to the walls. Weapons and armor lay abandoned and damaged, silent witnesses to a violent struggle. Flickering torchlight cast long, warped shadows, deepening the sense of despair. Dust hung thick in the air. Whatever grandeur this place once held was buried under layers of ruin.

Pale light filtered through narrow slits in the walls, casting a ghostly glow over the wreckage. The old man shuffled through it all, leading us to the final doorway.

As we passed a room on the right, Keenan paused. His eyes glistened. "This was my room," he whispered.

He looked up at me, sorrow etched across his face. I placed a hand on his shoulder, unsure what to say.

Throm stood near another room, staring silently into the dark. I could only guess it had been his.

Keenan clenched his jaw, tightened his grip on his sword, and pressed on.

The old man pushed aside a broken door, revealing a large common room with long tables and a podium, once used for speeches, lessons, and rites of passage.

Signs of battle were everywhere. Tables hacked to splinters. Chairs overturned and shattered. The air felt heavy, like the room itself remembered.

At the far end sat another old man in a large chair, cradling a helm in his hands.

He sat in silence, unmoving.

Throm and Keenan quickly approached. Throm knelt beside him, trying to meet his gaze, while Keenan stood silently at his side, waiting.

The guide who had brought us quietly vanished into thin air.

At last, the man in the chair spoke, his voice barely more than a whisper.

"The poor boys never had a chance," he said, placing a trembling hand on the helm. "They came in and killed the trainers first. Then they subdued the boys... beat them with clubs and staffs."

His eyes lifted, unfocused, as if staring through us. "Then they opened portals and took whoever survived. I tried to stop them," he continued, his body beginning to shake. "But they broke me... my frail body was no match."

I stiffened, startled by his words, and glanced at Keenan. He turned toward Throm, whose expression darkened as he slowly rose to his feet.

"The old man lowered his gaze. "I tried to save them," he whispered. "But they were taken... and they will be..." He trailed off into silence.

Throm exhaled grimly. "This old man is an illusion, a final message for any paladin who might return."

Keenan turned away and let out a frustrated yell, his grief and rage echoing through the ruined hall.

"This was Eldrin," Throm said quietly. "He was the master here for decades. A good man. He was close to retirement, I think."

We turned back to the flickering image. Eldrin sighed.

"I can't hold on much longer, but...but..." His image glitched, jittering with each word. "I have failed them...I have failed them...I have failed them..."

Throm raised a hand and dispelled the magic. The illusion vanished.

Chapter 19 - Bad News

He bowed his head. "May your spirit find peace, Master Eldrin. Teacher of many great paladins."

Merek let out a weary sigh. "He was one of the last I truly enjoyed speaking with." He paused, then added more softly, "I'm tired of watching friends die while I'm left to carry on. One day, I'll finally join my brothers in peace, without any more death."

We all stood in silence.

Then Keenan turned to Throm. "We need to check the armory."

Throm nodded. "There may still be gear left that could be important."

We followed them quickly to the armory, only to find the metal door torn from its hinges and the room completely empty.

"There were weapons here that could be devastating in the wrong hands," Keenan muttered, staring at the bare walls and shelves.

Throm exhaled. "Yes. But there's nothing we can do now, except hope they didn't get them."

Then his eyes narrowed. "The light is still emitting."

Keenan's eyes widened. "Maybe she survived."

Throm nodded and led us down a narrow corridor. We stopped in front of a door sealed with magic. He muttered an incantation, and the seal dissolved. As the door creaked open, he turned to us.

"We'll just be a moment," he said, stepping inside with Keenan.

Reeger muttered something about checking on something and wandered off, leaving me alone with Lily.

She had been unusually quiet. When she finally spoke, her voice was soft, almost fragile.

"Brother?"

I turned to her. "Yeah?"

"This time... we kill them all. So this never happens to anyone else again."

Tears streamed down her freckled cheeks. "Even if I have to die... I don't ever want to see something like this ever again."

I stepped forward and wrapped her in a hug. "Hey," I whispered. "It's going to be okay."

She wiped her face and looked up at me, managing a small, grateful smile. "Thanks, bro." Then, pushing me away, she added, "If you tell anyone about this, I'll beat you up."

I chuckled. "Don't worry. Your secret's safe with me."

Just then, Keenan stepped out of the room. "What secret?" he asked, raising an eyebrow.

I glanced at Lily, who shot me a warning glare and shook her head slightly.

I smirked. "Lily farted."

She sighed. "Yep. That's actually much worse."

I laughed, until Throm stepped out, his expression grim.

"She's alive," he said. "But she's asking to see Lily."

"Me?" Lily blinked in surprise.

Throm nodded.

She shrugged. "Alright," and disappeared into the room.

I turned to Throm. "How bad is it?"

Chapter 19 - Bad News

He sighed, the weight of the world in his eyes. "There aren't many paladins left. Maybe not enough to train new ones. But she says there's still hope, and to never give up, no matter how bleak things look."

He managed a small, weary smile.

"Hah," I scoffed. "Easier said than done."

We waited fifteen minutes before Lily returned. Her expression was somber at first... but slowly, a smile crept back onto her face.

"Now I've got a secret I can't even tell my brother," she teased.

I rolled my eyes. "Oh, really?"

She laughed. "Alright, enough of that though. It's time to go kick some demon butt! We need to get back to the mountain."

I smiled as Throm gave a slight bow. "Of course," he said, already heading for the door.

Keenan shook his head at me as he passed, whispering, "You two dragons think you're so special."

I smirked. "Well... yeah, a bit."

He smiled, shaking his head.

We found Reeger meditating in the courtyard. As we approached, he spoke calmly, his voice steady.

"In warfare, there is always sadness, fear, and death," he said. Then, rising to his feet, he placed a hand on mine and Keenan's shoulders. "But hope can never be destroyed as long as we fight for what we love."

Lily rolled her eyes. "Ugh, you elves. Go write a book or a song or something, sheesh."

We all laughed and made our way to the docks, where we waited for the fishermen to return.

To honor the fallen, we erected a memorial gravestone. Throm and Keenan cast a spell to keep the dead's likeness illuminated. As the gentle glow settled over the stone, they each looked down filled with reverence and sorrow.

When the ship finally arrived, we boarded in silence. The captain stood at the helm, eyeing us as we climbed aboard.

"How did it go?" he asked.

No one responded. The weight of what had happened hung too heavily in the air.

The captain nodded, sensing our grief. "I see," he murmured, then turned to his crew. "Head back to the mainland."

As the ship pulled away, Throm quietly gave the captain a brief account of what had transpired.

The captain listened, then smiled knowingly. "Eldrin was smarter than I think any of us realized."

We all turned toward him, confused.

He chuckled. "For the past seven days, he's been giving us crates to smuggle into town. We delivered the last one two days ago." His grin widened. "Pretty sure that's the 'armory' you lost."

Throm bolted upright. "This isn't some kind of joke, is it? Because I wouldn't find it funny if it is."

The captain smirked. "You know me as Ramus," he said. Then, with a dramatic pause and a sweeping bow, he added, "But my true name is Solvaris, paladin of the Second Order."

Merek snapped. "Wait... the Second Order? That order hasn't existed in over 1,500 years."

Chapter 19 - Bad News

The captain's smile only deepened. "Ah, my dear grumpy old Merek, we never disappeared. We've simply been hiding. And don't worry...there are more of us than you might think. Once the world reaches a tipping point, we're instructed to emerge and fulfill our secondary duty."

"And that is?" Reeger asked.

"To save the world, of course," Solvaris said with a wink.

I almost laughed. "Wait... if saving the world is your *secondary* duty, then what's your *primary* one?"

Solvaris grinned. "Preserving all paladin literature and weaponry. Everything's safe, stored in a vault beneath Grissom City."

Merek muttered, "Well, I'll be a worthless piece of metal..."

Throm smiled. "Given the circumstances, this is incredible news."

Keenan's eyes widened. "So the library and the armory weren't destroyed? Or stolen?"

Solvaris chuckled. "No, sir. They were emptied by us. We moved everything before the attack."

Then, turning to Throm, he added, "We may need to relocate the cache again. The dwarves' halls might be the last truly safe place left."

Throm nodded. "Agreed."

As the harbor came into view, the weight on our shoulders felt a little lighter. We still mourned the fallen, but knowing the Second Order had survived, and that the sacred knowledge and weapons of the paladins had been preserved, was more hope than we'd dared to believe in.

Just as we neared the harbor, the ship we watched earlier made a turn towards us.

Ramus chuckled. "Ah, so now they come for us, eh?" He folded his arms with a smirk. "Well... I think they're in for a surprise."

The other ship swung alongside ours, sails flaring as it matched our pace. Its captain grinned, smug, far too confident. Ramus, or rather Solvaris, met his gaze coolly.

"So," Solvaris called, "how can we help you, my little pirate friend?"

The pirate captain's grin twisted into something darker. "Now, now, Captain. That's no way to greet someone offering help."

Solvaris raised an eyebrow. "Help? By lightening our hold of fish, perhaps?" He gestured toward the cargo hold.

The pirate chuckled. "Not at all. I've simply heard rumors, dangerous people about, certain... assets being transported. Thought we might assist in keeping them safe."

Solvaris's smile faded. His voice dropped. "We're not easily persuaded."

The pirate leaned forward. "Of course not. But we're prepared to offer... protection. For a modest fee. Say, half the weapons you've been smuggling aboard."

Solvaris scoffed. "You won't get a single herring let alone weapons. And if you push this, you'll regret ever setting sail, and won't ever again."

The pirate's grin widened. "You misunderstand. I have something not even your paladin brothers can stop." He held up a glowing orb, pulsing with unnatural light. "So... why don't you tell me where the weapons are?"

Chapter 19 - Bad News

Solvaris hesitated, unsure of what the orb was, and surprised by the pirates' confidence.

Throm stepped forward, sword drawn at his side. "We stand with you, Solvaris."

Around us, the fishermen threw off their outer coats, revealing chainmail and weapon belts beneath.

Keenan grinned. "I've never seen more than two paladins fight at once. This is going to be awesome." He unsheathed his sword.

The pirate captain sneered. "So, you've all chosen death." He raised the orb,

And then a small voice sliced through the rising tension.

"Okay, you slimy, rat-infested, mold-covered, algae-eating son of a sickly goat," Lily snapped.

I blinked, trying to process her insult.

She kept going. "I've just had one of the worst days of my life. So, if you don't throw down your weapons and surrender right now, I will burn your ship to the sea floor and boil the ocean around you. Got it?"

Everyone stared at her.

Then the pirate crew burst into laughter.

The captain wheezed, "You're joking. This little girl is your secret weapon?"

I felt myself start to sweat. I turned to Lily. "Uh, Lil…"

She looked at me, eyes blazing. "Brother. Are they laughing at me?"

I swallowed hard. "Well… they don't know any better. Just stay calm…"

"I am calm," she stated flatly.

The laughter only grew.

I raised my hands. "Guys, seriously, stop laughing. She's had a really bad day…"

The pirate captain cut me off with a smirk. "This little show's been fun, but it ends now." He chuckled and tossed the orb toward the water.

Before the orb could hit the surface, a massive claw snatched it from the air.

Smoke poured from Lily's nostrils as she loomed over the ship, now fully transformed into her dragon form. She rolled the orb in one claw, then scoffed.

"This? This is your weapon? Pathetic!" she bellowed.

The pirate crew stood frozen, gaping at the enormous dragon perched on the back of our ship causing it to sink dangerously low in the water.

Lily casually flicked the orb off into the distant horizon. Then, with a single bound, she landed on the pirate ship, scooped up the captain in her jaws, and shook him like a ragdoll.

With a violent flick of her neck, she flung him after the orb. "Go fetch your little toy, you jerk!" Her voice cracked like thunder, shaking both ships.

She turned, eyes blazing, on the rest of the crew. "Anyone else want to laugh at me!?"

The pirates whimpered and shook their heads, frozen in fear.

"Good!" she bellowed. "You all work for me now. Understand?"

They nodded, cowering and mumbling agreements.

Chapter 19 - Bad News

Then Lily shrank back into her human form, beaming with pride. "Hey guys! I got my own ship! How cool is this?" She waved excitedly across the water.

I chuckled and shook my head. "Unbelievable."

"Hey, Keenan!" she called. "I'm Lily, the Pirate Queen! Fear me!"

Then she spun toward the nearest sailor. "Alright, we're taking this bad boy into port. Show me how this wheel thingy works."

The man scrambled to comply as the rest of us stood there in stunned silence.

"Well," Solvaris said at last, "that was... anticlimactic and incredible at the same time."

Throm sighed. "Yep. That's our Hammer."

We all laughed.

Solvaris glanced around. "By the way... which one of you is that good with illusions?"

Our group exchanged knowing looks.

"I guess you'll have to figure that one out yourself," I said, shaking my head with a grin.

We laughed again as Lily's triumphant voice echoed over the waves, barking orders at her new crew as her ship sailed ahead of us into port.

Chapter 20 - Into the Abyss

We arrived at the dock to find Lily standing proudly beside a pirate, his hat off and head bowed low. I stepped off the boat and greeted her.

"Hey, Lil. How's the pirate life?"

She shrugged. "Basically awesome. These guys treat me way better than you ever did, so I might stick with them for a while."

I laughed and shook my head. Keenan smirked as he approached.

"So, she's going with them?" he asked, grinning. "Ah, good, some peace and quiet at last."

Lily's nostrils flared. "Oh, really?" She snorted. "Well, just for that, I'm going with you guys." She turned to the pirate. "Listen here, you uh... what's your name?"

Before he could answer, she waved him off. "Never mind. Your name is Bob now. Bob, I'm gonna need you to take over for me while I'm gone. But don't you dare mess up my ship, or I will eat you. Got it?"

"Bob" nodded fervently. I struggled not to laugh.

"Good," Lily declared. "Now go find us some resources. We've got bad guys coming."

As Bob hurried toward the ship, she called after him, "And Bob! Don't kill anyone unless they're demons, or if they really, really deserve it!"

He nodded again as he climbed aboard, and the ship immediately set sail.

Chapter 20 - Into the Abyss

Lily sighed, watching it slip from the harbor. "Well, it was a good run as Pirate Queen. But I may have to retire from life at sea and settle for being a landlubber."

Throm shook his head as she walked past, then glanced at me.

I smiled. "Sometimes meeting your idols isn't all you hoped it would be, huh?"

He chuckled. "I suppose not."

We made our way toward the city center, where Gam met us. He listened intently as we recounted the Isle of Light, asking a few clarifying questions. When we finished, he sighed.

"There's a sliver of hope you might find those boys," he said. "But you'll need to go to the king to see if it's ready."

Throm nodded. "The portals?"

Gam nodded back. "I think they're close. I just spoke with Reggie, and…"

"Wait!" Keenan and I shouted together.

Nothing happened. We stood dumbfounded.

"Wait," Keenan repeated, staring at Gam. "Say his name again."

Gam frowned but obliged, speaking slowly. "Reggie…"

Still nothing.

I glanced at Keenan. "Why does he only appear when we say it?"

"I have no idea," Keenan muttered.

Gam looked between us, confused. "What are you two talking about?"

"Whenever we say Reggie…" I began, then winced.

Poof!

Reggie appeared, tapping his foot impatiently.

"You still look very alive," he said, annoyed. Gam cracked a smile.

"Sorry," I said. "We were just talking about portaling, and…"

Reggie's eyes lit up. "Oh! Yes, yes, yes, I just figured that out! The black stones we enchanted can now block the portals, though we're running low on reagents. Enough for most major cities and the dwarves under the mountain. The stones have the right resonance to stabilize the…" He paused, staring at us. "Well, never mind. You probably have no idea what I'm talking about anyway. Basically, the stones block portals within a certain radius."

He grinned. "And we even managed to create a returnable portal from the demon realm! You'll have to talk to the king about that one. I'm very proud of it. Although, to be fair, the dwarves did most of the work. I just swooped in and took all the credit at the end."

He beamed. "Glad you're not dying. Glad I could help. Gotta go!"

And just like that, he vanished.

I sighed. "Yeah… like that."

Gam chuckled. "Well, he must really like you. He doesn't do that for anyone else I know."

Throm's expression hardened. "We need to get back to the king and see if we can portal in to save the students."

"Whoa," Reeger cut in. "We don't even know if we can find them, or if they're even still alive."

Throm met his gaze, voice nearly breaking. "But as a paladin, I have to try."

Chapter 20 - Into the Abyss

I nodded. "We just have to be careful. No unnecessary risks. We can't lose anyone else."

Keenan shook his head. "No. Throm's right. If there's even a chance, we have to try."

"Okay," I said, "but let's talk to the king first. We need to make sure getting there, and back, is even possible."

Lily perked up. "All I heard was that we get to take the fight to the bad guys in their house." She grinned. "I'm definitely messing up their furniture."

We all stopped and stared at her.

"What?" she asked, looking around. "Do they not have furniture?"

We exchanged glances, shrugged, and then burst into laughter.

Lily huffed. "What?"

As evening fell, we all returned home. After a restful night's sleep, we set out before dawn, determined to reach the mountain with the strength needed to attempt a rescue.

As we walked, the question of teleportation gnawed at Kennan.

"Reg... the gnome... can do it," Keenan muttered, catching himself. "Why can't we?"

Throm chuckled. "He doesn't do it that often, and he's a lot smaller than us. Less mass to move."

"I suppose," Keenan said.

Lily laughed. "We could just fly."

I nodded. "In an emergency, sure. But flying burns a lot of energy. We should conserve our strength for when we really need it."

"I suppose," Lily said, then darted off the path to pluck a flower. She skipped back, grinning, and I smiled, remembering how much she loved them.

When we arrived at the mountain, we were led straight to the king, who greeted us with a smile.

"I have good news," he announced.

He repeated Reggie's report, then added, "We've placed enchanted stones all around the mountain, so the enemy can't open portals here, unless we allow it."

He hesitated, then continued, "We also sent a scout team to test the portals."

His expression darkened as he glanced toward a cluster of guards gathered near open ground, weapons at the ready.

"They should have been back by now," the king muttered, striding toward them.

Keenan stepped forward. "Can you open another portal? We can go check on them."

"No, no," the king said firmly. "This mission was meant to test the portals' safety. We can't risk more lives if they're being dropped into lava, a cage, or..." he gestured vaguely, "right into the middle of the enemy's mess hall, for all we know."

Throm nodded. "Without a return strategy, a suicide mission would be unwise."

We waited anxiously for the scouts' return. In the meantime, we filled the king in on what had happened on the Isle of Light.

Just as I was about to ask about alternatives, a portal suddenly opened in the middle of the assembled troops. Soldiers instantly formed ranks, weapons raised toward the shimmering gateway.

Chapter 20 - Into the Abyss

Several tense seconds passed before two dwarves stumbled out, coughing violently. The portal snapped shut behind them, and the troops surged forward to assist. Healers rushed in, then quickly stepped back after examining them.

"They just inhaled some smoke," one reported. "They should be fine."

The soldiers gave them space as the king stepped forward to question them.

"We emerged in a vast cavern," one scout said, still clearing his throat. "There was a large stone structure at one end and what looked like some kind of barracks, or maybe a prison, at the other. We could hear shouting now and then, and patrols moved through the area at random."

"Our main goal to find a stable anchor point for the portal was a success," the second scout added. "We finally found a small cave off the main path and placed it there. It took us longer to return because we had to make sure it was safe before using it."

The king turned to us, his expression hesitant. "I can fully support Throm and Keenan going in to check on their captured friends. However," he said, looking directly at me and Lily, "I strongly urge both of you to stay behind. If either of you is lost..." he paused, "then all hope may be lost."

I understood his concern. But I couldn't let Keenan go without me. Even with my memories restored, even knowing who I truly was, the life I had lived with him still mattered. He was my childhood friend, and that bond was just as important as anything else.

I placed a reassuring hand on the king's shoulder and offered a small smile. "I give you my word: I'll make sure we all come back."

He studied me for a long moment, as if he wanted to say more, then sighed. "Very well. It is, of course, your choice."

I turned to Keenan and Reeger with a mischievous glint in my eye. Then, raising my voice just enough, I said, "However… I don't think Lily should go. It's far too dangerous."

Lily exploded. "What? Too… what?! How dare you!" She planted her hands on her hips, fuming. "You can't go without me!"

I struggled to keep a straight face. "Lily," I said solemnly, "we simply can't risk you ruining their furniture."

There was a second of silence before realization dawned on her.

"Wait. Their... oh, you jerk!" she huffed. "'Too dangerous,'" she muttered under her breath, scowling.

I burst out laughing.

She glared at me. "I'm the dangerous one, you old softy!" Then she punched me in the shoulder as Reeger and Keenan chuckled at her outburst.

The king handed each of us a small stone, one for me, one for Lily, and one for Throm. Then he turned to Reeger and Keenan with an apologetic expression.

"I'm sorry. We only had three. I was originally going to give out just one, but since these two…" he nodded toward Lily and me, "are going, they each get one in case they get separated."

Chapter 20 - Into the Abyss

"How do they work?" Reeger asked, peering over my shoulder.

"Just throw them on the ground," the king explained. "The portal will open instantly. But keep in mind, these are all we have for now. If you can manage with just one, that would be best."

"How long do they stay open?" Throm asked.

"They're locked at thirty seconds," the king replied. "If you go through too soon, whatever's behind you might follow. And if you go through too late…" He shrugged. "Well, just don't go through too late."

I chuckled. "Good advice."

The king's expression turned serious. "If the worst should happen," he said, pausing, "and you're not back by morning, I'll send in the Hammers."

Lily perked up. "You called?" she said smiling.

The king chuckled. "Not you, Lily. However, I think you'll like this."

With a flourish, he explained, "The Hammers are a battalion of one hundred shock troops, trained to descend with unmatched force and destroy everything in their path, no matter who or what stands in their way."

Lily's eyes lit up. "Now that's what I'm talking about!" She turned to me with a smirk. "Hey, bro, you got anything cool like the Hammers? I doubt it. I bet something lame, like the healers, is named after you."

The king started to speak. "Well, actually…"

"No, no," Lily interrupted, waving a hand. "Don't ruin the moment. I'm having a moment. Let me bask in it."

She took a deep breath, closed her eyes for a few seconds, then exhaled. "Okay. That was a good moment."

She opened her eyes and looked around. "What?" she asked as everyone stared at her. "We've got demons to fight, don't we? Why are you all standing around?"

Then she turned and strode toward the waiting troops, muttering to herself, "The Hammers. How cool is that?"

The king glanced at me.

I shrugged. "Yeah, she's always like that. And don't worry, I'd be honored to have healers named after me."

Keenan shrugged too. "I'd be happy just to have a meal, or a cool sword named after me."

"Hey," Reeger said, nudging him. "Don't you already have some crazy spell and a sentient shield?"

"Eh," Keenan replied. "Fair point."

Reeger and I laughed.

After that, we finalized the plan with the king, where we'd search, how long we had, and what to do if things went wrong. One of the royal mages stepped forward and opened a portal with Keenan and Throm immediately stepping through.

I took a deep breath. After two thousand years, I was finally going to see their world, the world that had nearly destroyed ours. What would it be like? Who would we encounter? Would we survive?

Well, we had to.

I had made a promise.

Smiling to myself, I exhaled.

"Here we go," I said, and stepped through the portal.

Chapter 21 - Broken

As I stepped out of the portal, dim light illuminated the shallow, cave-like chamber. The rocky terrain crunched underfoot, and ahead, a narrow slit in the stone opened to the outside, where Keenan and Throm were already cautiously peering out.

I joined them and surveyed the landscape.

It was a nightmarish expanse of jagged, blackened stone and molten rivers that snaked through the earth like fiery veins. Towering spires of basalt jutted from the cracked ground, their surfaces scorched and pitted by relentless centuries of heat. The air was thick with ash, choking and heavy, making each breath a struggle. Waves of searing heat shimmered across the landscape, distorting the world into a hellish mirage.

Explosions of molten rock burst from deep fissures, sending glowing embers spiraling into the smog-choked sky. A dull red glow lit everything from below, cast by countless pits of fire that burned across the surface.

The ground trembled with distant rumbles, like the world itself groaned under the weight of ancient, infernal forces. Massive stone structures, ruined fortresses perhaps, stood half-sunken in the volcanic waste, their cracked walls inscribed with glowing runes that pulsed faintly. Deep tunnels and cave mouths gaped from the rock, magma veins illuminating their insides like open furnaces.

This world was alive with fire and death, an unforgiving wasteland.

Lily came up beside me, unconsciously grabbing my hand. Staring at the infernal landscape, she murmured, "Man, this is hard for me to breathe in. I can't imagine what it's like for you guys."

I smiled and gave her hand a reassuring squeeze. "You ready?" I whispered.

She looked up at me, her fiery grin returning. "Yeah. Let's go find some furniture!"

I chuckled, shaking my head. Behind us, Reeger approached quietly, his eyes fixed on the burning hellscape.

"I never imagined a place like this could exist," he murmured.

I nodded, then turned. "So, what do you think, Throm? Which way?"

Throm scanned the landscape thoughtfully. "I'm not sure."

To our left, a massive stone structure was built into the side of the cave wall, part castle, part barracks maybe, judging by its shape. Faint lights flickered in its windows, and glowing runes shimmered across its crumbling walls. Ahead and slightly right, a jagged outcropping overlooked a field of bubbling lava flows, bordered by towering stone pillars. Farther right, a much smaller, ruined building sat surrounded by scattered debris, too far to identify what it had once been.

Reeger squinted. "I think we're less likely to run into trouble if we go right... but we can't be sure."

"We could split up and cover more ground," Keenan suggested.

Chapter 21 - Broken

Throm shook his head. "Normally, I'd agree, but here? That's not a risk I'm willing to take."

"Alright then," Lily said, "right it is. But I want to check out that outcropping first, we might get a better view."

Without hesitation, she hopped down from our cave's ledge onto what looked like a path, or at least one free of lava. She waved us forward. "Come on, you slowpokes! Their furniture ain't gonna break itself!"

I smiled and followed, landing beside her. Keenan and Reeger dropped down behind me. Throm lingered, his gaze still fixed on the old fortress.

"Come on, Throm," I called.

He blinked and shook his head as if clearing a fog. "Right," he muttered before jumping down. But as we moved toward the outcropping, he cast one last look back at the ruined stronghold before following as if being called to it.

We advanced carefully. As we neared the outcropping, the faint sound of voices drifted through the heat-hazed air, muffled and indistinct.

Reeger held up a hand, motioning for silence, then crept ahead, disappearing behind a cluster of rocks.

We crouched low and waited.

It didn't take long. A few moments later, Reeger returned, shaking his head and motioning for us to follow.

As we caught up, he whispered, "You're not going to believe this."

We rounded a massive boulder and saw them.

Four figures were tied to large stones.

One was a man with the head of an elephant. Another was a small, frog-like creature. The third was a Minotaur, though unlike any I'd seen before, more mythic than real. And the last was a human. They were quietly bickering among themselves.

The human turned to the Minotaur, huffing, "You can't just charge in every time! You could at least wait for me to play a tune or something, y'know, amp us up a little?"

The elephant man rumbled, "Hey, lay off him. How could we have known what was going to happen?"

The frog spat onto the ground. "Man, I knew you guys were gonna get me killed. This place is drying me out; I can barely get my poison flowing."

Throm stepped forward. "Excuse me."

The four captives froze mid-argument and stared at us.

"Great," the human muttered. "Now I'm hallucinating."

The frog blinked. "Nope. I think these guys might be real."

The Minotaur grunted. The elephant-headed man muttered, "I should've just stayed with the cat lady. Exploring that old library would've been way better than this."

Keenan, thoroughly confused, asked, "Uh... what are you doing here?"

Lily rolled her eyes. "Nice, Keenan. Top-tier questioning. Ten out of ten."

The group stared at us for a long moment, then the human burst into laughter.

"Oh, you're serious?" he said, mockingly. "Well, you see, we went out for a picnic, and this seemed like just the spot!"

Chapter 21 - Broken

We stared at him.

"Sorry," Keenan muttered.

The elephant-headed man sighed. "Please forgive my friend. It's been a rough day. But if you could release us, we'd be grateful."

I looked at Throm, who shrugged. Lily did the same, then she stepped forward and cut the elephant man's bonds.

"You seem alright," she said. "But you can cut your friends loose. That way, if we have to kill them, it's not on me." She turned and walked back toward us.

"Nice touch," I said, shaking my head.

She shrugged. "What? Now they won't attack. They'll be too scared."

Keenan frowned. "Yeah, that's not how that works."

She smirked. "Always worked for me."

We shook our heads as the elephant man freed the others.

"So… can we get your names?" I asked.

The elephant man looked to the human, who quickly shook his head. "Better not."

"Why?" I asked.

"The less we know about each other, the better. If we get captured again…" He shrugged.

"You could come with us," Keenan offered.

"Nope," the human said. "We need to get back to our world. And I need to get my lute back." He groaned. "Ugh. They better not have damaged it."

The frog muttered under his breath, "Might poison him next time."

"What was that?" the human snapped.

The frog just stared at him.

"Well, thanks for the help," the elephant man said. "But we've got to go." He turned and started down the path from where we'd come.

The Minotaur approached Lily, towering over her. He placed one hand over his chest and gave a slight bow.

"Ahh," she said. "Manners." She mimicked the gesture, and he nodded before following the elephant man.

The frog sprang after them, leaping onto the Minotaur's shoulder. The human lingered for a moment, watching his companions as if weighing a decision. Then he turned back to us.

"Look," he said. "You want some advice? Don't get captured. Better to die." His voice faded, and then he turned and jogged after the others.

We watched them vanish into the distance.

Throm finally broke the silence. "I really would've liked to know who they are, and where they came from."

"Yeah," Keenan agreed. "And how did that guy get an elephant's head?"

"Right?" Lily added. "But they had a talking frog. How cute is that?"

I laughed. "Glad you didn't say that to his face."

Keenan smirked. "Now I kinda wish she had."

With that, we continued toward the other building.

As we approached it, we spread out cautiously, edging toward the entrance. Reeger slipped ahead and vanished inside. Moments later, he reappeared, held up two fingers, and pointed toward the door.

Chapter 21 - Broken

Throm entered first, Keenan close behind, while Reeger peeled off to scout the perimeter. Lily picked up a broken shield, frowning as she turned it in her hands. I followed Keenan and Throm inside.

It looked like an alchemy lab, potions, papers, spellbooks, and reagents scattered in chaotic disarray. Several cots lined the walls, each showing signs of struggle. One had been torn apart, as if someone had been dragged from it.

Keenan shook his head as he passed the ruined bed. "This place..."

At the back of the room, a wide doorway loomed. Just as Throm stepped toward it, a teenage boy burst through, nearly impaling himself on Throm's blade.

"Grab him!" Throm shouted.

Keenan lunged, but the boy slipped past him. I stepped in front of the door and caught him in a bear hug. He thrashed and kicked, shouting, "Let me go!"

Suddenly, something slammed into my head. Wings fluttered frantically as sharp claws raked across my face.

A shrill voice screeched, "Let him go!"

I winced as blood trickled down my cheek. "Uh... guys? Little help here?"

Keenan was already grappling with the attacker, while Throm placed a calming hand on the boy's shoulder. Almost instantly, the teen stopped struggling, his breathing slowed.

Throm gently lifted his chin. "Galen?"

The boy blinked. "Throm?"

Keenan, still fending off the winged assailant, paused. "Wait... Galen? Is that really you?"

The boy turned toward him, eyes wide. "Keenan? You're here too? I knew you'd come! ...but what took so long?"

Throm studied him, concern deepening the lines on his face. The boy's expression shifted, growing distant.

"Please don't hurt him, Keenan," he said softly, glancing at the creature Keenan pulled from my face.

Keenan sighed and released it, an imp, though far smaller than the ones we'd fought back in Grissom. It flapped over to Galen, landing beside him and puffing up its tiny chest in a show of attempted intimidation.

"You better not hurt him!" the imp squeaked. "He's been through enough!"

Galen suddenly looked at the imp, fear creeping into his eyes. His hands trembled. "Wait... they're illusions, aren't they?" he whispered. "They're not real..."

The imp frowned. "Nope. They're real," he said, glancing at the blood still trickling down my face.

"Yeah, thanks for that," I muttered, wiping it away with a weak chuckle.

Galen turned back to Throm, his composure crumbling. "We tried to be strong, but... it's been years since you were here. And they... they hurt us." His voice trembled. Panic flared in his eyes.

"Shh," Throm said gently, kneeling and placing a firm hand on his shoulder. "Let me take a look at you."

The imp zipped around anxiously. "What are you doing? You better not hurt him!"

Throm met the imp's glare, calm and steady. "I'm helping him forget the last few days...or at least the worst of it."

Chapter 21 - Broken

As Throm's magic worked, Galen blinked, his eyes clearing. A slow smile spread across his face.

"Oh, man... I knew you guys would come!" He reached down and scratched the imp's oversized ears. "Hey, I named this little guy Aegis. He helped me... uh..." He frowned. "Well, shucks. I don't remember. But I'm sure he did!" He laughed, still affectionately scratching the imp.

Throm knelt beside them and said gently, "Thank you for helping this boy. I am in your debt. If there's anything you need, just ask."

The imp crossed his arms and huffed. "Yeah, I got something. Get us the heck out of here!"

Throm smiled. "That, I think we can do."

"Wait," the imp said, eyeing him warily. "You're not gonna torture me when we get to your place, are you?"

"Of course not," Keenan said, stepping in with a reassuring tone.

The imp turned to him, eyes widening. "Huh. A Noctari that turned?" He grinned. "That's gonna make the boss real mad." He chuckled.

Keenan frowned. "What do you mean?"

The imp shrugged. "He doesn't like it when we switch sides. But I hate it here, everyone's cruel, and they all hurt each other." He shook his head. "No way to live."

Throm glanced at him. "So, Galen calls you Aegis, huh?"

"Oh, yes!" The imp puffed out his tiny chest with pride. "I saved him, and he gave me the name. Said there was a great warrior, one of his heroes, who had a shield and was called Aegis."

Throm smiled. "He was probably reading one of our old history books. That name goes back centuries."

The imp shook his head. "Nope. He said he watched him train. Said that one day, that warrior would come save him... and I could come along when he did."

Throm looked over at Keenan, who was visibly struggling to hold back tears. I placed a hand on his shoulder as he took a deep breath.

Softly, Keenan murmured, "I'm sorry I couldn't get here sooner, little buddy."

Galen shook his head. "I'm sorry, guys... it's the weirdest thing. I can't remember anything from the last few days." He let out a small laugh. "But I know two things for sure: this little guy here is my best friend... and you guys were always going to come for us. And now you're here."

His face lit up with certainty.

Galen leaned toward the imp and whispered, "See? That's him. And that's his shield," he said, pointing to Keenan's back.

The imp's eyes widened. "Whoa," he breathed. "So cool."

"Yeah," Galen said with a firm nod. "So cool, for sure."

Throm stood and looked at me and Keenan. "He's badly broken... but he'll heal in time."

We both nodded, trying not to think of what had happened to the poor boy.

Throm turned back to the imp. "Where are the others?"

The imp bounced nervously. "What do you mean, 'the others'?"

Chapter 21 - Broken

"The others they brought here, like him," Throm clarified, nodding toward Galen.

The imp looked around, as if searching for an answer. Galen spoke up instead.

"They should be back at the Isle... I think. I don't even know how I got here, to be honest. But Master Eldrin said we needed to prepare, and we were just about to leave for somewhere safe. They could be there." He shrugged.

Then, with a spark of excitement, Galen turned to the imp. "Wait 'til we get back, then we'll show you how paladins fight!"

The imp, only just beginning to grasp what Throm's magic had done to Galen's memory, nodded slowly. "Yeah... yeah, that would be great." He said quietly.

Throm's gaze hardened. "The others?" he pressed again, looking directly at the imp.

The imp hesitated, his eyes falling to the ground. "I'm not strong... or powerful," he said softly. "I could only save one."

Throm turned and slammed his fist into the wall, gritting his teeth. He didn't speak, but the strain in his posture said enough. Keenan backed up until he hit the wall and slowly slid down to the floor, burying his face in his hands.

I didn't know what to say. The odds had been low from the start, but this... this crushed whatever hope was left. As I struggled to find words, Galen walked over to Keenan and placed a small hand on his shoulder.

"Don't be sad," he said gently, smiling. "I'm sure you guys did everything you could to help... whoever it was you were trying to save. So don't be sad. You're gonna help save the world and stop the demons."

Keenan looked up through his tears, forcing a smile. "Well... looks like we were able to save at least one," he said, glancing at the imp. "With the help of a new friend."

Galen gasped. "Wait, my little buddy helped you guys too? That's awesome!"

"Yep," the imp said, grinning. "And now we're going back home. You can show me all that cool stuff you told me about."

Throm, still facing away, shook his head with a dry laugh. "This was not how I saw my week going," he muttered. "Standing in the demon realm, with the Hammer and Anvil, being comforted by the one we came to save... and the one doing the comforting is an imp who hates demons, in a torture lab... You can't make this stuff up."

I chuckled. "You should write a book about it."

Throm laughed under his breath. "I might if I make it through this."

"You better," I said smiling.

We shared a brief, bittersweet laugh, just as Lily burst in, breathless, her eyes wide with urgency.

"There's a patrol coming!" she hissed, her voice filled with urgency.

The moment of fragile levity shattered. Weapons were drawn, hearts hardened, and the air thickened as we waited for whatever was to come.

Chapter 22 - Brother

We quickly and quietly pressed ourselves against the wall on either side of the door as Galen stood there, confused, looking around. The Imp grabbed his hand and yanked him behind an overturned table.

"Where is Reeger?" I asked, keeping my voice low.

Lily shrugged. "That guy's a ghost," she whispered.

We heard voices approaching, though we couldn't make out what they were saying. Keenan mouthed, *Infernal,* and we waited. The voices drew closer, stopping just outside the doorway as Keenan listened intently, picking out words in his half-native tongue. After a brief exchange, the voices moved on, fading as they turned a corner down the path.

We all exhaled in relief.

"Well, that was interesting," Keenan said. "I didn't catch everything, but they're planning some kind of large-scale operation. Not all the clans are on board, so they're… weeding out the weak."

The Imp stepped forward and hissed, "Yes. They have been fighting for some time. This world is dying, falling apart, and they want to take another. One of their leaders is from there."

Lily and I exchanged uneasy glances, our stomachs sinking at the mention of him.

Lily fumed. "That backstabbing, dirty, rotten, no-good, lousy, friend-killing, stinky, dumb poo-poo head!" She panted after her outburst.

Keenan stared at her before bursting into laughter. "Wow. Did you get them all out, or are there a few more insults left in there?"

She shot him a glare. "Listen, buddy," she snapped. "He is the worst of the worst. He tried to kill us, his own mother, and he helped kill his brother, our creator. There aren't enough bad words in the universe to describe him."

"Okay, okay," Keenan muttered, glancing at me before turning back to her. "Please, continue."

She sighed. "I'm done. But, brother," she added, turning to me, "he can't take our home and kill our friends."

I smiled. "Don't worry. We're together again, and we've got some of the best fighters on our side."

Throm gave a faint smile. "I hope it's enough," he said. Then he pulled me aside and lowered his voice. "Listen, we need to learn more, how many of them there are, how they're getting through, but first, we need to get Galen back."

"Agreed," I said. "But who's going with him?"

Throm sighed. "I should be the one. You and Lily have a better chance of surviving anyway, and they won't trust Keenan or Reeger, especially not with the child, and certainly not with the Imp. I don't want to leave, but I can't let Galen stay in danger."

"Don't worry, Uncle," I said with a reassuring smile. "We've got this."

Chapter 22 - Brother

He chuckled. "'Uncle,'" he repeated with a sigh. Then, staring blankly into the distance, he added, "You know, despite everything, raising you, and being with Grom and Gam, those were some of the best years of my life. I wouldn't give anything in the world to change that."

I placed a hand on his shoulder and grinned. "Then let's kill them all and go back to living, just the four of us."

A loud crash shattered the moment, causing us to jump. We turned to see Lily smashing a table and chair, muttering, "Goodbye, furniture."

I laughed. "Alright, five of us."

Throm smiled, then gave a final nod, tossed the stone to the ground, and a portal bloomed open in a swirl of light. He turned to face me and Lily.

"You two better come back," he said.

I smiled. "Don't worry. We'll be back in no time."

"Or several hours," Lily added. "This place is huge."

Keenan shook his head as he walked out the door, and Throm, Galen, and the Imp stepped through the portal. Fifteen seconds later, it fizzled out, leaving only silence behind.

I stood there, staring at the empty space, thinking of Galen and all the others we hadn't been able to save. I exhaled and shook my head.

"Come on, bro," Lily said, watching me.

I turned, and she gave me a mischievous grin. "There's got to be more furniture out there, and none of it's safe."

I laughed. "Yeah, you're going to single-handedly keep every furniture maker in business, with bonuses."

"Wait," she said as we stepped out the door. "Do you think demons actually have furniture makers? Or do they just steal everything?"

I chuckled. "I have no idea, Lil."

She shook her head. "Well, if they do, we've got to take them out too. No way I want them getting bonuses."

I shook my head, smiling.

Keenan stood in the open, eyes scanning the horizon. He raised a hand, and we froze.

We exchanged a glance, then carefully moved toward him.

"What is it?" I asked.

His voice was low. "I don't know... but the sound has changed. So has the air. Something's wrong."

We moved quickly, slipping behind the rocks and making our way back to where we started at the outcropping.

"Where's Reeger?" I asked, scanning the terrain as we crept along.

"No idea," Keenan said.

When we reached the outcropping, we looked toward the old castle. It was completely dark, no glowing runes, no torchlight. Just stillness. Silence.

"I don't like this," I said.

A hand suddenly touched my shoulder. I spun around, sword drawn, only to find Reeger standing there, pale and unsteady.

Keenan stepped forward, catching him, eyes closing as he concentrated.

"What happened?" I asked.

Through labored breaths, Reeger rasped, "I was scouting around the building when three Noctari and a demon

Chapter 22 - Brother

stopped in front of the door and talked for a while. Then they left, so I followed them. They went down a passage that opened into a much larger area, full of demons. One of them was huge, yelling commands, fuming over something. I don't know what."

He winced, nearly collapsing as he gasped for air. I caught him, steadying him. His skin was cold and clammy.

Keenan glanced at me. "Poison."

"Can you do anything for it?" I asked.

He nodded. "I can try... but this isn't a skill I've had much cause to use." He closed his eyes, focusing on Reeger.

The air grew tense as we watched, waiting to see if Keenan's magic would be enough. Reeger's breathing was shallow, his lips pale, blood dripping from a shoulder wound. The silence pressed in around us like the pressure at the bottom of the ocean. Lily shifted uneasily, gripping her small black stone tightly.

I watched helplessly as my friend struggled to breathe, his skin growing paler by the second.

After what felt like forever, Keenan exhaled. "Okay... I think I got it. But he needs rest."

Reeger gave a weak smile. "Anyway... they had some of the biggest demons I've ever seen. Bigger than the ones you fought," he said, looking at me.

I nodded. I knew exactly how massive they could get.

"I tried to leave," he continued, "but I spotted a gargoyle. At first, I thought I imagined it moving, but I didn't. When I turned back, it stabbed me with a small blade. Must've been coated with the poison."

Some color returned to his face, and he managed to make a faint smile. "But now, there's one less gargoyle in the world."

We smiled at that.

The four of us paused to take stock of the situation. Our team was slowly getting smaller as we lost Throm and now Reeger. We were debating whether Reeger should return on his own, or if we all should.

Keenan sighed. "We still don't have anything new, just confirmation of what we suspected."

"Agreed," I said. "But knowing their world is falling apart... that makes them desperate. And desperate is dangerous."

Reeger, now seated and resting against a rock, looked at us apologetically. "I'm sorry, guys. I should've been more careful."

Keenan smiled. "Don't sweat it. How many times have you saved us by doing exactly that?"

Reeger gave a faint smile, closing his eyes.

"I think we should check out the castle," I said. "But we stick together. We use one stone to send Reeger back and the final one comes with us."

"Agreed," Keenan and Lily said at once.

"Hah!" Lily smirked. "Owe me a candy."

Keenan frowned. "Why?"

Lily stared at him, incredulously. "You don't do 'owe me a candy' anymore!?"

Keenan looked at me and shrugged.

I chuckled. "It's a game. When two people say something at the same time, whoever calls it first gets a candy from the other person."

Chapter 22 - Brother

Keenan shook his head. "Never heard of it."

Lily crossed her arms, shaking her head in mock disappointment. She turned to me. "Is this world even worth saving if they lost 'owe me a candy'?"

I laughed. "Maybe not. But we're gonna try anyway."

"Unbelievable." She muttered.

Keenan helped Reeger to his feet. I pulled out the stone and threw it down, activating the portal. Reeger gave us a nod, then stepped through, disappearing into the swirling light.

"All right," I said, turning to Lily and Keenan. "Let's stay close. No risks."

They exchanged glances, then turned to me with matching looks of innocence.

"Who, us?" they said in unison.

Keenan grinned. "Hah! Owe me a candy."

Lily gaped at him. "What!? You can't do that! You don't even play the game!"

"Well, I just did," Keenan said smugly. "And you lost. So, I guess that makes us even."

"No! That's not how it works!" Lily protested. "Now we both owe each other one! It doesn't cancel out!"

I just shook my head as we started toward the castle, their debate trailing behind me.

As we slowly approached one of the entrances, the arguing faded. We fell silent and crept toward the large doors. I glanced at Keenan, who gave a small shrug, then stepped inside.

The interior was a wreck. Dead demons littered the floor, their twisted forms sprawled across scorched stone.

Furniture was overturned, walls blackened, whatever happened here had been brutal.

"Think these were some of the ones that needed to 'get in line'?" Keenan muttered.

"Maybe," I said. "I'm just glad they don't get along. They're hard enough to fight on their own."

We picked our way through the carnage, stepping carefully over charred bodies and shattered debris. The smell of sulfur and burnt flesh clung to the air, making each breath heavy.

Eventually, we reached a small chamber in the back. The door was obliterated, and whatever had once been stored inside was gone.

Keenan frowned. "Notice anything odd? All the demons were killed the same way. Clean, efficient. Whoever did this knew exactly where to strike."

"That doesn't make me feel any better," I said, exchanging a glance with him.

Lily wandered over, letting out a dramatic sigh. "And worst of all, they destroyed all the furniture."

Keenan and I smiled.

"Tragic," I said dryly. "Now you can't destroy it."

"Right!?" she said, throwing her hands in the air in exasperation.

Keenan picked up a broken weapon, examined it briefly, then tossed it aside. "We're not going to find much more here. But at least we know their weak points now."

"I'll take whatever advantage we can get," I replied.

He nodded. "Let's move."

We exited the castle, speaking in low voices as we considered our next step.

Chapter 22 - Brother

"I think we should check out the area where Reeger got stabbed," I suggested.

Keenan hesitated. "What if we're spotted?"

"Only one way to find out," Lily said with a grin, already heading off in that direction.

I smiled and followed.

Keenan sighed, muttering as he trailed behind. "Sure, let's do the dangerous thing. Because, yeah, we can just turn into dragons."

Merek scoffed. "Yeah, well, they don't have me. Now quit whining and let's go."

Keenan smirked, shaking his head. "Got it, boss."

"Watch it, you little whelp," Merek shot back.

Keenan chuckled, and we continued on.

We followed the path Reeger had described, passing the spot where we'd found Galen before reaching the tunnel. Moving cautiously, we crept through the narrow passage, the air thick with the scent of damp earth and something fouler. The deeper we went, the louder the noises became: pounding footsteps, distant screams, metal crashing against metal. A battle.

We exchanged uneasy glances, then pressed on.

The tunnel curved and opened into a vast cavern, larger than anything we'd ever seen. It stretched into endless darkness, its jagged walls pulsing with a sickly glow of hellish energy. The air reeked of sulfur and decay. Towering stalactites hung like jagged teeth from the ceiling, and the uneven ground was strewn with ancient bones and rusted weapons.

Hammer and Anvil

Along the cavern walls, enormous obsidian chains held monolithic stone pillars in place. Crimson runes pulsed across them, feeding the chamber's unnatural energy.

The place was swarming with demons, thousands, maybe tens of thousands. At the far end, two massive figures barked orders. My blood ran cold as I recognized one of them: the younger brother. His once-elegant celestial form was now fully corrupted. His veins glowed red, his eyes burned with malice and hatred, runes carved into his skin like a dark manuscript of evil.

Beside him stood a towering demon, easily forty or fifty feet tall. Its mere presence radiated raw, crushing power.

Off to the side, five or six frost giants fought against a relentless tide of demons, while the two leaders watched and laughed.

Lily stepped forward instinctively, but Keenan grabbed her arm, holding her back.

"We have to help them," she whispered, her voice sharp with fury.

I placed a hand on her shoulder. "Lil... we wouldn't survive."

Tears welled in her eyes as she watched the giants fight, valiant, but hopeless. One by one, they fell. When the last warrior dropped, the demons erupted into a deafening cheer.

The massive demon raised his arms. "Soon, my brothers, we will leave this world to burn and march to our next conquest!"

The crowd roared.

Chapter 22 - Brother

Keenan leaned in, voice low. "There's got to be forty, fifty thousand demons here."

I nodded grimly, staring at the impossible army before us.

The demon's voice echoed across the cavern. "Those whelps shut us out two thousand years ago. Now, they will suffer for their arrogance. We shall inherit their world!"

Another roar of approval.

"They have grown soft. Their fortresses lie in ruins, their greatest weapons lost to history. They squabble while we gather strength. The dwarves are warriors, yes, but few remain. Their 'Mother' is gone, and there is no sign of their so-called protectors."

Lily trembled with rage. "Fat chance, fatso," she muttered.

I watched the younger brother. He still stood beside the massive demon, smirking, until something shifted. His expression sharpened. He tilted his head, as if listening to something distant. Slowly, he inhaled... and then looked out across the cavern.

Right at us.

Keenan stiffened. "Uhhh... that's not good. We gotta go."

We turned to retreat down the tunnel, only to find him standing there.

The younger brother. Smaller now, somehow. But unmistakable, blocking our path.

My heart pounded. I glanced back and he was still beside the massive demon, eyes closed. Yet here he was, too, smirking in front of us. An illusion. He must be projecting himself.

"We now have portals anchored..." the booming voice of the demon echoed behind us, still addressing the crowd.

The illusion stepped forward, grinning. "Well, well. What have we here?" His voice was smooth, amused. "Intruders."

He began to circle us, his gaze like a predator sizing up prey. Keenan drew his sword.

"Oh, please." The younger brother chuckled. "You could no more cut the air with that blade than harm me. Put it away."

Keenan hesitated, then reluctantly sheathed the weapon.

"Excellent," the apparition purred. "Now, tell me, how did you three escape the holding cells? And why wasn't I informed of my new guests?"

He kept pacing, eyes sharp and calculating. "You smell of the old world," he mused. "But we haven't brought anyone back today. So tell me..." He stopped in front of Lily, smiling in a way that made my skin crawl. "Did you enjoy the frost giant show?"

Lily's eyes burned with fury. She opened her mouth, but I cut her off.

"No. Don't."

The younger brother's smirk widened. "Ooooh, interesting," he said, turning to me. "So, you're the leader?" His gaze bored into mine, piercing, invasive. "Tell me, leader..." he said, mockery curling in every word, "why are you here?"

Before I could answer, Keenan stepped in, dry and unimpressed. "Well, we were looking for a vacation spot. This

Chapter 22 - Brother

place seemed perfect. Though, the neighbors are a bit noisy."

I sighed, closing my eyes and shaking my head.

The brother chuckled, shifting toward Keenan. "Well, well... A Noctari with a backbone and a sense of humor. That's rare."

Before he could say more, another voice rang out, strong and unwavering.

"Listen here, you little worm."

It was Merek.

His voice carried weight I'd never heard from him before. Pure authority. Unshakable.

"Your time will come to an end. Whether you succeed or fail, I swear, by whatever power I have left, you will pay for what you've done."

Silence fell.

Even the younger brother stilled. His smile faded, and when he spoke again, the smooth honey of his voice was gone, replaced by cold, calculating hatred.

"I never forget a voice," the younger brother said slowly. "And unless I'm mistaken... you are Merek. Some paladin from an order so insignificant, I can't even recall its name."

He stepped forward, his expression twisting with amusement.

"You were an obnoxious little creature the last time you graced the old world. So, tell me... are you here for a preview of what's to come?"

His smirk widened, tone dripping with mockery. "Well, I must say, I'm glad you survived all these years, *old friend*. If only so you can witness your precious world crumble.

Don't worry, I'll make sure you have a front-row seat as we tear it apart, piece… by… piece. And there will be nothing you can do to stop it."

The air hung heavy with his words.

Then Merek laughed.

His eyes narrowed. "Do you find something funny, old friend?"

"Yes," Merek said, calm and resolute. "Just that after all this time, you're still the same pompous fool. Your arrogance will be your undoing."

His voice rang with confidence. "So thank you. This was all I needed to hear to know we have nothing to fear from you… little puppy."

The brother's face contorted with rage. He let out a scream, his form flickering violently with raw energy, and at that Merek sent out a pulse of power. With a crack like lightning, the illusion shattered.

From deep within the cavern, a deafening roar echoed, shaking the ground.

The brother staggered in the distance, eyes blazing, screaming in fury. The cavern trembled with his wrath.

Merek said to us, unfazed, "I suggest you throw the stone and take us back. Now. Or we're dead."

"Good grief," Keenan muttered.

I didn't wait. I grabbed the stone from my pouch and hurled it to the ground. With a rush of air and swirling light, the portal ignited.

Chapter 23 - Giant

Lily stepped through the portal first. Keenan glanced at me, then followed.

Ten seconds.

I held my ground, watching as the younger brother sprinted across the cavern, thousands of demons at his heels. His furious bellow echoed through the chamber.

Fifteen seconds.

They surged toward the cave opening, closing in fast.

Twenty seconds.

As he came within earshot, I smiled and shouted, "Beware of traitors!"

His rage twisted into something darker as the words sank in.

Twenty-five seconds.

Laughing, I added, "How else did we get here?" Then, with a final smirk, I stepped backward through the portal.

I landed on the other side just as it snapped shut two seconds later. I chuckled. "Oh, that's really gonna mess with his paranoia."

Around us, dwarven warriors stood with weapons drawn.

Merek laughed out loud, amused. "You just had to get the last word in, didn't you?"

I grinned. "Maybe."

The king stepped forward. "What happened?"

We recounted everything that happened after Reeger went through the portal.

When we finished, I looked around. "Where is Reeger?"

"He's with the healers, resting," the king replied. "He should be back on his feet soon."

"And Throm?" I asked.

The king's expression darkened. "He's lucky you gave him your blessing to bring that imp. Otherwise, we'd have interrogated and executed it." He sighed. "He took the child and the imp to Grissom, said he needed to update Grog and Gam."

I nodded. "We need to get back too and come up with a plan."

The king agreed. "We've been preparing, but we're only a few thousand. Against what you've seen..." He shook his head grimly. "We have our tricks, but we'll be hard-pressed to hold out."

I smiled. "Don't forget you have us."

The king grinned. "Of course." He turned to the gathered dwarves and bellowed, "With the Hammer and Anvil, we cannot lose!"

A thunderous cheer erupted as the dwarves sprang into action, going back to sharpening weapons, reinforcing fortifications, and preparing for the battle ahead.

When the excitement faded, the king's tone grew solemn. "Even with your strength, we'll need allies. Grissom, Burke, and the elves will have to pull their weight. Even then..." He hesitated. "It may not be enough."

Chapter 23 - Giant

I exhaled, the weight of it settling over me. "I know. But whatever happens, we can't give up. If we stand together, even if we fall, we can't fail."

The king met my gaze and nodded. "Indeed."

We checked in on Reeger, who was already up and walking. "I'm fine," he assured us. "I'll join you on the way back to Grissom."

Without wasting another moment, we set out, leaving the mountains behind. As we made our way toward the city, Lily, quiet until now, stepped up beside me. Her eyes stayed fixed on the ground, voice barely above a whisper.

"What were their names?"

I glanced at her, confused. "Who?"

"The frost giants," she said, finally looking at me. Sadness lingered in her eyes.

"Oh." I paused. "I have no idea."

She sighed. "How many people fight to the end, never giving up... and no one will ever know their names?" Her voice cracked. "They were brave. And no one will remember them."

I nodded slowly. "I guess I never thought about it like that."

Another sigh. "How many from the first war, too? All those lives lost." She clenched her fists. "I hate bad guys."

I placed a hand on her shoulder. "Me too, sis. Me too."

We continued walking in silence, the path to Grissom stretching out before us.

When we arrived late that night, we stopped in our tracks.

The three frost giants were helping build fortifications around the city. Even more surprising, the people of Grissom were working right alongside them, laughing and chatting like it was completely normal.

We just stood there, staring in disbelief.

"I thought we were going to ease into this," Keenan muttered.

"Yeah... me too," I said.

As I stepped forward, a familiar voice called out, "Hey, guys!"

Something was off. The voice sounded... deeper. Bigger.

I turned and there was Philip, stepping out from behind a wall.

He was now seven feet tall.

Keenan blinked, leaned in, and whispered, "Yeah... I'll take whatever he's having."

"Philip?" I asked, still trying to process what I was seeing.

Lily stared, wide-eyed. "Why are you taller? And... kind of blue?"

Philip scratched the back of his head, grinning. "Well... they heard I didn't have any parents, so they asked if I wanted them to be mine."

His grin widened. "And I thought, how cool would that be? So, I said yes! They did some kind of ceremony, it was kinda weird and I had to drink this strange liquid. Next day..." He gestured at himself proudly. "Ta-da!"

Lily immediately turned to the frost giants. "Can I have some of that liquid?"

I shot her a look. "Knock it off, Lil. This is serious."

Chapter 23 - Giant

She waved me off. "Yeah, yeah."

"Philip, you can't just drink random stuff from strangers! What if it had killed you?"

He shrugged. "Frank said it was alright."

I rubbed my temples. "Frank said," I repeated flatly.

Keenan clapped a hand on my shoulder. "Well, that settles it. Frank said it was fine." Then, grinning, he strolled off before I could glare at him.

Philip went on, "Anyway, I told Gam what happened, and he asked if I could get the giants to help. Once I told them it was to stop the demons, they were all in!"

He beamed, standing a little taller, puffing out his chest like he was trying to look official. "It was very smart of you guys to bring me along."

I shook my head, an amused smile tugging at my lips. "Thanks, Philip."

He nodded. "Anything for you guys. You always treated me right."

As I turned to leave, I hesitated. "Hey, Philip?"

"Yeah?"

I glanced back. "Can you understand them now?"

Philip's grin widened even further. "Yeah. It's like their words just... make sense now. I don't know how, but I understand them in my head, clear as day. They said it's part of the bond. Family hears family or something like that."

Lily's eyes lit up. "So, you're like... half-giant now?"

Philip laughed, a booming sound that startled the nearby townspeople. "Maybe! All I know is, they call me family now. And I'm not letting them down."

I nodded, feeling a strange mix of pride and unease. "Then let's make sure we use that bond wisely. We're going to need every ally we can get."

His face lit up. "I guess now that I understand them. I technically speak two languages. That basically makes me highly educated."

I chuckled. "Alright, Professor."

As we walked away, I heard him murmur to himself, "Professor... I like the sound of that."

I smiled as we all headed toward our house and spotted Throm approaching, with Galen and the imp at his side.

Throm grinned. "Philip told me where the mirror is. I've heard about Frank, though, and I don't want to show up with these two without Keenan. Still, I think that's the safest place for these two right now."

The imp huffed. "Yeah, some people around here aren't exactly thrilled about my presence, if you catch my drift."

Lily stared at the imp.

The imp blinked. "What?"

Lily replied, "What, like a sand drift or a snow drift?"

"What?" the imp said, confused, looking at us, then back at her.

Lily continued, "How am I supposed to catch a sand drift? That's like trying to stop a wave or something."

The imp furrowed his brow. "Is this a human thing? Because I don't understand."

Lily shook her head. "You said it! You wanted me to 'catch your drift,' but you didn't say what kind of drift. Is it sand? Snow? Fog? I mean, how am I supposed to work in these conditions?" she said, exasperated.

Chapter 23 - Giant

The imp shrugged, looking completely lost as we tried not to laugh.

Keenan shook his head, ignoring Lily, and said, "If it makes you feel better, it took me over twelve years just to get them to talk to me, so I feel your pain."

"Ugh," the imp groaned. "Humans, am I right?"

We all smiled, and Throm said, "Well, shall we head to the cave?"

"Sure," I said.

Reeger, who'd been quiet until now, spoke up. "I'm going to rest, still not back to a hundred percent."

With that, Lily, Keenan and I set off with Throm, Galen, and the imp toward the warehouse. We entered and stepped through the mirror, emerging in the cave. Galen looked around in awe.

"This is so cool!" he said. "Throm, when you said you had a super-secret hideout, I didn't think you meant this cool."

Throm smiled. "Oh, just wait, it gets better."

We headed toward the living quarters when we heard the familiar thud of Frank's heavy footsteps. Keenan grinned. "Alright, guys, don't scream, don't panic. It's just Frank."

Just then, Frank rounded the corner, smiling, until he saw the imp. His eyes widened.

"You!"

The imp smirked, leaping off Galen's shoulder, and started circling Frank as the ogre reached for his club.

We froze, stunned.

Keenan asked, "What is happening right now?!"

Frank narrowed his eyes. "Alright, Tiny, you going down this time."

"I don't think so, big guy. You're too slow."

Frank let out a booming laugh. "We shall see!"

He swung his massive club. But before we could react, the imp dodged, scaled Frank's arm, and locked him in a headlock.

Frank flailed, trying to grab him. "Not fair! You have to stand still!"

The imp scoffed. "What? And let you flatten me? Not a chance."

Frank dropped his club, dropped to his knees, and gasped, "Not... fair..." before collapsing flat onto the ground.

We stood there shocked, our mouths open.

The imp climbed onto his back, raised his fists, and shouted, "I am the champion!"

Then Frank's shoulders began to shake. The imp scrambled off just in time as Frank sat up, roaring with laughter.

"Tiny!" he bellowed, arms wide.

The imp grinned. "Hey, big guy!" He jumped into Frank's arms, and the two burst out laughing.

Lily looked at them, then at us. "Your friends are insane. I mean, I thought I was going to be the crazy one. Well, crazy awesome, but seriously. You people don't have a single normal friend. And that concerns me."

We all burst out laughing.

As we gathered around Frank and the imp, Keenan asked, "Frank, how do you know him?"

Chapter 23 - Giant

Frank's smile faded slightly. "When I was with demons, after taken from home, I met Tiny. We friends but had to hide it. We do fake fights, so no one knew we friends."

Keenan shook his head. "Two weeks ago, the weirdest thing in my life was that I was a paladin." He exhaled and glanced around. "Now? Being a paladin is the easiest and most normal thing I have to deal with. I don't even know what to think anymore."

We all chuckled.

After getting Galen and the imp settled in, Frank showed us the upgrades they'd made to the cave with help from the frost giants. The place was turning into a real fortress.

"This place is really coming together," I said, smiling. "Nice work, everyone."

Frank beamed. "Don't worry. When bad guys come, Frank will bonk them."

The imp jumped up. "Don't forget me!"

"Yes!" Frank bellowed. "I bonk them, and Tiny jumps on their backs!"

The imp shrugged. "Eh, close enough."

We all laughed, enjoying the rare lighthearted moment.

We promised to return soon and after saying our goodbyes to Frank, Galen, and the imp, we headed out once more.

Chapter 24 - The Meeting

We went home and slept, waking up early to meet my uncles and Reeger at the inn for breakfast.

As we ate, we filled Gam and Grog in on everything that had happened. They listened intently, occasionally asking questions. When we finished, Gam pushed his plate back and sighed.

"Well," he said, shaking his head, "I guess the younger brother is still alive, and still wants our world."

I nodded. "Unfortunately, it sounds like they need a place to move to, so yeah... they're committed."

Grog grunted. "Over my dead body."

Throm smiled. "It might come to that, you old badger."

Grog grunted again. "There'll be piles of them if it does."

Gam shook his head and looked around at all of us. "Well... I sincerely hope it doesn't come to that. But for those of us who make it..." He placed a hand on my shoulder, and another on Throm's. "I'll remember this meal." He smiled.

Reeger sighed. "I suppose some of us won't make it."

Lily rolled her eyes. "Ugh, you guys are such downers. How about we all live and just meet here for lunch every week?"

We all smiled.

"Now that's a plan I can drink to," Keenan said, lifting his mug. We all raised our drinks in agreement.

Chapter 24 - The Meeting

After more conversation, we decided it was time to check in with Burke and the Order since we were eyewitnesses to everything. Reeger said he needed to return to the woods to warn his father and assess the situation, but he'd try to meet us back here tomorrow morning. So Keenan, Lily, and I headed off toward Burke. Reeger and Gam went to the woods, while Throm and Grog stayed behind to continue helping Grissom prepare.

When we arrived at Burke, we were welcomed into the castle and ushered in just as his sons and daughter arrived. Brom was sitting with his wife, while Victus and Oryn stood nearby. We walked up and bowed, but Brom waved his hand dismissively.

"None of that," he laughed.

Keenan looked around. "Where's Thalion?"

Brom shook his head. "Apparently, there's trouble in the woods. He was recalled."

"Hmm," Keenan murmured. "Reeger's headed there as we speak."

"Well," the queen said, smiling as her eyes drifted to Lily, "who is this young lady?"

Lily's mouth dropped open in mock offense. She playfully punched my shoulder. "She thinks I'm a lady," she said, then lifted her chin and stuck her neck out proudly.

I laughed and turned to the queen. "This is Lily, my little sister."

Cara's eyes lit up as she stepped forward, smiling. "That's so cool! And I love your hair," she said, pointing to the red streak that fell across Lily's cheek.

Lily grinned at the girl's excitement. "Oh yes, but remember, I'm waaay cooler than he is." She smirked. "He might be able to freeze things, but I spit fire."

Cara gasped. "Wait, you can spit fire?! Can I see?!"

"Sure," Lily said, taking a step back.

But before she could do anything, I jumped in. "Okay, okay, how about not in the castle?"

"Pssshh," Lily scoffed. "You're probably right. This is a very pretty place. I wouldn't want to ruin your furniture."

"Furniture?" the queen asked, raising an eyebrow.

I chuckled. "Don't ask. She has it in for furniture, apparently."

Lily snorted and muttered, "Only evil furniture."

Brom looked at me and asked with a smile, "So, are you finally going to explain how you beat the demons and how you freeze things?"

I paused for a moment, then realization hit me, I'd never actually told them who I was. I'd been so focused on talking to my uncles that I completely forgot.

"Brom," I said, feeling a little sheepish, "I'm so sorry, I forgot to tell you last time we were here."

He smirked. "Yeah, believe me, it was hard to believe Oryn when he said the only reason they survived was because of a dragon that came out of nowhere."

I sighed, feeling terrible for forgetting, but Brom just started laughing as the queen smiled warmly.

"Wait," Cara said, her eyes growing wide as she looked at me. "You mean... you're a dragon?"

I smiled. "Yes, I am, though I only recently found out. My memory was locked away for some reason."

Chapter 24 - The Meeting

Cara's eyes lit up. She turned to Lily with growing excitement. "But that means...!"

Lily nodded and grinned. "Yep. But waaaay cooler, remember?"

The two of them immediately started whispering and giggling. Keenan shook his head and muttered, "There's way too much power over there for me to feel comfortable."

We all laughed.

Then we started going over everything that had happened since our last visit, detailing all the events unfolding in Grissom. Perseus sighed and looked at his father, who sat deep in thought. The queen placed a reassuring hand on his shoulder, and he took a deep breath while looking around the room.

Rannoch interjected. "We'll be ready, Father."

Brom gave him a proud smile. "I know, son. But with their overwhelming numbers, if we don't coordinate with the other cities, they'll take us out one by one, no matter how prepared we are." He paused, then added with a grin, "However, we've secured the stones from the mage and placed them around the castle as instructed. So, they can't teleport in. And if they try to take anything, well, they'll pay dearly for it."

Perseus nodded. "We still don't know who they'll hit first or what tactics they'll use."

"True," Brom said. "But fortunately, I've got one of the best tacticians in the land at my side."

Perseus looked down humbly as the queen beamed at him.

Brom continued, "And I have some of the finest special forces." He walked over and clapped a hand on Rannoch's shoulder. "They can plug any gap, or even take down demons, no matter how big."

Rannoch nodded, smiling with quiet confidence.

Then Brom turned to Keenan. "And we've got a paladin and apparently, two dragons." He chuckled. "I don't think taking this castle will be as easy as they think."

Cara, still chatting with Lily, chimed in. "Dad, don't forget your secret weapon."

Brom turned to her with a grin. "Ah yes, our secret weapon." He chuckled and tapped her nose playfully. "We can talk strategy all day, but if things ever look grim, they definitely won't see you coming."

Cara smiled proudly.

Lily smirked and nudged her. "Oh, Cara, me and you are going to have so much fun kicking bad guy butt!"

"Now," Brom said, rising to his feet, "we were just about to discuss some news Oryn had before you arrived." He turned to him. "Oryn, what do you have for us?"

Oryn stepped forward and gave a respectful nod. "Our scouts within the Order have discovered two key developments. First, the elves will be of no help in the coming battle. They've closed their borders and are dealing with internal conflict. Second, the Noctari are massing in the east."

"What?" Keenan said, startled. "How many could possibly be left? I tried to find them years ago and could only track down small groups, five or ten at most."

Oryn nodded. "Exactly. They're experts at hiding and concealing their numbers. But we've infiltrated their caves,

Chapter 24 - The Meeting

hidden among the ruins of several cities, and it turns out their numbers are in the thousands."

Brom frowned. "Do we know why they're gathering?"

"We're not sure," Oryn admitted. "But all signs point to something significant. They've been summoned to a central location. That meeting is happening tomorrow night."

I glanced over at Keenan. "We could check it out. And if Reeger makes it back in time, he could come with us, he's stealthy."

Keenan chuckled. "Stealthy is putting it mildly."

We continued talking about the broader situation and the defenses being put into place. One by one, people began filtering out to take care of their duties. Eventually, only the king, queen, Keenan, and I remained in the court.

Brom looked at me. "You've fought them before. You've seen their home turf. What do you think our chances are?"

I lowered my gaze, thinking carefully. After a long moment, I let out a sigh and met Brom's eyes. He held my gaze, and in that quiet moment, he understood without me needing to say a word.

"Well," he said, trying to summon a smile.

The Queen tilted her head and gently took his large, weathered hands into her own. "No matter what happens," she said softly, "we have each other."

Brom looked down, fighting back tears.

Just then, Lily and Cara came bursting back into the room. Lily looked around and frowned. "Do you guys enjoy being miserable?... Sheesh," Lily said, waving her hand dismissively. "You are all always moping around like you just lost your favorite dog to a lava monster! We're not gonna lose."

Brom raised an eyebrow. "Lava monster…?"

The queen smiled. "Why can't we lose?" she asked.

Lily scoffed. "Because you've got us and Keenan. I don't know if you've noticed, but we basically kick butt and destroy furniture."

The queen smiled, her eyes twinkling. "That is true," she said, glancing at her husband.

He laughed softly. "Of course. And besides, we've got something they don't." He looked at each of us in turn. "Each other. I'd rather die among family and friends than live in fear and alone."

I grinned. "As the old saying goes, it ain't over till the fat lady sings."

"Wait," Lily said, looking confused. "What fat lady? Where is she? I can just kill her so she can't sing, and then we can't lose!" She grinned, clearly proud of her logic.

Brom shook his head. "Lily, it's just an expression."

She frowned. "Well, that's dumb. Who came up with that? It doesn't make any sense. I'm gonna slap whoever did." She turned to Keenan, hands on her hips. "Was it you and your Noctari people? Forcing fat women to seal poor country folk's untimely demise?"

Keenan looked at me, completely lost. "I don't know if I should be mad, hurt, or just confused."

I smirked. "I usually just go with confused."

Keenan sighed. "Alright. Confused it is."

"Come on," Lily scoffed. "Let's go talk some sense into Keenan's people! But first, everyone to the front gate, I

Chapter 24 - The Meeting

promised Cara a fireball." She laughed as she skipped out of the meeting room.

Brom watched her go, then turned to me. "Is she always like this?" he asked, as the queen chuckled beside him.

"Oh yeah," I said. "It never ends."

"Huh," he mused. "She's a handful then, isn't she?"

Keenan shook his head. "You have no idea."

Brom laughed.

"Wait till she fights," I said with a grin. "Then she'll be a handful for the demons."

Brom nodded, smiling. "And for that, I'll be thankful."

We made our way to the front gate. Outside, we were met by a large crowd of soldiers and townsfolk, all waiting expectantly.

I shook my head. "You're really putting on a show, huh, Lil?"

She smirked. "Cara said she was only going to tell a few people but come on, they need encouragement. A reminder of why we're going to win."

Then she turned to the crowd. "Alright, all of you worried about the future, here's why you don't need to be."

Without another word, she transformed. A massive roar erupted from her, shaking the ground. Then she launched a fireball into the sky, so large and bright it left me momentarily stunned. It was easily ten times the size of any she'd cast before.

As I stood there shocked, Keenan chuckled. "Okay... that was pretty awesome."

At first, the crowd recoiled in fear, but as the fireball faded, awe replaced fear, and cheers broke out. Lily shifted back into her usual form and gave an exaggerated bow.

She strolled over to me, still grinning.

"Lil," I said.

"Yeah?"

"I've never seen you throw a fireball like that before."

She avoided my gaze. "Yeah, well... maybe I've been practicing."

I followed her glance up to the castle ramparts where Cara stood watching. She gave a subtle thumbs-up, barely noticeable to anyone but us.

I shook my head. "Ah... I see now."

Lily laughed. "Whatever do you mean?" she asked, feigning innocence.

"Practicing, huh?"

She grinned. "Oh, she is so riding on my scales into battle. They won't even know what hit them."

I chuckled, shaking my head. "Wait, where did you two disappear to earlier, anyway?"

Lily smirked. "A lady never tells." She winked and turned, striding confidently down the road toward Grissom.

We arrived late and went to have dinner at the inn. Lily mentioned going for a walk, and we jokingly warned her not to set anything on fire. She sputtered and mumbled something about not being a child... probably. We laughed and headed inside to eat.

As Keenan sat down, he shook his head. "You know, if I wanted to walk this much, I would've been a merchant."

I chuckled. "Yeah, everyone trusts a traveling Noctari."

Chapter 24 - The Meeting

His eyebrows shot up. "Oh? You want to go there, huh?" he said, feigning mock indignation. "Don't think that just because you can turn into the size of a house, I can't still take you."

I laughed. "Alright, fair enough."

We ate in relative silence. Keenan, though, was uncharacteristically quiet. I kept an eye on him, noticing the weight of something pressing behind his usual bravado. Eventually, he sighed. I looked up and said, "Well."

He looked at me. "Well, what?"

I said, "Come on out with it. What's on your mind?"

He let out a soft laugh and sighed again. "The Noctari."

I nodded, waiting.

"I want to try and help them."

Another nod.

"But I'm afraid they won't listen," he admitted, glancing around the inn. "Instead of hiding in caves, being seen as freaks or unwanted... I just want them to find a home. A town. People who... love them."

"Love?" I echoed, tilting my head.

He chuckled. "Okay, tolerate."

I grinned.

He swirled the last remnants of his drink, sighing once more. "There was so much bad blood, but that was centuries ago," he murmured. "Why can't people just be better?"

"Hah," I said. "Yeah. Sadly, I don't have an answer for you."

He smirked. "Come on, you're supposed to be some wise and ancient being who knows all the things about all the stuff for all of history."

I nodded solemnly. "Wow, that does sound impressive. And if you meet this person, please let me know."

He laughed. "Okay, will do."

As we sat, the warm din of the inn surrounding us, my ears caught a conversation at a nearby table, an old sailor speaking with a young man.

"I'm telling you," the sailor said, his voice firm, "it came out of nowhere, faster than any ship I've ever seen."

"You know it started here?" the young man said. "They did something to it in the harbor!"

"Well," the old sailor huffed, "whatever they did, they should do it again. Those pirates had just about got us when she came sailing in, pure white, bright as the driven snow. And on the deck, I swear, stood a ghost and a red-haired woman. They slid up to the pirates and raked them with fire and shot the likes of which I've never seen. The pirate ship foundered in less than five minutes… Five minutes!"

The young man gave a low whistle as the sailor continued.

"And then," the old man said, voice dropping to a hushed reverence, "the red-haired woman saluted, and they whisked away like the wind and sea itself was carrying them. I always thought women were bad luck at sea, but by the mast, those two were angels sent from heaven." He took a long drink from his mug.

The young man chuckled. "Well, I'm glad they're on our side."

I smiled and glanced at Keenan, who was also grinning as he finished his drink.

"Glad that worked out," he said.

"Me too," I replied.

Chapter 24 - The Meeting

With that, we paid for our meal and headed home to sleep.

In the morning, we prepared for our trip to the ruins. We explained our plan to my uncles, and while they cautioned us to be careful, they admitted it was unlikely the Noctari could handle two dragons and a Paladin.

After packing our gear, we decided to wait for Reeger until midday before heading out.

"I hope he makes it," Keenan said. "I've gotten used to his scouting. It feels like cheating, but I'll take it."

I smiled. "Yeah, I remember someone who used to cheat all the time."

Keenan chuckled. "I guess you're right."

Lily shook her head. "Listen, if you're not cheating, you're not trying."

I raised an eyebrow. "You're talking about combat, right, Lil?"

She gave me a confused look. "There are rules in combat?"

Keenan and I burst out laughing.

I glanced up at the sun. "Well, it's about time to go. I don't want to get there after dark."

"Agreed," said Keenan.

With that, we grabbed our gear leaving a note for Reeger and set out.

Chapter 25 - Cern

The air outside was crisp, carrying the faint scent of smoke from hearths and the earthy smell of decaying leaves as fall settled in. Our boots struck the stone road at a steady rhythm, the sound echoing softly off the surrounding walls as we moved away from the inn

Lily skipped ahead a few paces, humming to herself, while Keenan adjusted the strap of his sword and muttered something about "too many walks for one lifetime." I smiled, feeling the familiar mix of anticipation and unease that always came before a journey.

As we walked, Keenan fell into silence, his brow furrowed as he brooded over the Noctari' plight. The weight of his thoughts seemed to press down on him, and for a while he said nothing.

"Ugh, you guys are so boring! I'm gonna find some flowers or something," Lily huffed, breaking the quiet.

I chuckled. "Alright, Lil, just don't wander too far."

She threw her hands up in exasperation. "What do you think I am, three years old or something?"

Even Keenan cracked a smile at that. As she skipped off, whistling a tune, he sighed. "I'm sorry. I just really want to help them."

I nodded. "Unfortunately, some may not want help... or won't change."

Chapter 25 - Cern

"Yeah, I know," Keenan said, exhaling heavily. His voice carried the frustration of centuries of failed attempts at reconciliation.

We kept walking in silence until Keenan suddenly stopped, and I felt it too. Instinctively, we moved back-to-back, slowly turning, scanning our surroundings.

"It got quiet," I whispered.

"Yep," he replied.

Lily's whistling had vanished.

"Do you think it's her?" Keenan asked.

"Could be. I don't think we're close enough to the Noctari yet, it's only been a short walk. We can still see Grissom in the distance."

Suddenly, Lily popped out from behind a boulder.

"What are you two idiots doing?"

"Good grief, Lil, you scared me," I said, shaking my head.

She smirked. "Aww, the big bad dragon's scared of little ol' me?" She laughed. "Come on, I found some pretty flowers, so my mission is accomplished."

"Where are they?" Keenan asked.

She just smiled and continued down the path.

We shook our heads and followed her. The landscape began to change, the remnants of the old road faded into disrepair, and small stone foundations and crumbling structures dotted the terrain like ghosts of forgotten lives.

Then the feeling returned. The hair on the back of my neck stood up. I glanced at Lily, who had stopped walking and was staring straight ahead.

"It's not me this time," she whispered.

We tensed, scanning our surroundings.

Hammer and Anvil

A soft chuckle drifted from behind a low stone wall about fifteen feet away. Then Reeger stepped out, grinning.

"Well," he said, "at least you noticed me. But you'd all be dead if someone actually meant you harm."

I let out a sigh of relief. "Come on, Reeger," I said, smiling. "You're stealthier than anyone in this world."

Keenan shook his head. "Just like when we were kids. I swear, one of these days you're gonna give me a heart attack."

Reeger smirked. "Seriously though, we need to work on your awareness. I've invested too much time in you two to see you taken out by an ambush."

I chuckled. "What about Lily?" I asked, glancing her way.

She threw her hands up dramatically. "Don't drag me into your fight. This is between you guys."

Reeger grinned. "Well, he's right, you should learn too."

She shook her head. "You guys and your silly games."

"As much as it pains me to admit," Keenan said, "he is right."

Lily shrugged. "Whatever. You guys would be dead without me." She started walking again, then suddenly turned back like she'd just remembered something. "Oh, and thank you, Reeger."

He raised an eyebrow. "For what?"

She flashed a mischievous smile. "For carrying my flowers for me." With that, she turned and skipped down the path.

Chapter 25 - Cern

Reeger looked confused. We watched as he slowly swung his pack around, unfastened the straps, and discovered three flowers carefully placed inside.

He stared in disbelief. "Not possible," he muttered.

Keenan and I burst out laughing.

Shaking his head, Reeger glanced toward Lily, now further up the path. "Oh, she's dangerous."

I smiled. "You have no idea."

Keenan grinned. "Glad she's on our side, then."

As we continued down the worn-out path, Lily suddenly stopped and looked around.

"Huh," she said.

"What's up?" I asked.

"It's weird seeing all of this the way it is now." She gestured toward an empty spot in the field. "I remember that was the Jeffersons' house, right there."

I thought back, the memory slowly resurfacing. "Oh yeah," I said, smiling. "And they had that tomato garden with those hot peppers you liked."

She smiled at the memory. "Yeah, and Mrs. Jefferson would always try to make them hotter for me."

"Yep," I said, still smiling.

She sighed, her expression turning somber. "It only feels like a month ago for me."

"I'm sorry, sis," I said softly. "For me, it's been over two thousand years."

"Yeah," she mumbled, her voice thick with emotion. "I miss her."

I put my arm around her shoulder. "Yeah, me too."

"Thanks, bro," she murmured. Then, realizing she had an audience, she quickly wiped the moisture from her eyes and forced a smile. "So, which city are we going to?"

She tried to sound cheerful. "Verdalis, with all its gardens? Or maybe Virethia, with its famous bakeries? Or…"

"Lil," I interrupted.

She had turned away, tears silently streaming down her face as she gazed into the distance.

"It's all gone, isn't it?" she whispered.

"Yeah," I said. "Destroyed, mostly in the war. The rest just fell into disrepair after that."

She sighed. "And no one rebuilt it?"

I shook my head. "No. Sadly, there was a lot of distrust toward humans for a century or two. They never really got over the Noctari conflicts. Then there were the wars with the islands a couple hundred years ago, which wiped out a lot of the population."

She exhaled heavily. "These guys really need to take better care of this place. I leave for a little bit, and everything goes the way of the dodo."

I smirked. "What's a dodo?"

"No idea," she admitted. "Just thought it sounded funny."

She grinned mischievously. "Like your stupid singing fat lady," she teased, punching me in the arm.

Laughing, I held up my hands. "Okay, okay, I get it."

She turned back toward Grissom. "Well, I can see they're at least rebuilding some cities. But some of the prettiest ones were under human rule on the southeastern end of the island."

Chapter 25 - Cern

I nodded. "Maybe once we beat them again, we can help rebuild this time," I said with a hopeful smile.

She nodded firmly. "Yeah. So let's get the Noctari on board already so they can help, cause I can't do everything for everybody."

Keenan piped up. "Yes, I agree," he said, smiling. "Let's get them on board."

Lily groaned in mock indignation. "Ugh! You two are always lurking in the background when we're trying to have a serious conversation!"

We all laughed and continued toward the meeting place.

The road narrowed as we pressed on. We continued down the poorly maintained dirt track until patches of cobblestone began to appear beneath our feet, fragments of the old world surfacing like bones through the soil. The ruins loomed ahead, silent and waiting.

"We should be getting close to Cern," I said.

Lily sighed but remained silent as we crested a small hill. Below us, the ruins stretched across the landscape, a once-grand city of white marble, now cracked and weathered, its pristine surface dulled by time and the elements.

Once-polished columns, fractured and leaning, reached toward the sky like skeletal remains of a forgotten civilization. The intricate carvings that once adorned the buildings had been worn smooth by centuries of wind and rain. Streets that had once bustled with life were now littered with rubble, overtaken by creeping vines and stubborn weeds clawing through broken tiles and shattered archways.

Hammer and Anvil

The great buildings that once reflected sunlight like mirrors were now tarnished, stained by soot and decay, their walls marred with deep fissures. Time and war had left gaping holes in their hollow, silent shells. Shattered fountains lay dry and abandoned, their basins filled with dust and dead leaves.

Despite the ruin, the city held a haunting beauty, a lingering echo of the splendor it once knew. The bones of its greatness remained, whispering stories of an age long past, of a people who built wonders only for time to reclaim them.

As we passed through, most of the buildings lay collapsed, massive marble blocks scattered in heaps all around us.

"This city was so beautiful," Lily murmured, resting her hand on a dirt-streaked piece of white marble. "When the sun hit it just right, the whole place would shine."

We continued until we reached what had once been a grand square. In the center, a massive obelisk lay toppled across the stone pavement.

Lily stared at it. "Okay," she said, narrowing her eyes. "Who ruined the spire?"

I glanced down, trying to suppress the smile tugging at my lips. But before I could regain my composure, I saw her feet appear in front of me. I looked up to find her standing there, hands on her hips, tapping her foot in irritation.

"It was you, wasn't it?" she accused. "Tell me. And this better be good."

"Okay, now hold on," I said, trying to frame the story in the best light possible. "It was after the Great War. There

Chapter 25 - Cern

were these giants, one in particular was proving to be rather... annoying."

"Worse than me?" she interrupted.

"Way worse."

She shook her head, unconvinced. "Continue."

"Well," I said, "I was trying to freeze him, but he kept dodging around the obelisk..."

"Spiiiire," she corrected, drawing out the word.

"Spire," I conceded, rolling my eyes. Keenan and Reeger stood off to the side, grinning ear to ear, clearly enjoying my predicament.

"Anyway," I went on, "this giant had hurt or killed a lot of innocent people, including children, and I finally had enough and, well... I may have... pushed it over on him."

Lily stared at me for several long seconds, then shook her head. "You got impatient, got lazy, and thought it would look cool," she said flatly. "Not thinking about the fact that it was the last cool thing left standing from the Masons... you jerk."

I chuckled. "How do you always know?"

She shrugged. "Eh, you're my brother. I know you better than anyone." Then, in an exaggeratedly dramatic voice, she added, "And it better not be cracked, because when this is all over, you're helping me put it back up."

I laughed. "Lily, those things weigh tons."

"Don't care," she said, shaking her head. "You're supposed to be the strong one, you figure it out."

I turned to Reeger and Keenan for support, but they both just smiled.

"Yeah," Keenan said. "And we're gonna watch you and make sure you do it."

"Not you too!" I groaned, laughing.

With that, we continued through the ruins and left Cern behind, making our way toward the meeting place just northeast of the city.

As we approached, Reeger held up a hand. "Let me check it out before we all move in."

Then he paused, glancing at Lily. She met his gaze and frowned. "What?"

He smirked. "Just saying, it seems like we've got more than one stealthy person in this group."

She shrugged. "I don't know what you're talking about. I just start fires and destroy furniture."

We all chuckled as Reeger slipped into the shadows, disappearing as the sun dipped below the horizon.

We waited in silence, scanning the area for any sign of movement. The ruins seemed to hold their breath, the wind dying down until even the vines hung motionless. After about thirty minutes, he returned, shaking his head.

"At first, I thought I was in the wrong place," he admitted quietly, "until I almost walked into a guard. So, I stayed back and watched. Eventually, someone climbed out of a hole in the ground to talk to him. Then more people started showing up. I'm not sure how big it is, but they've got something underground."

I racked my brain, trying to remember anything about this area, some clue about what could be hidden beneath us. Before I could come up with anything, Lily spoke up.

"Could be that underground theater the dwarves built back before the war."

I turned to her, surprised. "Lily, you might be right! How do you even remember that?"

Chapter 25 - Cern

She looked at me like I was an idiot. "Really?"

"Oh... right," I said, remembering she'd only been awake for a few days.

Smirking, she asked, "So, do you remember where the dwarves put their secret tunnel?"

I chuckled. "No, but I bet you do."

She grinned. "It's right over there," she said, pointing. Then, with a playful skip, she added, "And if I know my dwarf buddies, it's still holding up, because they build things to last."

Keenan and Reeger exchanged glances and shook their heads as they followed her.

"This is surreal," Keenan muttered.

Reeger nodded, whispering, "Like going back in time while still being in the present."

"Right," Keenan whispered back.

We arrived at what looked like the remnants of an old house foundation. Lily poked around for a moment, moved a dead bush aside, and pulled up a moss-covered stone. Beneath it, a ladder descended into the darkness. She grinned.

"Tada! Don't know what you guys would've done without me."

"Probably just gone and talked to them," I said.

She recoiled in mock disgust. "Gross. Where's the fun in that? Besides," she added, a mischievous glint in her eye, "this way, we hear what they think before we talk to them."

She smirked. "The more you know."

I shook my head, chuckling. "Yeah... the more you know."

We climbed down the ladder and landed in a small chamber, barely large enough to fit ten people comfortably.

A dark tunnel stretched out before us, roughly six feet tall and just as wide.

Suddenly, Lily's face lit up with excitement. She was practically bouncing around with glee. "Oh! I hope this still works. They told me be careful when I use it, but it was made for me!" She chortled, then turned to us with a dramatic flair. "Alright, boys, prepare to be amazed."

She leaned in and breathed lightly on what looked like ordinary rocks embedded in the wall.

In an instant, flames ignited and raced down the tunnel, illuminating the passage with a warm, flickering glow. The fire leapt from stone to stone, revealing carvings etched into the walls, dwarven runes dulled by centuries but still legible in the dancing light. Lily giggled with delight as the fire danced along the walls, her laughter echoing in the chamber like a child discovering a hidden treasure.

Keenan stared, wide-eyed. "How?"

Lily smirked, adopting an exaggeratedly regal tone. "Well, you see, I am particularly good friends with one of the chief builders. He likes to hide little surprises for me. Tuned this system to react to a bit of heat from my fire breath, told me to be careful when I used it." She laughed. "Naturally, I was going to test it out when he wasn't around, but I never got the chance until now. Oh, just wait till I tell him I... I…"

Her voice trailed off. The firelight flickered across her face as her expression shifted, the joy slowly fading.

"Kisago," she murmured.

"Yeah?" I said gently.

She hesitated. "Did he survive the war?"

Chapter 25 - Cern

I opened my mouth to answer, but she shook her head before I could speak. "No... never mind." She exhaled slowly. "I want to remember him like this."

Without another word, she started down the tunnel, quietly humming to herself. The sound was soft, almost fragile, but it carried through the stone corridor like a thread of hope weaving against the silence.

My heart ached for her. So much had changed so quickly. I wished she could just live, to have a moment of peace, free from the weight she now carried. But we were the Guardians. Protecting our world had to come first.

I felt Keenan's hand on my shoulder as Reeger followed Lily down the tunnel.

"You alright?" Keenan asked quietly.

I met his gaze and tried to smile. "I will be... once this mess is over."

Keenan nodded. "Agreed." Then, shaking off the heavy mood, he grinned. "Alright! As Frank would say let's go make new friends!"

I chuckled. "Alright, big man, after you."

He rolled his eyes but stepped forward, leading the way into the tunnel. The firelight stretched ahead of us, painting the walls in reddish-orange glow with the shadows dancing along as we moved.

Chapter 26 - Noctari

We walked for several hundred feet before the path curved sharply to the left. Lily suddenly stopped in front of a door, causing the rest of us to nearly bump into her. She stood motionless, breathing slowly, her eyes fixed on the worn surface.

I leaned in and whispered, "What's up, Lil?"

She didn't look back. "He would always leave me enchanted notes," she murmured, reaching out. As her fingers brushed the door, glowing red symbols slowly appeared across it.

Keenan leaned closer. "What does it say?" he asked quietly.

I squinted at the script. "It says, 'Smile. I left you a small present if you ever turn into a dragon in the theater. But don't abuse it, you little rascal.'"

Lily's eyes widened, and she gave me a sharp look. I chuckled. "Not yet, Lil."

A slow grin spread across her face. "Oh, this is gonna be awesome."

Reeger shook his head and pushed the door open. As it creaked aside, a low murmur of voices drifted out.

"How many people could fit in here?" Keenan asked, keeping his voice low.

I glanced around. "At least a thousand. This place used to sit right between the three great cities."

Chapter 26 - Noctari

Keenan nodded thoughtfully. "Hmm. Well, I guess we'll see."

Reeger slipped in first, followed by Lily and Keenan, with me at the rear.

We emerged into a hallway high above the main floor, overlooking the stage and vast rows of tiered stone seating. The theater was massive. Its domed ceiling was upheld by towering columns, each carved with intricate dwarven designs now worn by time. The air was cool and faintly scented with earth and aged stone. Cracks ran along the walls, ivy and moss sneaking in where the structure had faltered, nature's slow reclamation of once-immaculate craftsmanship.

Above the stage, a faded fresco clung to the ceiling, its once-vivid colors reduced to ghostly echoes. Dust-coated chandeliers hung in silence, their crystals catching dim glimmers of light like frozen stars. The space felt paused between moments, a hauntingly beautiful relic of long-forgotten performances and applause now reduced to memory.

As we crept to the edge, we saw hundreds maybe over a thousand Noctari, gathered in hushed groups, murmuring among themselves as they waited for someone to take the stage.

"Uhhh..." Reeger muttered, glancing over his shoulder. "How many Noctari did they say there were?"

"I have no idea," Keenan replied, stunned.

"I thought they were nearly extinct," I whispered.

He nodded, equally quiet. "Me too."

I took a slow breath. "Well... this is either going to be a massive breakthrough or a complete disaster."

"Yeah," Reeger said, shaking his head. "No pressure."

Keenan stood frozen, his expression blank with disbelief. "The way everyone talked about them," he muttered, "I thought there were only a couple hundred left at most."

"Yeah," I said, scanning the crowd below, "but these are mostly men. Which means the women and children must be somewhere else."

Lily sank into a chair with a tired sigh, looking drained. I exhaled slowly. "I'm not sure what to do now."

"Agreed," Reeger said. "This is way bigger than anything we expected. I mean, just this group alone is larger than any human army we've got. They could probably take Grissom on their own."

Keenan shook his head. "Come on, man, don't say that. Hopefully they are friendly."

"Fair point," I said. "Still... not knowing makes me nervous."

"Same," Reeger admitted. "But I think the best move now is to listen, learn, and decide what to do next."

Keenan and I both nodded. We found seats tucked away in the shadows. Luckily, the section had been reserved for dwarven VIPs, elevated, dimly lit, and far enough from the main crowd to stay unnoticed.

As I looked over the sea of Noctari, I was struck by their diversity. Their skin tones spanned from deep crimson to bright scarlet, some matching Keenan's dark red. Others shimmered with dusky violet or lilac, dark navy, bright sapphire, or even turquoise. Some bore charcoal, slate, or shadow-black tones, while others had warm earth tones, tans, olives, browns, blending in more easily with other races.

Chapter 26 - Noctari

Their horns were just as varied. Some curled thickly like a ram's, others jutted forward smooth and short, or long and ridged. A few had elegant, branching antlers like stags, while others bore slim, gazelle-like horns that swept back or curled under. Some bore clear marks of battle, chipped, cracked, or broken.

But their eyes... their eyes were mesmerizing. Most had no pupils, just glowing orbs in vibrant shades, fiery red, molten gold, silver, violet, icy blue, shadowy black. The range was astonishing. I hadn't realized just how much variation there was among Keenan's people.

"Hey, Keenan," I whispered. "Some of those colorings down there are incredible."

"Yeah," he murmured, still staring. Then I smirked. "So, how'd we get stuck with you?"

He let out a short laugh. "Oh, thanks. Super encouraging."

I grinned as Reeger shook his head, and Lily fought to stay awake beside us, already drifting.

After another twenty minutes, the crowd began to quiet as several figures of clear importance entered the theater. A group of Noctari made their way to the stage, and three prominent leaders stepped onto the platform, taking their seats.

A herald moved forward and announced, "Our leaders have arrived, and the meeting shall now begin. First, the facts will be laid out. Then, each leader will present their case. Afterward, there will be time for discussion before a vote is held to determine our course of action."

A ripple of murmurs passed through the crowd.

The herald continued, "As you all know, we have lived in obscurity for centuries and that secrecy has kept us safe. In the shadows, we thrived. But now, we stand at a crossroads. Portals have begun opening, and an emissary from the demon realm has approached us with an offer: an alliance. They propose we join them in conquering this world and finally step into the light. This meeting will determine the answer to that and the future of our people."

The theater fell silent.

Then the silence cracked as murmurs and excited chatter burst through the crowd.

Lily sat up, rubbing her eyes. "What did he just say?" she asked, squinting down at the herald in disbelief.

The herald raised his hands for quiet. "The first to speak is Maldras Vex'thir of the city of Verdalis."

He stepped aside, and a towering Noctari strode forward. Maldras exuded an intimidating presence, deep red skin, piercing golden eyes, and thick ram-like horns, one broken clean in half. His worn leather armor clung to a broad, battle-tested frame, and his every movement radiated authority.

With a crooked smile, he called out, "I think you all know what I'm about to say."

A hush swept the room, the weight of anticipation growing heavy.

"It is no secret that I've long advocated stepping out of the shadows to claim what is rightfully ours. Our oppression has lasted long enough. The humans, the dwarves, they've hunted us, driven us into hiding, treated us as vermin for two thousand years. And for what?"

He took a step forward, voice rising.

Chapter 26 - Noctari

"Why should we continue to skulk in the dark, living like criminals, burdened by false guilt for simply being who we are?"

A wave of murmurs rose, some tense, others eager.

Maldras's voice thundered. "We outnumber them two to one. Why do we cower? Why live in fear? The demons are not our enemy. I don't trust them, and I don't have to like them, but they haven't been the ones keeping us in chains. They offer power. And what have the dwarves ever offered us? Nothing. They've raided our homes. Slaughtered our people."

He paused, then sneered.

"And the humans?" His tone dripped with contempt. "They look at us like we're thieves. Like we don't even have the right to exist. Maybe it's time we take their cities. Their lands. Let them learn what it feels like to be powerless."

Lily leaned in. "I bet he's a lot of fun at parties."

Keenan groaned. "He's not wrong... but he's so wrong."

I nodded. "Yeah."

Maldras scanned the room, his gaze piercing the crowd. "You know where I stand. You know what I'm willing to do."

With that, he returned to his seat.

The herald stepped forward once more. "Now speaking: Vaeltharis the Emberborn of the city of Virethia."

Vaeltharis rose and glided to the front of the stage with effortless grace and a confident smile. His skin was a pale tan, touched by a faint red undertone that surfaced when the light struck him just right. His jet-black eyes held a sharp, calculating gleam. If not for his tail and the subtle horn-bumps on his forehead, he could almost pass as human.

"Friends," he began, his voice calm and deliberate, "as Maldras has stated, one path before us is to ally with the demons and seize this world for ourselves. But at what cost?"

He let the question hang in the air, the silence stretching taut.

"I propose patience. Let the war continue. Let both sides bleed each other dry. And when the time is right, when they are weakened enough, we will be in the strongest position to choose. We can side with the victor... or, if fortune favors us, eliminate them both."

He paced slowly, hands folded behind his back, his tone never rising above a cool, reasoned cadence. "The key is not haste. It is advantage. We must act only when it most benefits us."

He paused at center stage, bowing slightly, the smile still fixed in place. "We owe it to our people to be clever, not impulsive."

With that, he returned to his seat.

Keenan leaned in. "I don't trust that one at all."

"Yeah," I murmured. "He's got that 'slimy politician' energy."

I turned to say something to Reeger only to realize he was gone.

Good grief, I thought. That guy.

Lily remained still, her eyes locked on the stage, silently watching.

Chapter 26 - Noctari

The herald stepped forward once more. "And for our third speaker: Azmira of the Azure Veil, from the city of Cern."

A tall, slender woman gracefully walked to the front, her movements smooth and deliberate. The room fell into an expectant hush. Her skin shimmered in deep shades of purple and blue, and her silver eyes gleamed with unsettling depth. A flowing cloak swirled around her as she moved, and her long black hair veiled part of her face. Notably, no visible horns adorned her head.

She surveyed the crowd with a calm, knowing smile.

Azmira began to speak, and the moment she did, her voice wrapped around the room like silk, smooth, calm, but laced with something unnatural.

"As you all know," she said, "I have long supported stepping out of the shadows. But I do not crave war, nor do I wish to unravel what we've built in exile. Still, we are at an impasse, one we cannot ignore, no matter how much we long for peace. If we must choose a side, let it be not by fear or fury, but by reason."

She paused, letting her words settle in like dust on stone.

Lily muttered under her breath, "Do you feel that?"

I glanced over. "Feel what?"

"There's magic in her voice," she whispered, brow furrowed.

Keenan leaned in. "What? How?"

Lily shook her head. "Not sure."

"I do not love humans or dwarves," she continued. "But the demons? They are far worse. They have no reverence for beauty, for history, for the artistry of life. They would burn everything if it suited their whim. If we must choose evil…" Her voice lowered, growing colder, "…let it at least be the lesser one we understand."

Her silver gaze swept the room like a blade, sharp and searching.

Suddenly, Lily hissed, "Duck."

Before I could react, she and Keenan dropped low. "Why?" I began, turning toward her, but it was too late.

Azmira's eyes locked onto mine, and she smiled.

"Perhaps," she said smoothly, "we should ask our guests what they think."

I froze, silently chiding myself for not listening to Lily.

She sighed, rising to her feet. "Nice job, doofus," she muttered.

The hall erupted. Murmurs turned to shouts.

"Kill them!"

"Get them!"

Noctari all around us rose in alarm, bodies tensed to strike.

But Azmira's voice cut through the clamor, sudden and sharp.

"There will be none of that," she commanded, "not until we hear what they have to say."

A dozen armed Noctari rushed in and surrounded us. Without a word, they guided us from the balcony, down toward the stage.

And then we stood there, face-to-face with the three leaders, finally seeing them up close.

Maldras was unmistakably a warrior. Scars crisscrossed his face and arms, the marks of countless battles.

Chapter 26 - Noctari

Towering nearly seven feet tall, his sheer presence was enough to make most people think twice before speaking.

Vaeltharis, in contrast, was lean and wiry, exuding quiet cunning. He watched us with a smirk, eyes constantly calculating, as if measuring every word and movement for how it might benefit him.

Azmira, however, looked at us with a warm, almost intimate smile, like a friend welcoming long-lost companions. If we hadn't known better, we might've believed it. She had the kind of presence that made you want to trust her... to tell her anything she wanted to know.

"So," she said, her smile widening, "why are you here?"

Lily crossed her arms. "Okay, first off, your magic doesn't work on us, witch." She paused, frowning. "Or... sorcerer? Wait..."

"Mage," I whispered.

"Right, that," Lily said, refocusing. "Your magic doesn't work on us, mage. So maybe skip the mind games and get to the point."

Azmira's smile flickered, just for a moment, before she let out a soft chuckle and dropped some of the sweetness from her voice. "Well, aren't you three interesting?" she mused. "But no matter how I phrase it, the question stands, why are you here? And why have you brought Daemon back to us?"

Her gaze shifted to Keenan, who froze like he'd been slapped.

I blinked. "Daemon?"

Azmira tilted her head. "Oh, you didn't know his birth name? How tragic. Though I suppose Keenan is... acceptable."

Keenan and I stared at her in disbelief. Lily glanced between us, confused.

Azmira continued, her voice smooth as silk. "Your parents were murdered, weren't they? By dwarves, if memory serves. Though I doubt they ever told you that."

Keenan finally broke out of his stupor, his voice steady. "Yes, I know about my parents. But that's not why I'm here."

Azmira's smile deepened. "No," she said softly. "I suppose not. A conversation for another time, perhaps."

Vaeltharis leaned forward, eyes narrowing. "I would like to know why this Noctari stands with these humans and wears the mark of a Paladin."

Azmira let out a pleasant laugh. "Oh, you haven't heard?" She clicked her tongue. "Tsk, tsk. Your network of spies is slipping, dear."

Vaeltharis scowled. "Just spit it out, Az. We don't have time for this."

Her eyes flashed at the nickname, but she quickly masked her annoyance with another sweet smile. "He became a Paladin two weeks ago, actually. Busy saving lives, fighting monsters, making the world a better place." She turned her gaze back to Keenan, savoring the moment.

Maldras scoffed and shook his head. "Enough. If he's a Paladin, that's all the more reason to kill him."

His golden eyes burned with fury as he glared at Keenan.

Chapter 26 - Noctari

Azmira sighed theatrically. "Maldras, darling, the adults are speaking. Be quiet until we need something smashed, hmm?"

The room fell still.

We all stared, stunned by how casually she dismissed him. Maldras looked ready to explode, but instead, he glared at her, nostrils flaring, then took a single step back and folded his arms tightly.

Azmira turned back to us, all warmth again. "Now," she said sweetly, "I'll ask one more time before Maldras here practices his culinary skills on all three of you."

Vaeltharis chuckled under his breath, but a sharp glance from Maldras shut him up immediately.

Azmira's silver eyes locked onto mine.

"Well?" she said, voice soft but full of authority. "We are waiting."

Chapter 27 - Complications

Lily started to smile. "Do you have any furniture?" she asked.

"No, no," I replied, as the Noctari exchanged confused glances.

Keenan quickly stepped forward. "We've come to ask you to join us and work together in protecting our world."

Maldris laughed. Azmira smirked. Vaeltris crossed his arms and said smugly, "Really?"

"Yes," Keenan affirmed. "We were going to offer you a place to stay, a safe haven." He glanced around, hesitating. "But there are... a lot more of you than we expected."

Maldris glared. "You humans and your arrogance. You think you're the ones who'll protect us? You can't even protect yourselves from us."

The crowd murmured in agreement. Cries of "Here, here!" and "Yes!" rippled through the Noctari.

Emboldened, Maldris stepped forward, a confident smirk on his lips. "You've come to bargain but you should be begging for our help."

The Noctari erupted in cheers, but Azmira and Vaeltris exchanged uneasy glances, seeing the room shift.

Keenan held his ground, meeting Maldris' gaze. "It's better for all of us to work together than to fight each other."

Maldris snorted. "Do they teach you that drivel in Paladin school?" He smiled cruelly.

Chapter 27 - Complications

"No," Keenan said evenly. "That's just common sense."

The subtle jab landed. Rage flared in Maldris' eyes. "Listen, pup," he bellowed. "What gives you the right to come in here and insult me? I'll have your tail hung on the hearth, you clanless coward!"

Keenan didn't flinch, but for a moment, I saw the old Keenan flash through, and I worried what might happen.

But I should have been watching Lily.

She stepped forward, deliberately, to the center of the stage. Her eyes blazed with fire.

"Okay, Mr. Tough Guy," she said, her voice sharp with irritation. "I've survived too much and come too far to let blowhards like you jeopardize my world and my friends. So, if you're looking for a fight, you big oaf... come over here and pick one with me."

I hadn't seen her this angry in a long time. Her hair glowed like embers. Her eyes flickered like flames. Smoke curled from her nostrils. She was staring daggers at Maldris.

He burst into laughter. "You see this?" he roared to the crowd. "See how weak humans and this outcast have become? He's too much of a coward to fight, so they send a little girl to challenge me!"

Still laughing, he stepped forward, towering over her. But Lily didn't move. She stood her ground, furious.

I muttered under my breath, "Please don't kill him, Lily."

Azmira glanced at me, a flicker of surprise in her eyes. Then she looked back to the stage. A slow smile spread across her face. "Oh, this should be interesting," she murmured.

Lily smirked. "Well?" she taunted. "You gonna fight me or just stand there blowing hot air all day like a volcano that never erupts?"

Maldris snorted, staring down at her, trying to figure out the trick.

Lily tapped her foot, clearly unimpressed. "Well?" she said again. "Are you going to do something, or just stand there like a statue?"

He let out a short laugh. "There's no honor or worth in killing a child." He turned away dismissively.

Lily's eyes blazed hotter. "Don't you dare turn your back on me, you filthy Noctari coward!"

He froze.

Lily smirked. "Oh, that got you, huh?"

I shook my head and started backing up. So did Keenan. Azmira and Vaeltris exchanged wary glances, then followed our lead.

Maldris turned slowly, seething. "What did you say?" he growled, pulling his massive war maul off his back.

"Ooo, that did do it, huh? Cowardly little Noctari," Lily taunted, her tone razor-sharp.

I shook my head again. She was really trying... which was terrifying.

Azmira leaned in, whispering, "This is a bad idea. She should stop saying that."

I sighed. "Trust me. This is beyond my control."

Azmira just shook her head. "It's her funeral."

I hesitated. "No... but it might be his."

Azmira looked at me in shock.

Chapter 27 - Complications

Maldris took a step forward as the crowd erupted in bloodthirsty chants. "Kill her!" and "Destroy her!"

He grinned, feeding off their frenzy. "Well," he said, striding toward Lily, "I always give the people what they want, little worm. And they want you dead."

He hefted the massive hammer and swung.

Lily barely stepped aside, her lips curling into a smile. "Oh, I see why you stay hidden. You can't even hit a little girl."

Snarling, he swung again. And again.

Each time, Lily slipped just out of reach, her movements effortless. Her cool composure only enraged him more. His strikes grew wild, sloppy.

Then slowly, his stance shifted. He began to adapt, reading her rhythm, adjusting his timing.

And finally, he caught her.

The maul slammed into her ribs, crushing them. Her small frame rocketed into the wall with a sickening crash.

The world stopped.

A flash from two thousand years ago hit me, the moment she fell, the moment I rushed to her, barely keeping her alive by freezing her in time.

It took everything I had not to transform into a dragon right then and tear Maldris apart.

But I knew Lily had a plan. Or at least... I hoped she did and I needed to trust her.

Maldris stood over her, breathing hard, arms raised in triumph. The crowd erupted in thunderous cheers.

He let out a bellowing laugh, basking in their cheers and in his triumph.

Keenan stepped forward, but I held out a hand, my eyes locked on Lily's motionless body.

The room fell silent.

Then...a laugh. Soft, raspy... but unmistakably hers.

Maldris turned, the triumph on his face giving way to disbelief.

Lily was standing.

Blood ran from her lips and dripped from her nose. She clutched her ribs, gasping for air. But despite everything, she was smiling.

Maldris stared, stunned. "Not possible," he muttered.

Lily coughed, then smirked. "So," she rasped, "are you gonna finish the job... or just stand there looking stupid?"

He didn't move.

"What kind of magic is this?" he demanded.

She grinned. "Noooo..." she drew the word out, taunting. Then her expression shifted. "Then it's my turn."

The air pulsed with heat.

Lily began to change.

Her hair flared red-hot, smoke billowed from her nostrils, and her eyes ignited with blinding white fire. Her body grew, shifted, until a roar shook the very foundations of the theater.

The walls lit up, ancient glyphs glowing to life, playing scenes of a fire dragon locked in battle against hordes of enemies.

We watched in stunned silence.

I chuckled under my breath. Oh, Dorrim, you old scoundrel. Even after all these centuries, he'd left Lily one final gift.

Chapter 27 - Complications

Now fully transformed, Lily loomed above the crowd in her dragon form. She flicked her eyes to the glowing murals, smirking, then dropped onto all fours and lunged.

With one claw, she snatched Maldris off the ground. His war maul clattered to the floor.

She brought him close. Her voice rumbled deep and powerful. "Well? What now, little pup?"

Maldris stared into her blazing eyes. Defeated, he muttered, "Do your worst, dragon. I won't beg."

Lily bared her teeth in a wicked grin.

She opened her jaws and stuffed his upper body inside. Gasps. Screams.

I sighed. "Alright, Lil. I think you've made your point."

She paused, then pulled him back out and set him gently on the ground, laughing. With a shimmer, she shifted back into her human form. "You should've seen your face," she teased, giving him a playful smack on the back.

Maldris just sat there, stunned.

Lily plopped down in front of him, watching him quietly.

Azmira muttered "A dragon…" then leaned toward me and whispered, "I've never seen him so subdued. And I've known him for thirty years."

I nodded. "She can be annoying, but she has a way of getting to people."

Finally, Maldris looked at Lily.

She smiled at him. "Thank you for not begging. I hate it when people beg."

Then she stood and extended her hand.

Maldris hesitated, confused.

"We can be friends now," she said simply.

Slowly, the massive Noctari rose to his feet, towering over the much smaller girl. After a long pause, he reached out and clasped her hand.

Lily grinned. "See? We can be friends. We just gotta beat each other up sometimes."

A small smile tugged at the corner of Maldris' mouth.

As he turned away, a few other Noctari began approaching, murmuring among themselves and stealing cautious glances at us.

Keenan shook his head. "What the heck was that, Lil? Are you crazy?"

Lily blinked at him. "Uhhh... duh? Where have you been? You're just figuring this out now?"

I tried to smile, but no words came.

Lily turned to me, concerned. "What?"

I opened my mouth but still couldn't speak. I just smiled.

Then realization hit her. "Oh! Sorry, bro," she said, rushing forward to hug me. "I didn't even think about that. Please don't be mad at me."

I chuckled, wrapping an arm around her. "I'm not mad." I took a deep breath.

Keenan glanced around at the Noctari. "Well, that definitely made an impression."

"Yeah," I said with a wry smile. "Good or bad? Yet to be determined."

Lily scoffed. "Uh, clearly good. Look... no more fighting. See?"

Chapter 27 - Complications

The energy in the room had changed. The once hostile Noctari were now quiet, subdued, whispering among themselves and casting glances our way.

Right then, Reeger appeared beside us. A few Noctari noticed him, but none said a word.

"So," he asked, "what did I miss?"

Lily gasped. "Are you kidding me?!" She gestured dramatically. "You just missed one of the greatest shows this theater has ever put on!"

Then, more softly, she looked up at the glowing glyphs still faintly visible on the walls. "I got to see Dorrim's last gift to me."

Reeger raised an eyebrow. Keenan quickly filled him in. Reeger shook his head. "Of course you did," he muttered, eyeing Lily as she smirked.

"Wait," I said, narrowing my eyes. "Where did you run off to?"

Reeger grinned. "The demons had one of those gargoyles spying on us. When it spotted us up in the balcony, I tailed it before it could report back."

"And?" I asked.

He smirked. "Not as flashy as Lily", she gave a small, proud bow..." but I tricked it into turning to stone... then shattered it. Now it just blends in with the ruins."

Lily blinked. "Wow. That's kinda dark."

Reeger gave her a look. "Says the girl who pretended to bite a guy in half."

Lily laughed. "Ohhh, the look on his face." She shook her head, still chuckling to herself.

The Noctari had begun to leave. Vaeltris had already slipped out, and as Maldris reached the doors, he paused.

He glanced back at Lily and gave her a small nod, silent but respectful, before disappearing through the exit.

Azmira finally approached us, a thoughtful smile on her face. "Well," she said, glancing at Reeger, "you four have certainly given us much to think about... and even a bit of a show."

She looked at Lily, who responded with an exaggerated curtsy.

"But," Azmira continued, "I'm not sure how much this will actually change."

I shook my head. "You know the demons will destroy everything when they come. We should work together."

She nodded slowly. "Yes, you and I know that. But most Noctari have spent so long hiding that the idea of stepping into the open, let alone fighting alongside men and dwarves, is... unsettling."

I sighed. "As you may have guessed, Lily and I are protectors of this world. We'll fight for any good in it, no matter the race."

Azmira smiled faintly. "I appreciate that. But I fear very few will stand with you in the end." Her gaze drifted to the door, her expression tinged with sadness. "And Maldris... his hatred for the dwarves runs deep after what they did to his family."

Keenan crossed his arms. "What about Vaeltris?"

Azmira shook her head. "He's just as likely to feed you bread as stab you in the back. He'll switch sides the moment it benefits him. But his people love him, and he tries to do what's best for them, so he stays in power."

I studied her. "And what about you?"

Chapter 27 - Complications

She sighed. "I want what's best for my people." A pause. Then she met my eyes. "And I'll do whatever I must to achieve that. Even if it means fighting a dragon."

She turned to Lily with a sly smile. "Though my survival instincts would prefer otherwise."

Lily grinned. "Mine too. You're the prettiest Noctari I've ever seen, and I'd hate to have to eat you."

Azmira laughed. "Well, I'd hate that as well."

She continued, "We've decided to take this discussion back to our people. Since you crashed our meeting this time, the next one will be in a smaller, more secure location." She shook her head slightly, then met my gaze again. "Once a decision has been made, one way or another, I'd like to meet with you again to discuss it."

I nodded. "You're welcome in Grissom anytime."

She offered a faint smile. "I doubt I'll be traveling that far. But if you come to the obelisk…"

"Spire," Lily muttered under her breath.

Azmira glanced at her but continued, "…one of my people will find you and bring you to me." She exhaled. "Come back in two days. I should have an answer for you, and hopefully we can make plans from there."

She shook her head. "Don't expect good news… but I suppose there's always hope."

With that, she bid us farewell and left.

The four of us stood in the now-empty theater, the conversation replaying in my mind.

Lily, however, was smiling.

Keenan raised an eyebrow. "Okay," he said with a chuckle, "what are you grinning about?"

"Oh," she replied absently, "I was just replaying the glyphs in my head." She stood and looked at me. "You know he was my favorite, right?"

I smiled. "He knew it in the end, too."

"I hope so," she said quietly.

I swallowed hard, forcing back the emotions rising in my throat. "You know it was the Architects who kept you safe until I got there, right?"

Tears welled in Lily's eyes. "Yeah," she murmured. "I went in to save them, but I was too reckless... and got hit."

I nodded. "They rallied around you. Fought with a fury that put berserkers to shame, just to protect you."

A single tear slipped down her cheek. "Really?"

"Yep," I said, my own eyes stinging at the memory. "And I made sure the demons knew they'd been stood up by artists and sculptors." I smiled softly, though the ache lingered.

Lily sighed and shook her head. "Oh, Dorrim..."

She wiped her tears away, straightened her shoulders, and her usual spark returned. "Well," she said, voice regaining its energy, "this theater better survive, because we have to come back so I can show you guys the glyphs again."

Reeger shrugged. "Why not just show us now?"

Lily gasped dramatically. "Are you kidding? If I showed you now, you'd lose your best reason for living. Not happening."

We all laughed, the tension easing for a moment.

Chapter 27 - Complications

As we stepped out of the theater and began the walk back to Grissom, our smiles faded, replaced by a heavier silence. One question weighed on all of us: what would the Noctari decide?

And more importantly... when the reckoning came, would they stand beside us, or against us?

Chapter 28 - Devastation

As we approached the city, a faint smell of fire and smoke hung in the air. We exchanged uneasy glances.

"Well, that can't be good," Keenan muttered.

We quickened our pace. At first, nothing in Grissom seemed out of the ordinary. But when we looked toward the mountains and the elven forest, the horizon glowed with an eerie orange hue, flickering even against the night sky.

Reeger stared hard, then shook his head. "No... it must be the warrens, maybe somewhere near the beach," he murmured.

When we reached the city, it was alive with movement even at this late hour. People rushed through the streets, guards stood alert at the gates and outer walls. We made our way straight to the inn, one of our designated meeting point in times of crisis.

Sure enough, Throm and Grog were at the bar, weapons within reach.

Reeger strode up. "Any word?" His voice was tight.

Throm shook his head. "It started burning two, maybe three hours ago. No word since. But if I know my brother, he'll have sent the Hammers to help and scouts to gather information. Hopefully your people don't need the help," he added with a glance at Lily and a small smile, "but the Hammers are a force to be reckoned with."

Lily nodded. "They have to be. They're named after me."

Chapter 28 - Devastation

Reeger tried to look composed, but the worry in his eyes was plain. He exhaled sharply and began shedding extra gear. "I need to head that way."

Lily sighed and set down her pack. "Come on, guys. Let's help him out."

Keenan nodded and followed suit. I looked at my friends and my sister. We didn't know how bad it was, but none of us hesitated. We were going to help our friend. I smiled.

Grog chuckled and hopped off his stool, grabbing his axe. "I'm coming with you."

We turned to him, surprised.

He raised an eyebrow at our looks. "What? You've never seen a real dwarf fight. About time you did." He cracked his thick fingers and grinned. "Who do you think trained the Hammers? My boys'll end any threat still breathing, but it wouldn't hurt to stretch my legs."

Keenan smirked. "Grog, you forget, I've seen Throm fight."

Grog squinted at Throm, then looked back at Keenan. A rare laugh rumbled from his chest. "Like I said, you've never seen a real dwarf fight. Now come on. Let's go save the pointies."

Reeger shook his head, a reluctant smile tugging at his mouth.

But before we could move, the door burst open.

A gravely wounded elf staggered inside, then collapsed to the floor.

"Saevel!" Reeger cried, rushing to him and cradling his head.

Keenan dropped to his knees beside them, working swiftly to assess and stabilize the elf's wounds. Saevel was a mess, covered in cuts and gashes, his left side badly burned. He drifted in and out of consciousness as Keenan worked.

At last, Keenan exhaled. "Okay. He should be stable, but he's in rough shape."

Grog emerged from the kitchen holding a small vial. He handed it to Reeger with a gruff nod. "Drink," he said flatly. I was surprised, healing potions were incredibly rare and very expensive.

Reeger took the bright red liquid and gently pressed it to Saevel's cracked lips, slowly pouring it in. The elf sputtered but managed to swallow. Gradually, his breathing steadied, and his eyes fluttered open.

He scanned the room, then focused on Reeger. "We've lost the wood," he rasped. "Your father sent me to find you, to ask for help. But... it may already be too late."

Reeger's expression darkened. "What of the stones? Didn't they help?"

Saevel shook his head weakly. "Your father didn't trust them. They were never placed except by a few elders who brought them into their homes. That saved some of us from the first wave."

The room went still as Saevel continued. Portals had erupted across the forest, spewing demons in relentless waves. At first, the elves held their ground, but the tide kept growing, more portals, more demons.

"Eventually, Thaylan ordered me to find you," Saevel said. "To ask for aid. But I think... he knew it was hopeless. The last I saw, he and fifteen warriors were making a final

Chapter 28 - Devastation

stand at the Greatwood in the center of Calen near the elder's garden. But there were hundreds of demons, some as big as trees."

Throm leaned in. "Did you see any dwarves?"

Saevel shook his head. "No. But as I left the woods, I heard battle coming from the mountain."

Keenan frowned. "I wonder if Brom knows…"

"I think Thalion was dispatched to seek aid," Saevel added. "But I don't know if he made it out or how well the humans will fare."

I allowed myself a small smile, thinking of Brom and Victus cutting down demons, and hoping they were still alive.

Throm exhaled sharply. "You should go. We've wasted enough time."

"Agreed," I said, grabbing my weapon as the others followed suit.

Saevel tried to rise but stumbled. Reeger caught him. "No," he said firmly. "You need to recover."

The elf set his jaw. "No. My place is with you, now more than ever. You might be the last leader we have left. We need to keep you safe."

Reeger blinked, clearly taken aback. Then, understanding softened his expression. He placed a firm hand on Saevel's shoulder and smiled.

"Then my first command is this: rest for three hours. Then come find me. Don't worry, I won't engage unless there's a real chance at victory. And I've got two secret weapons they're not expecting." He glanced at Lily and me, grinning.

Lily and I exchanged a knowing look and smiled, earning a puzzled glance from Saevel.

"All right," Grog said, cracking his knuckles again. "My axe is crying for some demon blood. Let's go."

As we filed out the door, Throm helped Saevel into a chair and brought him food.

Outside, the smell of smoke had grown stronger, thick and pungent in the cool night air. Without hesitation, we made our way through the northern gate. Once we were a few hundred yards from the city and out of sight, I turned to Lily.

"How's your energy level?"

She grinned. "You read my mind."

In a flash, we both shifted forms. Lily bellowed, "All aboard the demon-butt-kicking express!" as she lowered her neck. I chuckled.

Reeger and Keenan climbed onto our backs without hesitation. Keenan shook his head in disbelief. "Given the situation, this is probably the worst time to say this... but riding a dragon is awesome."

I laughed, then turned to Grog, who stood rooted to the spot.

"Grog?" I asked, pausing.

He slowly shook his head. "It's one thing having you two as our guardians. It's another thing entirely to step on one of you." He took a step back, then another, clearly torn.

"Come on, Grog, it's no big deal," I said.

"Says you," he muttered, staring up at me in awe.

I sighed. "Don't make me carry you in my claws."

The old Grog surfaced instantly, eyes narrowing into a glare. "You wouldn't dare."

Chapter 28 - Devastation

I glanced at Lily, who was already grinning mischievously. Before Grog could react, she snatched him up in one of her claws and launched into the air, his protests and colorful dwarven curses echoing behind her.

I grinned and stretched my wings. "Been a while, big guy. Let's see if we still remember how to fly."

"You better!" Keenan called from my back. "I can't fly!"

Laughing, I kicked off the ground and soared into the air.

As we neared the woods, the devastation became unmistakable. Entire sections of forest were scorched to ash, flames still licking at the edges of massive blackened clearings. The air stank of smoke, sap, and death.

Reeger pointed to a landing spot, and we descended into a charred clearing. The remains of homes and trees lay scattered across the ground, mingled with the lifeless bodies of elves and demons.

"Lily, stay with them and look around," I said. "I'm going to put out some of these fires."

With that, I launched back into the air, scanning the destruction from above. I doused two of the worst blazes, then turned to a third when cheers rose from below.

Circling back, I descended once more and spotted nearly a hundred dwarves emerging from the tree line, weapons ready but held low. They approached me with heads bowed, then dropped to one knee in reverence.

"Kisago, we are honored that you would join us in battle," one of them said.

"Tholdrun?" I asked.

He looked up sharply, startled. "You... know me?"

I chuckled. "One sec."

With a flash of light, I shifted back into human form. His eyes widened in disbelief, and he bowed again, deeper this time.

"No, no," I said quickly, holding up a hand. "None of that. But I'd like to know what happened here."

He straightened, nodding. "We had watchtowers set up and spotted the portals almost right away. We assumed the elves needed help, so we pushed in about an hour after the first sounds of combat. Resistance was light until we reached what was left of one of their cities, here in this clearing. That's when we ran into a couple of the big ones."

"How are your numbers?" I asked.

Tholdrun turned to glance at his men. "We're still near full strength. We lost two, took down forty-seven demons and both giants that killed our own."

I nodded, solemn. "Please record their names."

He nodded. That was something I'd begun after the Great War, ensuring no sacrifice was ever forgotten. Whenever I could, I'd return to read those names aloud, one by one.

"What about the elves?" I asked. "Any survivors?"

His expression darkened. "Not yet. Just bodies." He paused. "We separated them from the demons and burned the enemy corpses."

"Well done," I said quietly. "I'm proud of you."

Tholdrun stood a bit taller at that. "What are your orders now?"

"If I hadn't shown up, what would you have done?"

"Report back. Let them know the stones aren't working."

Chapter 28 - Devastation

I shook my head. "No. They were never used. I have it on good authority."

He gasped. "Why would they refuse them?"

I exhaled slowly. "I don't know. But I intend to find out."

With nothing left to fight and no survivors to aid, the dwarves began their march back toward the mountain.

I flew to the clearing where Keenan was still picking through the fallen, searching for anyone clinging to life. Reeger was quietly burying the elves they'd found, his expression grim. Lily was dragging demon corpses into a growing pile. Grog was nowhere in sight.

I landed and asked, "Where's Grog?"

Keenan, clearly exhausted, stood and wiped his hands on his tunic. "No idea. He wandered off that way," he said, pointing into the woods.

I looked to Reeger, who frowned. "There's nothing in that direction."

A few minutes later, Grog returned, his axe streaked with blood and his face set in a grim scowl.

"Well, he clearly found something that way," Reeger muttered.

Grog looked straight at me, shook his head, and said one word: "Possessed."

Reeger and I sighed in unison. Keenan tossed a shattered shield onto a pile of broken weapons.

"Well, I don't..." Keenan began, but Reeger sharply signaled for silence.

I immediately moved to stand in front of the group, my gaze locked on the direction Reeger pointed. Lily shot into the sky, circling above. It was one of our old tactics, she'd rain down fire from above while I served as bait. Keenan and Grog flanked me, and I lowered my wings slightly to shield them. Reeger vanished into the woods.

A few tense moments passed.

Then came a bird call, followed by a response. And another. Reeger emerged from the tree line, five elves cautiously stepping out near him. They eyed me warily, until Reeger clasped their hands in greeting, relief washing over his face.

"Please tell me there are more of you," he said.

The lead elf, who introduced himself as Traeliorn, shook his head. "We were the only ones watching the northern slopes by the sea. When the fighting started, we were ordered to hold position. But when the fires weren't contained and we heard nothing else, we broke orders and came back."

He paused, voice heavy. "But it was too late. The forest was burning, and we couldn't find the elite guard or the elders anywhere."

Reeger nodded grimly. "We haven't found them either."

"They knew exactly where to strike," Traeliorn murmured, his brows furrowed. "I don't understand how they caught us so completely off guard. It's... incomprehensible."

Reeger stared into the distance. "Pride," he said quietly. "Thinking we always know better."

"What was that?" Traeliorn asked.

"Nothing," Reeger replied, shaking his head.

Chapter 28 - Devastation

I watched him, heart aching. The weight of the loss was etched across his face. I remembered the day our creator, mentor, and eldest brother gave his life to save our world. The memory flared in me like a spark to dry tinder. Anger simmered, but then I heard his voice in my mind:

Emotion is a strong thing, a gift, but never let it control you, or you'll become a fool.

I smiled at the blunt wisdom. He wasn't wrong.

Emotion is powerful.

But control is even more powerful.

Lily landed beside us, and the elves instinctively stepped back, hands tightening around their bows.

She chuckled. "Relax, I have no plans to roast any elves today."

I shot her a warning look.

"Oh," she added, glancing around. "Too soon?"

Keenan tried to suppress a grin. Grog grunted. "I like her."

The elves explained they had been heading for the beach, following an ancient fallback plan dating back centuries. Few had believed an invasion could ever truly happen, and the strategy hadn't been reviewed in generations.

We agreed to go with them. Relief washed over their faces. Their eyes flicked between me and Lily, and the tension in their shoulders eased. They knew their odds of survival had just risen significantly.

Lily and I shifted back into our human forms. The elves stared, shaking their heads in quiet awe.

We moved cautiously through the forest, silence broken only by the soft crunch of leaves beneath our feet. Occasionally, we passed the bodies of fallen elves, but more often, demons lying twisted and broken. The elves had made them pay dearly.

As we neared the beach, the lead scout raised a hand for silence. The group spread out, eyes scanning every shadow. After a tense moment, one of them motioned us forward.

But hope died the moment we stepped out of the trees.

The beach was a graveyard. Burned ships lay in ruins along the shoreline, and the sand was stained dark with blood. Bodies were everywhere, the elves had made their last stand here.

Reeger broke into a run, sprinting across the devastation until he came to a charred vessel surrounded by corpses. He dropped to his knees beside a fallen figure, his father surrounded by dead elite guard faithful to the end. Wordlessly, he took his hand, grief etched deep into his face.

I bowed my head, heart heavy. This island had been home to the last great elven stronghold, the final creation of the Eldest, apart from Lily and me. And now... it was gone.

Lily sat down in the sand, drawing absentminded patterns with one finger, her expression distant.

"I can't believe it," Traeliorn whispered, eyes scanning the wreckage. "How did we fall like this? We knew they were coming. We had the stones. They should've stopped the portals..."

I didn't have the heart to correct him.

Keenan kept searching the debris, desperate for anyone he could still help. But the truth hung heavy in the air.

The devastation was complete.

Chapter 28 - Devastation

Maybe six or seven elves remained alive, perhaps a few scattered across distant islands, but this... this was the end of a once great people.

I turned to ask Grog a question when a sudden ripple in the air made us all freeze.

A portal tore open, crackling with dark energy. From it emerged a massive demon, easily twenty feet tall, flanked by several smaller demons. He snorted as he took in the devastation, a cruel smile curling across his face. Then his eyes locked onto our small, battered group.

"Who has the authority to treat with me?" he bellowed.

Grog stepped forward, gripping his axe, fire in his eyes.

"Grog," I said sharply.

He glanced back at me, and I shook my head with a small smile. "Not yet."

I stepped forward. "I do."

Lily sprang to her feet, glaring, while the elves spread out, bows drawn and ready.

The demon exhaled a plume of smoke, eyeing me for a long moment. "So be it."

One of the smaller demons muttered something guttural and venomous.

I glanced at Keenan, who leaned in and whispered, "Colorful language. Fairly sure you've been insulted."

I smirked, then looked back up at the towering demon. "Well? Are you here to surrender?"

The demon blinked, visibly thrown off for a second, then burst into a jagged, guttural laugh.

"Oh, you're either brave, stupid, or a jester," he sneered. "But I admire the bravado, little human."

Hammer and Anvil

I gave a faint, unbothered smile.

Lily leaned toward me and whispered, "Now?"

I shook my head. She sighed, disappointed.

The demon's grin widened. "No. I came to offer you mercy, though it may be the last you'll ever get. We've proven your kind is no match for us. We don't need to slaughter every last one of you... but we will."

He bared his jagged teeth. "One by one, your people will fall. The elves were the best you had..."

Grog snorted.

", and they were crushed in a single evening."

The demon pressed on. "So tell me, will you surrender this world, or must we continue the bloodshed?"

I opened my mouth to answer, but Keenan stepped forward first, a smirk on his face.

"You're scared," he said.

The demon's eyes narrowed.

Keenan chuckled. "That's what this is, isn't it? You got lucky. You hit the elves hard and fast, but now you're worried. You think we'll rally. You're trying to bluff us while we're still hurting. But the truth is, you're not sure you can win. How pathetic."

The demon's expression twisted into a snarl.

I raised a hand calmly to Keenan and looked at the demon. "He's not wrong though. Your kind revels in pain and chaos. So why offer peace? Why parley, unless you're not sure?"

The demon's sneer faltered for a breath, then returned in full force. "Some among my kin may wish to limit the bloodshed," he said slowly. "But you're right, human."

His voice dropped to a low, menacing growl.

Chapter 28 - Devastation

"I am not one of them."

He took a step forward, the ground trembling beneath him.

"You whelps will not hinder my celebration of victory tonight, for it was I who brought this destruction upon you and there is nothing..."

A sharp twang split the air.

An arrow struck the demon in the throat.

I turned to see Reeger already notching another. His expression was cold. "So, you are responsible," he said flatly.

Five more arrows followed, thudding into the demon's neck, clustering around the first. He staggered, choking on his own blood.

"Kill them, you fools!" he sputtered, clutching his throat.

The smaller demons lunged, but they didn't get far.

Grog spun into action, cleaving three in half with a single swing. Another he split clean from head to toe like he was chopping firewood. The last demon barely had time to react before Grog's blade smashed into its skull, knocking it out cold.

The elves loosed a volley of arrows, raining down on the towering demon with relentless precision. He tried to strike back, but he was no match. Seconds later, he crashed to the ground, gasping and seething, then finally laying still.

Reeger came to stand beside me, quiet and calm.

"It's good," he said softly, "to no longer be consumed by vengeance. It's a destructive companion. But those responsible for my father's death have been brought to justice. Now... we can focus on saving what's left of this world."

I placed a hand on his shoulder. "I'm sorry, my friend. Truly."

He offered a faint smile. "As long as the four of us make it, I think I'll be okay."

I nodded. "Then let's make that happen."

Lily strolled over, arms crossed. "Well, that stunk."

We all turned to her.

She shrugged. "Didn't even get to scare anyone by transforming."

We laughed.

Grog shook his head. "At least we know they can't portal into the other cities. But the woods aren't safe anymore."

"Agreed," I said.

The five remaining elves approached. One stepped forward. "Since you are the last of the elder line, we will follow you wherever you go."

Reeger grasped each of their hands in turn. "I'm honored to have you by my side."

I looked over at Grog and grinned. "You must be getting rusty. You missed that last demon, you only knocked him out."

Grog snorted. "Gam always wanted a prisoner to question. Old habits die hard."

I chuckled. "Yeah... though I'm not sure how much he'll tell us."

Grog shrugged. "We'll find out."

Chapter 28 - Devastation

With that, we secured the unconscious demon and left the forest behind, heading toward the mountain.

Chapter 29 - What Now

We arrived at the mountain just after midnight and collapsed into the barracks of the outer city. A few hours of restless sleep passed before dawn stirred us awake. By then, the prisoner was already gone.

The king awaited us in the same meeting hall where we had first met. As we walked to join him, I noticed several of the Hammers stationed throughout the town, their presence a silent reminder of the night's cost.

He waited patiently as the four of us entered, accompanied by the six elves we had rescued from the forest. Once everyone was seated, he asked us to recount what had happened. Some of it he already knew from the Hammers' report, but he listened intently when the elves spoke, their voices heavy with grief.

When they finished, the elves retreated to the back of the room, heads bowed, whispering softly to one another. Silence lingered until the king finally exhaled a heavy sigh.

"This is a terrible blow. Archers of that caliber would have been vital in defending the towns. And losing the wood entirely... devastating."

Reeger shook his head. "They wouldn't have come to your aid. They would have stayed in the forest and died there alone." His voice carried sorrow sharpened into bitterness, and it broke my heart to watch him lash out at their memory.

Chapter 29 - What Now

"We would have come to yours!" the king exclaimed, slamming his fist on the table.

Reeger nodded. "I have no doubt. And you did, last night. But my people would not have come to yours. Too preoccupied with pride and petty quarrels."

Keenan placed a hand on his shoulder. Reeger sighed. "Now we have no home. No future."

The king's expression softened. "You are welcome under the mountain. You shall be kin to us, if you accept."

The elves stirred, surprised. Rarely were they invited beneath the mountain. Lily grinned and smacked the king's back. "Aww, you old softy."

Reeger bowed his head. "We are honored. We accept and will defend you until the battle is won."

Despite their sorrow, curiosity flickered in the elves' eyes at the thought of seeing within the mountain. The king sighed. "Their goal is clearer now. It isn't just conquest. Anyone descended from the Eldest or Mother is a target."

"They're using divide and conquer," Keenan added. "They'll wear us down until nothing's left."

The king nodded grimly. "But we can't meet their hordes in open battle."

"And we can't take the fight to their world," I said. "We don't have the numbers."

"So, what now?" the king murmured.

Lily shook her head. "Man, you guys are a barrel of laughs. We win. Duh."

I smiled. "A simple plan. I like it."

The king smirked. "More importantly, how?"

Lily crossed her arms. "What do you do if someone's bigger and stronger?"

Silence. She put her hands on her hips. "It's a miracle you survived without me."

We waited. "Okay," she said, "you chip away. Take their weapon while they sleep. Spoil their food. Cut their supply lines."

Keenan smirked. "So... annoy them to death? Like you do to us?"

"Exactly!" she exclaimed, then paused. "Wait... I'm not annoying. I'm fun."

Keenan laughed. I nodded. "So... guerrilla warfare."

She blinked. "Wait...we have gorillas? And you're just now telling me!?"

"No," I said, amused. "Guerrilla warfare."

Her eyes widened. "And they know warfare!?"

Keenan chuckled. "Yep. This is fun."

Reeger laughed, while the king looked thoughtful. "That, we can do for a few days. But if they're preparing a full assault, we're in trouble."

"Agreed," I said. "At least we can harass them, buy time, and gather intel."

The king signaled a guard, then frowned. "The problem is, we only have so many portal stones and then who do we send? Our best warriors risk leaving us defenseless. The inexperienced risk dying when every life counts."

He sighed. Keenan finally spoke. "What if we send a small team first, just to find a weak spot? We set up an anchor. Once it's safe, we bring in the Hammers. Destroy what we can and get out fast."

The king jumped up, nodding. "Okay... that could work." He began pacing, his footsteps echoing against the stone walls.

Chapter 29 - What Now

"Agreed," Reeger said.

I nodded. "Our group can go first, set the anchor once we find a good location."

The king looked at us and sighed. I smiled. "I know. But we've been there before. We know what to expect, and we already have a rough idea of the layout."

Reeger turned to the elves. "You'll have to stay behind. Find Saevel and bring him back. He's probably searching for me, in the forest, maybe toward Burke or Grissom. I doubt he'd come here."

The elves looked ready to protest, but after a moment, they nodded and slipped out.

"We should go soon," I said. "After last night, they'll be celebrating. Hopefully, that means they'll be distracted."

Reeger smirked. "Even after we killed the leader of the attack?"

I nodded. "Yes. They never lead with their best. The first wave is pawns, meant to test us. When the real force comes, whatever hits us first will be nothing compared to what follows. But it will still hurt."

Reeger, Keenan, and the king all nodded. The king turned to a guard. "Bring the portal stones." Moments later, the mages entered, beginning preparations.

He looked at me with a small smile. "Your gnome friend has been helpful. You can now set timers on the return stones. They'll stay open for as long, or as short, as you need."

I grinned. "That's nice. Waiting last time was... unnerving."

The king chuckled. "This time, we'll set the return point just outside the gates. When you come back, you're welcome to bring friends. Just try not to bring too many."

I laughed, then paused. "Wait... where's Grog?"

The king nodded. "He went back to Grissom before you woke up. Something about no one else knowing how to make a proper breakfast."

"Of course," I muttered, shaking my head before turning to the others. "You guys ready?"

Keenan and Reeger both nodded.

Lily snorted. "I was born ready."

We all turned to look at her.

"What?" she said. "I was! I was literally born at full size, ready to fight."

Her eyes widened, and she glanced at me. "Wait..." She hesitated, then winced. "Were we even born?"

I laughed. "I doubt it. Probably just created or something."

She looked down, shaking her head. "My whole life is a lie."

Keenan smirked. "It's like the chicken and the egg."

"The what?" Lily asked, narrowing her eyes.

I sighed. "No, Keenan." But it was already too late.

She turned to him, smirking. "Explain!"

He grinned. "Which came first, the chicken or the egg?"

She stared, then laughed. "That's the dumbest thing I've ever heard. Clearly, the..." She trailed off, brow furrowing. Then she looked back at Keenan. "Wait... is this some kind of weird Noctari riddle?"

Chapter 29 - What Now

He laughed. "Nope. Just a question people have been asking forever."

"No," she said firmly. "That's stupid. We've never asked that before."

I straightened, adopting a mock-serious tone. "Well, it's a philosophical question debated for centuries. Even the wisest scholars haven't reached a consensus."

She stared at me for a long moment before declaring, "Whatever. You guys are dumb. Let's go burn down some furniture!"

The king leaned toward me and whispered, "What is with the furniture?"

I shrugged. "I have no idea."

The mages activated the portal. The king handed us two stones, and with a nod to one another, we stepped through.

We emerged in the same place as before and quickly, quietly made our way toward the tunnels. More guards patrolled the paths now, but they didn't seem particularly concerned. Their eyes wandered, their steps sluggish, as if annoyed to be on duty at all. Slipping past them was easy, and we entered the tunnels unnoticed.

On the other side, we stepped once again into the vast expanse where we had seen the younger brother and his demons the day before. Three paths stretched before us.

To the right stood a massive stone castle surrounded by smaller structures, shouting and chaos echoing from that direction. Straight ahead, smaller buildings resembling houses were scattered about. To the left, a crumbling warehouse loomed in the torchlight and lava glow, heavily guarded by sentries.

Keenan closed his eyes, concentrating. When he opened them, he said, "The place on the left has a massive magical signature. Hard to pinpoint the type. Could be interference... or everything all at once."

"I don't like the sounds from the right," Lily muttered, shivering. "Nope. Don't like that at all."

"So," Reeger said, arms crossed, "middle is unknown. Left is unknown, but with magic."

Lily plopped dramatically onto the ground, pointed at me, and declared, "You pick. But there better be furniture, or you're fired."

I chuckled, glancing between the options. "What do you guys think?"

Keenan leaned toward the magic. Reeger preferred the house-like structures. I sighed. "Thanks, guys. Super helpful."

I thought back to our childhood, Keenan always leading us into trouble, Reeger or my uncles always bailing us out. I smiled.

"Keenan," I said.

"Yeah?" he replied.

"You were always good at finding the best trouble."

Keenan glanced around. "And that's... good?"

"Yep. I've got a good feeling about the left."

Reeger chuckled. "Looks like I'll have to bail you two out again."

We both laughed, but Lily narrowed her eyes.

"Wait, what? What's this 'bailing out'? There's a story here."

"Not now," I said as we headed toward the ruins.

Chapter 29 - What Now

"Oh no, no. You can't do this to me!" Lily huffed. "I need to know what happened! What did you two do? And more importantly, why wasn't I invited?"

"Because you were frozen," I said flatly.

She crossed her arms. "That's not a good enough reason. You should've unfrozen me sooner."

"Lily, you know I didn't have my memory back at that point."

She shook her head. "That sounds like a *you* problem."

I tried not to laugh as we made our way carefully toward the structure. When we arrived, we spotted six guards aimlessly wandering the area in front of the doors.

"How do you want to do this?" Keenan whispered.

"Not sure," I admitted. "But we should at least figure out what's inside before we attack."

Reeger nodded. "Be right back." He grinned and disappeared into the shadows.

"Be careful," Lily called after him with a smirk.

He shook his head but didn't stop. We waited silently for at least half an hour before he returned.

"Hey, remember those orbs in the cave?" Reeger asked.

"Yeah, the soul orbs, I think they were called," I said.

"Well," he said, glancing back at the structure, "this place is full of them. Some are massive."

"Really?" I grinned. "Sounds like a jackpot."

"Okay then," Lily said, springing to her feet.

I grabbed her arm and pulled her back down. "What are you doing?"

"What?" she asked, annoyed.

"No dragons unless we absolutely have to," I said, shaking my head. "We can't let them know we're alive."

She huffed. "Fine."

Then, before any of us could stop her, she casually strolled into the open.

The guards immediately snapped to attention, ran towards her and surrounded her. The lead demon stepped forward, eyes narrowing.

"Who are you? How did you get here?"

Lily laughed. "Are you serious right now?"

A Noctari guard behind her shoved her down. She stood slowly, brushing herself off, eyes locked on him.

"You will pay for that," she said coldly. Then, raising her voice, she announced, "I have one question!"

She paused dramatically. "Well, shoot. I guess I have *two* questions."

The guards exchanged confused glances.

"First," she said, hands on her hips, "where is your *nicest* furniture?"

They just stared at her, mouths slightly open.

"Hmmm. No response," she muttered. "Not the brightest bunch." Then she spun around and glared at the Noctari who had shoved her. "And now for my second question... Which came first, the chicken or the egg?"

The guards blinked, bewildered.

"She's crazy," one Noctari muttered.

Another whispered, "No... that's actually a good question."

"Kill her," the lead demon growled shaking his head.

Chapter 29 - What Now

Lily gasped dramatically. "Oh no! If only there were actually *smart* people here who knew what a distraction looked like!"

"Oh, shoot," I said, chuckling. "That's us."

We leapt from behind the rocks, catching the guards off-guard and taking them down in seconds.

Lily just stood in the center of the chaos, shaking her head. "Honestly," she muttered, "do I have to do and explain *everything*?"

Suddenly, Lily went rigid. "He's here," she said, eyes scanning the room.

A chill ran down my spine. I felt it too, the weight of his presence. Then, a hazy figure materialized before us. Though indistinct, his cruel smile was unmistakable.

"So, you fools decided to come back," he sneered. "I've been waiting for you."

The projection began circling us, his sharp gaze sizing us up. "You must be desperate... bringing a little girl to fight your battles."

He sniffed the air twice, then burst into laughter. "Oh, you've got to be kidding me."

I glanced at Lily, who looked at me with concern.

"You reek of dwarves," he went on, still laughing. Lily and I both let out small sighs of relief. He hadn't recognized us.

"So tell me, are they that weak? So few? Or just too cowardly to come here themselves?" His grin widened. "And if you stink of dwarves, then surely... you know of the elves."

His gaze locked on Reeger. "Tsk, tsk, tsk. Such foolishness. Such pride. Just like their creator."

My fists clenched, and I bit my cheek, fighting the urge to lash out.

I stole a glance at Lily, she was seething.

The figure drifted towards me, expression shifting to something more curious. "You were here before... but there's something different about you." He frowned, as if searching for the thought. Then he waved it off. "No matter. Your plans are known. You'll soon be taken. And once we have you, we'll learn everything."

He smiled wickedly as he was about to speak.

CRACK.

We all turned as several pieces of wood clattered to the floor. Lily stood with a broken chair in one hand and another gripped tightly in the other, her eyes glowing red.

She grinned. "You talk too much."

The figure scowled. "Listen here, you whelp..."

CRACK. Another chair shattered against the ground.

"You were saying?" she interrupted.

"I will not be..."

CRACK.

His image flickered.

That's when I realized what she was doing. I glanced at Keenan and mouthed, *Dispel magic.* He nodded and cast the spell. In an instant, the projection vanished.

"Good job, Sis," I said. "He was far away and his connection was weak."

Reeger smirked. "Breaking his concentration with chairs? Honestly? Brilliant."

"So what now?" Keenan asked.

I turned to Lily with a grin. "I think the furniture in this building needs to be destroyed."

Chapter 29 - What Now

Her eyes lit up. "Now we're talking."

"Let's call in the Hammers."

As we were about to open the portal, the apparition suddenly flickered back to life, his face twisted in rage.

"You little whelps won't avoid me forever. All you're doing is prolonging your suffering."

"Maybe," Keenan said, smirking. "But before you capture and kill us... we're gonna blow up your energy warehouse."

The figure laughed, though I caught a flicker of unease in his eyes.

"Oh, please. It would take..."

Lily cut him off. "Oh, I dunno... maybe a hundred dwarves?"

She tossed the portal stone to the ground.

Seconds later, the Hammers poured through.

"Men!" Lily bellowed, her voice echoing like a warhorn. "There's furniture in that building, and it all has to die!"

With a thunderous cry, the dwarves surged forward, axes raised, their boots pounding like rolling thunder. They tore through the structure with the fury of a storm, splinters flying, beams collapsing, the clash of steel and stone reverberating across the cavern.

The apparition lingered at the edge of the chaos, seething. His eyes burned with malice as he hissed, "You and your little band of miscreants will be my personal slaves for the rest of your miserable lives. And you will suffer in ways you cannot imagine."

I smirked, the words sliding off me like dull blades. *Yeah, I've heard that before.* I didn't bother to answer, only held his gaze until his form flickered and vanished.

Then came the horns, shrill, urgent, followed by the roar of shouting. Troops spilled from the castle and surrounding barracks, a tide of armored bodies rushing to meet us.

"One minute!" I shouted over the din. "We need to get out of here!"

The Hammers were already finishing their work. One of them clutched a soul orb, its eerie glow pulsing like a heartbeat, bringing it for the mages to study. I dropped another portal stone, its runes flaring to life, and set the timer for sixty seconds.

Everyone rushed through, but I lingered, watching the enemy forces close in. Winged demons swooped low, their screeches splitting the air, while hulking brutes thundered across the ground, their weapons gleaming.

I stepped through with ten seconds left as a handful managed to follow. They were cut down instantly by the waiting dwarves, axes cleaving, blades flashing, and two of the creatures were sliced clean in half as the portal snapped shut behind me with a final crack of energy.

We exchanged tired but triumphant smiles. It wasn't a massive victory, but it was something, and more importantly, it was a spark of hope, a surge of morale we desperately needed.

The dwarves clapped us on the back, their laughter booming, their congratulations loud and heartfelt, as we made our way toward the king. He stood atop the walls, watching our return with the quiet pride of a commander

Chapter 29 - What Now

who had seen too many defeats. When we reached him, he gave a single, satisfied nod.

"I take it the mission was a success?" he asked, voice steady but eyes gleaming.

"Yes," I said, glancing at our group with a smirk. "And we got to really upset the younger brother, which is always a bonus."

The king chuckled, deep and gravelly. "Make 'em angry so they make mistakes."

Keenan grinned. "Oooo, I like that."

Lily huffed, crossing her arms. "You guys do know that's my line, right?"

We began making our way through the gates and into the mountain, exhaustion settling over us like a heavy cloak. The promise of rest was almost intoxicating after everything we'd endured.

"No, seriously," Lily continued, refusing to let it go. "That *is* my line. I said it like two thousand years ago. So, clearly, I said it first. Which means it's mine."

We all just shook our heads, smiling despite ourselves, as we finally headed to bed.

Chapter 30 - The Decision

We woke early, ate quickly, and packed our gear with restless urgency. The mountain still hummed with activity as dwarves continued to prepare. The king oversaw it all, his voice carrying across the stone courtyards. Before we left, he pulled us aside, lowering his tone.

"Be back here this evening if you can. It's important."

We pressed for details, but he offered none, only a grim look that lingered in my mind as we set out for Cern.

By late morning, the fallen spire rose before us, gleaming against the ground like a shard of light.

Keenan glanced around. "What's so special about this ob..."

Lily's glare cut him short. "Spire," he corrected quickly.

I smiled. "It was built long ago to point toward the heavens, a reminder of how small we are... and where we came from."

Reeger frowned. "I thought we all came from here."

"Right," I said. "But the power that created us came from above."

Lily sighed dramatically. "Oh yeah, Cern's full of deep, philosophical, make-you-think kind of stuff. But I do love how shiny everything is."

At the spire's base, a Noctari emerged from the shadows, signaling us to follow. He led us into the ruins of a

Chapter 30 - The Decision

shattered building, where only one corner still stood. Inside, Azmira waited, her expression stormy.

I sighed. "Didn't go well, I take it?"

She studied me for a long moment before answering. "I don't know what you did, but the demons are furious. They've moved up their timetable and issued ultimatums."

I glanced at Lily, who smirked knowingly.

Keenan leaned forward. "What did they say?"

Azmira exhaled sharply. "They opened a portal in the middle of our leaders' meeting."

One of her guards snorted. I muttered, "Well, that's rude."

Azmira nodded. "Yes. But they don't care. They demanded we join them, and they're accelerating their attack plans. Their leaders seemed... rattled."

I couldn't help but smirk. Azmira caught it, shook her head. "So, it was you. Well, if you wanted them angry, you got it."

She continued, voice tightening. "When Vaeltharis asked for assurances, land, survival, if we joined them, the demon went into a rage. He screamed that we should join simply because we're kin. When he finally calmed, I was more certain than ever we couldn't trust them."

Her arms crossed. "And as you all know, trying to strong-arm Maldras is a terrible idea." She glanced at Lily. "Unless you're her."

Lily smirked. I shook my head. "Yeah, she has a way with people."

Azmira's lips curved faintly. "Indeed. I'm one of the few Maldras listens to. But I think he just wants to marry me, unite our tribes, make us stronger." She shrugged. "So, there's that."

Her tone hardened. "The demon had had enough. He demanded allegiance. I refused. Maldras snorted and declared neutrality."

Her eyes darkened. "The demon snarled, 'Then you will all be dead.' Vaeltharis tried to talk his way out, but the demon roared, 'No more talking!' and called him a sniveling coward. Then, before anyone could react, he killed Vaeltharis."

Keenan's eyes widened. "What?"

Azmira nodded grimly. "Maldras killed the demon on the spot. The lesser ones fled. He bellowed after them that any demon entering our lands would be killed on sight."

Reeger hesitated. "So... you'll join us?"

Azmira sighed. "No. I lobbied for it, but with Vaeltharis dead, their forces are scrambling for a successor. My people will follow me, but most still want to remain hidden. Maldras will do whatever it takes to keep his warriors alive. For now, that means fortifying and waiting."

Lily laughed. "He'll fight in the end."

Azmira blinked, surprised. "How can you be so sure?"

Lily grinned. "I don't know. Sometimes I just get a feeling about people."

Azmira studied her, thoughtful. "That remains to be seen. My people aren't warriors. When the real fighting begins, we can do little. But we have healers, some of the best in the land." She sighed. "Mostly, though, we are artists. Lovers of beauty. Nothing makes us happier than sharing our creations. But for now, we share only among ourselves. I want us to break free, to show the world what we can do."

Chapter 30 - The Decision

Her voice dropped. "But what kind of world will be left if the demons win?"

Lily hopped up, hands on her hips. "Don't worry! We have so many secret weapons, the bad guys will probably just get tired of them and die!"

I closed my eyes, shaking my head. Keenan gave her a flat look. "Yeah... that's not how that works."

"Whatever," Lily said breezily. "Just trust me. We basically can't lose because... well..." She paused, shrugged. "We just can't."

Azmira smiled faintly. "I can't argue with your reasoning, mostly because I have no idea what you just said. But I do hope you're right." She rose, signaling the meeting's end. "If my healers can help, send people to us. We'll do what we can."

I stood up. "I'm sorry you won't be joining us, but I appreciate the offer. I hope you weather what's coming. And maybe, when all this is over, we can be friends."

She nodded. "I hope so too. But I have a feeling this storm will leave the world looking vastly different when it passes."

Lily grinned. "But you guys are artists, right? So that's like... a reset. New canvas, new masterpiece. This could be great for you!" She paused, tapping her chin as if weighing the thought. "Unless you run out of paint. Or break your brush. But I guess you could always make more... maybe even better ones."

Azmira glanced at me, shaking her head with weary amusement.

"Yeah, it never changes," Keenan said with a smirk.

Reeger nodded. "Never a dull moment."

Suddenly, Azmira stepped closer to Reeger, her gaze locking onto his. He shifted under the intensity, clearly uncomfortable, until she finally spoke.

"I'm so sorry for your home."

Before he could respond, she embraced him. The hug was brief, a tear glistening in her eye as she stepped back, bowed slightly, and turned away. Her guards followed in silence.

Reeger blinked. "Well... that just happened."

"Yeah," Keenan said softly. "She sees things others can't. Cuts right through you."

"A little unsettling," Reeger muttered.

Lily grinned. "Imagine trying to throw her a surprise birthday party."

I laughed. "Lily, never change."

"What?" she said, indignant. "She'd just look into your eyeballs and know everything. Like, 'Thanks for giving it away, eyeballs! I thought you were on my side... sheesh.'"

We chuckled as we made our way back toward the mountain.

By the time we arrived, the sun was sinking low, painting the peaks in gold and crimson. The outer city was tense, the Hammers on full alert. The meeting hall was locked down, guards searching everyone who entered with grim determination.

Inside, the air was thick with anticipation. Brom sat with his wife and three children beside Thalion. The council from Grissom was present, and even Reggie was there, fidgeting nervously, though he managed a smile when he saw us.

Chapter 30 - The Decision

The moment Reeger spotted Thalion, he strode forward and embraced him, catching the elder elf off guard. Thalion returned the hug warmly.

"It is good to see you, Reeger."

Reeger stepped back, eyes searching his face. "How did you survive?"

Thalion's smile held, but he shook his head. "That story is for another time. Just know this, your father was proud of you. He knew you'd endure this mess."

Reeger's gaze dropped, tears welling in his eyes.

Meanwhile, Keenan approached Brom, shaking his hand and greeting the family. "Where's Victus? I thought he'd be here."

The king smiled. "Out front... He was difficult to pry away, but since I brought a secret weapon," he said, winking at Cara, "so he let me go."

I glanced at Lily, who smirked and mouthed, *Secret weapon* I shook my head, smiling.

The King of the Mountain cleared his throat, his voice carrying authority. "We've gathered here for an emergency meeting because of the threat we face. If anything happens during this meeting, follow me into the tunnels. We'll get you back to your cities safely."

Brom and the council members nodded gravely.

"As you all know, the elves have been attacked, their lands fallen. As far as we're aware, only eight elves remain, two of whom are in this room. Black-flagged ships were seen docking at the elven harbors, and earlier today, we lost contact with our scouts in elven territory. We must assume the area is no longer safe, and that enemy forces may be massing in the woods."

Reeger's jaw tightened, his expression grim.

"Two of the remaining elves have volunteered to scout the area and report back. They know the terrain and may discover what happened to our men.

"This mountain can withstand all manner of attacks. We've been preparing for this our entire lives. If any of you wish to fall back here, you are welcome. But understand, there will be rules, and certain areas will be off-limits. If you choose to stay and defend your homes, I respect that. Just know you will have a place of refuge if you need it."

He scanned the room, letting his words sink in.

"I believe we need a battle plan, one that ensures we're prepared for what's coming and can work together for survival."

Brom nodded. "We've been stockpiling food and resources. The halflings have been brought inside the city walls. Greenholm is empty now, save for two watchtowers. Those towers reported movement near the forest border earlier today, but they have strict orders not to engage and to fall back to Burke if necessary."

The dwarven king nodded. "How long can you hold out?"

Brom sighed. "Hard to say. We have stout, brave men defending the city. As long as our walls hold, we can last until the food runs out. At the moment, we should sustain for at least half a season, possibly more."

The king turned to Gamreal, who exchanged uneasy glances with Ancelot, Renard, and Millhouse, the latter fidgeting nervously. Finally, Gamreal spoke.

Chapter 30 - The Decision

"We are the least prepared for this war," he admitted. "Our walls are weak, and even with the Frost Giants' help, we won't hold for long."

Thalion blinked. "I'm sorry... did you say Frost Giants?"

Gamreal grinned. "Yes."

"Fascinating," Thalion muttered, then gestured for him to continue.

"We have a few hidden places where our people can take shelter," Gamreal said. "But I fear Grissom will fall quickly, which gives them both ports."

The king gave a solemn nod, then turned to Reggie, who smiled nervously.

"The majority of the mages have already left the tower," Reggie explained. "They're scattering our documents, tomes, artifacts, anything we don't want falling into enemy hands. Once they've finished, they'll regroup wherever the fighting is fiercest and assist as best they can."

"Excellent," the king replied. "And what about you?"

Reggie's smile faltered, replaced by quiet resolve. "I have one final task to complete, something I hope will make a difference. I'll be at the tower."

The king gave him a final nod as Reggie sat back, lost in thought.

At that point, Throm stepped forward, his voice low and deliberate. "What we're about to share cannot leave this room."

Keenan leaned in, voice low. "Where was he hiding?"

I whispered back, "No idea."

Throm's tone was grave. "We may have found a way to neutralize the younger brother... possibly even kill him."

Lily and I exchanged a glance, the weight of his words sinking in.

"The Paladins have been developing a special, well, 'poison' is the closest word," Throm continued. "But essentially, it disrupts everything tied to the demon world. For demons, it would either kill them outright or paralyze them."

Reggie leaned forward, eyes gleaming with intrigue.

"The ingredients were rare beyond imagining," Throm said. "We managed to produce only a single, large dose. But if it works, it could drag him back to the level he was at two thousand years ago. Maybe weaker. It could give us a fighting chance."

Keenan's eyes narrowed. "Was this Project Redsun?"

Throm smiled faintly as Keenan nodded. "I knew it was something big," Keenan muttered.

"The problem," Throm went on, "is that it has to be injected directly into his bloodstream. Which means we'll need to get close."

The room erupted. Voices overlapped, disbelief and panic colliding: *"Impossible!"* ... *"We can't do that!"* ... *"How would we even try?"*

I stayed quiet, staring at the floor until Lily's face slid into view upside down, lying on her back with a grin.

"Penny for your thoughts?" she teased.

I looked at her. "Wait, you have issues with every other saying, and that's the one you use?"

She shrugged. "Well, yeah. I'll only pay you a penny, but for my thoughts. I'm thinking at least five gold."

"Incredible," I muttered, shaking my head.

Chapter 30 - The Decision

"I know, right? Why are my thoughts worth so much more than yours? Doesn't make sense... well, it makes *cents*... but whatever. Anyway, the important thing is, you've got an idea. And even though it's not worth as much as mine, we'd still like to hear it."

At that, I realized the room had gone silent. Everyone was staring at us, caught between awe and disbelief.

I exhaled as Lily stood.

"Me and Lily will just walk up to him and do it," I said.

Reeger folded his arms. "And how exactly are you planning to manage that?"

Keenan chimed in. "Well, you're taking us too."

"No," I said firmly. "We have to go alone."

Gamreal stepped forward. "No, you don't. We'll all go. It'll look like we're coming to entreat with him."

"Ooo, good idea," Lily said, nodding toward Gam. "He'll think we're surrendering. Won't see the attack coming." She punched her palm with emphasis.

I shook my head. "This will likely be a one-way trip. Even if we manage to kill him, there'll be demons everywhere. They won't take it well."

"True," Gamreal agreed. "But there's no reason to go in alone."

"That's right," Lily added. "Because friends who stick together also, apparently, kill their little godlike-man child of evil together."

Keenan shook his head. "It's like... the stuff she says... I don't even know what to do with it."

Reeger muttered, "Join the club."

The king finally spoke, voice steady. "It is decided. Once he arrives, you will approach as a group and inject him."

"Seems simple enough," Brom said. "But how in the world are you going to get close?"

I shrugged. "I still don't think he knows about us. We'll transform. That should give someone else the opening they need."

Throm looked at Gam. "Can you place the knife?"

Gam cracked his knuckles with a grin. "Then you hammer it home."

"Haven't been in a fight like this in a while," Gam said matter-of-factly. "Or... ever."

Suddenly, a guard burst in, one of the elite, clad in black armor. The moment I saw him, I knew something was wrong.

"Sir," he said, bowing to me and Lily before turning to the king. "Mother has left."

The king shot to his feet. "What do you mean, left?"

"She told the guards, 'Well done, and please stand fast, my loyal dwarves.' Then there was a flash of light, and she was gone."

Shocked glances rippled through the room. *Is she safe? Why did she leave?* Questions churned silently, but the king straightened, his voice calm and commanding.

"Well, you heard her. Stand fast. And that's exactly what we'll do."

Another guard entered, whispering urgently into the king's ear. The king sighed.

"So it begins," he said. "Come."

Chapter 30 - The Decision

We followed him up to the walls. The sun was setting, painting the horizon in fire and blood. Below, a vast force emerged from the tree line, tens of thousands of troops armed and laden with supplies, spreading across the rolling hills like a tide.

"We need to move now, before we're cut off," Brom urged.

But the king only smiled. "My friend, the dwarves have not been idle all these years. We'll get you back to your city without them ever knowing you left."

Reggie raised an eyebrow. "So, you figured out portals too?"

The king chuckled. "Not exactly."

He led us underground, where steam-powered carts stood waiting on iron rails stretching deep into the tunnels.

"Just in case," he said with a knowing smile.

Brom let out a low whistle. "This is incredible. And you've had this connection to my city all this time?"

The king merely smiled.

Meanwhile, Gam turned to the council. "We need to get you back to Grissom."

Brom and his family departed, chuckling at the cart and explaining to Cara why teleporting was a bad idea, magic leaves a signature that can be tracked. They arrived safely a short time later. The Grissom council, minus Gam who chose to remain, also made the journey through the tunnels.

"They'll likely try to keep everyone awake all night," I said. "Maximum fear impact when morning comes, if they're still operating the way they used to."

The king nodded. "The guards are in position. You all need rest. Get some sleep. We'll wake you if anything changes."

But I didn't sleep. I returned to the wall, watching as the enemy crept across the fields, remembering when this had happened before, long ago.

Why are we doomed to repeat ourselves? I wondered.

With a heavy sigh, I stepped down from the wall.

The night was restless for everyone except Grog, who could apparently sleep through a hurricane. After a quick breakfast the next morning, Grog, Gam, Throm, Keenan, Reeger, Lily, and I made our way to the king, who was once again surveying the field.

As we walked, unease gnawed at me. What happened during the night? What would we see now?

Chapter 31 - The Battle

We arrived and stood atop the wall, gazing out over our small, embattled world.

"Well," Keenan said quietly, "I guess this is it."

"I suppose so," I replied.

Before us, the once-peaceful countryside writhed with tens of thousands of demons and Noctari. Portals shimmered, held open by hovering orbs, and more creatures poured through in endless waves. Grissom and Burke were already under siege, though the enemy had stopped just short of the dwarven walls. In the distance, flashes of magic lit the sky from the mage tower, too far to see clearly, but we hoped Reggie was holding his own.

"Any word from the Noctari?" Reeger asked.

I shook my head. "None."

"They'll come," Lily said with stubborn certainty. She exhaled sharply. "Well? When do we go in and make our presence known?"

I sighed. "We wait for their backline to show. Shouldn't be long now."

Unfortunately, I was right. A moment later, the hills split open as a massive portal tore into existence, easily a hundred feet tall. The dwarven king muttered something under his breath. Lily turned to me with a resigned sigh.

"Well... here we go," she said.

A colossal demon stepped through, fifty, maybe sixty feet tall, armed with a hammer the size of a house. His wings unfurled like storm clouds, his tail snaked across the ground, and his skin glowed with molten red heat. His eyes were pits of endless black. Then the younger brother followed, stepping casually through, smirking as he surveyed the battlefield. Four hulking demons carried a massive throne, setting it down with a crash. The giant demon sat, watching the chaos with grim satisfaction.

A dwarf spotter, peering through a gnome-crafted eyepiece, shouted, "There's a breach in Grissom!"

Reeger snapped his gaze to the city. "The frost giants are holding it, trying to plug the gap," he reported.

I closed my eyes, inhaling deeply, trying to steady the emotional storm inside me. I hated death. I hated fighting. I hated all of this. And yet... this was what I was made for: to keep them safe.

Throm, Grog, and Gam approached, nodding. Everything was ready. The only question left was whether it would be enough.

I looked up at the sky and exhaled. "Well... here we go."

Turning to my friends, who had stood beside me through everything, I smiled.

"My friends," I began, voice tight with emotion, "I can't ask any of you to go further. This task is for me, Throm, Gam, and Lily. I ask that you stay here and defend the dwarven city."

Grog snorted. "Fat chance."

Keenan grinned. "I agree."

Reeger smirked. "Besides, who's going to keep you two out of trouble if I stay behind?"

Chapter 31 - The Battle

Gam chuckled. "Well, lad, looks like you've got quite the entourage."

I looked down, heart full. The decision was already made, and I couldn't have asked for better friends. Their loyalty gave me strength.

"You all understand this could be a one-way trip," I said. "Even if we succeed, we'll be surrounded, and more will keep coming."

Grog laughed, hefting his axe. "Perfect. Target-rich environment. Won't have to worry which way I swing."

I smiled. "Very well. Let's see if we can do some damage."

Throm nodded, and together we climbed down from the wall. Passing through the gates, we walked straight toward the massive demon.

To our surprise, the enemy ranks parted, allowing us through. They knew we were here to negotiate or at least pretend to. That didn't stop them from mocking us, spitting in our direction, hurling insults as we passed.

Lily was unusually quiet. Keenan leaned over. "You okay?"

She gave him a small smile, unfazed by the jeering. "Yeah. Just conserving energy." She exhaled. "This is going to be tough." She opened her mouth as if to say more, then simply smiled.

"It's been fun," she said softly.

Keenan looked ahead. "Yeah... yeah, it has."

We reached the massive throne. The demon atop it threw back his head and laughed, his voice rumbling across the battlefield.

"So, you've come to surrender?" he bellowed, gaze sweeping lazily over us. "Let's see... three dwarves, an elf, two humans and the runt." His grin turned cruel. "What is he? Your pet? Or maybe some kind of slave?"

Keenan stepped forward with a smirk. "Oh, he is not going to like this," he muttered, then raised his voice, steady and strong.

"I am Aegis, Protector of the Innocent, Wielder of the Bulwark of Kings."

The demon stared, stunned for a moment, then burst into laughter.

"You? A paladin?" he scoffed. "They must be desperate. Or the Noctari have gone mad." He slapped the younger brother's shoulder. "Can you believe it?"

"Just wait, you big oaf," Merek muttered.

The younger brother only looked irritated.

"Well," the larger demon said, turning back to us, "about your surrender then?" He grinned.

I stepped forward before he could continue. "Yes. About your surrender."

The demon snorted, displeased at being interrupted, but then a slow smile spread across his face.

"You must be the little whelp who messed with baby brother."

"Don't call me that," the younger brother growled.

The large demon laughed. "Well, I'm sorry, but I won't be surrendering."

Laughter erupted from the demons surrounding us.

"Good," Grog muttered. "All the big ones are gathering to watch. That buys the cities more time."

Gam and Throm both nodded.

Chapter 31 - The Battle

"Keep them talking," Throm whispered.

But the younger brother scowled. "Enough. If they won't surrender, let's kill them."

The large demon waved him off. "Sure, go ahead. Kill them."

The younger brother smiled darkly. "Don't mind if I do. It's been a while."

He stepped forward, his tarnished white robes billowing, his skin pulsing with black and red energy. The stench of the demon world clung to him like smoke, choking the air. His lips curled into a cruel smirk as he drew his weapon.

"Well, Lil, you ready?" I asked.

She smiled. "Yep."

The younger brother froze, startled. "What did you say?"

In that instant, Lily and I transformed, power surging through us as we stepped forward until we stood toe to toe with him. A smirk tugged at my lips as Lily moved beside me.

"Remember us?" I asked.

His surprise faded, replaced by twisted amusement. "I can't believe you two survived everything," he sneered, then laughed darkly. "Oh, I've been waiting for this. Never thought I'd get to kill you both myself."

His eyes turned pitch black. Power rippled off him in waves, his body pulsating with vile energy. "Now you will feel the power of two worlds joined!" he screeched. "I am unstoppable!"

I smiled. "You think that... but we're just a distraction."

His grin faltered. "What?"

Suddenly, Gam leapt from Lily's shoulder, driving a dagger deep into his flesh. The younger brother screamed in pain.

At the same time, Throm launched from mine, his hammer glowing with raw energy. With a roar, he slammed it down onto the dagger, unleashing the full force of a dwarven spell into the wound.

He staggered back, howling. "ARRRGGHHH! What did you do?!"

I smirked. "Something the dwarves have been working on for a long, long time. I don't know all the details, but its supposed to cripple your magic."

He raised a trembling hand, trying to cast. Nothing.

"No... Not possible!" he roared. "No matter! I'll crush you with my bare hands!"

The larger demon laughed, clearly entertained.

The younger brother lunged, but before he could reach us, a blinding flash split the sky. A divine presence descended, halting all movement.

Everything stopped. Demons and mortals alike froze in awe.

Father had arrived.

"You fool!" Father's voice thundered. "Do you have any idea what you've done? The chaos you've unleashed across realms?!"

The younger brother staggered back. "Father..."

"Don't 'Father' me!" His voice cracked the very ground. "You killed your brother! You nearly killed your Mother, I just carried her to the healers myself. If she had

Chapter 31 - The Battle

died..." His eyes burned with divine fury. "We wouldn't be having this conversation."

"But... Father..."

"No buts!" His wrath shook the battlefield. "We are stewards of this power. Stewards! And you twisted it into something monstrous. Now you will face judgment."

The younger brother collapsed, tears streaming. "Please, Father... please..."

For a moment, Father's expression softened. He lifted his son gently, embracing him.

But in an instant, the younger brother's face twisted with malice. His hand flashed, driving a dagger deep into Father's side.

"You disgust me," he hissed.

Father staggered, collapsing.

I tried to move, but an invisible force held me back.

The younger brother sneered. "Now you'll all feel my wrath. The galaxy will kneel before me. This world is just the beginning!"

He loomed over Father, eyes blazing. "You're weak. Prideful. Brought low by the same poison that killed your son and nearly took your wife."

Despair swept over us like a suffocating fog. *This is it,* I thought. *We've lost.*

Then, Father rose.

Gasps rang out across the battlefield.

The younger brother's smug expression shattered.

Father shook his head. With a snap of his fingers, the younger brother froze, locked in place by divine power.

"What did you do to me?!" he shrieked.

Father's eyes brimmed with sorrow. "It's too late for you, my son."

"Let me go!" he screamed. "I'll kill you, you old fool!"

Father sighed. "Your brother... your mother... they warned me. I knew you'd try to betray me. I wanted to hope. But you're so lost... I don't even know who you are anymore."

The younger brother thrashed, screeching in vain.

"No," Father said firmly. "It is time for judgment."

A blinding light engulfed them both. In an instant, they were gone.

Silence fell.

Then, after several long seconds, the large demon threw his head back and laughed.

"HAHAHAHAHA! Finally! That little whelp was so annoying! Save this, protect that, don't kill everyone, we need subjects, blah, blah, blah!"

His gaze fell on us, cruel and hungry. "Now... bring the rest!"

More demons poured from the portals, towering monsters, twenty to thirty feet tall. A tide of destruction was coming through.

My hope shattered.

Then Reggie appeared, grinning.

"Did you miss me? Of course you did!" he chattered. "Sorry it took so long, but I finally figured it out!"

He held up a small box. "This is it!"

As he opened it, he began chanting words of power.

The large demon's eyes widened in horror. "NO!" he roared, hurling a massive spear straight at the gnome.

I lunged to intercept, but I was too slow.

Chapter 31 - The Battle

The spear struck Reggie square in the chest, impaling him and pinning him to the ground.

He gasped, suspended, blood trickling from his lips. His eyes dimmed, but he managed a weak smile.

"Too late," he whispered.

The box slipped from his hands as his body went limp.

The instant the box struck the ground, a colossal shockwave erupted outward. Energy surged across the battlefield, ripping through the air like lightning. Every portal flickered... then shattered into shards of nothingness, their echoes ringing like broken glass across the hills.

The massive demon bellowed in rage, his voice shaking the earth. "That's it!" he howled. "No more waiting. I'll kill you all myself!"

I braced, but he was enormous, three times my size, pulsing with raw power. He charged, each step pounding like thunder.

A streak of flame cut through the air. Lily slammed into his back, clawing, biting, spewing fire with all her fury. Her flames licked across his molten skin, but they barely left a mark.

I lunged at his leg, desperate to bring him down, but he thrashed wildly, trying to dislodge her. His massive fist connected with me, and I flew backward, crashing into the dirt with bone-shaking force.

Dazed, I forced myself up, vision swimming.

Around us, the battle was unraveling. Demons swarmed the walls. The frost giants in Grissom faltered under the tide. Burke's walls partially collapsed with a deafening crash, smoke and fire rising into the sky.

Hammer and Anvil

I staggered to my feet just in time to see him seize Lily, yanking her from his back.

Time slowed.

He twisted her wing until it snapped.

Her scream tore through me like a blade.

Then he slammed her into the ground, crushing one of her legs.

Lily gasped in pain, trembling, but still tried to rise. She couldn't fly, could barely stand, yet she summoned the strength for another blast of fire.

He caught her by the throat, lifting her effortlessly.

"Now you die, little runt," he growled.

I rose, every nerve burning, and just as he raised his hand to finish her, I slammed into him with everything I had.

It was like hitting a mountain.

I managed to knock Lily free, but he only dropped to one knee. His burning eyes locked on me, fury blazing.

His rage had a new focus.

I stood between him and Lily, ready.

But he was too strong.

Again and again, he knocked me down. I kept rising, but my body was failing. Desperation surged as I summoned frost, too weak, only a short burst escaped.

He screamed in pain, stumbling back.

And then it hit me. *Idiot. The frost hurts him.*

I should've focused on that from the start.

For a moment, we locked eyes, each measuring the other.

Then he grinned, slow and cruel. "You're out."

Chapter 31 - The Battle

A rumbling chuckle rolled from his chest as he stalked toward me.

I swiped at his eyes, but he was faster.

He pummeled me, blow after crushing blow.

The end crept closer.

Another strike hurled me across the field. I landed hard beside Lily. She was still trying to rise, broken but defiant hurling insults at him.

My vision blurred. My strength faded.

The demon towered over us.

This is it, I thought. *We've lost.*

Then, voices. Strong. Defiant.

Three small figures stepped between me and the massive demon.

"You leave our boy alone," Throm growled.

"That's right," Grog added. "If you want him, you'll have to go through us."

I tried to protest, but I could barely breathe.

The demon snarled. "Three dead dwarves, coming right up."

I heard the crack of Throm's smite, the clash of Grog's axe. I struggled to rise, but my body failed.

A heavy impact. A dull thud. Another.

Grog's battle cry cut short by a sickening crunch.

Silence.

Through the haze, I saw them, Throm, Grog, and Gam, lying motionless.

And standing over them, sword clutched in his hand, was Keenan.

He was barely upright. His shield gone. His body bruised, bloodied. His left arm hung limp. But still, he stood.

"Not my friend," he rasped, dragging himself forward. His leg seemed broken, dragging behind him.

The demon snorted in amusement.

A twang of a bowstring, an arrow struck the demon's hide. He growled, hurled a rock toward Reeger's position. No more arrows followed.

Keenan reached him, swaying, barely able to lift his sword. His breath ragged, his strength nearly gone.

I forced myself up, staggering forward.

Keenan turned to me and smiled, tired, proud.

Then the demon's massive hand struck him.

Keenan flew like a ragdoll.

I screamed. "No!"

The demon turned to me. I unleashed everything, pain, sorrow, rage.

A blast of frost exploded, slamming into him.

He staggered, but kept moving, inch by inch through the storm.

I was losing strength. Running out.

Then, a spark.

A flicker of energy surged into me. Someone was still alive, barely, pushing what little power they had left into me.

It wouldn't last long.

The demon smiled, wicked and knowing, pressing forward through the ice.

Despair crashed over me.

It won't be long now.

Chapter 31 - The Battle

I strained everything. My vision blurred. My body shook.

I'm sorry, my friends. I'm so sorry. I tried.

Just as I was about to collapse, ready for it to end,

A flash of light.

A surge of energy unlike anything I had ever felt.

It was as if all the loose magic in the world had suddenly become mine. Power flooded my veins, more than I'd ever dreamed possible.

I glanced down.

The king's daughter, Cara, had teleported in. Her hands blazed with radiant light, her eyes fierce.

"You leave my friends alone!" she shouted.

She poured her energy, her very life force, into me.

It was too much.

The sheer force of it overwhelmed me, threatening to tear me apart from the inside. My veins burned, my bones felt as though they might shatter, and my body seemed to unravel under the pressure of it.

Then, a calming touch.

A steadying presence.

The Queen of Burke stood beside me, her hand resting gently on my leg. Her touch was cool, deliberate, guiding the wild torrent before it could consume me. The chaos inside me bent to her will, the storm of magic finding shape instead of destruction.

A slow smile curled on my lips.

I turned back to the demon.

Now I was the one smiling.

And I unleashed everything.

A devastating storm of power erupted from me, a blizzard of fury and grief. The demon's wicked grin vanished, replaced by raw horror as ice exploded outward, jagged shards encasing his body, freezing him to the core. His molten skin cracked, steam hissing as frost spread across him like a living curse. He staggered back, shrieking, his voice echoing across the battlefield.

"Help me!" He screamed, calling the other demons.

None came.

His army was in chaos. Brom's forces rallied, driving them back over the collapsed wall. Dwarves surged forward, axes flashing, fighting desperately to reach me and Lily. Even warriors from Grissom stormed into the fray, their battle cries rising in one final, desperate push.

Behind us, Lily had recovered enough to fight. Her eyes blazed as she unleashed a wall of fire, a roaring inferno that sealed off the demon's escape. Flames towered high, hemming him in, forcing him to face us alone.

And at that moment, I remembered something the Mother once told me:

"Ruling with love creates those who will die for you. Ruling through fear ensures they flee when you need them most."

As the demon screamed, abandoned by his own kind, I saw the truth of her words.

He was alone.

But we were not.

His eyes burned with hatred... but beneath it, I saw fear.

Chapter 31 - The Battle

With one last, rage-filled glare, he let out a howl as the ice consumed him completely. His body froze solid, locked in place, a monument to his own arrogance.

I exhaled, ragged and spent, my chest heaving as the storm faded. My vision swam, but I forced myself to look around.

That's when I saw them, Maldris and nearly five hundred Noctari warriors, charging in from the south with a thunderous roar. Their weapons gleamed in the fading light as they smashed into the demon flank, carving through them like a storm unleashed.

Lily grinned, her face streaked with soot and blood. "See? Told you our new buddy would show up," she said. "Now, I gotta go help them."

Without another word, she spun, flames bursting from her mouth. She scorched a swath across the battlefield, splitting the demon ranks in two. The Noctari roared in triumph, weapons raised high, as they tore into the fractured enemy lines with renewed fury.

I tried to smile... but my vision was blurring.

"Uncles..." I whispered, the word trembling from my lips.

I turned, searching for Keenan. I had to find them. Had to make sure they were okay.

But everything around me began to fade.

The clash of steel, the roar of fire, the cries of battle, all of it grew distant, muffled, as though the world itself were slipping away.

The light dimmed.

The world slowly faded to black.

And I collapsed.

Chapter 32 - The Aftermath

My head swam as I slowly came back to consciousness. I was lying on my back, something heavy pressing down on me, pain, soreness, the weight of exhaustion. My chest rose and fell in shallow breaths.

I stirred, blinking against the darkness. Faint light flickered against the stone walls, shadows dancing like restless spirits. As I sat up, slowly, painfully, my memories came rushing back in jagged fragments.

Lily sat nearby, arms crossed, watching me with that familiar mix of impatience and affection. She snorted. "Took you long enough. Three days out cold, like a baby. And it's not like you even fought that long."

"What?" I muttered, disoriented, my voice hoarse.

"Asleep," she repeated, rolling her eyes. "For three days. Did that last hit scramble your brain? Forget our language?" She stood, leaned out the door, and yelled, "See! Told you he was gonna be okay!"

Footsteps echoed down the passageway, hurried and purposeful.

I looked around groggily. "What happened?"

"Uhhh, we won. Duh." Lily grinned, her tone light but her eyes betraying the weight of what we'd lost.

"How?" I asked. "And where are we?"

She stretched, feigning nonchalance. "We won because I'm amazing, obviously. And we're under the mountain, sooo…"

Chapter 32 - The Aftermath

"Lily," I said, voice unsteady as I fought back tears. "Who's still alive?"

Her smile faltered. She hesitated, staring at me for a long moment. Then she stepped forward and wrapped me in a hug, her voice dropping to a whisper. "It's gonna be okay."

I wanted to respond, but the footsteps reached us. Two Noctari entered the room, followed by Azmira.

Startled, I jumped to my feet. "You can't be down here! We need to hide you before the dwarves see you and..."

Lily chuckled.

"Lily, this isn't funny!"

Azmira smiled softly. "It is. A little bit."

"What?" I stared at her, baffled.

Then Throm walked in, grinning wide.

"They can be here," he said, "because I said they could."

Relief crashed over me like a wave. "You're alive!" I ran to him and pulled him into a hug, clinging as though he might vanish.

He chuckled, patting my back. "Yes, I'm alive."

"I don't remember what happened," I said, struggling to hold back tears. "You all went down, and after I passed out..."

Throm nodded. "From what I was told, you got back up and froze the demon. Then some young girl joined the fight and put up a protective barrier around us all. You collapsed again, and she held the shield for forty-five minutes before passing out herself. That gave the dwarves and

Brom enough time to reach us. Azmira brought in healers and started helping everyone."

Azmira gave a warm smile. "Happy to help," she said. "After all, you saved us too."

I shook my head slowly. "This has to be a dream. It doesn't feel real."

Throm grinned. "Oh, it's real. But, it'll take some getting used to. I never thought I'd see Noctari under the mountain. But once they let Keenan in, I figured anything was possible."

"Wait..." I froze. "Keenan? Where is he? Is he okay?"

Throm's smile faded. He looked down. "We tried to..."

"Where is he?" I cut him off, panic rising like floodwater.

Azmira stepped forward and gently placed a hand on my shoulder. "Halvar, please. Breathe. Calm down."

"Calm down?" My breath hitched, my chest tightening. "He's my best friend."

Then, from the doorway, a familiar voice called out.

"Well, I'm glad to see you're finally awake. We've got a lot of clean-up to do, and I'm not doing it all myself."

"Keenan!" I ran to him and picked him up in a bear hug.

He hugged me back, but something felt wrong. I stepped back quickly, my eyes scanning him. That's when I saw it. His left arm was gone, and he limped slightly on his left leg.

"Are you okay? What happened?"

Keenan sighed, his voice heavy. "When the fighting started, a bunch of the big ones tried to flank you and Lily. Reeger, your uncles, and I went to stop them. We managed

Chapter 32 - The Aftermath

to take out two. Then Lily went down. And when you fell... your uncles charged in. That left two of the big ones. One went after Reeger. The other... well, he went berserk and started wailing on Merek and me."

He paused, glancing at where his arm used to be. When he looked back at me, his eyes were wet with tears.

"I got knocked down, trying to hold my shield up. The blows kept coming. The shield was cracking. My arm had gone numb. I knew I was done. But Merek... he just chuckled and said, 'One last trick, boy.' Told me I did good and that he was proud of me."

His voice broke, but he pressed on. "I heard him charging up something big. When the hammer came down... there was this massive discharge, an explosion. The shield shattered. Merek was gone. My arm wouldn't move. The pain was unreal. But the demon was thrown back, killed by the blast."

He swallowed hard. "I tried to get up. Saw Gam go down, it looked bad. I knew I had to help. I forced myself to my feet, started to walk toward him. Then I saw Throm go down. Then Grog... which made me sick to my stomach."

His gaze dropped. "I made it to them, but you were still down. So I thought... I have to protect you guys. I walked over to the large demon, but when I got there, I knew I couldn't stop him. So I just... looked back at you. Thought about all the good times we had. Then smiled."

His voice grew quiet. "Then... boom. I got hit. Hard. Everything went black.

"When I woke up," he added softly, glancing past me, "an angel was standing over me."

"Ugh," Lily groaned. "He talks like this now. It's so annoying."

I followed his gaze to Azmira. She looked down, blushing.

"Oh no," I said, laughing. "I see."

"Ugh," Lily groaned again.

I laughed and turned back to Keenan. "I'm just glad you're alive." Then I looked at Lily. "And you too."

She smirked. "Someone's gotta look out for you."

I chuckled, but then paused, glancing at Throm. I was afraid to ask. "What about Grog and Gam?"

Throm sighed, his shoulders sagging. "Gam is... not doing well."

My stomach dropped. "And Grog?"

Throm managed a faint smile. "Turns out he's incredibly hard to kill."

Azmira chuckled softly. "Yeah. Once we got him conscious, he grabbed his axe and went right back into the fight. He sure is stubborn."

Throm smiled. "You have no idea"

I let out a shaky breath of relief, but my thoughts stayed fixed on Gam. "Gam?" I asked quietly.

Throm's smile faded. He shook his head. "He's in the next room. He... doesn't have much time."

I didn't think. I just ran, tearing through the doorway and down the hall, the others close behind.

When I entered, my heart sank.

Gam lay in bed, his skin pale, even for a dwarf. Both legs were crushed, twisted beyond recognition. His entire body was wrapped in bandages, bruises covering what little

Chapter 32 - The Aftermath

skin was still visible. His breathing was shallow, labored, short, each rise and fall of his chest a battle.

I knelt beside him. Softly, I asked, "Gam... how are you doing, Uncle?"

He stirred. His eyes fluttered open, and when he saw me, he managed a faint smile.

"Aye, boy... there you are." He coughed, his breath gurgling in his throat. "Knew you'd make it," he said, voice weak. "But me... on the other hand..." His words drifted off as his eyes closed again.

Tears spilled down my cheeks as I turned desperately to Keenan. "Please. Lay on hands, or Azmira, can you do anything?" I looked around, pleading with anyone, everyone.

Keenan stepped forward, his face grim. "I did," he said quietly.

My heart pounded. "What do you mean you did? Shouldn't that have healed him?"

Keenan shook his head. "I can heal one, maybe two major wounds. But he was too far gone. I only managed to bring him back this far." His voice faltered. "Even then...he won't last long. But... he wanted to say goodbye to you."

Tears blurred my vision.

"Maybe I can freeze him," I choked out. "Maybe that would..."

Throm placed a firm hand on my shoulder. His voice was steady, but his eyes were wet. "It's okay, son. Sometimes... you have to learn to let go."

"No," I gasped, breath catching in my throat. "No."

I clenched my fists. "All this strength, and I can't even save one person?"

Throm nodded solemnly. "No, you can't. But that's life. And Gam wouldn't regret a thing. He'd do it all over again. The best we can do now... is remember and honor his sacrifice."

I looked up at him, my voice barely a whisper. "I'm supposed to be the old, wise one. And here I am... breaking down like a child."

Throm gave me a sad smile. "We all need to cry sometimes." He glanced over at Gam. "I had my tears yesterday."

Gam stirred again. His eyes opened, locking onto mine. He smiled weakly. "Hah... knew you'd make it, my boy."

I knelt beside him, still crying. "Yes, Uncle. I made it. I'm here."

"Good... good." He sighed. "Then I did my job. You're safe... you are safe, right?" His eyes looked distant, confused, searching.

I swallowed hard. "Yes, Uncle. I'm safe. You did good."

"Good, good," he murmured. "Needed to be sure... before I go. Gotta do some traveling, I think…"

His voice trailed off. His eyes closed again, lips barely moving.

Throm stepped forward, resting a hand on Gam's forehead. "Be at peace, my friend," he said quietly.

Gam coughed once more. His eyes opened one final time, finding mine. He smiled.

"Good...good," he whispered.

Then his eyes closed for the last time, and he slipped into his final rest.

Chapter 32 - The Aftermath

I sank to the floor and cried until I had no tears left. I don't know how long I stayed there. But when I finally looked up, Lily was still there, the last one left, standing silently, waiting for me.

I sighed. "Sorry, Lil."

She shook her head gently. "No, no. It's okay," she said, her voice soft.

I drew a shaky breath and forced myself to stand. Just as I turned to leave, Grog entered. We locked eyes for a moment. Then he walked over and pulled me into a crushing hug.

He held me tight, solid and steady, then stepped back.

Looking up at me, he smiled. "You know... he was proud of you."

I smiled faintly. "I know."

"We all are." His voice wavered, and I caught the glint of moisture in his eyes before he turned away.

"He would have wanted you to know that," he said firmly. Then, clearing his throat, he added, "Anyway, I'm off. Gotta show these runts how to cook, since apparently everyone forgot how in the last twenty years."

He reached the door but paused in the doorway, glancing back at Gam one last time. With a slight bow of his head, he murmured, "Goodbye, old friend."

Then he walked away.

I exhaled and turned to Lily with a small smile. "Well... shall we go check on everything else?"

She grinned. "That's the spirit!" She hopped up and headed out the door, and I followed close behind.

Spotting a nearby guard, I called out, "Can you take me to the king?"

The guard bowed. "Of course."

He led us to a planning room where several Noctari, Azmira among them, were deep in conversation with a group of dwarves. I walked over to Throm.

"So... where's the king?"

Throm scratched his head. "Oh... the king is gone."

My stomach dropped. "What?"

"No, no," Throm said quickly, realizing his mistake. "I mean he left, he's not dead. He went to help clean up another island with the Hammers." He chuckled. "Sorry about that."

I let out a breath. "Good. I don't think I could handle another death right now."

Throm smiled, his expression steady but kind. "For now, I'm in charge."

I nodded toward the Noctari. "And them?"

Throm's expression brightened. "Now that the demon threat is gone, we're talking about rebuilding. Turns out, these Noctari can work stone almost as well as we can. They want to restore Cern, and we're going to help them."

"About time!" Lily chimed in. "I miss Cern. They better make it better, or else it won't... be better." She sighed, shaking her head. "That sounded way cooler in my head."

I laughed, the sound easing some of the heaviness in the room.

Looking around, I asked, "What about the dwarves?"

Throm's smile faded. He sighed. "We lost almost thirty percent of our forces."

I gasped. "What?"

Chapter 32 - The Aftermath

He nodded grimly. "But we won. And now we need purpose. Rebuilding's as good a place to start as any. Not everyone's thrilled about the Noctari being under the mountain, but... they're too tired to argue. Hopefully, they become friends before they remember they used to be enemies."

Peeking past Throm, I spotted Keenan giggling with Azmira. I shook my head. "That's going to take some getting used to."

Throm sighed. "Yeah. Hurts my brain to watch or think about."

Lily crossed her arms and muttered, "Annoying."

"What about Grissom and Burke?" I asked.

Throm nodded. "Still standing, but there's a lot of cleanup left. We've already cremated all the demons, thanks to Lily."

She gave a dramatic bow.

I smiled.

"At least there's no more fear of invasion," Throm added. "And for now, everyone's working together. You should check in on Grissom and Burke though. I know you had friends there, and they'd love to know you're still breathing." He shook his head. "Honestly... it'd be good for you too."

I nodded. Most of the soreness in my body had faded. "I could go for a walk." I glanced at Lily. "You coming?"

She smirked. "Yeah. Just in case you pass out again. Who else is gonna drag your sorry butt back?"

At that, Keenan walked over. "If you're heading to Burke and Grissom, I want to come with." He glanced at Azmira. "If that's okay with you?"

She smiled. "Of course. I've survived this long without you. A couple more days won't kill me."

Keenan winced. "Ouch."

Lily made exaggerated gagging noises as she walked out of the room, and the rest of us burst into laughter.

As we started to follow, I paused and took a deep breath. Keenan and Throm looked at me, waiting.

"What?" Keenan asked.

"Reeger," I said quietly.

"Oh, he's fine," Throm replied with a laugh. At that Lily poked her head back in and said, "Though his face is all kinds of messed up, which, honestly, is fine. Men shouldn't be that pretty."

I blinked. "What?"

Keenan chuckled. "That rock that knocked him out clipped him across the face. He's got some pretty gnarly scarring now."

"Ah." I nodded. "But he's okay?"

"Oh yeah," Keenan said. "He was back on his feet pretty quick. I think he's in Burke with the other elves, going over rebuilding plans with Brom."

"Wait... Brom made it too?" I asked, surprised.

Keenan grinned. "Yep. Whole family did, thanks to Cara and her mom."

I let out a long breath. "Good. I really don't want to lose any more friends today."

Lily, Keenan, and I grabbed our packs and set out. As we walked toward Burke, we talked about the battle, reminiscing over everything that had happened. Some memories brought laughter, others quiet reflection, filling in pieces of the fight we hadn't seen. The road was scarred, littered with

Chapter 32 - The Aftermath

reminders of the war, but the air felt lighter now, touched with the promise of hope and rebuilding.

As we walked, I recognized a spot near the road. I stopped and pointed to the ground. "We need to put a statue here."

"Oh yeah," Lily said, nodding enthusiastically. "Two massive dragons, three dwarves, a Noctari, and an elf, all fighting off demons, standing together in victory!" She grinned, but when she noticed me staring quietly at the spot, her smile softened. "Or... just one statue. For Gam. That might be better."

I chuckled, and she smiled gently.

"No," I said. "Just one statue. And it needs to be huge."

"Yeah?" Keenan asked. "How big are we talking?"

"Thirty feet," I said, grinning.

Keenan let out a low whistle. "Dragon-sized, then."

I nodded. "It'll be of the biggest gnome I ever met, and the one who saved us all."

They fell silent.

Lily spoke first, her voice quiet. "I forgot... he was the one who closed the portals."

"Wait, what?" Keenan looked confused.

I nodded. "Yeah. I was too slow. I couldn't save him. But Reggie saved all of us. He stepped up in a way that no one else could." I told them what happened, how he'd rushed in, how he'd made the ultimate sacrifice to seal the portals for good.

Keenan stood still for a moment. "Reggie..." He glanced around, as if half-expecting him to appear. When he didn't, Keenan sighed. "I'm gonna miss him."

I placed a hand on his shoulder. "Me too."

Lily suddenly stepped ahead of us, walking backward so she could face us. "But," she said, grinning, "we build the statue. Thirty feet tall. Right here. Facing the horizon, so you can see him from all three cities. That way, it's like he's still here watching over us."

I smiled. "I like it."

Lily leaned in with a conspiratorial smirk. "And it just so happens... I know a guy who'll do it cheap."

I laughed, and Keenan raised a eyebrow. "You mean... all the dwarves?"

Lily smirked. "Well, I don't mean to brag, but... yeah. They basically love me."

We all chuckled as we continued walking. The weight of our losses still hung heavy on our hearts, but the thought of honoring Reggie, and remembering the good times, brought a warmth that helped carry us forward.

Chapter 33 - The Good, the Bad, the Sad

As we approached Burke, the once-beautiful walls loomed before us, scarred and broken. Sections had collapsed entirely, leaving jagged piles of stone debris scattered across the ground. Soldiers and citizens worked shoulder to shoulder, hauling rubble, resetting beams, and patching breaches with whatever materials they could find. The air smelled of dust and ash, but beneath it was the faint scent of bread and stew.

When we reached the gate, a weary guard recognized us instantly. His eyes widened, and he signaled for us to follow him without hesitation.

The deeper we went into the city, the less ruin we saw. Streets were swept clean, stalls reopened, and laughter echoed faintly from corners where children played. It looked almost normal again. Yet beneath the surface, a quiet somberness lingered. People spoke in hushed tones of what had happened, their words circling back again and again to Cara, the dragons and the miracle they had performed.

Inside the king's hall, Brom stood over a table covered with charts and maps, his brow furrowed in concentration. Several unfamiliar men flanked him, along with his wife, their faces drawn but determined. When we entered, Brom looked up, and his expression broke into a broad smile.

"Ahhh, my friends!" he said, clasping my hand warmly. "I'm glad you're okay." He turned to Lily, his eyes softening. "Ahhh, you'll want to see Cara, I imagine." He nodded to a guard and gave Lily's shoulder a reassuring pat before pulling Keenan into a quick hug.

Keenan blinked, confused. "What was that for?"

The king smiled knowingly. "It's not often a small decision creates ripples we can follow all the way to their end and see the impact."

"Okay…" Keenan said, still not following.

"You wanted to be a paladin, yes?"

Keenan nodded slowly. "Yes, but…"

"Yes!" Brom interrupted, clapping him on his good shoulder. "Because of that, you learned a healing spell. Because of that, you saved my wife. Because of that, she encouraged Cara to help. And because of that…"

Lily leaned in, muttering under her breath. "If he says 'because of that' one more time…"

Brom grinned. "…Cara teleported you and her mother to help Halvar kill the demon. And because…" He smirked at Lily, who shook her head. "…of that, we're all still here."

Keenan looked down, trying to process it all. He opened his mouth to speak, but Brom raised a hand.

"No, no, don't ruin it for me," he said with a smile. Then his expression darkened. "We lost almost twenty percent of our people. I'm grateful my family survived, but my people are my family too."

He was about to say more when the doors burst open and Cara ran in, her face alight.

"Lily!" she cried, rushing forward and wrapping her in a fierce hug.

"See?" Lily said, grinning. "I told you we'd be awesome together."

Chapter 33 - The Good, the Bad, the Sad

"Right?" Cara laughed. "And when I helped your brother with the ice thing, that was amazing!"

Her mother shook her head. "Well, you did pour a little too much into him."

Cara shot her mother a look, then softened. "I know. I was scared and just wanted to help. And... I'm sorry, Halvar. I didn't mean to almost kill you."

She hugged me, and I smiled. "It's okay. Turns out your mother has quite the talent for channeling and controlling magic," I said, glancing at the queen, who nodded knowingly.

"But... what happened after I passed out?" I asked. "I've heard bits and pieces, but I'd love to hear what happened to you all."

Brom smiled faintly. "Well, they started on the walls, and we repelled the first couple of waves. Right around the time they began breaking through, we saw you locked in a fight. That's when Cara ran up to her mother and said, 'We need to help Lily, she's hurt.' She was pretty upset, but I was about to lead Rannoch and his men to plug the gap in the wall."

He paused, his eyes distant. "That's when she teleported them both. I saw where she went, and without thinking, I knew I had to get to them. So I charged out." shaking his head. "Foolish of me, but all I could think about was getting to my girls." His voice softened, a faint smile tugging at his lips.

"I pushed through their lines and quickly realized I was in trouble. But strangely, I wasn't being attacked from behind. When I finally turned to look, I saw Victus and Oryn at my side, and Rannoch with forty or fifty men behind us, driving forward. So, I turned and kept fighting. They stayed with me all the way to where you had fallen."

He glanced at Victus. "We suffered losses," he said quietly. Victus gave a solemn nod, his jaw tight.

"Oryn only made it halfway," Brom continued, his voice low. "He was cut down stopping one from hitting me from behind."

For the first time, I noticed the sorrow in Victus's eyes. He was usually so stoic, but now his gaze was heavy with grief. He hadn't known Oryn long, but clearly, the loss had struck deep.

Cara chimed in, her voice trembling. "Yeah, once you passed out, I didn't know what to do. So, I did the only thing I could think of, I put a shield around you and your friends. Everyone looked so hurt, and I didn't want them to get hurt anymore."

"Well, thank you," I said with a smile.

Eryndra picked up the story, her voice quiet but steady. "She held the shield as long as she could, but I couldn't help her. I was going to... well, explode," she admitted, glancing down. "But then Brom showed up. I told him to get down, but he saw what I was about to do. He ran up, hugged me, and said, 'If you're going, then I'm going too.'"

She paused, looking at Brom, who smiled gently, his hand brushing hers.

She laughed softly, shaking her head. "I thought about it. But then Cara collapsed, and the shield fell. If I had gone through with it, I might've killed her. I couldn't do that. So instead, we did our best to surround you and protect everyone."

Chapter 33 - The Good, the Bad, the Sad

Her voice grew heavier. "As we were slowly being beaten back and had just about run out of room, a massive wave of Noctari arrived. A big one led a charge into the demons while a woman with a band of smaller Noctari tried to get to you. They told us to move aside, but Brom refused."

Brom shrugged, spreading his hands. "How was I supposed to know?"

"And just as things nearly came to blows, Lily showed up and said they were friendly," Eryndra explained. "So we let them through. Their leader was a woman named Azmira. They started healing whoever they could and helped carry the injured back to the dwarven city."

"The fighting was dying down at that point," she continued. "With most of their big fighters dead or gone, the rest began retreating toward the woods. But the dwarves poured out of the mountain, cutting them off."

Brom nodded, his eyes gleaming with admiration. "They pulled off this incredible shield wall with pikes and spears. I've never seen anything like it. The demon's forces broke against it like waves on a rocky shore. The wall held, and they were taken down one after another. We'll have to teach that to our men," he added with a grin.

I turned to him. "Have you seen Reeger and the elves?"

Brom smiled. "Ah, yes. They're looking into building some homes in Greenholm with the halflings, at least until they can start cleansing and restoring parts of the forest."

"Good," I said. "Do you know if and when they're coming back?"

He nodded. "They should return in the morning with plans and ideas."

He let out a long breath, then smiled. "But for now it's almost dinner time. We're celebrating by opening the stores we saved for a siege since they won't be necessary anymore. So please, join us!"

"Of course," I said, smiling. "We'd be honored. And we might as well stay until morning, if that's all right."

"Of course!" the king bellowed, laughing. "You are always welcome."

That night, we joined the city-wide feast. The king and queen gave speeches, thanking both us and their people for the victory. They toasted to health and happiness. We laughed and told stories late into the night, reliving memories of those we lost as well as tales of the past, before finally heading to bed.

The next morning, we gathered once again in the king's hall. Reeger, Thalion, Saevel, and the other five elves were already there, deep in conversation with the king. We thanked him and his family for their hospitality, then greeted Reeger, who agreed to accompany us to Grissom. We were all eager, and a bit anxious, to see what had happened there.

Lily grinned. "Hey Reeger, I think your face is getting better."

Reeger rolled his eyes and looked at me. "She won't stop talking about it. Be honest, how bad is it?"

I smiled. "Well... let's just say the rest of us finally have a chance with the ladies now."

Reeger groaned while Lily and Cara burst out laughing.

Chapter 33 - The Good, the Bad, the Sad

After saying our goodbyes, we set off toward Grissom.

"Have you heard anything about Grissom?" I asked Reeger along the road.

He shook his head, his expression darkening. "Some of the reports aren't good."

I sighed. "I don't know if I can take any more bad news after Gam." My voice broke with emotion.

Lily looked down, silent. Keenan placed a comforting hand on my shoulder.

Reeger nodded solemnly. "So... he's gone, then?"

I nodded.

"I think I'll write a song for him," Reeger said softly.

I smiled. "He would've been honored."

Reeger nodded again. "He was the one I could really talk to, about anything. No matter the subject, he always listened. Always had some wisdom to share."

"That's true," I said. "He had a mind for that sort of thing."

"Though I think Throm and Grog know more than they let on," Keenan added with a small chuckle.

"Definitely," I agreed.

As we neared Grissom, our hearts sank. The docks were charred and blackened. The entire western wall was a ruin of crumbled stone and ash.

"Looks like half the market district's gone too," Reeger murmured, squinting ahead.

We exchanged uneasy glances, steeling ourselves, and moved forward.

"Upper hill's damaged pretty badly," he added a moment later, his voice quiet.

When we reached the city's edge, the full scale of destruction became clear. The walls were scorched and shattered, debris scattered at odd angles. Yet amidst the ruin, there was hope: Noctari and humans working side by side, clearing rubble, sharing jokes, helping each other rebuild.

"Well," Keenan said, "I hate that it had to happen this way... but I'm glad to see more of my people being accepted."

I looked around and nodded. "Yeah. Nothing breaks down prejudice quite like saving each other's lives."

We passed a burned-out building, and our hearts nearly stopped. Lying in the street, eyes closed, body dusted with soot, was Frank.

"No!" Keenan shouted, rushing toward him.

Just as he reached him, Frank suddenly bolted upright and shouted, "One hundred! Ready or not, here I come!"

He turned and spotted us, breaking into a wide, soot-streaked grin. "Friends!" he bellowed, enveloping us in bone-crushing hugs.

"Wait one moment, I have little friends to find!" he said, turning and bounding off. For a troll, he was strangely agile and stealthy. We heard children laughing in the distance as he lumbered toward them.

Keenan stared after him in disbelief. "Did we die or something? Why is there a troll playing hide-and-seek with kids and no one is bothered by it?"

Before we could answer, a familiar, overly self-important voice spoke behind us.

"Hey, guys."

Chapter 33 - The Good, the Bad, the Sad

We turned and saw Philip, now easily eight, maybe nine, feet tall, leaning against the charred remains of a house, trying to look casual.

A loud crack sounded, and part of the structure collapsed beneath him. He tumbled over with a grunt.

"Ugh," he muttered, standing up and dusting himself off with a sheepish grin. "Forgot I'm a little bigger than I used to be."

We couldn't help laughing.

"So... what happened?" I asked.

"I think the beam just broke," Philip said, brushing dust from his arms. "Don't worry, I can fix it. I'll be more careful about what I lean on..."

I shook my head, chuckling. "No, Philip, I meant here. In the city. During the fight."

Philip straightened up, his face shifting into that overly serious look he always wore when he had something important to say, the kind of look that meant he would deliver his words at his own pace, no matter how long it took. It made all of us smile despite the heaviness of the subject.

"Well," he began, "the fighting started, and it wasn't long before the walls went down. My new parents and I came in with our clubs and boy, they were not ready for us." He laughed at the memory, his deep voice booming. "But even with the three of us, and some help, we couldn't hold them back." His smile faded. "We were pushed back."

Just then, Frank's voice echoed through the streets: "Found you!" followed by the delighted squeals of children.

Keenan shook his head, muttering, "This can't be real."

Philip smiled knowingly. "Yeah, it's weird how much they like him, but just between you and me…" He leaned in conspiratorially. "I think he might be closer to their age mentally."

We all struggled to keep straight faces, nodding solemnly in agreement.

"Anyway," Philip continued, "we'd fallen back to the city center and were heading up the hill when we saw a bunch of kids being chased out of a house by a demon."

At that moment, Frank reappeared, four children riding on his massive shoulders, all of them laughing wildly. He gently set them down and plopped next to us, still grinning ear to ear, as Philip went on.

"That's when this guy showed up," Philip said, gesturing toward Frank.

"I did?" Frank asked, eyes wide with innocence.

Philip sighed and shook his head. "Frank, tell them what happened."

Frank blinked. "When?"

"When the kids were in danger," Philip prompted patiently.

"Ohhh," Frank said, nodding. "Yeah! So I came out and bonked them. They used to be friends, but Keenan was right, they bad. So, I bonked them and bonked them until I got tired of bonking."

Philip burst out laughing. "I'm sorry, I don't know why, but the word *bonk* gets me every time."

I grinned. "You're not the only one."

Philip was still chuckling. "Anyway, I guess there was some commotion at that point. They started to retreat, not sure why, but they seemed pretty spooked."

Chapter 33 - The Good, the Bad, the Sad

"What about Jeffries?" I asked, glancing around.

"Oh, he's fine," Philip replied. "He was up protecting the council. The enemy didn't quite get that far, I guess."

Then his tone shifted, more somber. "But... we lost almost half the city."

"Half?" I repeated, stunned.

Philip nodded. "Yeah. Including Mrs. Belfree."

"No..." Keenan said quietly, his voice breaking.

Philip gave a sad sigh. "Yeah."

Keenan managed a faint smile. "She used to make the best bread and always gave me some as a little boy."

"I remember," I said softly, shaking my head.

"Oh, also, the red-headed lady showed up near the end," Philip added, brightening a little. "Boy, oh boy, she's a whirlwind of destruction."

We all stared at each other.

"Wait... *The Lady in White* is back?" I asked.

Philip shrugged. "If you mean that ship thing, yeah. Said they were gonna be here for a bit, until they met some friends or something."

We exchanged looks, then, saying goodbye to Philip, took off quickly toward the docks.

As we passed a burnt-out building, something shiny caught my eye. I bent down, picked it up, and froze. The others stopped and turned back. I just stood there, staring at it.

Reeger walked over and sighed. "The anti-portal stones. The ones Reggie made."

"Yep," I said quietly, thinking of the little gnome and how we'd first met him. "I'm gonna miss him." A faint smile tugged at my lips.

"Yeah, he was crazy, but in a good way," Reeger replied, smiling too.

"Wait," Lily asked. "Crazy like me?"

Keenan shook his head and started walking away. "Nope. Can't do it. A world with both Lily and Reggie as friends? That's too much for me."

We all laughed and kept moving toward the docks, telling Lily more about Reggie as we walked.

As we approached, we spotted her, white sails billowing gently, gleaming against the ruined skyline. Just the sight of her brought a strange sense of comfort. One dock was still standing, though several piers were splintered and damaged.

The lady appeared at the gangplank, smiling. "I'm glad to see you've made it. I want you to know that I helped as much as I could. Stopping their ships until there were none left."

I smiled. "We appreciate it."

"Yea, a lot," said Keenan.

She nodded. "Thank you for the friend."

"Yeah…" I said, glancing around. "Where is she?"

"She's here," the lady replied.

I looked around. "Where?"

The woman nodded toward the water, then turned and spoke to someone unseen. "Yes, that girl is the one who set you free."

I looked over at Lily, who just shrugged.

Suddenly, a massive tentacle shot up from beneath the ship and, before I could react, snatched Lily into the air and yanked her underwater.

Chapter 33 - The Good, the Bad, the Sad

"Lily!" I shouted, running to the edge of the dock as the water churned and bubbled.

"Remember," the lady said calmly, "she needs air."

An instant later, Lily burst from the water, gasping as the tentacle gently placed her back on the dock. She landed on all fours, soaked and panting.

"I think... a squid just hugged me," she said between breaths.

"Well, technically, she's a kraken," the lady said, smiling.

I chuckled. "Only you, Lil. Only you."

The lady continued. "Apparently, this one was released when Lily threw her out to sea. I found her defending the waters she believed had been given to her. We talked and agreed to be friends. Now she lives beneath my hull, and we sail together."

Lily stood, dripping wet, and looked at me with wide eyes. "Well, no one's ever going to say Lily doesn't give good hugs, so here I come, Kraken-squid-thing!"

She transformed into a dragon mid-sentence, scales flashing in the sunlight, and dove back into the water with a roar of delight.

Reeger just stood there, shaking his head, his scar catching the light as he rubbed at it absently. "I mean... you can't make this stuff up. If I wrote a book about this, no one would believe it." His voice carried a blend of disbelief and weary amusement.

Keenan laughed, shaking his head as if trying to clear the absurdity of the last few minutes. I couldn't help but join him in laughing.

Then Lily clambered back onto the dock, dripping wet, her grin wide enough to split the world in two. She shook herself like a dog, sending droplets everywhere, before reverting to her human form with a flourish.

"See?" she said, chest heaving, eyes sparkling with mischief. "That one was better."

We all stared at her for a moment, then burst out laughing again.

"Better?" Keenan managed between chuckles. "You just got hugged by a kraken, Lil. That's not better, that's insane."

"Insane is better," she shot back, wagging a finger at him. "Normal is boring. And besides, she liked me. You saw it. That was a *friendly* hug."

Reeger groaned, rubbing his temples. "Friendly hug? Lily, it dragged you underwater. That's not friendly, that's attempted drowning."

"Semantics," Lily said, waving him off. "You're just jealous you didn't get a hug."

I shook my head, smiling despite myself. "Only you, Lil. Only you could turn a near-death experience into bragging rights."

She puffed out her chest proudly. "Exactly. And when they build statues of us, mine's gonna have tentacles wrapped around me. Kraken Lily the Pirate Queen. Has a nice ring to it."

Keenan rolled his eyes, but there was a smile tugging at his lips. "If anyone ever does write a book about this, they'll have to put you on the cover. Although no one would believe half of it."

Chapter 33 - The Good, the Bad, the Sad

Reeger chuckled, finally giving in. "Fine. But I'm telling you, if I write it, I'm leaving out the part where you called it a squid. That's just embarrassing."

"Hey!" Lily protested. "Squid, kraken, whatever. It's still a hug."

The laughter faded into silence. The sea lapped gently against the dock, the sails of *The Lady in White* billowed softly in the evening breeze, and for the first time in what felt like forever, the world seemed calm.

I looked at each of them, Reeger with his scarred face, Keenan with his missing arm but unbroken spirit, Lily dripping wet and grinning like a child, and felt a warmth settle in my chest. We were battered, scarred, and grieving... but we were alive.

And somehow, impossibly, we were still laughing.

I exhaled, the weight of our experience closing around me like a curtain. "Yeah," I said softly, more to myself than anyone else. "That one was better."

Chapter 34 - The End?

I walked through my childhood city, each step stirring memories. Compared to thousands of years, my time here had been brief, yet it still felt like home, sometimes even more than the mountains. Perhaps that was because of my three uncles, who had filled this place with laughter, wisdom, and warmth, making it something more than stone and timber.

We arrived at the old house they had once shared. Its walls sagged, part of the roof collapsed, debris scattered across the floor like forgotten echoes of the past. I stepped inside, the air heavy with dust and silence, and made my way to the corner where Gam used to sleep. Sitting down on his bed, I let the memories wash over me.

When I was young, he would have Keenan and me perch on the edge of the mattress while he spun his tales. I used to think he made them up, weaving fantasy from nothing, but now... now I wasn't so sure. His stories had carried the weight of truth, fragments of history disguised as bedtime adventures. We would listen, argue, and debate, trying to piece together what had really happened.

As I looked around, something caught my eye, a book sticking out from beneath the mattress. I pulled it free, brushing away the dust, and studied the leather-bound cover. Etched into it was a name: *Gamreal Stonehide*. I smiled faintly. I had never even known his last name.

Chapter 34 - The End?

Opening it, I was greeted by his familiar handwriting, bold yet uneven, the kind of script born from long nights scribbling by candlelight. My chest tightened as I read the first paragraph:

"Great news, I've become an advisor to the king. Or rather, soon-to-be king and my best friend. Of course, Grog is here too, because where would we be without our favorite berserker and cook? I know it's early, but I genuinely believe we'll accomplish great things together, and I can't wait to see what comes our way. I'm going to document it all here, because I think one day people might want to read the story, especially about Throm. I'd like for him to have it all written down. Excited for the future, the adventures, and the challenges that await us. -Gam"

A hand settled gently on my shoulder. I turned to see Keenan standing behind me, his expression quiet, respectful. I quickly closed the book and looked up at him.

"The stories?" he asked softly.

I nodded. "Yeah... he was the best storyteller."

My eyes blurred with tears as I rose, glancing around the ruined room. "Well... I guess that means we'll have to tell them now."

Keenan chuckled, though his voice was thick with emotion. "I suppose so."

We gathered a few keepsakes for Throm, who had chosen to remain in the mountains. Grog, on the other hand, had fallen in love with the inn in Grissom. Though he was welcome back, he decided to stay there, which left me with a pang of sadness. After all those years together, it felt like even in victory, pieces of us were still breaking apart.

Reeger sighed as he tucked away a trinket. "Well, all good things must come to an end."

"That's stupid," Lily shot back immediately.

Reeger laughed. "This one's true, Lily. You can't beat all our sayings into submission."

She muttered, "Then get better sayings. I'm a good thing, and I plan on living forever just to spite your stupid saying."

We all laughed, the sound easing the heaviness, as we packed up and headed to the inn. It had escaped most serious damage, and we wanted one last meal together before returning to the mountains in the morning.

Around the table, silence lingered at first. Lily and I had escaped without visible scars, though her wing and leg still ached in dragon form. Reeger and Keenan bore their wounds more openly, but all of us carried hurts, some carved into flesh, others etched into the heart.

I lifted my mug, forcing a smile. "Well... we made it back. Like we promised."

"Agreed," Keenan said, raising his own.

Reeger lifted his with a faint grin. "To friendship."

"I can get behind that," Lily added, clinking her mug against ours.

We drank, laughter slowly returning as we swapped stories of the past, tales of battles, mischief, and the ones we had lost. For a few hours, grief gave way to memory, and memory gave way to joy.

That night, we slept at the inn, then rose early and began our journey back to the mountains.

Chapter 34 - The End?

We arrived just in time for the service, though I suspected they had waited for us. The hall was filled with solemn faces as names were read aloud, every soldier who had fallen, every dream they had carried, every hope they had left behind.

Gam's name was saved for last.

And just as it was spoken, a light broke through the mountain ceiling.

It was Mother.

As she descended, the entire hall fell silent. The dwarves dropped to one knee, their armor clattering softly against the stone. Lily and I bowed our heads, while Reeger, Keenan, and Azmira stood frozen in awe, their eyes wide as if they were gazing upon a dream.

She landed softly, barefoot, her glowing white robe flowing like liquid light.

"My brave and loyal dwarves," she said, smiling. Her voice radiated warmth, a comfort so pure it seemed to ease every ache in the room. "The only reason I can return here is because I am tethered to my husband's life force. And the only reason he allowed it... is because you saved my life, by acting selflessly, allowing me to live."

Her gaze swept across the chamber, lingering on faces lined with grief and pride.

"I know you have made many sacrifices," she continued, her tone reverent. "I had to be here to honor them, and those left behind."

As she moved through the crowd, she touched each dwarf gently on the head, offering a quiet blessing. Some wept openly, others bowed deeper, but all seemed transformed by her presence.

When she reached Reeger and Keenan, she smiled.

"Well," she said, "I would like to thank you both for helping my eldest creation find his way home."

They nodded, still overwhelmed, their usual wit silenced by awe.

Then her eyes found Azmira, who for once looked uncertain, her hands trembling slightly.

"And thank you," Mother said gently, "for healing those you could. It means the world to me."

Azmira swallowed hard, then nodded, humbled.

Finally, she turned to Lily and me, pulling us both into a warm embrace. Her touch was radiant, like sunlight breaking through storm clouds.

"My son would be so proud of you two," she whispered. "And I have been allowed to offer you a choice, to come home with us. To finally rest... and leave behind these lives of protection and destruction."

I froze, stunned. The thought of leaving, especially with Mother, had never even crossed my mind.

"I... I don't know what to say," I managed, my voice shaking.

She smiled patiently, as though she had expected my hesitation.

Lily sighed, her usual bravado tempered by something deeper. "Who's going to protect this world if we leave?"

Mother looked at her kindly. "That is no longer your burden. This world must now write its own story and walk its own path."

"I see," Lily murmured, fidgeting. "So... what happens if we don't go with you?"

Chapter 34 - The End?

I glanced at her, surprised, but then I understood. This was what we were made for: to protect, to fight, to serve. And while we had done so gladly... we had never thought about what came after.

Mother's smile was calm, timeless. "Then it will be a very, very long time before we meet again. But rest assured, we will meet again."

Lily glanced at me. I smiled, and in that silent moment, we agreed.

She turned back to Mother with a mischievous grin. "Well... we did do all this work cleaning up their mess. And honestly... there's still furniture around here I haven't even met yet."

Mother gave me a quizzical look. I shook my head, smiling despite myself.

"So," Lily said, "I think we're going to stay. For a bit. And make sure only the good furniture survives."

Mother's smile deepened. "Very well." She turned to the dwarves. "Stay strong, my wonderful creations. I pray peace will follow your long lives."

With that, she began to rise toward the cavern ceiling, her light trailing upward like dawn breaking through the clouds. With her ascended the spirits of the fallen dwarves. I watched as Gam's spirit drifted upward. He turned, smiled at me, and gave one final thumbs-up before vanishing into the light.

The dwarves buzzed with excitement, voices rising in awe and reverence, as we made our way toward Throm.

He was beaming, his eyes alight. "How about that?" he said. "Now that was amazing!"

"I agree," I said, smiling, my heart still heavy but warmed.

Just then, a soldier ran up, breathless, panic in his eyes.

"Sire!" he gasped. "There's a portal opening!"

"What?" Throm said sharply.

"It's one of ours, sir."

Throm didn't hesitate. He took off running with the soldier, and the rest of us followed Keenan, Reeger, Lily, Azmira, and I sprinting after him, hearts pounding.

We arrived at the portal just as the sounds of fighting echoed from the other side. Steel clashed, voices shouted, and the air trembled with violence. Throm stood silently, nodding to the guards as they formed a defensive perimeter, weapons raised.

"Can we go through?" I asked, tense.

Throm shook his head grimly. "No. It's a one-way portal. They can only come through."

I nodded, and we waited, every muscle taut. The sounds of battle grew louder, closer, and then, just like that, the portal vanished.

We stood in stunned silence, the air heavy with dread.

"Well, that was a letdown," Lily muttered, frustration dripping from her voice. "We don't even know what happened!"

Throm's expression darkened. "That's not good. My brother only carries four or five of those stones, and only for emergencies."

We were debating what to do next when another portal suddenly flared open, its light harsh and unstable. A demon stumbled through, confused, and was immediately cut down by the dwarves.

Chapter 34 - The End?

"I don't like this," Throm muttered, his jaw tight.

Then a dwarf stepped through the shimmering light. He was one of the Hammers, his armor dented and smeared with blood. He bowed quickly, then straightened, his voice flat but urgent.

"Your brother requests immediate reinforcements. We've located a stronghold on another large island. I must return at once. Anyone ready to fight must come now."

The portal flickered behind him and collapsed. He pulled a small stone from his pocket and smashed it against the ground, reigniting the portal in a blinding flash.

"It will only last sixty seconds," he warned. With another quick bow, he stepped back through.

I looked at Lily and smiled as we started forward, the glow of the portal shimmering like liquid fire before us. Its light rippled across her face, catching the mischievous grin she wore even in moments like this.

Then I felt a hand on my shoulder.

"If you two are going, I have to," Reeger said. A faint smile touched his scarred face, brief and almost amused then it faded into steady resolve.

Keenan grinned, his voice steady despite the weight of his missing arm. "Even with one arm, I can still do some damage."

Just then, another hand touched his shoulder. He turned to find Azmira standing close, her usual stern gaze softened into something warmer.

"Not without me," she said, her voice quiet but resolute. She drew a small dagger from her belt, its edge gleaming, and in her other hand an orb pulsed faintly with light.

"Besides... it's been a while since I've had a proper adventure."

For a moment, I simply looked at them, my friends, my family, scarred and battered but unbroken. My heart raced, not with dread, but with pride.

I smiled, lifting my chin toward the portal. "To the king," I said, my voice carrying more weight than I expected.

The portal flared brighter, humming with power, its edges unstable yet inviting.

And together, Lily, Reeger, Keenan, Azmira, and I stepped through.